THE ERNE WARDER

Steve & Anne,
your support is such
a blessing!
I think you'll most
only enjoy this, but
"get it," too!
much love - Aaron

THE ERNE WARDER

Aaron T. Babcock

Morning Dove Press
Nova Scotia, Canada

Published by Morning Dove Press
Eastern Canada's Christian Publishing House
Nova Scotia, Canada

The Erne Warder
Text and Images Copyright © 2023 by Aaron T. Babcock

All rights reserved. The use of any part of this publication reproduced, transmitted in any form or by any means, electronic, mechanical, photocopying, recording, or otherwise stored in a retrieval system, without the prior written consent of the publisher — or, in case of photocopying or other reprographic copying, a licence from the Canadian Copyright Licencing Agency — is an infringement of the copyright law.

Edited by Morning Dove Press
Designed by Aaron T. Babcock

Cover design, illustrations and photo editing by Aaron T. Babcock

Original source images courtesy of:
1. Front cover — Jakob Owens / Unsplash (https://unsplash.com/@jakobowens1)
2. Framed portraits on back cover: a) Young Man -Stocksnap.io CC0 1.0 Universal (CC0 1.0), b) Young woman - FreePik.com c) Mature African man - Kazi Mizan https://unsplash.com/@kaziminmizan
3. Back Cover Archer / Canine — Freepik.com and Adobe Stock
4. Maps — selected graphic assets sourced from Freepik.com

A Morning Dove Press Book
Paperback ISBN 9781738742165
E-Book ISBN 9781738742172

Published and printed in Canada
morningdovepress.ca

Dedication

First and foremost, this book is dedicated to the One non-fictional Person whose Name appears inside its pages: Yeshua Ha Mashiach, better known to most as Jesus the Christ, Jesus of Nazareth, son of David and Son of God — Source of my creative talents and Whose truth inspired the subplot of this fictional adventure.

It is also dedicated to my loving wife, Stephanie, who vetted select plot points during the creation of this work, my long time friend Peter who for a lifetime has supported all my creative efforts, my brother Jeremy who encouraged me to get it published, and all the friends, loved ones and even personal adversaries who loosely inspired some of the characters and events of this story.

A very special thanks to my publisher, Morning Dove Press, for catching the vision of what this story is about.

Thank you all for making this possible.

THE ERNE WARDER - MAP SECTION

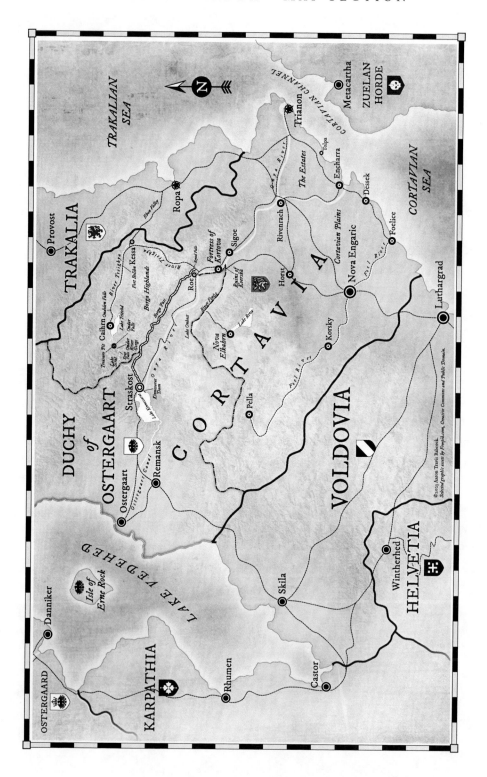

KINGDOM OF CORTAVIA

THE ERNE WARDER - MAP SECTION

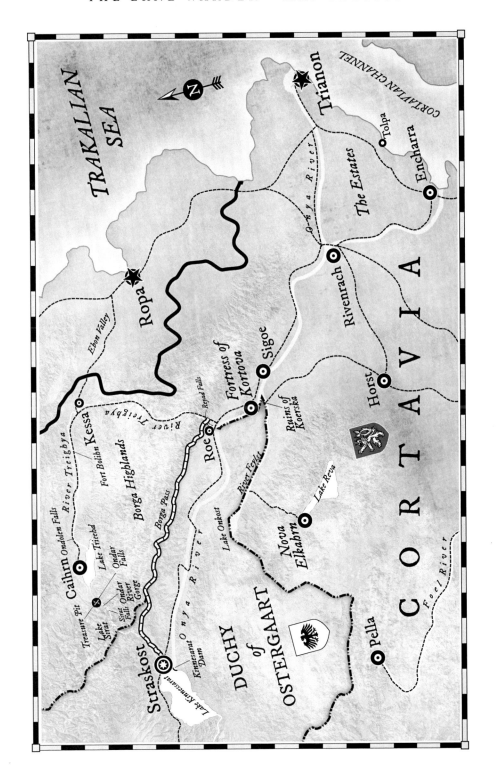

CORTAVIA - ONYA RIVER DETAIL

THE ERNE WARDER - MAP SECTION

LAKE TRIEEHD REGION

THE ERNE WARDER - MAP SECTION

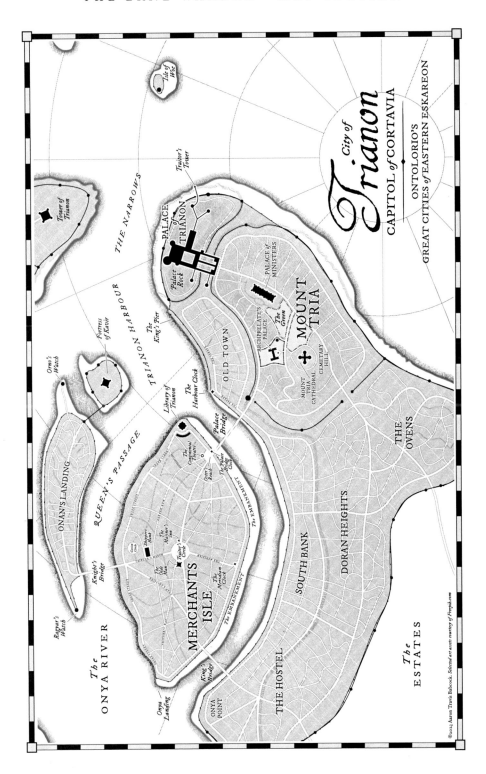

CITY OF TRIANON

THE ERNE WARDER - MAP SECTION

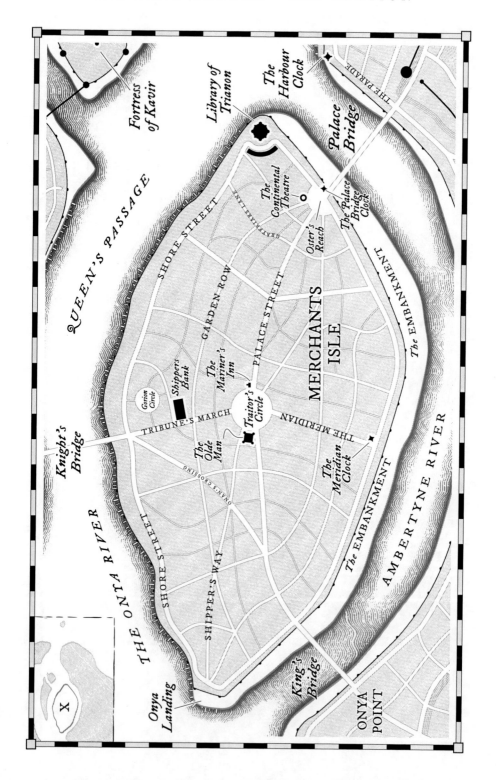

CITY OF TRIANON - MERCHANTS ISLE

THE ERNE WARDER - MAP SECTION

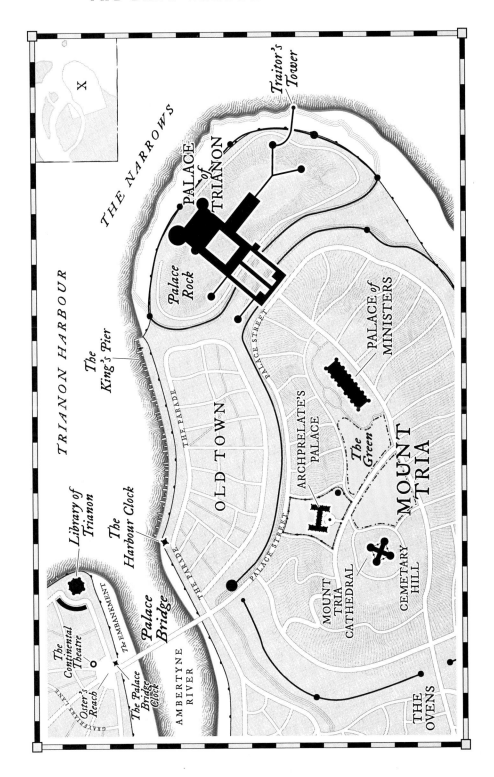

CITY OF TRIANON - MOUNT TRIA

THE ERNE WARDER - MAP SECTION

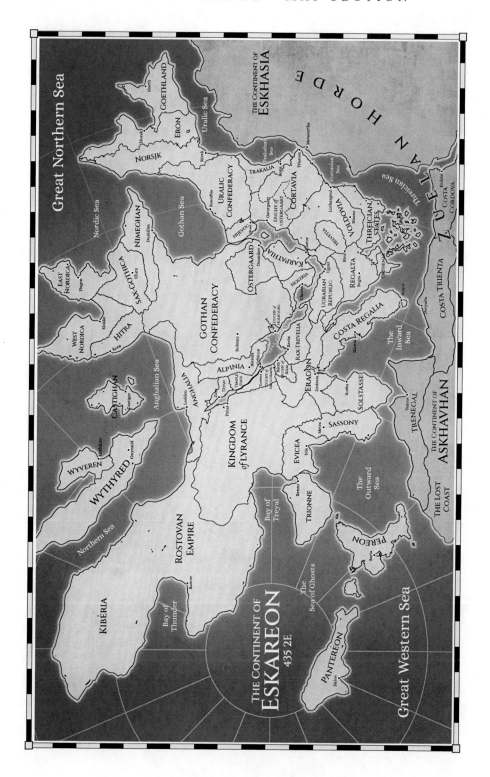

CONTINENT OF ESKAREON

Erne

A sea eagle or "fish eagle", mostly in reference to the white-tailed eagle. Any of the birds of prey in the genus Haliaeetus in the bird of prey family Accipitridae.

Warder

From the archaic verb "to ward" which means to guard or protect. Thus, a "warder" is one who guards, protects, defends; a guardian.

THE ERNE WARDER

CHAPTER ONE
The Name

Arghan's neck had escaped the axe once in his life. This time there would be no axe. He'd be burned at the stake. That is of course if he were caught.

He cupped his hand behind his ear and peered back down the trail, fixated on the spot where it turned a corner some distance behind him.

Nothing. Better run anyway. May not have the option later.

He grabbed the hem of his grey woolen cassock, spun his walking staff parallel to the ground, and bolted into the treeline, inhaling the fresh scent of pine needles and the earthy musk of moss, mushrooms, and rotting bark as he raced through the brush.

He burst through a dense stand of evergreens and tumbled headlong into a copse of thorn bushes. Razor-sharp barbs gouged bloody lines across his hands and face. He winced and slipped his arms inside his baggy sleeves, twisting his trunk from side to side until he broke free. He leaped over a fallen tree and continued.

Some shortcut. Would it really make up the time difference?

His weekly hike through the forest of Glenhava south of Mount Mora usually took four hours, not counting the return ascent to his home in the monastery on Precipice Peak, the towering crag whose steep granite cliffs shone in the late afternoon sun above the treetops in the distance. But that was on a normal Risenday[1] when ritual ceremonies were kept like clockwork. This was no normal Risenday. It was the third Risenday of Repose[2]. Another package was sure to have arrived if only he could find it in time. Any deviance from his schedule would attract unwanted interest, and he was already under suspicion. Why else had the new Abbot sent his guards to escort him back from the village of Cairhn after High Mass?

He skidded to a stop and arched his head southward. *A sound?* At first, there was nothing but the gentle rustling of pine branches and the squeaking, chattering fuss of two chipmunks chasing each other through the canopy. But there it was again — a faint bellow echoing from the hillside below.

Wolves? No, not wolves. Hounds. At least one hound.

Borgrel's farm lay just beyond the tree-line in that direction. Perhaps that ambitious fox he'd told Arghan of had sought another of his chickens and met Borgrel's new mastiff instead? No hungry fox was a respecter of Risenday. No mastiff of Borgrel's either.

No cause to stop.

Arghan turned and leaped over a rock. He was back on the trail now.

He rounded the towering granite boulder that marked the entrance to what his fellow Cantorvarians called the Oratory, a circular area that brothers in centuries past had cleared and surfaced with stones gathered from the forest. At its heart stood the Witness of Time, a flat-topped stone holding an ancient iron sundial.

Arghan scurried toward it, scanning the forest perimeter. The space was empty save for the ring of boulders monks sat on during gatherings there. He took one more look over his shoulder and placed his walking staff beside the stone. He reached inside his belt pouch, produced a scrap of parchment, and read it.

At precisely three of the dial at Time's Witness, on the third R of R, defy

---

1. Risenday – The first day of the week according to the Common Calendar.
2. Repose – The sixth month of the year according to the Common Calendar, late summer.

the shadow of the gnomon³ thence thirty paces past the ring of stones. At Sorto's trio stand and face the golden eye. At one hundred paces less three toward its gaze, beneath the bleeding rock, it is concealed.

Arghan looked down at the Witness and squinted.

The shadow of the gnomon? What shadow?

He brushed aside his long ashen bangs, knelt down, and drew closer to the dial.

Still nothing.

He looked up at the massive pines that surrounded the Oratory and then downward at the stand of birches that had overgrown the area. He snorted and gripped his chin and upper lip, wringing the sweat from his grizzled beard. He stood up and took a few paces back from the stone, glancing from it to the trees and back again. He spotted the sun's glare through the branches and held out his arm to gauge the trajectory of its rays.

He grabbed his staff from the Oratory floor and spun in the opposite direction his arm had pointed. He hastened to the side of one of the rock seats around the Oratory perimeter then slowed his pace. He counted out each step, weaving in and out of the birches, correcting his course each time. At thirty paces he stopped.

"Sorto's trio," he whispered, "what on Earda⁴ does he mean by that?"

Arghan scanned the forest floor. He gripped his beard again, this time pulling a few thorns out of its curly strands. He used his staff to brush aside the debris at his feet. *Nothing but grubs.* He rested the end of his staff amid a pair of tiny bushes and allowed his eyes to fall out of focus as he looked at it.

Sorto's trio. Sorto's trio.

He jerked his head up again and looked deeper into the forest. Three bulky oaks grew within a footfall of each other at the bottom of a tiny slope. Arghan dashed toward them.

A rusted iron stewing pot sat over a pile of stones between the trees.

---

3. Gnomon – The gnomon is the part of a sundial that casts a shadow.
4. Earda – The name of the world where this story takes place.

He smirked and shook his head. *I should expect as much from a librarian*, he mused. The trees must represent the heroes who told stories around the cooking fire in the great playwright Sorto's masterpiece, *The Three Swordsmen of Pereon*. It seemed his young apprentice Gavek's constant ramblings about the books he was reading had finally proved useful.

Arghan jumped on top of the pot and surveyed the forest through the gaps between the oaks. He stopped when the summit of Cauldron Rock came into view above the distant treetops. He was used to seeing it from the monastery on Precipice Peak, where a toppled stone lying partly inside the pool of water on its summit resembled a ladle resting against the edge of a pot — hence its name. But from this particular vantage point, it looked nothing of the sort. The toppled rock was levered over a boulder and its upward edge formed an arch. The sun shone directly through the centre of the elliptical space below it.

"The golden eye," he said. Arghan jumped out from the stand and began counting his steps again, inwardly at first, then aloud, "…forty-eight, forty-nine, fifty, fif—"

Hounds bellowed again from the south. This time he was certain. *At least two hounds.* Neither sounded like a mastiff. They were coming closer. Had they not yet caught that fox? Perhaps it was Borgrel's neighbour with his hunting dogs now giving chase? He looked up again at Cauldron Rock and estimated the remaining distance. He bolted ahead, bounding over rocks and shrubs as he went.

His toe snagged a root, invisible below the ferns. He tumbled over a thicket and fell face down into a sunken clearing. A solitary granite boulder stood at its edge, nearly as high as a house. He looked up its steep, shadowed face at the red leaves on the vines that grew from the soil between its fissures.

"Blood vine," he muttered. *The rock that bleeds.* Arghan's staff was lying just in reach of his fingers. He drew it forward and braced himself with it, rising to his feet. He shuffled forward. The hounds sounded very close now. He dropped at the foot of the boulder and groped inside its darkened overhang.

Come on… Come on.

Arghan strained forward. He scowled as his lateral muscle tightened to its full extent. His fingertips grazed a smooth surface. An oil-tanned scroll cylinder rolled within reach. He clutched it and stuffed it inside his tunic. He scurried past the rock and slid behind a shrub for cover and peered back into the clearing through its branches.

Footfalls pounded. Twigs snapped. Arghan cocked his head toward the opposite side of the clearing. *Two feet, not four?* He could hear heaving, gasping breaths now. The breaking and springing of branches grew louder. The hounds shrieked.

It was no fox they were chasing.

A young girl burst from the midst of the thicket, tumbling into the clearing the same way Arghan had. She darted to her feet and scrambled up the blood vine. She had almost reached the top of the boulder when a loaf of bread fell out from beneath her tattered garment. She reached out to catch it but it bounced off the tip of her fingers and landed on the forest floor. She slid on top of the rock and turned back to look down at the bread, wheezing.

Two black dogs emerged from the bush, then a third. They barked and howled at the girl, bearing their teeth. Foam dripped from their jaws. These were no hunting hounds. These were the kind that only ate what they killed.

The third dog circled to the right, nearing Arghan's position. Arghan looked over to the rock and noticed a gentler slope of earth leading up its side, not visible to him before. His eyelids widened. He glanced at the girl, who hugged her own trembling torso. The hair on the dog's back spiked. Its howling deepened into a growl. Arghan took a breath, reached into his cassock, and pulled out the cylinder. He thrust it between two low branches at the base of a tree and jumped to his feet.

"Back, mongrel!" He batted the dog in the ribs with his staff. It reeled back, whimpering. The other two lunged forward and latched onto the loose skirting of Arghan's robe. With two spinning motions, he struck each canine between the eyes. With two more he thrust the tip of his staff behind their tails. They wailed and scampered back into the woods. Arghan kicked the third between the legs and it galloped away even faster than the rest.

He wiped the sweat from his brow and turned to look up at the girl. Tears streaked down her face, washing away some of the dirt on her skin. She stared back at him with sky-blue eyes; her curly blonde locks fell over her face, disheveled.

"You're okay now, my dear. Come down the back side, over there." Arghan pointed at the slope he had seen.

The girl shook her head. Still gasping for air, she struggled to speak. She pointed over Arghan's head. "L-look—"

Arghan cocked his head toward the sound of leaves rustling across the forest floor.

"Stay right there," growled a man's voice, a short distance behind Arghan. "Turn around slowly so I can see you."

Arghan complied. An archer in light armour drew his bow and pointed his arrow at Arghan's chest. Arghan scowled when he saw the symbol emblazoned at the centre of the bowman's surcoat. *The Grand Prelate's arms. A soldier in the Theocracy's Alpinian Guard. Likely one of the Abbot's men, from the village.*

"Who are you?" the archer demanded.

"I am brother Arthos, acting Prior of the monastery of Cairhn." Arghan pointed behind his head toward Precipice Peak.

"What are you doing so far from it on a Risenday, let alone out here?"

"I take a ritual journey to the forest Oratory each Risenday. Ask the Abbot."

"I see no trail marked with prayer stones here." The archer glanced to the right and left, then back at Arghan.

"I don't suppose you're in the habit of relieving yourself in the middle of a sacred trail? I know I'm not," said Arghan.

"I suppose not," said the archer. He lowered his bow but kept his arrow nocked.

Arghan glanced up at the little girl and back again. "What of this lass here? What's your business with her?"

"She's a fugitive of the Church."

"A fugitive... of the 'Church'?" Arghan cringed every time he had to use that sacred word to refer to the Palace of Orbicon. Ruled by the Grand Prelate, the theocracy headquartered there dictated all matters of faith across the continent of Eskareon, using the iron fist of the Alpinian Guard to enforce its will. Centuries before, its founders had massacred the holy nation chosen by the Father of Lights to carry His message of salvation to the world: the Tzyani people, of whom only a scattered remnant now survived, cowering in sequestered enclaves. Afterward, Orbicon had forbidden the dissemination of all sacred texts written by the Tzyani prophets, and had murdered Petros, leader of the first Eskaran[5] disciples to believe their message. Petros' followers would later become the Cantorvarians, who pretended to renounce the contentious tenets of their faith to avoid persecution while practising them in secret, behind the closed doors of monasteries like the one on Precipice Peak.

The archer pointed at the ground. "Stole a loaf of offertory bread, right out from under the Abbot's nose she did, in the middle of First Mass. I've been after her ever since."

Arghan looked down at the loaf at his feet. A few desperate bites had been taken out of it. He closed his eyes and took a deep breath. "Is there so little grain in all of Cortavia that the Abbot may not spare one loaf of bread for a suffering soul such as she?" He pointed up at the girl.

"She committed a sacrilege. A witch in disguise, no doubt."

"You're serious?"

"Abbot's rule, not mine. Step aside."

"What will you do to her?" Arghan took a step closer to the archer, clenching his staff.

The archer raised his bow again, this time pointing it at Arghan's head. "Step. Aside."

The girl shifted her weight. Her heel caught some loose stones and she slipped onto her back. She flipped over and tried to scurry away on her knees. She slipped on the wet moss she had been lying on and skidded back down the rock face, catching herself on the blood vine. The

---

5. Eskaran – the demonym used to denote a native inhabitant of the continent of Eskareon.

archer raised his bow over Arghan's head and released the string.

"No!" Arghan lunged forward. He whipped his staff over his head and struck the archer's knuckles, sending both the archer and the bow crashing to the ground as the arrow thudded into a tree near the far side of the rock.

The archer rolled onto his back and reached for his sword. He had it half drawn when Arghan landed a sharp kick under the man's wrist. The sword slipped free of its scabbard and spun through the air. Arghan grabbed it by the hilt and whizzed the point downward, stopping it less than an inch in front of the man's throat.

"You will leave this place and not return, is that understood?"

The archer nodded, his eyes bulging. Arghan grabbed him by the front of his surcoat and lifted him up. With a flick of his wrist, he sliced through the archer's shoulder strap. The soldier's quiver fell, catching one of the rocks near the ground, and sending arrows tumbling out in all directions. Arghan spun the man around by the shoulder and kicked him in the buttocks, sending him stumbling toward the edge of the clearing.

"Now run." Arghan glared at the archer as the man dashed back into the woods. "And tell the Abbot I'd like to discuss this incident when I see him tomorrow." He pitched the archer's sword deep into the woods.

He fell to his knees, trembling, adrenaline still coursing through his veins. He closed his eyes and groaned, lifting his head skyward. "Shepherd King, spare my brothers from wrath for my failure." He felt the sensation of hair brushing against his cheek and slender arms around his neck.

"Thank you," the girl said.

Arghan opened his eyes. The child who stood before him looked no older than ten. Beyond her frazzled, golden locks stared the face of what looked to him like an angel, caked in mud. She appeared much the way he had imagined his own daughter may have looked at that age, had he ever been blessed to lay eyes on her.

"What is your name, child?"

"Grace."

"Ah, your mother is Agape, of the lakeshore?"

Grace noticed the silver cross dangling below Arghan's neck. She stepped backward. "Yes. She's in her bed. Has been for days. I was hungry, so I—"

"It's alright, dearest. Fear not. Come." Arghan rose and held out his hand while he pointed at the loaf of bread with the other. "There's better food than that where I live. We'll make sure your belly is filled and then minister to your mother, agreed?"

Grace nodded. Arghan turned, walked to the edge of the clearing and knelt down. He retrieved the cylinder and stuffed it back inside his robe.

"Are you that old saint people say lives up on the mountain?" said Grace, pointing northward.

Tears welled up in the corner of Arghan's eyes. "No, Grace. You must mean Abba Ardwynn. He died three weeks ago. I'm only his disciple, brother Arth—" Arghan stared down at the mess of arrows on the ground. "My name is Arghan. Arghan of Danniker. I am no saint."

The piquant aroma of hot beef stew wafted through the air inside the vaulted expanse of the refectory. Monks sat on benches at two long tables that ran the length of the room, breaking their Risenday fast with smiling faces. None spoke a word or made a sound except to excuse the occasional belch, or to slurp back some final sips of broth. The first to finish scoured the corner of his bowl with a piece of bread and waved down a server for a second helping. Others soon followed, using the opportunity to cast a curious gaze at the meal's unexpected guest of honour.

Little Grace perched on the edge of a bench at the head table beside the man they all knew as brother Arthos, her chin only inches above her bowl, gobbling away. A few monks exchanged curious looks through the dim, flickering candlelight. Some gestured toward the front, while others nodded their heads in the same direction and grinned. One monk lifted his goblet in Arghan's direction as if to toast and nodded as he made eye contact. Arghan returned the gesture, his smile quickly receding into the brooding expression that preceded it.

Bright light flashed through the row of pointed-arch windows at the side of the room, framing the silhouettes of the monks' heads against the white plastered wall on the opposite side. A few moments later thunder rumbled in the distance. A gust extinguished some candles at the table nearest the outer wall and a monk rose to shutter the offending window.

Arghan patted Grace on the shoulder and whispered into her ear, "Just show your empty bowl to brother Eathid here if you want more. He'll look after you in case I'm called away." He looked into the eyes of the monk who sat to Grace's other side. The burly man nodded, then looked at Grace. He smiled through bushy black whiskers and winked. Grace grinned and kept eating.

Arghan pushed his bowl away and started tapping his fingers on the hardwood tabletop. He started to rise but halted when the chamber door swung open. He and the others turned their heads toward the threshold. Another monk stepped through the door, carrying a bulky leather satchel slung over his shoulder. With a sigh, he lifted its strap over his head and tossed the bag onto a nearby chair. He stepped forward and bowed, pulling back his hood as he rose. His complexion was much darker than that of the other monks, though his short, black curly hair showed nearly the same amount of grey as Arghan's. His ebony eyes searched the room for a moment. He turned and walked toward the table where Arghan sat. He stopped when he noticed the young girl sitting in his place. His eyes met Arghan's azure gaze. He looked at the girl and back again. Arghan nodded toward the door along the exterior wall. The man walked past the table, opened the door, and stepped outside. Arghan wiped the corner of his mouth with a napkin and followed.

Both men raised their hoods and tucked their arms inside their sleeves. They crossed the terrace outside the compound's main building and stopped under a pavilion beside the parapet wall that lined the edge of the cliff beyond it.

Arghan stepped near the edge of the parapet and surveyed the valley below. Lightning streaked landward in the distance, striking the mountain range on the far side of Lake Trieehd, illuminating the proud, snow-capped summit of Mount Raenik and its lesser cousins Veygar and Indiad in a nigh-daylight glow. The lights of the village of Cairhn, a community nestled along the lakeshore nearest the monastery, barely penetrated the advancing fog. The storm was heading their way.

Arghan turned and faced his counterpart. "So? What news have you, Pattron?"

"What news have I?" Pattron shook his head. He dropped his chin and stared up at Arghan. "Perhaps you'd like to explain what that child's doing here?" He pointed his thumb toward the refectory door.

"In a minute. What about the scroll, has he—"

Pattron held up both palms. "Gavek's still working on it; holed up in the library. Refused even to break his Risenday fast until he was sure."

"And? Anything?" Arghan stepped closer to Pattron and looked into his eyes.

"It's authentic, just as we hoped. Archaic Tzyani script. A near-complete copy of the testament according to the prophet Gion[6]."

"Yes!" Arghan's eyes flashed with excitement. He clenched his fists, shook his arms, and spun on his heels. "The Name... does the scroll reveal the Shepherd King's name?"

"Yeshua. His name is Yeshua."

Yeshua. Arghan recited the word over and over in his mind. The name he yearned for so many years to know. The secret name. The hidden name. The forbidden name. *Yeshua. The Shepherd King's name is Yeshua.*

Arghan shook his head. "I told you Cybella's finds were genuine. It's quite possible the entire collection predates the great purge."

"It would appear so," said Pattron, "but your daughter's playing a dangerous game now my friend, helping us. She sent you another letter, hidden inside the scroll." Pattron reached inside his tunic and produced a roll of parchment which bore Cybella's mark: the red wax seal of the Crown Princess of Cortavia. He tossed it to Arghan.

Arghan gasped and snatched the letter from the air. He spun away and ripped it open. He unrolled the parchment and paced back and forth,

---

[6]. Gion – This is pronounced with a "J" sound used for the "G" and in one syllable. It is identical phonetically with the Earth name "John".

his eyes racing from one side of the page to the other and back again. Then, as fast as he'd begun, Arghan froze and let his arm fall against his hip, clenching the parchment.

"Something's wrong."

"What?" Pattron sprung to within inches of Arghan's face.

"Cybella... she's... she's coming here. To lake Trieehd. To Cairhn. Wants to see me." Arghan stared into Pattron's eyes, searching.

Pattron stood silent for a moment, his mouth gaping wide, his eyes darting left and right. "When?"

"Sometime tomorrow."

"Is she mad? Cybion's already watching us like a hawk. A royal visit now is just the kind of attention—"

"Says she's coming in secret. Minimal escort."

"Yes, but it's only been just over a month since King Eriohn's death. She may be the heir apparent, but she dare not leave the capitol so soon. Not only will it rouse suspicion, but who knows what the Archprelate may do in her absence?"

"He'll do nothing. Her coronation as queen may have to wait for the new year, but she became Grand Royal Arbiter of the Church the minute Eriohn breathed his last. Solstrus cannot act against any royal citizens without her approval."

"Solstrus has already acted. Cybion's here poking around, isn't he?"

Arghan nodded. He sighed, massaging his face.

Pattron continued, "Cybella's authority over the Library may be the only thing preventing the whole collection from being seized. If the scrolls are destroyed the truth will be destroyed along with them. What if Solstrus is already aware — not only of what's buried in the crypts under the Library of Trianon, but of Wardein's efforts to smuggle the texts out, and Abbot Cybion's here to build a case against us and not just a new abbey?"

Arghan returned to the parapet and stared into the darkness below the cliff toward the Oratory. "One of Cybion's guards caught me in the woods this afternoon while searching for the cylinder. There was an altercation." He swallowed and looked back at Pattron.

"Oh dear God—" Pattron turned away and folded his hands behind his neck. "Why?"

"He was chasing that little girl in there," he said, pointing at the refectory door. "He was going to kill her." Arghan related the rest of the afternoon's events as Pattron paced from one side of the pavilion to the other.

Pattron stopped and placed his right elbow against one of the pavilion's columns. He exhaled and rested his forehead on top of his arm. "Why am I not surprised?" he pushed himself off the column and turned to face Arghan. "Do you have any idea what Cybion may do when he hears of this? He can't come up here, Arghan. Not now, especially not in force. Not when so much is at stake."

"I know, dear friend. I know." Arghan gripped Pattron's shoulder. "But what could I do? Look at her." He pointed toward one of the windows. "She's starving. Said her mother is bedridden. By all indications, it has to be the pestilence. I saw more children like her roaming the village streets today. Half the fishing fleet is beached. How many more of their parents lay ill, I wonder?"

Pattron crouched and squinted, looking across the courtyard to the row of windows into the refectory. He grunted and turned back toward Arghan. "Go on."

Arghan continued, "The woman's name is Agape, of the lakeshore."

"The same whose husband died a fortnight ago?" Pattron said, frowning as he looked back toward the refectory.

"The same. I'd like you to go find her after first light. Perhaps one of the medicines in that satchel of yours may yet revive her if she's not too far gone?"

"No."

"But—"

"Cybion's edict. We're banned from ministering to the villagers, remember?"

Arghan pounded one of the columns with his fist. "To hell with the Abbot's edict!"

Some of the monks inside the refectory got up and looked out the windows. Pattron turned his back to them and walked toward Arghan, who now rested his back against the column. Arghan slid down it to crouch near the pavilion's smooth stone floor. "What was the old man thinking when he named me his successor?" He groaned, rubbing his eyes. "You're clearly more spiritual than I'll ever be. Forgive my outburst."

Pattron knelt down and faced his friend. "That may be true," he said, pressing his palm against the left side of Arghan's chest, "but you've got a bigger heart. Ardwynn would have it no other way. Now..." Pattron scanned the lines of dried blood on Arghan's face left by the thorns. He lifted Arghan's chin and pressed down on each of his friend's cheekbones, exposing the lower part of Arghan's bloodshot eyeballs. His eye sockets looked sullen and dark. "How long has it been since you've slept?"

"Three days, maybe four."

"The nightmares again?"

"Yes. Every night."

Pattron sighed. "Well, I've got something in my case for that at least. I'll fetch it for you." He got up and headed for the refectory.

"Pattron... ?"

Pattron stopped and looked back at Arghan.

"Thank you."

Lightning danced across Lake Trieehd's waters. A sudden gust shot up across Precipice Peak, knocking the bell inside the monastery's chapel tower into motion. Its clapper struck its lip three times before coming to rest again.

A voice rose above the sound of the wind, "Please help my momma. You gotta help my momma..."

The men turned toward the sound. Grace stood at the threshold of the pavilion. The refectory door hung open in the distance, knocked by the wind against the building's stone exterior.

Grace stared at Pattron with a searching, desperate gaze. Somehow, her brilliant blue eyes seemed to defy the darkness. Pattron looked at Arghan who — catching the movement in the corner of his eye — looked back at his friend. The pair looked at one another for a moment. Pattron took a breath and held it. Moisture glistened at the edge of his eyes. He exhaled, looked back at Grace, and nodded.

CHAPTER TWO
Exposed

"More wine, eminent one?" The young servant bowed and extended a pitcher across the table.

"No. Leave us." Cybion raised his hand, rings twinkling in the candlelight. He flicked his fingers toward the back of the room. The servant bowed again and crept backward until he scooted out the chamber door.

The slender young man standing to the right of Cybion's chair leaned over the table, took hold of the Abbot's goblet, and slid it toward himself. "If it's not to your liking I could send for some—"

Cybion grabbed the novice's wrist. "It's as fine as they come in this backwater province, Faelis." He glared at the fair-haired priest. He pushed Faelis' arm away and sprung from his seat. He rounded the side of the table and paced toward the curtained archway at the front of the circular chamber. He spun back to face the table, flapping his gold-embroidered, black velvet robe like the wings of a crow. The flames on the candelabra next to him danced on their wicks. His dark, puffy eyelids constricted. "I've simply no thirst for it while the matter at hand remains unresolved." He spun away again and thrust open a set of heavy curtains, exposing a pair of windowed doors. He peeped for a moment through one of its panes. "What's keeping him? How hard can it be, tracking down one little wretch?" He flung both doors wide open and took a few steps onto the balcony, leading with his chin. Raindrops pelted his forehead. He squinted and held his arm up in front of his face, recoiled by the wind. Cybion shifted from side to side, looking out over the balcony rail into the darkness. He ran his fingers through his long black locks, reshuffling them across his balding scalp.

Faelis crept to within a few feet of Cybion's back and stood behind him. "Storm's getting worse. Perhaps he's held up somewhere for the night?"

"He wouldn't dare," huffed Cybion. He turned back and pointed his finger. "I may expect such carelessness from one of those fools in the local garrison but not from a member of the Grand Prelate's own Alpinian Guard. He'll come back here with that little witch in tow or I'll see to it he never draws a bowstring again." Cybion clenched his fist and hammered his opposite palm with it.

Faelis turned and began to clear the table. "It's a pity the Archprelate sent so few of them with you. If he had, perhaps the village folk would show you the respect you so richly deserve, your eminence."

"It is very much a pity, Faelis," said Cybion. "But one cannot blame His High Reverence for that. Alpinian Guards are in short supply these days. Most are held up keeping the Gothan-Lyracian war from spilling over onto the Grand Prelate's doorstep. And, as dim-witted as these country folk are, one cannot blame them entirely for their ignorance of spiritual matters. No, for that, one need look no further than that pile of beer-guzzling nature lovers up there." Cybion pointed out the window toward the silhouette of Precipice Peak. "I'm not sure what I hate worse, their incessant singing or their complete disregard for the Grand Prelate's book of edicts. Imagine the irreverence. The indignity. The ignorance! Do any of those backwater curs know their place; know the order of things? How can they even dare dream of salvation when they show so little regard for those whose station it is to judge who is worthy of it? I tell you, if I accomplish nothing else in this God-forsaken province I'll bring that lot to heel, if not to an end."

"That is indeed your mission here, is it not, eminent one? What are—" Faelis flinched at the sound of knocking.

"You were about to ask 'what am I waiting for'?" Cybion closed the double doors and scooted back to his seat. "Damning, incontrovertible proof of their heresies, that's what. The late king favoured them for some reason, as does his heir apparent. If I prove the Archprelate's suspicions, not even the Grand Royal Arbiter herself will be able to stop him from taking swift and decisive action against them." Cybion raised his eyebrows and waved his hand. "Now, see who's there."

Faelis scampered to the door and opened it.

Two men in light armour entered, holding their helmets. They circled the table and stood on the opposite side of it, facing Cybion, and bowed.

The taller of the two spoke, "Hail, eminent one. We've news to report."

"Out with it then, Captain."

"Perhaps it's best if my man explains, my—"

Cybion's nostrils flared. "I don't give a damn if one of your hounds come here to tell me the tale, as long as its news that insolent little rat is hanging from a rope somewhere." He turned his gaze toward the second man, the archer from the forest. "Now did you or did you not catch her?"

"Ah, may I, your eminence?" The archer winched and motioned with his helmet his intention to set it down on the table.

Cybion sighed and nodded, waving his hand at the tabletop.

"She got away, your eminence, but—"

"What's that you say?" Cybion's face grew red. He tilted his head to the side and glared at the captain.

The archer cradled his bandaged left hand with the fingers of his right. He glanced at his captain and then back at Cybion. "I chased her all the way to the forest. I had her all but cornered until..."

"Until what, man? Wag that tongue of yours before I have it cut out!"

"Until someone intervened."

"What?"

"It was the Prior, my lord," said the Captain. "He was in the forest and defended the girl. He disarmed sergeant Pinion here before he could exercise your wishes. Told him he wants to speak with you about it on the morrow."

Cybion's eyes widened. He glanced at Faelis and then back at Pinion. He sprung from his chair and leaned over the table. "Disarmed... you?"

"That's right, my lord."

"How old are you, soldier?"

"Twenty-nine, sire, ah, I mean, your eminence."

"You're a member of the Grand Prelate's own guards and a monk, at least twenty years your senior... disarmed you?"

"It's true, my lord. As fast as the wind, he was. Before I knew what was happening my arms lay on the forest floor and—"

"Rubbish," said Cybion. "Don't insult my intelligence, soldier. There's no need to concoct such a tale to conceal your incompetence. Just admit you failed. Captain, relieve this man and throw him in the stockade for a week. Perhaps then he—"

"No, wait," said Faelis. "It may not be as preposterous as you think, Abbot Cybion — if I may be so bold?" Faelis left Cybion's side, walked and stood at the edge of the table with the Abbot to his left and the soldiers to his right. He addressed Pinion, "Did he use both his hands and feet to take you down, sergeant?"

"He did."

"And he caught your own sword in the air?"

"Yes, how did you—"

Faelis grinned and gestured with both hands toward Cybion. "The all-seeing One has smiled on you, your eminence."

"What on Earda are you babbling about, Faelis?"

"These sound very much to me like the skills the elite sea knights of Ostergaard were once famous for."

"You mean the Erne Warders?" said the captain.

"Yes," said Faelis.

"Impossible," said Cybion. "The Grand Prelate himself ordered them all destroyed years ago for their heretical treachery."

"I mean no dishonour, Abbot," Faelis continued, "but perhaps you aren't as aware of our national history as us native Cortavians are, yourself being from Lyrance. Have you heard the tale of the Erne Warder who saved the life of young prince Eriohn II twenty years ago and became our king's friend, only to be condemned to death a few years later for his role in the massacre at Koerska?"

"You mean the war criminal, Arghan of Danniker?" interjected the captain.

"That's the one," said Faelis, pointing at the man.

The soldiers turned to get a better look at Faelis. Cybion lifted his hands off the table and fixed his eyes on Faelis as well.

"Well, the king spared his life and instead condemned him to spend the rest of his days in the dungeon at the Palace of Trianon. But there's an old rumour that Eriohn I later freed him in secret, still grateful for the life of his son. If it's true, it's a pity because young Eriohn II was lost at sea four years ago, making it all for nothing. It ruined the king. He was never seen publicly after that, not until his state funeral, that is."

"Come now, is there any evidence to back up this conspiracy theory of yours, Faelis?" said Cybion, "I'd leap at the chance to put any or all of these Cantorvarians to the axe blade — you know that — but to implicate the late king may put the Archprelate decidedly on the wrong side of the grand royal arbiter and future queen."

"He did all I said he did, your eminence, I swear to it," said Pinion.

"What's more, I've seen him work in the monastery's vineyard," said the captain. "There's biceps the size of tree trunks and a stomach flatter than the plains of Nova Engaric under that baggy habit of his, though I've never seen him remove his linen undergarment, not even during the hottest days of Sunren[1]."

"So he's modest. Isn't that one of these monks' cherished virtues? Why's that significant?"

"When I was attached to the Archprelate's force at the Cathedral of Trianon one of Eriohn's old prison guards — a former sailor — had a falling out with the Palace and found himself out of work," said the captain. "He asked me for a position guarding one of the Archprelate's properties in the city in exchange for his sharing a little secret the Archprelate may have wanted to hear. He told me that when the prisoner everyone

---
1. Sunren – the fifth month of the year, mid-summer.

supposed to be Arghan of Danniker died some years ago he was tasked with burning the corpse. Only there was no tattoo of the Sea Eagle on the man's chest and neither ear had ever been pierced. He'd fought alongside the great Sea Knights fending off the Zuelan invasion of 410. He'd know one to see one. He insisted the corpse was no Erne Warder."

Faelis interrupted, "There you have it, your eminence, if the Prior of Cairhn monastery is a fugitive Erne Warder — that makes him a heretic of heretics, doesn't it?"

Cybion's scowl widened into a devilish grin. His eyes darted from one man to another. He stepped away from the table and walked to face the double doors. Lightning flashed through its panes. He spun to face his company trio.

"Captain, assemble your force at the village watchtower at midday tomorrow, leaving a token guard to watch over the construction site. I'll meet you there and brief you on my plan. If Arghan of Danniker is truly hiding right under our noses and wants to take issue with how I do things, he'll soon regret it."

Pattron watched the fog banks rise like creeping fingers off the glassy surface of Lake Trieehd as the first rays of dawn danced across its waters. Little Grace, ahead by a few steps, tugged his hand as the pair rounded the bend leading to the lakeshore road.

"It's not far now, just aways down this path to the water's edge, see?"

A modest, weather-worn shack stood against a low, earthen embankment about thirty paces away. Its front door faced the pebbled beach to the west of the village of Cairhn, isolated from the other shanties that dotted that part of the shore. A small rowboat floated aimlessly offshore, tethered by a long rope to an old wooden stake driven into the beach. A few fishing nets and several sun-bleached pieces of driftwood floated in and out with the waves, teasing landfall.

"Yes, I see it." Pattron slipped on the muddy path and sidestepped two puddles while trying to correct his stride. With his free hand, he adjusted the shoulder strap of his leather satchel then shook the cool wet dew from his fingers before stuffing it back inside his cassock.

"I'm quite grateful that you decided to come see momma after all," said Grace.

"Hmm." Pattron looked up and down the path, walking on his toes for a moment.

"I know you didn't think it was a very good idea, but she really needs your help."

Pattron squinted and arched one eyebrow. "Really, what makes you think that — about me not thinking it was a good idea, I mean?"

"Abba Arghan told me; said you think he's crazy."

"Abba Arghan told you that? Did he tell you to call him 'Abba' too?" Pattron knew that apart from Arghan's daughter Cybella, he was the only living soul he was aware of who knew Arghan's real name. The consequences of it getting out could be severe, not only for him but for the entire monastery. Yet somehow he'd trusted a ten-year-old girl with such knowledge?

"No," replied Grace, "just 'Arghan'. 'Arghan of Danniker', I think is what he said it was in the woods. I added the other part. That's what they'll call him someday, after all."

Pattron let the girl's hand slip out of his and watched her walk on for several paces. He cocked his head and scratched his forehead. He held his satchel strap away from his chest with his thumb, tapping his chest with the other four fingers repeatedly. *He really isn't sleeping at night, is he? Telling her he would be revered as a saint someday? Has he finally gone mad? He of all people should know that's impossible.*

"Come on! Mamma's in there." Grace ran back and grabbed Pattron's hand again. She pointed in the direction of the house and tugged him forward. He stumbled a little but soon regained his stride.

Grace led him to the narrow wooden doorstep of the shack. He froze when he finally saw it up close. His respiration quickened into short, shallow breaths. The door had come off its lower iron hinge and hung at an angle off the one remaining. A page of parchment fluttered in the breeze, nailed at the centre of its uneven boards. On it was written an edict, punctuated by Abbot Cybion's personal seal. It forbade entry under the penalty of death, declaring that the house and all that it contained, living or otherwise, was damned.

Grace stood behind Pattron. "When you pray for her, don't forget to say the Shepherd's real name — the one you read upon the scroll."

Pattron trembled. "The what? Wait, when did you—" he spun around to face her.

Grace was gone.

Pattron's head darted from left to right, his eyes scanning up and down the beach, then out over the lake. "Grace?"

Nothing.

He scampered around to the left side of the shack, crossing behind it, and emerged past its right side. His pace slowed as he took position again in front of the door. "Grace?"

Nothing.

He looked at the ridge at the top of the waterfront's steep embankment. "Grace?"

Nothing.

"Where did?..."

He grabbed his shoulder strap and it slipped up and down against the edge of his neck. He tiptoed away from the door and ambled back toward the muddy path.

A deep, feminine groan echoed from inside the hovel. Pattron stopped. He fiddled with his strap again. He looked at the parchment on the door, then down at his satchel, and allowed his eyes to fall out of focus. *None of my medicines can do her any good at this stage.* He clutched his strap's brass buckle and held it in place. His eyes came back into focus on the tattoo that covered the fleshy area between his thumb and index finger. The drawing depicted the Owl of Trenegal perched atop a helmet, clutching the Hospitaller's Cross in its talons.

An oath is an oath. How many times had he said that to others? Had he forgotten his pledge?

He stepped toward the door and paused. He licked the dryness from his lips. A breeze blew in from across the lake. He pulled the parchment off its nail and threw it into the current of air. He pulled the door latch and stepped inside.

The stench of rotting fish and stale vomit invaded his nostrils. He gagged. He grabbed some gauze from his satchel, doused it with some water from his waterskin, and held it over his mouth and nose.

The front room was shadowy and dank. An empty pot sat atop a pile of ashes inside the cabin's crude stone hearth. Water dripped from between its loosened roofboards. Empty bowls were strewn across a rough wooden table. A single door hung partially open in the middle of the room's back wall.

Another moan sounded from behind the door. "Eldabar, is that you?"

The woman's dead husband, thought Pattron. *She's delirious, no doubt.*

Pattron spotted an oil lamp hanging from a hook beside the door. He grabbed it and placed it on top of the table. He retrieved his knife and flint from his satchel and soon had it lit. He lifted the gauze back to his mouth, pushed the door open with his elbow, and with his other hand raised the lamp and looked inside. A woman with long golden braids lay sprawled on top of a shoddy, rope and wicker bed. A thin linen gown clung to her body, filthy and soaked with sweat. Pattron shuddered when he noticed her wrists and ankles were chained to the bedposts.

Cybion's men had left her there to die?

"Agape?" Pattron's eyes were as wide as the full moons were on the second day of Repose. He crept near the bed and knelt beside it. Black pustules oozed from Agape's legs and arms. Her eyelids were red and swollen, and her lips cracked and bloody. Reddened sores dotted her face.

He gasped and shook his head. "Father of Lights!" He set the lamp on top of the bedpost and made the sign of the Three-in-One over his chest and head. "This is madness." He sprung to his feet and scampered back toward the door.

A burning welled up inside his heart. Grace's words echoed inside his mind, 'When you pray for her, don't forget to say the Shepherd's real name'. He dropped the gauze from his mouth and let it fall to the floor. A language he'd never heard burst from his lips. The hand that had held the gauze burned as though it had touched a stone next to a fire. He spun around and marched toward the bed. Tears streamed down his cheeks.

He laid his bare hand on top of Agape's forehead.

"In the Name of Yeshua, get up!"

Something that felt like the torrent of a waterfall shot through Pattron's arm and his fingertips. He collapsed to his knees, trembling. Pattron heard four clicks and looked up just in time to see Agape's chains glow and fall off her ankles and wrists. Agape shot upward and opened her eyes. She screamed and jumped out of the bed, running through the open doorway and across the front room. She burst through the cabin door and ran out onto the beach.

Pattron stared at his hand, still trembling. He squinted at the sunlight now beaming through the open door. He stumbled to his feet, catching himself against the door frame. He threw off his satchel and cloak, ran across the room, and then outside.

In the distance, Agape stood roughly ten strides[2] offshore, chest-deep in the lake, thrashing, sending splashes of water in all directions. She tore off her filthy gown and threw it into the lake. She disappeared below the waters. Pattron raced across the beach and then into the shallows. He dove into the lake and swam to the spot where Agape had disappeared. He stood up and poised to dive below the waters again when Agape suddenly burst from the surface, laughing. She batted some water at Pattron, spraying him in the face. Pattron's gaze fell on her naked body. His jaw dropped open. Agape's fair skin was smooth and clean. Her eyelids bright and soft. She looked back at him with a broad smile, her teeth white and gleaming in the sunlight.

Wide-eyed, Pattron shook his head and averted his gaze. He looked toward the shore and took Agape by the shoulder. "Come with me, dear lady, let's get you dry."

About an hour later the pair sat on driftwood on either side of a crackling fire. Pattron held a fish pierced with a stick, turning it over the flames while a teapot came to a boil atop the coals. Agape closed Pattron's cloak tighter around her neck and held out her other hand toward the fire. She looked at the back of her hand and then flipped it over to see her palm.

---

2. Stride (abbr. s) - a unit of measure roughly equal to one Earth metre.

"I can't believe my eyes. I don't know how to thank you... friar, I—"

"Call me Pattron. Brother Pattron. But don't thank me, thank the Shepherd King and that remarkable little girl of yours."

"What?"

"I still don't understand all that just happened, but it wouldn't have if not for her. She led me here. Insisted I see you. She took off somewhere before I found you."

Agape wrinkled her brows. "That's impossible."

"Why? What do you mean?"

Agape stood up and beckoned Pattron to follow her. She took him by the hand and led him up a second path on the far side of the shack. The pair reached the top of the embankment and stepped onto a field covered in wildflowers. A few feet away stood two piles of rocks in front of patches of disturbed soil. Bleached planks rested in front of upright stones with names carved into them. The one on the left read 'Eldabar'[3] and the one on the right read 'Grace.'

Pattron's knees buckled and he fell on them to the ground. He lurched forward and held his face in his hands, weeping. "Father of Lights, I know not how or why you visit us so, but for this and all your ways I worship thee." He raised his hands heavenward and gazed toward the clouds.

"The pestilence took them a fortnight ago," said Agape, tears streaming down her cheeks. "I've no hand for fishing, so when Eldabar fell ill I sought work in the village. One of Cybion's guards took a liking to me and... he forced me into their service, for 'comfort' he said. When I failed to show up the day my family died the guard sought me out and caught me as I finished burying them. I was already showing the signs. When he saw my marks he struck me down and then chained me to my bed. Later that day I heard the sound of pounding on the door. There I laid until you freed me."

Pattron stood up and put his arm around Agape. "And free you'll stay,

---

3. "Eldabar" - Compound name. "El" is from the Hebrew (לא), meaning "God", and the word "dabar" (Hebrew: רָבָד) means "word", "talk" or "thing". Thus the name "Eldabar" in this context means "The Word of God".

my lady. Come. There's shelter for you in the monastery. Prior Arthos will see to it, surely. Is there anything left for you here? Anything you wish to retrieve from your house?"

Agape shook her head. She held her arm against her chest and rested her chin in her palm, looking back at the graves.

"We'd be wise to set fire to your cabin before we leave," said Pattron. "The Shepherd King saw fit to deliver you from your chains and sores, but whatever brought them upon you in the first place may linger there. The fire will drive it away. Will you help me?"

Agape nodded. Pattron took her by the hand and led her back down the embankment.

They had just passed the corner of Agape's shack when Pattron skidded to a stop. He shuffled back, nudging Agape to stand against the wall.

"One of Cybion's men," he said, raising his index finger to his lips. He pointed toward the campfire still burning on the beach. A soldier stood with his back to them, looking down at the fire. With his foot, he lifted the sharpened branch Pattron had used to roast the fish he'd caught, then crouched to flip open the teapot Agape had left on the coals.

Pattron swept his hand over his forehead and winced. *What was I thinking, lighting that fire? They must have seen the smoke on their way to their posts.*

The soldier twitched his head and reached for something on the surface of the beach. He lifted the object and held it up to his eyes. It was the parchment that had been nailed to the door.

"Garrock, look what I found," said the man, waving the notice in the air. He turned and looked directly past the corner of the house where the pair stood.

Pattron jerked his head back behind the corner of the shack and pushed Agape tighter against the wall. "We've got to get out of here, now." He grabbed her hand and began to run for the path leading to the gravesites.

"Wait," she said. "Garrock is the one who—"

The pair recoiled when a barrel-chested, brutish figure appeared at the top of the embankment.

Garrock scowled, hissing through a set of half-missing teeth. "What manner of witchcraft is this then?" He leered at Agape, catching sight of the narrow, open gap in the cloak she wore. He hopped down the embankment, clutching the handle of the studded club hanging from his belt. He leaped forward and pulled Agape's cloak apart. Agape reeled back, closing it again.

Pattron lunged in front of Agape, holding both palms outward. "Leave the woman be. There's no witchcraft at work here."

"Ah, so she deceived us then? A little chimney soot rubbed in a few places maybe, all to scare us off? Whore probably killed her man and kid, y' know. Caught her buryin' them a while back I did. What's your business with her, black one? Here to take her 'private confession', are ye?" He cackled, lifting his head into the air.

"That's enough," said Pattron. He took Agape's hand and strengthened his footing.

"I don't know, Garrock, 'tis lookin' like witchcraft to me." The other soldier emerged from behind the corner of the shack, holding out one of Agape's chains. "Looks as though it's been burned clean through, and this was lying on the beach next to the fire. Somebody ripped it off the door they did." He waved the parchment with his other hand.

Garrock turned, squinting at the chain's severed lock. "Demon fire and unholy defiance…"

Pattron spun his head to look into Agape's eyes and tugged on her hand. "Come!"

The pair sprinted for the embankment. Something whizzed through the air behind Pattron's head. Points of light and pulses of red clouded his vision. He fell to the ground, choking on soil and blood. He rolled onto his back and looked up. He saw Agape leaning over him, sobbing. The other soldier came into view over her shoulder, dragging her away. He felt his satchel strap being slipped over his shoulder. His torso thudded as it fell back to the ground.

Another voice sounded from somewhere above Pattron's head, distinct from the rest, "What's this business here?"

"Sir, we spotted smoke coming from the beach and found this Askhavahni[4] Cantorvarian[5] here conspiring with that whore Cybion declared damned," said Garrock. "Look at the potions he carries in this bag of his."

"It's 'Abbot Cybion' to you, soldier."

"Sorry, sir."

"Give it here. Now, is this true?" said the third voice.

" 'Tis, sir, and look at this," said the second man.

For a moment there was nothing but the sound of surf hitting the shore and gulls squawking overhead.

"Hmm. Good work. Bind them both. Take them to the Abbot. Could be just what he's been looking for. Then get back to your posts. Understood?"

"Yes sir," said Garrock and his partner, nearly in unison.

Pattron felt the world turn around him and the sensation of rope burning across his wrists. The world spun again and his body fell limp over what felt like a pauldron grinding into his stomach. Blood rushed to his head. He struggled to open his eyes. Beyond the swaying motion of his captor's leg, he saw the blurry image of little Grace standing in the grass at the edge of the embankment.

He smiled as his vision faded to black.

The sun had burned off the night's rain by the time Arghan's meager crew had reached the hillside vineyard far below the priory. Now, it hung over the midday sky like a watchful taskmaster, dictating a schedule Arghan was no longer sure he could keep. In years past, nearly sixty monks had laboured in the vineyard at harvest time, joined by paid helpers from the village. Now fewer than a dozen men toiled there under his supervision. He wiped the sweat from his brow and sat down on the grass, leaning against one of the posts at the edge of the field. He cocked his head and shook out the last precious ounces of water from his canteen.

He gazed out over the endless rows of trellises and contemplated

---

4. Askhavahni – A native of the tropical southern continent of Askhavahn.
5. Cantorvarian – the monastic order headquartered at the Priory of Cairhn on Precipice Peak.

all the unharvested grapes they contained. *We'll never finish in time,* he thought, *now that Cybion's ordered most of the brothers to help the villagers build his monstrosity.* He stared down the hill toward Cairhn and scanned the site where hundreds of men swung picks and shovels, excavating the foundation of Cybion's new abbey, the structure destined to replace the clifftop complex Arghan had called home for just over two decades. If its architect's ambitious schedule continued unabated, in ten short years there would be no more Cantorvarians. No more singing. No more winemaking. No more worship and work. 735 years of tradition would come to an end.

An unfamiliar voice called from the top of the hill, "Arthos of Threicia. Is the prior called Arthos among you? I must speak to him."

Arghan sprung up and crouched behind the vine-stake he had been leaning against. He reached inside his hip-satchel and took out a small telescope. He spied through it, past the vines toward the crate stacks half way up the hill. Brother Kavar stood talking to a slender figure in a blue silk cloak and feathered cap.

Royal squire, looks like. Can't be older than sixteen.

Kavar pointed toward the bottom of the hill and the cloaked youth took off in Arghan's direction. Arghan turned his scope toward the barn and courtyard at the top of the hill. The guard who Cybion had stationed there had left his post.

Where have you gone now?

Arghan put his telescope away. He marked which row the squire had followed and crept up the next row over, crouching behind the trellises. He watched the squire walk past him, taking note of the rest of the young man's attire.

One dagger, left side. No sword.

Arghan scooted under the lowest trellis and emerged directly behind his visitor, still crouching below the branches. He grabbed the hem of the squire's cloak and yanked it back, pulling the youth to the ground. "What the devil are you doing here, you fool?"

The young man spun around to right himself.

Arghan grabbed the squire's shoulder, preventing him from rising to his feet. "Stay below the vines."

"What? Where did you come from, I didn't hear or see—"

"You weren't meant to."

"Who—"

"I am the man you seek. Speak the password."

"What? I—"

"The password." Arghan grabbed the teenager's cloak, tightening it around his throat. He pulled him closer until they were face to face.

The squire's eyes bulged, fixed on Arghan's face. "R-Revelation..."

Arghan scowled. Without blinking, he searched the teenager's expression for any sign of deceit. He slowly released his grip and rested his hands on his thighs.

The squire gasped, clutching his throat. Spittle dripped from his mouth. As if to remember his station, he straightened his back and attempted to deepen his voice. "Ugh... Now you. How do I know it's you? Speak the oath."

The oath. The very mention of it brought a flush of heat behind Arghan's ears. He studied the squire's eyes again. His chest filled with air. He closed his eyes and chuffed through his nostrils.

> *"At Erne Rock I'll take my stand;*
> *with my twin swords defend this land.*
> *The heartland's throat I shall ward,*
> *'gainst all who serve the devil's horde."*

Arghan opened his eyes and glared at the squire.

The youth's face broadened with a goofy, boyish grin. "I can't believe it. Me, kneeling before a real, live Erne Warder."

The squire's right hand skimmed across his belly, reaching for his left hip. With a snap of his left hand, Arghan arrested the squire's wrist in a vise-like grip. With a flick of his right wrist, he whipped the youth's dagger into the air, catching it by the hilt.

"Slowly." Arghan released the lad's arm, holding the dagger pointed toward his face.

With a groan, the squire shook his wrist, then reached past his dagger scabbard and retrieved a parchment scroll sealed in red wax, just as Cybella's other letters had been. Arghan snatched it from him. He spun the dagger with his fingers and held it by its blade, extending the hilt toward the squire's hand.

"Forgive me," said Arghan. "Precautions must be taken. Maybe someday you will understand. Where does she lodge?"

"I... I was told not to say."

"That sounds wise. How many accompany her?"

"Again, I'm forbidden to—"

"Understood. You came here on foot or horse?"

"Horse. She's hitched to the roadside of the barn."

"Circle clockwise 'round the field there, following the bottom of the culvert." He pointed to a spot some twenty feet from their position. "Approach the barn from the western side, and from there turn the far corner to collect your mare. Take the road west from the barn, through the forest. You'll soon find a crossroads and signpost. From there you can find your way back to Cairhn, or wherever it is you must return to. Clear?"

"Understood." The squire started to rise.

Arghan grabbed the youth's right bicep. He whispered in a sullen tone. "Tell princess Cybella her father sends his love."

The squire looked away and back again. He opened his mouth as if to speak, then stopped. He nodded and then scurried into the culvert.

What was it the courier wanted to say, but couldn't? Arghan watched the teen until he disappeared behind the rocks and thicket at the southwest corner of the field. Squinting, He looked down at the construction site, then back up the hill toward the barn. He marked the sun's position in the sky. *What on Earda keeps you, Pattron?* He sprung to his feet and jogged up the hill toward the barn, leaving his grape basket and tools behind.

Arghan approached the monk who had greeted his visitor. He leaned close to the man's ear. "Hail, Kavar. Did you see where Cybion's man went?"

"No, brother," the olive-skinned monk replied, "not where, but when. He left just after that young squire showed up looking for you."

"That's what I was afraid of. I'll be in the barn. Alert me if anyone else approaches."

"Is something amiss?" asked Kavar, wiping his forehead with the towel that hung around his neck.

"I pray not, but stay alert. Carry on as normal."

"As you wish, brother." Kavar grinned. "The Shepherd King guide you."

"And you, brother." Arghan patted Kavar on the shoulder and then marched into the barn. He scanned the horizon as he closed its two doors behind him. He turned his back to the doors and ripped open the letter. He unrolled it in front of a ray of sunlight that beamed in through the hay loft window and read:

Situation urgent. Meet me at midnight. Village pier. Come alone.

Arghan sensed his pulse quicken. The veins inside his neck tightened against his sweat-soaked collar. Had the prospect of seeing his only daughter for the very first time caused that or was it the nature and brevity of her message? He sunk into a bale of hay and reached for his canteen and frowned once he remembered it was empty. He yanked it off his neck and threw it at the barn door.

"Father of Lights, what now? All our hopes rest in her." Arghan sighed and dropped to his knees. He turned around and rested his elbows on top of the bale of hay. He bowed his head and wept. "Remember Your faithful ones, Father of Lights, the monks of Precipice Peak. Its elders are my fathers, its juniors are my sons. All are my brothers. Grant me strength and wisdom in this hour to do right by them. Grant that Pattron and I have not failed them."

The barn door creaked open. Kavar stumbled through the opening, kicking up dust.

"Brother Arthos, riders approach from the south!"

Arghan shoved the letter inside his satchel and sprung to his feet.

"Stay in the barn. Watch from the window. If I do not return, flee with your field-brothers to the Oratory. If no word comes from me by nightfall, head for the caves of Mount Trobus. Understood?"

Kavar nodded. He ambled to a nearby window, crouched at its sill, and peered through the crack between the shutters.

Arghan pushed the barn doors open. Hinges creaked over the sound of cicadas singing from the vines beyond the lawn outside. Horse hooves rumbled up the road. Pommelled helmets gleamed in the sunlight, bobbing up and down above the hedge row beside the road. Arghan strode to the centre of the lawn and turned toward the place he expected the horsemen would make an appearance.

Six riders galloped around the corner and onto the lawn, swords already drawn, led by the captain of the Grand Prelate's modest contingent and his men at arms, followed by members of Cairhn's volunteer citizen garrison who marched on foot. They split into two groups and flowed past Arghan until they formed a circle around him. The man he recognized from his encounter in the woods, sergeant Pinion, took a position several paces in front of him and aimed a loaded crossbow at Arghan's head. Yew bows creaked behind him. He looked around the circle, staring each man in the eyes, and then turned his view back to the sergeant. He heard the sound of a cart and a team of horses rumble up and stop just behind the hedgerow.

Cybion's shrill voice cut through the air, "Make way!"

The soldiers parted again as Cybion strutted up beside Pinion and stopped, staring at Arghan as if to expect a response. By now the monks working in the field had all started to tiptoe to the edge of the trellis rows. The ones who arrived first stopped and stared.

Arghan looked at the men to his left and right, then past them to the monks now lining the edge of the clearing. He gave them a reassuring nod then turned to face Cybion. He bowed and said, "Your eminence."

Cybion smiled and cocked his head. He glared at Arghan with his beady brown eyes, looking past his prominent nose and powdered cheekbones. He sauntered to his left, passing one of the mounted men, and walked to within a few feet of the monks. He grabbed a few grapes from one of the crates stacked before them and spun back in the direction from where he came and pranced back to the spot he started from. He tossed a few grapes in his mouth and chewed.

He turned his head and spit. "My protégé seems to think you're the war criminal known as 'Arghan of Danniker'. Are you?"

Arghan stared back at Cybion, motionless. He knew it was only a matter of time before this encounter would come.

"I see," said Cybion. He turned and looked behind him. "Bring the wagon."

A man whistled and slapped a pair of reigns, driving a pair of horses on top of a wagon that carried an iron cage. Inside it was a man and woman, hooded and bound at the wrists. Arghan gasped and gritted his teeth when he recognized the robe and brown hands of the male figure as those of his friend and brother Pattron.

"Stop there," said Cybion. He motioned to one of the village militia. "Bring them out."

A militiaman opened the cage, pulled each prisoner out, and led them to a spot in front of Cybion. He pushed them to their knees.

"Take off their hoods."

Pattron and Agape shook their heads, blinking in the sunlight, both gagged at the mouth. As Pattron's vision came into focus he widened his eyes and shook his head at Arghan, shouting through the gag.

"You know, I knew your lot was up to no good here but I really thought I'd have to go to a lot more trouble to prove it," said Cybion. "Imagine my surprise when these two just dropped into my lap this morning. Now get this—" Cybion looked around the area, finding the eyes of all the soldiers and monks who were watching. He pointed at Pattron. "This one claims to have performed some sort of miracle to heal this dying wretch after being led to the site by the whore's dead daughter, and that one — the erstwhile wretch — shows no sign of the pestilence my men say she so clearly had only a week ago. Now, call me daft, but I'm not quite sure which one of them is in league with the evil one. Do you know?"

Arghan raised his eyebrows and dropped open his mouth. He looked at Agape, then stared at Pattron, searching his eyes. Pattron nodded.

"Ah, I see you're at a loss too," said Cybion. "Did I mention she was found wearing only your friend's cloak? Probably heading out to the woods for a salacious romp, or perhaps coming back from one, I haven't figured that one out either."

The soldiers erupted with laughter.

Arghan narrowed his eyes and wrinkled his nose.

Cybion slid Pinion's dagger from out of its sheath and snapped it up under Pattron's throat. He nodded to one of the captain's men and the man stepped up, drew his own knife, and did likewise to Agape.

"Now. Are you... the war criminal... Arghan of Danniker?" Cybion tightened the dagger blade against Pattron's neck as a bead of blood trickled down it and soaked into Pattron's collar.

"I am Arghan of Danniker," said Arghan.

Armour rattled behind Arghan, followed by a thud. A rider dismounting? Footsteps thundered toward him. He spun to face the threat but met the captain's boot too late to stop it from hurdling deep into his stomach, emptying his lungs. He fell to the ground, wheezing.

"Seize him. Expose his mark. That'll prove it."

Arghan felt two men grab him by the arms and pull him upright. He looked at Pattron and stammered, "Fear not brother. We're all in the Shepherd's hands now."

Cybion jumped forward and slapped Arghan across the lips. "Heretic!"

The soldiers drew their daggers and slit the hems of Arghan's linen shirt and ripped it off of him, exposing his muscular chest and back. A turquoise-hued tattoo depicting a sea eagle in flight clutching a fish in its talons covered most of his left pectoral muscle.

"Do you see that?" Cybion turned and shouted to the monks standing amid the vines. "Your prior here bears the mark of an Erne Warder, a heretic, a devil worshipper, and an enemy of the Church and your most holy Grand Prelate divine, the only true oracle of the Emperor-God. Decide this day whom you will follow, whether it is me, the Grand Prelate's true representative, or this pretender, this traitor, this hellspawn!"

"Follow neither of us, brothers," said Arghan, straining to breathe and wrestling against the arms of his captors, "follow the Shepherd. Only He can truly lead you."

Cybion grabbed a club that hung from Pinion's waste and struck Arghan on the side of the neck. Arghan collapsed and lay motionless on the ground.

"Choose!" screamed Cybion, glaring at the monks. One by one they walked forward and stood beside each other, shoulder to shoulder. None of them knelt.

Cybion threw the club on the ground. "Bind the Erne Warder. Bind them all." He pointed at the monks. "Take them up the mountain to the monastery. I'm sure we'll get to the bottom of this there. Who knows what they've been up to all this time?"

The foot soldiers fanned out and bound each of the monks with rope, connecting a length of it from one man's wrists to another's. The monks watched as the Grand Prelate's guards shackled and blindfolded Arghan, then dragged him to the caged wagon and threw him in it, followed by Pattron and Agape.

Inside the barn, Kavar raced to the back wall. He grabbed a bale of hay that was leaning against it and threw it aside, exposing a hole in the boards. He slithered under the wall and emerged near where the young squire had earlier hitched his horse. He bolted for the treeline and watched for a few moments as the soldiers began to march, following the wagon. He waited until the party had passed then darted into the woods and up the hill.

CHAPTER THREE
Accused

Kavar lurched against the stony corner of the gatehouse wall, heaving. He squinted back down the hillside at the twisting path far below. Cybion's party continued to march up the road toward the compound. Brother Arthos' command to rendezvous at the Oratory now seemed moot. There was but one thing left to do.

Kavar gritted his teeth, swallowed, and pushed himself off his rest, stumbling through the entrance leading to the outer courtyard. He raced to the chapel and burst through the front door. He limped to the base of its bell tower and seized the rope. *One pull more than the hour. Seven rings instead of six.* With any hope, the other brothers making the return journey from the Abbey site would hear it and stay away.

Kavar bounded through the chapel's side entrance and out under the colonnade which connected it to the dormitory and the refectory kitchen below. He reached for the latch of a door but stopped at the sound of a familiar voice.

"Brother Kavar!" Gavek's wiry figure came running out from the library on the opposite side of the courtyard. He lurched to a stop beside the well which stood at the midpoint between it and the dormitory and studied his fellow monk. "I heard the warning bell. What's happened?"

"Gavek," said Kavar, panting as he leaned against a column. "Cybion's seized both Arthos and Pattron, the field-brothers from the vineyard too. He's marching them all up here; should be here any moment. Come, we must warn the others. If we hurry perhaps we can all escape." He opened his hands toward the refectory.

Gavek looked back and forth between the gate and the library door. "No. Go. I'll catch up." He waved his hand toward the dormitory. "Hurry."

"What? Where—"

"Just go!"

Kavar nodded, reluctantly. He rolled off the column and stumbled into the dormitory door.

Gavek raced back across the courtyard and into the library. The sound of his footsteps echoed off the vaulted ceiling as he bounded across the smooth stone floor. He weaved and dodged his way through a maze of shelves, sending loose pages fluttering through the air. He reached the scriptorium at the back of the room and slid beside a broad oak table, glancing down at the maps and drawings strewn across its surface.

He shook his head. *No time for any of that.*

He looked at the row of writing desks that stood along the outside wall below four tall, arched windows. His eyes darted from table to table. Codices lay open on every one of them.

If only there were time!

Horseshoes clacked across the courtyard, followed by the rumbling of marching footsteps and wagon wheels.

Gavek rushed to the nearest desk. He grabbed the codex on top of it and stuffed it inside a canvas sack that hung from a hook on the wall. He scanned the room and spotted the rope used to hoist a candle chandelier. He snatched a knife from the desk and leaped on top of the oak table. He tied the rope around one of the columns and then cut off the slack.

The shadows of four figures spread across the library's sunbathed vestibule. Armoured footsteps clattered just beyond the threshold.

Gavek jumped down. He tied the rope around the canvas sack and thrust open one of the windows above the desk.

Footsteps clomped across the library floor.

A high-pitched voice called beyond the shelves, "Search it all. Leave nothing unturned. Bring me anything that appears particularly old, especially scrolls."

"As you wish, Master Faelis," answered a deeper-toned male voice.

Gavek reached through the open window and tied the other end of the rope around the head of a stone gargoyle. He threw the sack out the window. The rope zipped over the sill until it sprung taut. Gavek shut the pane and dove under the table seconds before one of Cybion's guards turned the corner.

He held his breath and watched the soldier march up to the edge of the table. A shiver ran down his back. The polished detailing on the knight's greaves indicated he was one of the Grand Prelate's elite Alpinian Guards. His pulse quickened when he spotted something resting on the floor through the gap between the knight's legs. The leather cylinder Arghan had given him the night before lay near the desk's lower shelf. In his haste, he'd neglected to hide it. He glared at the soldier's legs. *Come on, move, move!*

The soldier strode to the other end of the room. Gavek exhaled and peeked out from under the table. The cavalier rifled through another codex with his back to Gavek. Gavek strained across the aisle and knocked the cylinder off the shelf. It tumbled to the floor. The guardsman twitched at the sound. He clutched his sword hilt and looked back over his shoulder. Gavek scurried back under the table as the man strode to the source of the sound. Sweat trickled down Gavek's forehead. The man knelt down. Gavek closed his eyes and recoiled, guarding his face with his forearms. The knight grabbed the cylinder and rose as quickly as he'd descended. Gavek bit his knuckle. *No. No, no, no!*

The knight called out toward the front of the room, "Master Faelis, come look at this."

Footsteps echoed from beyond the shelves until the hem of a flowing black cassock came into view.

"Give it here," said Faelis. The apprentice held the scroll casing close to his eyes and rolled it over in his fingers. He slid its top off and shook out its contents. He unrolled the scroll and scanned its aged surface. His mouth contorted into an indignant grimace. "Good work, Lieutenant. Come with me. The rest of you, keep searching. There must be more where this came from." He hastened to the open door and faced the courtyard. "Abbot Cybion, We've found something." Faelis marched out the door and the lieutenant followed.

Gavek rolled out from under the table and sprung to his feet. Two other soldiers remained inside the library, rifling through the shelves, tossing books in all directions. The sound of pages tearing grew louder. The men had to be nearing the back of the room. He sped to one of the shelves that stood against the inside wall and stood on his tiptoes. He pulled one of the books on the top shelf and the bookcase sprung open, revealing a hidden doorway. Gavek scurried inside it and gripped the latch. He held it for a moment and look back into the scriptorium, listening to the mayhem. The library had been the joy of his life since he was a child. What would become of it? He took a deep breath, closed the door, and disappeared into the darkness, feeling his way along the cold stone walls of the passageway.

The carriage transporting the caged trio stopped next to the courtyard well. Arghan, Pattron, and Agape huddled on their knees inside the cage, all of them bound with their hands behind their backs. Only Arghan was hooded; the others were gagged.

Footsteps plodded toward them. "Leave them here. They're not going anywhere. Come with me. We're to search the chapel. The Alpinians will come to fetch them when it's time."

The carriage rose as if a weight had been lifted off it and the sound of footsteps trailed away. Arghan leaned against the cage bars and cocked his head northward, straining to discern the nature of the commotion echoing from the library.

He whispered through the black hood that covered his head, "Pattron? Agape?"

Pattron managed a muffled affirmative through his gag.

"I'm hooded, are you?" Arghan asked.

"Uh-uh." *Negative.*

"Are any guards in earshot?"

"Uh-uh."

"I'm facing north, toward the library, correct?"

"Uh-huh."

They're ransacking the library, looking for evidence, he thought. Arghan prayed Gavek had already fled.

"Listen to me. We've not much time. I've got a plan to get us out of this, but you'll have to trust me."

Agape's eyes bulged as she looked at Pattron. Pattron nodded back to her with all the assurance he could convey.

"Cybion's brought us here to prove his point. I won't let him. He means to stage some kind of a trial, no doubt. Otherwise, he would have had us killed already."

"Mm. Mm!" Pattron's change of tone signaled alarm. Or did it?

Another set of footsteps clapped across the courtyard, softer than the others. Arghan felt the air stir against his chest as the sound of flapping fabric passed before him and stopped.

"Father Pattron, Father Arth—"

"Gavek? Hide yourself, they'll see—"

Gavek inhaled as if to speak but stopped, gaping at the sight of the erne tattoo on Arghan's chest. His gaze traced up Arghan's torso until it fixed on his mentor's hooded face.

"It's— it's okay, Father. I'm crouching between the carriage and the well and I've counted them all. They're busy turning the monastery upside down, for now."

"Well done. I assume it was you who rang the warning bell?"

"No, Kavar did."

"Kavar? I told him to—"

"Well, he didn't listen, obviously. Probably had something to do with the others being captured?"

"No matter. You've got to get out of here. Don't let them catch you.

Head for—"

"No, I won't leave you. I'm sorry, I tried to hide all I could but there was no time. The soldiers barged in, and in my haste I—"

"They found the scroll I retrieved from the woods?"

"Yes, I'm sorry. They did. They did. Please, is there anything I can do to help?"

Arghan's eyes moistened behind the dark canvas that obscured his face. Since the day he'd found the orphaned toddler wandering the vineyard twenty years before, Gavek had become the closest thing he would ever have to a son. He'd grown up to become what Arghan considered to be not only the smartest of all the brothers but the bravest too.

"It's not your fault, son. It's mine. Can you reach Pattron's gag? The lady's also? Don't remove them. Just try to loosen them enough so they can lower them with their jaws and speak."

Gavek nodded and reached through the bars. The pair of soldiers who had left for the chapel suddenly burst out of the sanctuary's side door. Gavek yanked his arms back and leaped below the carriage, watching their feet. The pair sprinted under the colonnade and into the dormitory door. Gavek exhaled and tried again.

Pattron shimmied the loosened rag down with his chin. He took a deep breath, coughed, and spit. "Ugh. That fiend, Cybion. That fiend!"

"What happened?"

"Glory happened, brother, glory. The evil one's retribution followed swiftly thereafter."

"I don't understand—"

"The Name, brother, the Name. The Name from the scroll. What power there is in that Name!"

"It's true," said Agape. "I was as good as dead until brother Pattron arrived and healed me with the power of the Shepherd King. If you'd only seen me before. If you could only see me now."

"What of your daughter, Grace? Tell me that dear little one is safe?"

Agape and Pattron exchanged glances.

"She's safer than any of us, brother," said Pattron.

"What?"

Another pair of soldiers jogged out of the door from the other end of the dormitory and opened the double doors leading into the monastery's great hall.

One of the men shouted back to the doorway they'd exited, "Bring two chairs from the refectory. Cybion wants them set up in here."

Pattron continued, "I think we're running out of time."

"Agreed," said Arghan.

"The Father of Lights is with us, brother," said Pattron. "That's all you need to know."

"I certainly hope so, but you're both still tied up, are you not? I'm in chains. If He plans to work a miracle I welcome it, but I've no plans to wait around for one. My trust in the Father of Lights isn't the issue here. It's Cybion I'm worried about. If we play this wrong we'll all end up tied to fire stakes come morning."

Agape shifted her weight. "What would you have us do, then, Prior Arthos?"

"Call me Arghan, please. All of you. I'm done running. Done lying. I swear to you, my brother, my son, my love for you — for God — has always been real. The rest is... a pack of lies. I lied to protect you. I lied because of the lies they told about me and my brothers-in-arms. Those devious hypocrites in the Palace of Orbicon."

Pattron rested his head against Arghan's shoulder. "What do you want of us, brother? Name it."

"Gavek, my son, I assume you used the passages I showed you to make your way here?"

"I did."

"Use them to access the gallery above the great hall and watch over us from there. If anything goes wrong inside, I want you to cause a distraction and if possible, provoke as many of Cybion's men as you can to give you chase."

Gavek still held the knife he'd used to cut the rope inside the library. He looked at it and responded, "I'm sure I can think of something."

"Good. Use the passages as I showed you and they'll never find you. Come nightfall, if you've not heard from us, escape through the catacombs and join the others at Mount Trobus."

"And us?" asked Pattron.

"Whatever charge Cybion lays against you, no matter how bogus it is, you must plead guilty, both of you."

Pattron's and Agape's eyes met once more.

"You can't be serious?" said Pattron. "Isn't there—"

"Trust me, brother. It's the only way."

Rugged fingers squeezed an old wound on Arghan's shoulder and forced him to the floor. He winced and rose to his knees, flexing his wrists as he struggled to loosen his bonds. The same fingers ripped his blindfold away. Water splashed across his face, flooding his mouth and nostrils. Gasping, he shook his head. Light invaded his corneas. He blinked and surveyed his surroundings.

As predicted, he was kneeling at the centre of the monastery's great hall. What better place was there than this for the pretense of justice? For centuries, this long chamber was where monastic elders met to discuss internal matters related to the administration of the order and also for any group discourse deemed unbecoming of the sanctity of the chapel, such as the settling of disputes or disciplinary hearings. His presence there could mean only one thing, or so he hoped. There would be a show trial under a cloak of legitimacy, not unlike another one he'd faced so many years before.

The hall's double doors creaked open. Arghan squinted over his shoulder. The captain of the guard stood immediately behind him with his sword drawn, glaring. The shadows of two figures cast across the light beaming beneath the man's legs.

Good.

Cybion and Faelis led a procession through the portal, followed by two of the guards who prodded the captive vineyard workers to move inside, as well as a few other monks he presumed were captured on the way back to the peak. Behind them walked several of the residents of the surrounding area, including Borgrel and his quarrelsome neighbour,

Toda. The fact that the two men appeared together under the same roof was proof enough to Arghan that they both had been forced to attend. Arghan smiled. It would appear most of his brothers had escaped, heeding the warning signal.

A voice shouted from outside the door. Kavar and the kitchen staff clamoured inside, hustled by a man-at-arms bearing a mace.

Kavar, the fool. Now he too was a prisoner.

Cybion and Faelis strutted to the top of the wooden platform at the front of the room and sat down on two simple wooden chairs.

Cybion leaned toward Faelis, cupping his hand behind his apprentice's ear. "I see no proper ecclesiastical thrones in this hovel, so I suppose these will have to do, though if you ask me they'd be better used if holes were cut in them and they were turned into piss-pots."

Faelis giggled and straightened one of the tassels on his master's robe. He gestured for Cybion to look at the walls. "What do you make of those?"

Tapestries hung from floor to ceiling between every window. Each of the ornate fabrics depicted icons of influential leaders of the Cantorvarian order down through the centuries. Most fabrics were faded and worn but the one nearest the stage blazed with brilliant colours. It featured the image of Arghan's mentor, the late Prior of Cairhn, Ardwynn of Castor. The image depicted the saint standing in front of Ondolen falls, a pilgrimage site on the river Treighya some 3 leagues[1] from the monastery. The white-bearded figure made a sign of blessing with his right hand and in his left held a scroll on which were written in archaic Tzyani script the nine virtues according to the prophet Polos: Ardvay, Kos, Packra, Rainya, Kovosk, Genya, Fideila, Sophode, and Kahn-yodar. Translated these are Love, Joy, Peace, Patience, Kindness, Goodness, Faithfulness, Gentleness and Self-Control.

Cybion answered, "I think they prove these fools are guilty of heresy in defiance of the orders of the Grand Prelate. Their tattered fibres should make tomorrow's fire burn all the hotter." He raised his voice and

---

[1]. League – standard common measure, equal to one thousand strides, roughly equivalent to an Earth kilometre.

pointed two fingers at one of the soldiers who stood against the wall. "You there, tear those down immediately. I'll not have the eyes of dead heretics sully this holy proceeding." He stood and watched as the guard moved from tapestry to tapestry.

Most fell off their hooks without issue. Those that didn't, he pulled until they tore.

"Gather them up at the back. We'll use them to light the fires tomorrow."

Arghan rattled his cuffs. "Cybion, you fiend. Is there no end to your spite?" He lifted his right knee as if to stand.

The captain batted Arghan's back with the flat of his sword. "Silence!"

Gleeful arrogance faded from Cybion's face, replaced by a cold, emotionless stare. "Speak again — except to answer a question — and I'll have your tongue cut out and fed to you, understood?"

The muscles in Arghan's jaw rippled as he clenched his teeth. He leaned on both knees, lifted his head toward the ceiling, and closed his eyes, trying to calm his mind through prayer. It was no use. Guilt infected his thoughts. Lying about his identity had finally caught up to him and now had imperiled his brothers. Had he dealt with things differently in the woods, the Theocracy might have ignored their reclusive sect in the back woods of northern Cortavia for seven more centuries. Better yet, he could have gone through with his plan to jump off Ondolen falls many years ago and saved them the grief. But something in Ardwynn's voice that fateful day had restrained him at the edge of the rushing tumult: his compassion, tranquility, and peace. No other man he ever knew possessed those virtues in such great abundance as his old mentor. It's what had inspired him to seek them for himself for the past twenty years. The quest for Sophode and Kahn-yodar was all that restrained him now. Barely.

"Bring in the others accused," said Cybion, waving at the guard stationed at the door.

Arghan opened his eyes, his head still facing the ceiling. His gaze fell on the timber beams that supported the hall's steep wooden roof. A face looked back at him from the shadows of the carved wooden screen of the hidden gallery above.

Arghan's eyelids widened. He repressed the urge to smile.

Gavek held his finger to his lips and winked. He reached between the bars, held his knife blade to the rope that suspended a massive chandelier above the floor where Arghan knelt, and nodded.

Arghan lowered his gaze as Pattron and Agape were marched in front of the stage. He shook his head in disbelief after Pattron passed his view. Little Grace appeared behind him, leaning against Cybion's chair. She held her finger to her lips and winked the same way Gavek had. Agape then passed in front of Arghan and the moment she no longer obscured his view, Grace had vanished. Arghan looked for her to the right and left of the stage. Where has she gone? How did she get here in the first place? How long had he lain unconscious from Cybion's blow to his neck? Was he hallucinating?

Cybion rubbed the gold medallion around his neck. "This tribunal is now in session. Bailiff, read the charges."

A villager took centre stage and looked at Arghan as if to plead for forgiveness. He cleared his throat and read from a parchment, quivering, "Court is now in session, Abbot Cybion of Lyrance presiding. The accused are as follows: Prior Arthos of Cairhn monastery and Pattron the physician of Cairhn monastery, conspiracy to commit grand heresy. Prior Arthos of Cairhn monastery, wilful deception of high church officials in the form of concealing his true identity as a convicted heretic and fugitive of the church, the war criminal and former Erne Warder known as Arghan of Danniker, and avoidance of lawful punishment by said officials, also aiding and abetting another fugitive of the church believed still at large. Pattron the physician of Cairhn monastery, also known as the Hospitaller, the practice of witchcraft, and the woman known as Agape of the lakeshore, the same."

Cybion knocked his rings against the armrest of his chair. "Prior Arthos, how do you plead?"

Arghan looked at Pattron. His friend slouched as if in pain, his head bandaged; clothes disheveled, yet his eyes twinkled with cheerful defiance. He smiled, glanced at Agape, then back at Arghan, and nodded.

"Guilty," said Arghan, straightening his back.

The onlookers murmured. One of the cooks who stood beside Kavar leaned over to him and whispered, "Is he mad, brother? Everybody knows the only way out of this is to plead innocent and try to prove it. He's choosing certain death."

Cybion clawed at his armrest and glared at Arghan. A guilty plea precluded any need to present evidence. He'd be denied the pleasure. Despite Cybion's vitriol, he was still bound by Theocratic law. He'd be forced to deliberate without a public review of evidence and then pronounce a sentence. He faced Pattron. "And you, Pattron of Trenegal, how do you plead?"

"Guilty."

The murmurs intensified. Even the guards began whispering to each other.

Cybion pounded his fist. "Silence!" He pointed at Agape. "And you?"

Agape's chin quivered. A tear escaped her eye. Her gaze darted from Pattron to Arghan and back again.

Pattron smiled and nodded. Arghan did the same.

"Guilty."

Cybion stared at Agape's face, blinking. He inhaled sharply, nostrils flaring. He snapped his head from side to side, releasing popping sounds from his neck. He gripped his armrest, then sprung to his feet. He leaped down from the stage and stood in front of Arghan, trembling.

"What is it that you hope to accomplish here today, baby-killer?"

Tension shot through Arghan's temples. He swallowed, burying nausea that rose in his gut at the sound of Cybion's insult.

"Liberation." Arghan looked up into the gallery and met Gavek's eyes. He twitched his head toward the chandelier.

Gavek chopped the rope, striking with such force that his wrist banged against the carved wooden mantle above him, knocking the knife from his grasp as his other hand let go of the rope. With a whizzing sound, the rope whipped through the steel rungs that hung it from the ceiling. The chandelier's iron fittings rattled as it plummeted toward the floor. Gavek's knife tumbled through the air until its blade plunged deep inside Faelis' right shoulder. Faelis screamed and fell out of his chair. Arghan kicked Cybion onto his back just as the chandelier hit the floor, pinning Cybion beneath it. The captain swung his sword, cutting the air behind Arghan's head. Arghan dodged. The captain's sword landed with a thud, wedged into the timber floor. Arghan thrust his wrists to either side of the blade, severing his bonds. He grabbed the captain's sword hand by the wrist and snapped it into a lock, forcing the knight to release the hilt. He spun the knight's arm over his shoulder below the elbow, breaking the joint and sending his captor screaming onto his back. He snatched the captain's sword from the floor and whipped it toward Cybion's throat. The remaining guards lunged toward him, weapons drawn.

"That's far enough," shouted Arghan over the captain's agonizing cries. "One step closer and I'll take his head." He kicked the chandelier off Cybion's chest, grabbed him by the scruff of his robe, and yanked him to his feet. He tightened his arm into a choke hold around Cybion's neck, pointed the sword toward Patron and Agape, and glared at the guards. "One of you cut them loose, now, or the Abbot dies." He spoke into Cybion's ear, "Tell them. Tell them!"

The guards hesitated. The occupants of the room stared silently, eyes gaping wide.

Cybion coughed, tears streaking from his eyes. He nodded to one of the captain's lieutenants and stammered, "Do as he says. Do as he says!"

The officer shuffled toward Pattron and Agape. He drew his dagger and paused to glance back at the Abbot and Arghan. Cybion gasped. With two quick strokes, the officer cut the pair's bonds, then backed away.

"Now make way for us, make way!" Arghan backed through the crowd of onlookers, dragging Cybion with him. He nodded for Pattron to follow.

"Come on," said Pattron, throwing his arm over Agape's shoulder. The pair scurried past Arghan and ran out the door.

Arghan sneered at the guards. "Not one of you is to leave this room until a count of a thousand, is that understood?"

The guards all glanced at the captain, who was still writhing and groaning on the floor.

"Is that understood?"

The lieutenant nodded. "Yes."

CHAPTER FOUR
Hunted

Arghan burst from the great hall's doors and shoved Cybion forward. Across the courtyard, the cavaliers' horses grazed at hay troughs, tied to a hitching post near the courtyard well. Arghan spotted Cybion's own mount and pointed. "We'll take yours, 'eminent one'." He kicked Cybion in the buttocks. "March."

Cybion stumbled into the centre of the courtyard, wheezing. He fell against the well wall and clutched his throat. Arghan yanked off the remains of his own bonds, seized Cybion's wrists, and forced the cleric to hold them behind his back. Cybion moaned and whimpered while Arghan tightened the rope into a sailor's knot.

Pattron grabbed his satchel from below the driver's seat of the cage wagon. "I hope you've thought this through. We're deep in it now, aren't we?" He slung his bag over his should, hastening past the well, and jumped into the captain's saddle. "Agape, dear lady, here." He reached out for her hand and pulled her onto the horse. "Hold tight."

Arghan threw Cybion over the hindquarters of his own horse and jumped into the saddle. He winked at Pattron. "Head for Lake Daena. There's a cabin there on the North shore. Wait for me there." He pointed toward their refuge on Mount Trobus, far from the lake he'd just mentioned, keeping their true destination hidden from Cybion.

Pattron nodded, playing along. "You're not coming now?"

Arghan tugged his horse's reins and slapped its rump with the slack. The horse spun toward the exit. "I'm off to greet our special visitor. Pray I'm not too late." He dug into the horse's side with his heels. "Yah!" The horse sped across the bridge and headed down the mountain path.

Pattron followed for a while then stopped where a brook intersected the trail. He watched Arghan disappear behind a bend then turned his horse, cross-stepping it through a shaded patch of tall grass onto another path and headed north.

"Clever," said Agape, looking back over her shoulder. "The prior rides westward toward Lake Daena while we head North. But where to?"

"The caves of Mount Trobus," said Pattron. "There's an old mine and a quarry there that our ancient brothers cut stone from while building the monastery. It's been a secret place of refuge for the order during persecutions over the centuries. The last time it was used was during the Zuelan war of 410 when they sacked the village. We'll be safe there."

Agape rested her head against the back of Pattron's shoulder, tightening her arms around his waist. "What about Prior Arthos — Arghan? Where—"

"I don't know," said Pattron, cupping his free hand over hers. "He's playing a gamble. If it pays off we'll have all the help we need."

"And if not?"

"He'd better think of something. Either way, he's on his own — for now."

Lieutenant Veksire rushed to his captain's side, wide-eyed with disbelief. The veteran horseman lay writhing in agony across the floor, his right arm dangling at the elbow. Hesitating, he looked back toward the stage. Faelis lay slumped against the seat Cybion had mocked barely a half hour before, hyperventilating.

Veksire glared at one of the men-at-arms then pointed at the helpless priest. "Beihdrir, see what you can do for him."

"Have the monks no physician?" said the soldier as he stepped onto the stage.

"No. The dark one who just ran out of here is their physician. Now get to it!"

"Yes, sir!"

Veksire shook his head. "You there," he said, pointing at Kavar. "You work in the vineyard, yes?"

"Y-yes," said Kavar, wiping the sweat from his face.

"Keep any spirits in this place?"

Kavar glanced to the left and the right, surveying the faces of his fellow monks. "Uh, yeah, we do."

"Fetch me some. At once." He snapped his fingers. "Joron, go with him. Don't let him out of your sight."

The foot-soldier clicked his heels and then ran to where Kavar stood. He grabbed the monk by the arm and pushed him toward the door.

As he waited, Veksire's gaze fell to the floor where the severed rope end lay atop the overturned chandelier. He furrowed his brow then shuffled closer, sliding on his poleyns[1]. He grabbed the rope and lifted it close to his eyes, studying its tip. His gaze shifted to the gallery screen above the stage. "Rollo," he said, pointing at another of the knights, "take command of the militiamen and tear this compound apart. The Erne Warder's got an ally on the loose somewhere here. I want him found. Go!"

"As you wish, my lord." Rollo signaled the others to follow him.

"And Rollo—"

"Yes my lord?"

"Burn the library to the ground."

Rollo grinned and sped away.

"Sergeant Pinion," continued Veksire, "take your hounds, bring your best marksman, and accompany Rovard and Galio on horseback. Track down the fugitives. Tell them I'll kill every last one of these monks and burn this place to the ground unless they surrender themselves and hand over the Abbot in one piece."

"And if the Abbot's found dead?" said Pinion, marching past the lieutenant.

---

[1]. A poleyn is a piece of metal armour covering the knee.

"Kill them all. Bring me their bodies."

Pinion nodded. "Regyar, you're with me." He turned and bowed to Rovard and Galio as they took the lead. "Sirs — we follow you."

Kavar scampered inside with the infantryman named Joron close behind, both sidestepping the other soldiers as they stormed out the door. Kavar ran to meet Veksire and handed him a bottle. "This is the stiffest stuff we've got, which I'm sure is what you're after if you mean to do what I think you do."

Veksire yanked out the cork with his teeth and then handed the vessel back to Kavar. "I do. Give it to him. All of it. Joron, fetch me that torch on the wall."

Joron bounded to the wall and retrieved the flaming staff. He handed it to Veksire, who drew his sword and began turning it over the flame.

Gavek scrambled through the dark passageway leading out of the great hall's hidden gallery. Shouts echoed from the chamber behind him. A scream pierced the air. Icy chills rippled down his neck. Had they seen him cut the rope? Had they heard him running away?

His elbow slammed into a wall, knocking the tiny candle he carried to the floor. Just as it landed, he lurched forward to right his balance and snuffed out its flame.

More shouts. He abandoned the candle and clawed his way along the musky walls. Soon, streaks of light pierced the darkness through the cracks in the secret door leading back to the library. He nudged it open and surveyed the room.

Nothing.

Gavek scurried inside and ran to one of the desks along the wall.

Clamouring reverberated from the library door. Footfalls echoed through the bookshelf aisles. Gavek dropped to his knees behind one of the rows, peering past the tomes. Soldiers marched inside. One after another they lit torches and threw them over the shelves, igniting the parchment, linen, and wooden contents of the room almost instantly.

"There," cried the tall knight named Rollo, "let's see how you curs like that! Come men, there's more to be done. Zurken, watch at the door. See to it no one comes in or out."

"No!" said Gavek, straining to control his volume. *No, no, no!*

The young scribe leaped to his feet, fuming. He paused to stare at the growing flames as if to memorize the scene.

He slid to one of the desks, grabbed an open codex, and stuffed it inside his robe. On and on he went until there was no more room inside his garment. Smoke wafted across his face. Coughing, he lunged to grab the map of Cortavia he'd left open on the study table.

The long row of shelves that divided the room began to crack and pop from the heat. The shelf beyond it collapsed, knocking the whole structure toward Gavek, who reeled against the wall. Remembering the sack he'd left hanging outside the window, he scrambled atop the chair next to it, kicked open the window, grabbed the rope, and dove outside.

His body slammed against the compound's curtain wall and his knuckles raked across its granite surface. He slid down the rope. One of the volumes dropped out from beneath his garment and plummeted down the cliff face. He watched it fall, counting the seconds until it disappeared below the treetops. Nausea washed over him.

He looked up. "Father of Lights!" The stone gargoyle that anchored the rope stared down at him. He tightened his grip and pushed against the wall with his legs, just far enough to view the sack of books dangling under him. Not too far below, a narrow ledge followed the rocky contour of Precipice Peak along the foundation of the wall.

It's the only way, he thought. But could he make it?

Summoning what remained of his strength, he lowered himself down the rope until he reached the canvas sack. He let it slip through his fingers until all that was left to hold on to was the edges of the book inside. He swayed there for a moment as a gentle breeze blew up from the valley below.

He lined up his feet with the ledge and let go.

Shadows danced across the trail like spectres celebrating the impending night, cast by the swaying trees that lined the trail. Arghan raced his mount deeper into the forest, squinting against the rays that flashed through the branches.

How many years had it been since he'd driven a horse to the brink like this? Twenty? Twenty years since the war. The bloody, brutal war. The Grand Prelate's war. And now, like no time had passed at all — every twitch of his knees, every nuance in his voice, every flick of the reigns — flowed out of him by instinct. The same instinct that led him to strike, to maim, even perhaps... to kill? There were at least a dozen ways to take down the captain that didn't involve destroying a limb. Had twenty years as a monk come to naught?

Arghan bit his lip and tried to bury his thoughts. Another skill honed to perfection as an Erne Warder. Don't think, act. He was on another mission. *Mission? What mission? You're running for your life again!*

Woods gave way to a clearing at the crest of a hill. Arghan pulled up the reigns and twisted in the saddle, peering at the treeline behind him.

Silence.

Cybion moaned, coughed, and vomited over the horse's rump. "Curse you, Danniker. There's a special place in the underworld reserved for sinners like you."

Arghan swatted Cybion with the reins. "Shut up, I'm thinking."

Cybion was valuable leverage, but keeping this pace was unsustainable with his portly hide burdening the horse. If he was to make the midnight rendezvous with Cybella and give his friends ample time to reach safety, he needed to get rid of Cybion somewhere in the hope that he'd be discovered by pursuers and blab the ruse that Pattron had followed him. But where?

He turned forward again and squinted. What was that blurry shape swaying above the road in the middle of the clearing? A gust of wind told his nose it was a half-rotten corpse hanging from a noose on a gallows pole.

Arghan urged the horse across the clearing until it closed to within a few strides of the ghastly figure. He sprung up in the saddle and severed the rope with his sword. The ghoul crashed onto the trail, its head severed from the impact. He swung the blade a second time, releasing the rope from its anchor point. He slid out of the saddle. "That'll do." He stooped to gather it. As he spun back, his toe clipped the dead man's torso. He stumbled, righted himself over the ragged figure, and recoiled, blinking. *That's too short to be the body of a man. A boy?* Arghan gazed at the brilliant streaks of rose and amber clouds that filled the sky and listened again for galloping hooves.

Still nothing.

He crouched over the corpse for a better look. The remains of a white and green robe appeared below layers of filth and blood. *A choir boy?* It was then he realized who it was. His mouth dropped open and his breathing sharpened.

Cybion wriggled, kicking his horse's hind legs with his knee. "What are you doing?"

"Shut up!" Arghan jerked his head in the direction of the figure's severed skull. The head was still covered in a canvas bag and the victim's writ of execution was still tied below its chin. Nostrils flaring, he snatches the parchment and held it close to his eyes, then crumpled it and threw it to the ground. He pointed at Cybion, trembling. "You ordered this." Arghan grabbed the severed head and yanked off the canvas. He stomped toward the horse and dragged Cybion to the ground. He pulled the Abbot up by the collar and shoved the half-decomposed skull into his face.

"You told me Kevid had drowned! This says... this says he was hanged — and for what?"

Cybion's eyeballs bulged. Colour drained out of his face. "I... I..."

"Yes, you know, don't you? Well, read it."

"I—"

"Read it!" Arghan dropped the skull and pressed the writ against Cybion's face.

"Executed for... for... w-wilful disobedience... o-of a ch-church elder..."

"Wilful disobedience? That's not what it was at all, was it? You needed to shut him up. Do away with him. The rumours were true, weren't they? What you and Faelis—" Arghan's neck strained, his teeth flashing as he spoke, "—what you both did to him!"

Arghan shoved Cybion to the ground, rendering the Abbot unconscious as his head struck a stone. Arghan collapsed, weeping and hyperventilating. He grabbed the rope, fingers racing, tying one loop after another until the knot was complete.

"To hell with the plan." Arghan slid the noose around Cybion's neck. He whipped the rest over the gallows arm and hurried to tie the other end to the horse's saddle horn. He poised to slap the horse on its rump. One command was all it would take to send the steed galloping, lifting Cybion to a well-deserved fate.

A child's voice pierced the air, "Abba Arghan, what are you doing?"

Arghan jerked his head. A chill cut across his neck. "Grace— h-how?"

An incandescent aura enveloped the tiny figure before him. It was as if he could see her, and yet see through her all at the same time.

"Is this the Kahn-yodar[2] Abba Ardwynn taught you?"

Arghan's gaze dropped toward his arms and hands, illuminated by Grace's glow. He sobbed. "No, it's not. It's not."

Grace stepped forward, Her eyes searching his, dreamlike and wistful. "What is the fifth principle of Kahn-yodar? Better the slow march of justice—"

"Than swift hand of revenge." Arghan's breathing slowed.

Bellowing echoed through the forest. Arghan looked into the tree line. *Pinion's hounds.*

He turned back to find Grace had vanished.

Arghan raced to untie the rope. He slipped the noose off Cybion's neck and used the cord to lash him to the gallows pole, then vaulted back into the saddle and sped down the path to lake Daena.

---

2. "Kahn-yodar" - Ancient Tzyani words meaning "self control". See chapter 3: Accused.

CHAPTER FIVE
Rendezvous

Gavek circled the base of the north watchtower and crept along the ledge near the compound's northwest wall to reach the base of the monastery's main gate. Trembling, he stumbled between the stone arches that supported the bridge above him. A breeze of cool mountain air bathed his face. He sighed, chuckling as he wiped his brow. "Many thanks, Eternal One. I needed that."

He peered over the edge into the narrow gorge that separated Precipice Peak from Mount Mora. As a boy, he'd often wondered what it would be like to be one of those eagles who nested along the north face of the ravine. Now, for the first time in his life, he was looking up at them. He'd spent his life buried in books, reading someone else's adventures. Now he was living his own. Someday he would tell the tale... if he survived. What a thrill! The heat radiating from the stones along the wall — the dizzying vertigo of distant treetops — the distracting freedom of mountain birds flying blissfully by — he soaked it all in while he crept along the ledge.

He stumbled and muttered, "You made capers like this sound so easy for your three swordsmen, Sorto[1]. Did you ever try it yourself?"

---
1. A great playwrite and novelist of a bygone era. See chapter 1, scene 1 for first reference.

He limped ahead, bracing himself against the side of a shadowy alcove under the bridge, and approached a heavy timber door set into the cliff he believed led to the tunnels ancient brothers had carved below the monastery. By them, he could reach the bottom of the well at the centre of the courtyard or a number of other exits throughout the compound, at least that's what Father Arthos had told him. What had his accusers called him? Arghan of Danniker? The butcher of Koerska? The secrecy, the subterfuge; it all made sense now, sort of.

Several minutes later he was a hundred paces past the well, deep inside the mountain. The occasional storm drain above him cast very little light, forcing him, as before, to feel his way through the darkness, relying on his keen memory of Arghan's descriptions to keep him headed in the right direction.

He stumbled into a stack of bones, knocking them down, revealing the tunnel he'd used earlier to reach the courtyard from the library. *Ah, there you are.* His escape route set, he pressed on to find a place where he could observe the occupiers in the hope of finding an opportue time to slip away. He took the centre passage. If his sense of direction proved true, it would lead him back to the very place his flight began, the great hall. But soon it split again. He veered left. Murmurs echoed from the passage to the right. *What's that sound?* He scurried back down the other route, following the noise.

He turned a corner and spotted a beam of light shining through a grate above the tunnel, interrupted by the occasional shadow that moved across the stony floor. He crept under it and peered inside. Light twinkled beyond the bars. Soles paced across the grate. Metal plates clinked and rattled. *Men in armour?*

"Will he make it, sire?"

Kavar's voice!

"Perhaps. Perhaps not. Not every man can lose an arm and live."

The lieutenant's voice? What's his name?

A door slammed open— or shut? Gavek couldn't tell.

"Lieutenant Veksire, we've found something!"

Veksire. An Alpinian name to be sure. No, perhaps even Regalian. Ah, southern Alpinian. That's it.

"Let's have it, then, Rollo."

Feet shuffled followed by a moment of silence.

"Never mind the Captain. It's not the first time you've seen a knight less an arm. Your report, cavalier."

The infirmary! Gavek was below Pattron's infirmary. It was the Captain's scream that chilled him as he fled. They'd moved him here for suturing, bandaging? 'Less an arm'? What did—

"Uh, yes lieutenant. This. We found it in the jail carriage, among the Prior's things."

"The fugitive's things, cavalier. He ceased being a Prior the minute he did... this."

"Yes, sir."

Footsteps. *A parchment crinkling?*

"By the golden spire, now we have him!" said Veksire.

"What?" said another voice, not Rollo's or Kavar.

"It seems Archprelate Solstrus was right in his suspicions. Mark the quality of the paper and the fine, delicate hand with which the note is written. These heretics have a sympathizer in the royal court, one sympathetic enough to come all the way here to meet them."

"You know I can't read! Does it say where? When?"

"Tonight. Midnight. The village pier."

"Capital! Let's go."

"Indeed, Beihdrir. Summon Joron to the courtyard, and select some of the best militiamen to accompany us. We'll set out for headquarters immediately after they're assembled."

"Yes sir."

Footfalls trailed away.

"What about me?"

"Rollo, you stay in command of the rest of the local troops here at the monastery. Post a guard at this door to watch over the Captain and Faelis. Oh, and interrogate this one, for all we know it was poison not drink he gave the Captain. Maybe he knows more than he's letting on."

Kavar objected with a burst of breath, his voice quivering, "No! I tasted it first, right before your eyes, I—"

"Shut up! Come with me," said Rollo.

Heavy footfalls, mixed with Kavar's screams and the sound of something heavy being dragged across the floor. A final set of footsteps marched away, the light faded and the sound of a door slammed. Silence.

Gavek's eyes bulged. He hiked up his robe and raced back down the passageway, headed for the well. Simply escaping was no longer an option. He had to find Arghan and warn him, somehow. The sympathizer Veksire mentioned — was it the person who had couriered the manuscripts he'd been translating? If they were arrested, the source of the texts might be discovered, even possibly destroyed.

He scurried up the ladder inside the well and peeked over the edge, eyes darting while he surveyed the courtyard. Heat radiated across his cheek. He cocked his head toward the source. Though the sky betrayed the onset of night, the courtyard looked as bright as day, illuminated by the blazing inferno spilling out of the library's windows. On the south side of the area, torches burned at every doorway. Silhouettes inside the dormitory windows and sounds of ruckus from every direction told him the militia were still busy turning the monastery upside down. He marked one silhouette on the drawbridge. A guard stood watch. How could he get past him? The horses remained; where were their knights? Footsteps approached. Gavek ducked seconds before Veksire strode past him, shouting commands.

"All of you follow me. Joron, drive the jail wagon. If all goes as planned we'll make use of it again tonight I'm sure. Yah!" Veksire spurred his horse and sped off over the drawbridge, followed by his other men. Joron leaped into the driver's seat and whipped the reins.

That's it. Gavek vaulted over the retaining wall, bending his knees to soften the sound of his landing. He rolled under the carriage, nearly clipping his toes under one of its wheels. He clung to the axles and hoisted his body up under the vehicle as it passed through the gate.

Arghan pushed the rowboat away from the dock and gripped the oars, turning away from the glow beyond the western hills above lake Daena to chart his course by the star that shone in the northern sky above Ardwynn's old cabin. He'd hitched Cybion's horse outside it and left a lantern burning on the floor to convince his pursuers he was hiding inside. How long this ruse would fool Veksire's posse remained to be seen, though the first phase of his plan showed promise.

A few minutes before he had left, he watched torchlights cross the barren hilltop where he had left Cybion bound. As predicted, the force split in two. Two torches went back toward the village, ostensibly to return Cybion to safety. The others continued down the trail toward the lake. But it was the sight of a much greater light that drove him forward. Crowned with fire, the monastery atop Precipice Peak glowed in the night.

Grimacing, he rowed the oars, cutting the water at just the right angle to propel his narrow, two-man craft speeding across the lake. If only Ardwynn were there, calling out the strokes as in joyful, sunny days of old. Perhaps that's why he and his old mentor connected so well. Both sons of the great lake Vedehed; he of the sprawling shipping port of Danniker in Ostergaard, Ardwynn of the Karpathian fishing hub of Castor; they both loved the water. It was there that Ardwynn had trained him to look past his pain and focus on the task at hand. Arghan imagined him there now, sitting in the seat opposite his as a familiar ache shot through his shoulder. His combat prowess remained sharp as ever, evidenced by the ease with which he dispatched the Captain, but after years of hard labour in the vineyard, it now came at a cost. He longed for some bergaroot[2] to chew on. He'd spotted some growing near the dock, but there was no time to harvest it considering how stubborn its hold would be on the lake bed this time of year, even after sundown.

Arghan dropped the oars, allowing the craft to glide. "A stubborn hold." He stared out over the surface of the lake, letting his eyes fall out of focus as gentle waves lapped against the side of the hull. Visions of

---

2. Bergaroot – An aquatic plant native to the rivers and lakes of Cortavia, known for its anti-inflammatory and pain killing properties.

another frantic race, on another night, another boat, another time filled his mind. For a few fleeting moments, he relived that fateful morning during the war of 410, when the seemingly unstoppable Zuelan Horde — nomadic tribesmen from Eskhasia who had conquered it and every other known continent save his own — had finally invaded Eskareon by way of Cortavia's river valley and had driven its defenders back as far north as Koerska, where soldiers from Ostergaard, including the Erne Warders, had stopped them in their tracks.

The voice of Arghan's old commander echoed in his mind, 'With Koerska in their possession, the Zuelans will control the Onya river indefinitely. We must break their stubborn hold, and do it tonight, in the same way one lays an axe to a stand of bergaroot. Only then can we drive them back into the sea.' That's what Omhigaart Thurn had said that night he ordered the raid on the Tzyani enclave of Koerska to unseat the Zuelan invaders he claimed were held up in its riverside citadel. Only it wasn't Zuelan troops who were locked up in the tower at all, was it? It was...

Arghan shuddered and sobbed. The last glistening reflections of the sunset flickered like flames across the rippling water, just like the fire that blazed across the oily remains of the incendiary rounds he had ordered fired from his shipboard trebuchet[3] against Koerska's stockade. That night, like this one, he had rowed with all his might toward the tumultuous inferno, compelled by his victims' screams...

Arghan fell on the empty seat in front of him, his soiled face awash with tears. "Father of Lights, forgive me. Forgive me."

Hounds howled from the lakeshore. Arghan looked over the bow. Two torches emerged from the clearing in front of the cabin. Their pace slowed. It appeared the riders had dismounted and were proceeding on foot. He looked over his shoulder to gauge the distance left to the mouth of the Daena river, whose rapids would propel him to Lake Trieehd. He gripped the oars again and prayed he wouldn't be late.

---

3. Trebuchet – A medieval catapult for hurling heavy stones, often employing a long sling (https://www.thefreedictionary.com/trebuchet).

Shivering, Gavek pulled up his hood and hunched outside the window while raindrops tapped the glass. Inside the stockade, Veksire and the others stripped off their metal armour and donned the deep violet cloaks of the Alpinian guard.

"Arm yourselves lightly," said Veksire. "We'll take him with speed on my signal, understood?"

"Yes sir," shouted the men.

"Don't lay a hand on the person Danniker meets tonight. No doubt they're worth more to the Archprelate alive."

The men nodded. Veksire strode to the door with Beihdrir, Joron, and Regyar close behind. As he was about to reach for the door it burst open, halting the company in their tracks.

"Lieutenant!"

"Galio, what news? Why—"

"We found Cybion bound to a gallows post in a clearing on the path to lake Daena. Rovard and I thought it wise to return him safely to his residence, he is the Archprelate's nephew after all."

"And Rovard?"

"Stayed with him to stand watch."

"Good work, and Pinion?"

"He and Regyar continued the pursuit. We believe Danniker headed for a cabin on lake Daena. That's what Cybion told us."

"I wouldn't be so sure," said Veksire, opening the door. "Danniker's evaded capture for over 20 years. Do you really believe he'd be that careless?"

"I suppose not," said Galio, scratching his head.

"No matter. We know where he's going. Shed your armour. Meet the rest of us in the harbour tower as soon as you're ready."

"Sir!" Galio clicked his heels as the others filed out the door.

Gavek scampered to the corner of the building. He watched the soldiers march out of the courtyard then looked back into the barracks. Galio's back was to the window. He bolted for the gate.

Cairhn's tower clock struck twelve. Arghan lifted his oars out of the water, allowing his craft to drift near the dock. He scanned the village skyline, inhaling the moist air. Lanterns burned through the falling rain, flickering, rocked by the wind swirling off the water. The village's narrow lanes lay silent, save for the raucous singing beyond the walls of the tavern on the boardwalk. A couple stumbled out the door, laughing and zigzagged their way up the hill toward the cemetery. The harbour bell tinkled, nudged by the wind.

Arghan traced the length of the pier and spotted a cloaked figure pacing below a lantern.

"Cybella..." he whispered. Did she come alone? Kneeling on his seat, he paddled the craft between the fishing vessels crowded under the dock. He secured it to the pier and started up the ladder to the deck. A silhouette rose from a dingy below him. He halted and jumped back into the skiff and grabbed his sword, spinning to face the figure.

"Oh, you," said Arghan, lowering his weapon.

The young squire who had visited him in the vineyard held out his palms. "We thought you might not show. Her Majesty was expecting you to approach from the town, why—"

Arghan leaned over him. "Has she brought no men at arms?"

The squire shook his head.

"You mean you're all there is?"

The squire nodded. Arghan huffed and shook his head. He gripped the sword underhand and scrambled up the ladder. *What the blazes is she thinking, coming here without a military escort?*

He sprung onto the dock. The female figure stood at an angle to him, peering inland with a curl of golden locks just visible over her shoulder.

Arghan approached her and brushed her elbow. "Cybella, it's me, your father. It's so good to finally—"

The woman flinched and turned to face him. Arghan's jaw dropped. He recoiled, allowing the sword to slip out of his fingers, dropping it to the deck with a clang. The beautiful blue eyes that met his gaze were set amid eyelids marked with the lines of time. This was no maiden of twenty. This was...

"Silla." Arghan took a step forward, tilting his head. He closed his eyes and then opened them again. The last time he had seen her was from behind the bars of a prison cell. That night, standing on the cold stone floor of the dungeon below the Palace of Trianon, he had kissed her fingers, finally letting her hand slip away into the darkness.

"Hello, Arghan." Silla smiled and stepped forward, pulling down her hood. She cupped her hand to his cheek and studied his face.

The sweet smell of perfume flooded Arghan's nose. He closed his eyes, enthralled by the memory of it. He pulled her wrist away and glared. "What trickery is this, Silla? Where's Cybella? You've no idea what danger we're in. I need to—"

"I didn't think you'd come had you known it was me who summoned you. I didn't have anyone else to turn to. I need your help."

"Need my help? Why? What's going on, Silla? Where is Cybella?"

"She's disappeared, Arghan."

"Disappeared? What do you mean? What happened?"

"She had a private audience with Eriohn just before he died. She left the palace the same day with her private bodyguards and sailed north from Trianon. Nobody has seen or heard from her since."

"Sailed? Where?"

"Nobody knows."

"Who's acting as head of state then?"

"Eriohn."

"Eriohn's dead."

"No, I mean my stepson, Eriohn the Second."

"Eriohn the Second? He's dead too — lost at sea. What—"

"Shortly after Cybella departed, a Voldavian nobleman; a ship captain called the Liester[4] of Luthargrad, sailed his ship into Trianon harbour with Eriohn the Second on board. He claimed to have rescued him from a band of pirates camped on the Eskhasian[5] coast. In Cybella's absence, the Archprelate has been pressuring the Palace of Ministers to recognize Eriohn II's claim to the throne."

---

4. Liester – a rank of nobility, roughly equivalent to a count.
5. Eskhasian – Eskhasia is the large continent to the east of the continent of Eskareon.

"What? Solstrus can't do that! Cortavian law expressly states—"

"I know it well," she said, nodding, "'upon the death of a monarch, their designated successor cannot be contested regardless of line of succession.' Well, not when the heir designate is charged with a crime against the state; in this case, heresy. Solstrus has proof of it, or so he claims."

"Heresy?" Arghan lurched forward. He gripped her shoulders and stared into her eyes.

Silla's eyelids narrowed. "Come now, you know all about it, don't you?" She bit her lip, eyes moistening. "Solstrus has been spreading the story among the Palace of Ministers that she fled Trianon to escape justice. There's a warrant out for her arrest. What have you gotten our daughter into, Arghan?"

"What have I gotten her into? She contacted me of her own accord! Otherwise, I might never have known she even existed, no thanks to you."

"Why should I have told you about her, Arghan?" She shook her head and pushed him away. "You're a convicted war criminal and she was made Eriohn's heir designate. She was better off not knowing anything about you."

"Perhaps, but she had a right to know, regardless."

"Well, you'll be happy to hear my late husband agreed with you. Eriohn insisted she know the truth when he fell ill four months ago and I finally acquiesced. But after what happened since, I regret that decision. He refused to tell me what he said to her after that, including whatever made her leave so suddenly the day he died. Her swift departure only heightens the perception of guilt. As far as I'm concerned it should be you going down for this, not her!"

Arghan stepped to the edge of the dock and looked up to the mountains beyond Lake Trieehd. The terrible shame of his decision that fateful night in Koerska stung all the more deeper coming from the lips of the woman who once adored him.

He shook his head, still looking over the waters. "You're right. It should be me. But she is a brave, brilliant young woman with a keen sense of justice, honour and duty. Though we've never met, she and I have forged a bond through our letters which I cherish dearly. Were you to hear what she confided in me, perhaps then you might understand. Some things are worth fighting for, Silla."

"Worth her very life, Arghan? I'm positive Solstrus has something to do with her disappearance. He's out to destroy her; and Eriohn II, for reasons I can't comprehend, has lent his full support. You more than anyone knows the fury of Temple justice. They'll find a way to execute her!"

"Not if I can help it." He returned to where she stood, stooping to retrieve his sword from the deck on the way. "The All Seeing One as my witness, I swear to you, I will—"

A robed figure ran out from the alley beside the tavern, arms waving. "Prior Arthos, run! It's a trap!"

Gavek?

A bulky figure seized Arghan's apprentice, forcing him to the ground.

Arghan squinted landward. A silhouette skulked behind a stack of crates where the dock met the boardwalk. Another scurried up behind some barrels along the opposite side. Some of the lights he'd seen during his approach from the water had been snuffed out.

"Get to your boat."

"What? Why?"

"I said get to your boat, now!" Arghan clenched Silla's arm and pulled her toward the ladder. Her gown snagged something on the equipment piled next to her.

Silla tugged at her skirt. "I can't. I'm stuck."

A cohort of militiamen stormed out from behind one of the warehouses beside the dock and formed a line, blocking the exit. The silhouettes that stooped behind the crates stood up. A chorus of swords being drawn rang out. The men marched down the dock.

Veksire emerged from the darkness and stood under a lamppost. "Give it up, Danniker. There's nowhere to run."

Arghan glanced back at Silla. "Get down, stay low." He took a few steps forward and faced Veksire. "Who said anything about running."

CHAPTER SIX
Confrontation

Veksire and his men closed ranks. Arghan tightened his grip on his sword and strode to the centre of the dock. "What do you want?"

"Surrender, of course."

"I can't do that."

"I'm not offering you the choice, Danniker. Stand down and we'll let the woman live. Resist us and you'll both be destroyed." Veksire took a few steps and pointed to the place where Silla hid. "You there, step out where we can see you." He attempted to pass but Arghan moved to block him.

Arghan glanced over his shoulder. "Stay put, Silla." He glared at Veksire. "That woman happens to be the Queen Mother, you fool. Show some respect. Cybion's not the only one with friends in high places. You will let her leave in peace or suffer the consequences."

The men locked eyes.

Followed by a pack of wailing hounds, horsemen rounded the same corner the drunks had turned on their way to the graveyard. They galloped behind the ranks guarding the dock and dismounted. Sergeant Pinion pushed through the soldiers, fuming.

"Lieutenant, wait," shouted Pinion. He waved back toward the men.

"Bring him here."

Struggling to control his writhing captive, the man-at-arms called Regyar dragged Gavek through the crowd.

Pinion drew his dagger and called to Arghan, "Do as the Lieutenant commands or I'll slit his throat!"

Gavek slammed his elbow into Regyar solar plexus, loosening the yeoman's grasp. The militiamen rushed forward. Gavek bolted and dove off the dock. Pinion grabbed his bow and fired an arrow through the hem of Gavek's robe.

Distracted by the commotion, Veksire glanced over his shoulder. Arghan spun his hips and kicked, burying the ball of his foot deep in Veksire's stomach, dropping him to the deck with a thud.

"Silla, run!" Arghan kicked Veksire's sword into the water. Galio and Beihdrir lunged at him. Arghan's blade flashed as he weaved between them, striking their weapons away. With two more spinning strikes, he sent the knights tumbling in opposite directions. He bolted toward Silla, slashed her skirt free, and pushed her toward the ladder. "Run!"

Arghan spun to face the militiamen, now only a few steps away. Pinion loosed another arrow. Arghan dodged as the projectile grazed his temple.

Silla screamed and dropped to the deck. Her young attendant scrambled to the top of the ladder.

Arghan dashed to her side. "Silla!" Blood gushed from the arrow shaft in the middle of her chest, dripping through the planks.

The young squire cradled her in his lap. "Your Majesty!"

Colour drained from Arghan's face. Another sword whizzed through the air. Arghan blocked it with a clang of his blade. He screamed and dove into the pack, tackling two soldiers to the ground. He sprung to his feet, releasing a flurry of steel and sweat upon the rest. One by one the militiamen fell, clutching severed limbs and oozing punctures. The knights regained their weapons and set upon Arghan with renewed fury, grazing him at times, but in the end, they too were no match for the wrath they had unleashed. Arghan leaped over Galio's severed head as Beihdrir's body fell limp, splashing into the lake. Veksire rushed him with a dagger and lost the hand that held it. Another thrust to the chest and the officer was finished.

Pinion fired again, followed by a shot from Regyar. Arghan sliced the first in mid-air seconds before the other one pierced his left shoulder. Arghan grunted, stooping to snatch another fallen sword. He dodged another volley and flung the two blades through the air in quick succession, dropping the two archers where they stood. He screamed at Pinion's hounds and they whimpered away.

Arghan lumbered back toward the end of the dock, stumbling over the corpses and the wounded as he went. He broke off the feathered end of the arrow and forced the rest through his shoulder, grateful that by chance and haste Pinion had fired a bodkin point and not a broadhead. He grabbed one of the militiaman's discarded torches and forced its burning tip into his wound.

Gavek emerged from the top of the ladder, lake water sloshing from his saturated robe. He stared at Arghan for a moment, eyes bulging, body stiffened. He looked out over the piles of men. Some moaned, and others lay silent, all contorted like discarded dolls.

Arghan fell to his knees beside Silla and the squire. "Is she breathing?"

"Barely."

"Gavek, go fetch one of the knight's horses."

Gavek stared across the dock.

"Gavek!"

Gavek shook his head and shivered. "Uh, yes, Father Arthos." He took a few uneasy steps, then trotted down the dock.

Arghan held out his arms. "Give her to me. What's your name, son?"

"Reighgus, sir."

"Reigh, go help him. Fetch a horse for each of us. Hurry. There's no time to spare."

A silhouette darkened the canvas roof of Pattron's tent, back-lit by a flickering campfire. "Brother Pattron, awaken! Hurry."

Pattron rubbed his eyes and muttered, "As if I could sleep after all this." He sprung up from his modest prayer altar. "What is it, Holberht?" He dashed through the door flap and stepped into the vaulted expanse of the Cantorvarians' underground refuge.

Holberht pointed to the crowd gathered around the dinner table in the centre of the camp. Pattron hastened past him, breezing through a cluster of tents as he headed toward the murmuring group.

Agape emerged from a nearby curtain and touched Pattron's arm as he passed. "What's the matter?"

"I've no idea," he said, touching her hand. "Come, I may need you."

Pattron raced ahead, not noticing Agape turn back.

Pattron pushed through the crowd. "Make way." He gasped when he saw Arghan standing inside the circle. "Saints and angels help me."

Arghan leaned over Silla's body, trembling. "Help her, Pattron, if you can, please."

Pattron traced the line of her blood-soaked silk gown and stopped at the place where a broad-tipped arrowhead protruded from her chest. He commanded the bystanders, "You, fetch some clean rags and pillows. You, hot water, go. You, bring a torch. And someone fetch me my—"

"This?" Agape handed Pattron his satchel of medicines.

"Bless you, yes. Well done."

Arghan's knees buckled.

Pattron shouted, "Someone get a chair for the Prior, and some water!"

A few monks scurried to Arghan's side, one lifting him under his elbow while another pushed one of the nearby wooden benches under his legs. Agape grabbed a water jug from the end of the table and handed it to Arghan, who guzzled it back, splashing half its contents all over his beard as he swallowed.

Pattron spotted the oozing wound in Arghan's shoulder. "Agape, there's bergaroot extract in my satchel. Blue vial. Give him all of it, with some wine from that bottle there, if you please."

Agape nodded and did as he said.

Gavek and Reigh emerged from the basket of a crude elevator driven by block and tackle at the edge of the cliff near the mouth of the cavern. They careened down the steps to the cave floor.

"Father Pattron," Gavek said, panting, "is she, will she—"

Pattron bent over Silla, nostrils flaring, eyebrows curled inward. "I don't know yet." He inspected the gold embroidery on her collar while he listened to her breath. "This can't be princess Cybella, this woman looks older than forty, who—"

Reigh ran his fingers through his frazzled hair. "Her Majesty the Queen Mother; the late king's wife, Silla Raventhern."

Pattron rolled up his sleeves. "Agape, the green bottle next. For me, please." Agape rifled inside the bag again and tossed the item to Pattron, who poured the contents of the vessel over his hands, looking over at Gavek. "What happened exactly?" He pressed two fingers against Silla's jugular.

"We... he..."

"Her Majesty and I went to the dock to meet him," interjected Reigh. "Soldiers arrived. There was a struggle. The Queen got shot. He—"

Gavek whispered into Pattron's ear while he stared back at his mentor, "Father Arthos... he killed or maimed nearly all the soldiers. Not one of them stood by the time he was done."

Pattron glanced at Arghan, who looked back at him through sullen, darkened eyelids. Arghan dropped his head. Pattron looked down again and tore off the Queen's gown. He inspected her wound, grimacing. The bloody arrowhead projected through her left breast. "Roll her on her side. Careful. Agape, the clean rags, put them on the table. Some more in your hands. Douse them with the same potion I used on mine. When I give the signal, press down over the wound, yes?"

Agape nodded and did as he said. Pattron felt for the back end of the arrow shaft only to find it had already been snapped off. He grabbed the torch one of the monks had retrieved and forced it against the entry wound. Silla shrieked. He rolled her onto her back and pulled the remainder of the arrow from her chest.

"Now!"

Agape pressed down the rags. "What next?"

"Keep the pressure on. Firm, but gentle." Pattron turned and searched inside his satchel. He pulled out a hollowed rod, some thread, and a needle.

Silla gurgled and spit up blood. Her head tilted to the side. Arghan leaped from his bench and back to the side of the table.

Agape gave Pattron a darting gaze. "She's stopped breathing!"

Pattron dropped his instruments and pressed both hands against her chest, applying thrusts in rhythmic intervals, stopping periodically to blow air into her mouth. "She's not responding, I don't... the arrow... it must have pierced her heart... I don't understand how she is still breathing... I—I don't..." He stepped back, wiping beads of sweat from his forehead. *Closing the wound will accomplish nothing if she's bleeding inside. How is she still alive? If only little Grace were here.* What was it she said to do in the cabin at the lakeshore? Would it work again?

Pattron leaped on top of the table, straddling Silla's body. He placed his hands on her head and spoke the Name, as he had before.

Silla opened her eyes. Arghan took one of her hands. She convulsed, throwing Pattron aside. She groped Arghan's chest. He leaned forward to hear her whispering. A moment later her hands fell limp and her gaze grew vacant.

Pattron dropped his hands to his side and stared at Agape. Agape shook her head as tears streaked down her face. Was she wondering the same thing he was? Why had the saying of the Name worked for her and not this woman?

Reigh fell onto Silla's chest, bawling. "My lady, my lady, forgive me, I've failed you."

Pattron slipped off the table. "I don't... I don't understand." He tottered up the stairs leading to the look-off. Agape went after him.

Pattron reached the edge of the cliff and fell to his knees, staring out over the night sky.

Agape knelt beside him and rested her head on his shoulder. "You did all you could."

Pattron nodded and put his arm around her.

Arghan's eyes welled up with tears. He snorted, gritting his teeth. He took another few gulps of wine and then dumped the contents of Pattron's satchel onto the tabletop. He grabbed a handful of dried bergaroot, tossed it in his mouth, and headed to the staircase.

Gavek jumped in front of him, looking past Arghan's shoulder at Silla's body. "What did she say to you?"

"That's none of your business, son. Step aside."

"No, look at you! You're exhausted. Haven't you—"

Arghan gripped Gavek's shoulder. "You've done so well. I'm proud of you beyond words, but I've no time to argue. Stay here, all of you, until I return. This isn't finished."

Gavek stepped back. "Where are you going? Tell me that at least?"

"Back to the Peak."

Galdir's helmet struck the wall, rousing him awake. Blinking, he caught his halberd before it fell and wiped the raindrops from his face. He surveyed the drawbridge across the chasm outside the monastery. Clear. Just like it was an hour ago, and the hour before that. He leaned under the archway of the main gate to read the clock of the chapel tower.

"Come on, Lorred," he muttered, "if you don't show again, and I catch you sleeping, so help me..."

Hoofbeats clacked nearby. Galdir whipped his head in the direction of the sound. He flinched, hitting the wall with his back. A man sat on horseback at the end of the bridge, holding a torch.

"Who goes there?" said the militiaman, pointing his weapon.

"Arghan of Danniker. I'm here to discuss terms of surrender."

"Surrender? What—" Galdir looked into the courtyard and back again. He stepped backward, eyes fixed on Arghan. He waved his hand in the air until he caught the cord of the warning bell and rung it. Another guard came running.

"What is— God above!" The other guard held out his weapon, trembling.

"It's Danniker. Go get Rollo. Now! Says he wants to discuss his surrender—"

"Not mine, his," Arghan growled.

The two guards stared at him for a moment, gaping.

Finally, Galdir spoke, "You get Rollo. I'll stay here."

"I'll get Rollo. You stay here," said the other, nodding. He scampered off across the courtyard, armour rattling as he went.

Galdir stared at Arghan, studying his form. Arghan's chest rose and fell with steady breath, still bare from when Galdir had seen it stripped in the vineyard, the tattoo of the sea eagle barely visible now beneath filth and spattered blood. Arghan glared at him through long, sweat-soaked, and matted grey locks. Galdir swallowed. Footsteps approached. The knight named Rollo stepped into the torchlight of the gatehouse, followed by several militiamen.

Scowling, Rollo drew his sword and stepped forward. "What do you want?"

"Your surrender."

Rollo grinned. He and his men erupted in laughter.

Arghan kicked one leg over the horse and slid off the saddle, landing on the bridge. He threw the torch on the ground and approached them. He rested his left hand against the dual scabbards he now wore on his hip.

"Recognize these?" he said, tapping the scabbards.

Rollo's gaze fell to Arghan's hip. The engraving of the sacred mountain on the belt buckle. The embroidery on the leather. An Alpinian guardsman's arms, to be sure.

"Your comrades are fallen. The choice is yours whether you fall too."

"Why you—" Rollo rushed at Arghan, sword raised above his head. Arghan drew both swords. With one he parried Rollo's downward blow. With the other he struck his side, dropping the knight to his knees. He kicked Rollo's wrist, knocking his weapon into the chasm. Rollo lunged again. Arghan blocked him with his boot.

"Yield!"

"To hell with—" Rollo spat on the ground. He looked back at the soldiers. "Well, don't just stand there, attack!"

The men held their positions, exchanging glances with each other, also looking at Rollo, then Arghan, and back again.

"Men of Cairhn, I have no quarrel with you," said Arghan. "Wouldn't you rather be in your beds tonight than running Cybion's errands? In all these years we've been a part of this community, have I — have we Cantorvarians ever done anything but good to you, your wives, your children? Can you say the same for that slave driver?"

The militia looked to their own leader.

He shook his head. "No. What would you have us do?"

"Follow me and you'll all get a share of the Abbot's treasury, you have my word." Arghan forced Rollo to the ground. "For starters, tie this one up."

Cybion kicked off his silk sheets and reached for the wineglass on his night table. His trembling fingers glanced the glass and it crashed to the floor.

"Curses!" he said, stumbling out of bed. He zigzagged across the room to his wine cabinet, whining and groaning.

Hounds bellowed from his courtyard. He gasped and shuffled to the window. He shrieked and covered his mouth. On the cobblestone patio below his window, the knight called Rovard dropped his sword and fell to his knees while Arghan of Danniker held a blade to his throat.

"Hellspawn! Devil!" cried Cybion, spitting.

Militiamen stormed into the courtyard, carrying torches. A club pounded his front door.

Cybion raced to his night table. A crackling sound sent a shiver up his neck and he buckled at the sensation of shards slicing his flesh. He fell on his backside, clutching his foot. Blood oozed from wounds where jagged glass pierced his skin. Whimpering, he plucked the pieces out one by one and stretched to pull his night table drawer onto the floor. He snatched a key from the clutter that had fallen out and limped toward a painting hanging on the wall opposite his window.

Heavy footsteps thudded up the stairs.

He yanked a framed canvas from the wall, revealing an iron door. With slippery, blood-soaked fingers he poked and scraped the key against its metal exterior until he found the keyhole and turned it. He pulled out several large canvas bags and stumbled backward, clutching them against his chest.

The door slammed open against the chamber wall. A bag slipped from Cybion's arms, then another, until all of them fell, bursting on the floor, releasing a deluge of gold coins.

Arghan stood in the doorway, silhouetted against the hall. A Sovereign[1] rolled against his boot and he stooped to snatch it from the floor. "It's over, Cybion. You're coming with me."

---

1. Sovereign – the highest denomination in Cortavian royal currency.

CHAPTER SEVEN
Exodus

Exhausted by the tumultuous events of the preceding day, Arghan surrendered to sleep that morning, unable to resist the inevitable, no matter how hard he tried. The nightmare unfolded as it always had; a torturous reliving of a tragedy his conscience would never let him forget...

A towering inferno blazes across the water, glowing in the night. Arghan orders a ceasefire and commands the oarsmen to take his ship in for a better look. Beyond the palisades, the rest of Koerska is engulfed in flames and smoke. Where is the signal of victory; the general's banner? Had the Zuelan defenders prevailed? How could they with their troops trapped inside the tower he set ablaze?

The water being too shallow now for the *Riverhawk*, he disembarks on a launch with a scouting party, taking the oars himself. Then he hears it. The pounding, thrashing, and screaming. Desperate voices cry out from the windows above him. They aren't the voices of Zuelan soldiers, but of women, children, and old men.

He screams and doubles his speed. A woman jumps from a window and splashes into the river. There's no use trying to save her. The sticky liquid floating on the water — released from the exploding clay pots hurled by his shipboard trebuchet — will soon ignite.

He grabs a rope and grapple from the locker, hurls it over the top of the stockade, and scales the wall.

A chill breaks the heat behind his ears. A young woman with dark braided hair stands atop rubble piled in front of the door, struggling to clear it while faces crowd the door's tiny window, screaming at her to hurry. Arghan sprints over to help her, but it's no use. Ox carts and the corpses of the animals that once towed them are too heavy, even for him. The woman collapses, crying and screaming, "My babies, my boys. Blessed Creator, save them, save them!"

Arghan spots a window higher up. He throws his hook again and scrambles up the side of the wall. Inside, a crowd huddles, desperately pushing against the door. Timbers fall from the floors above, engulfed in flames, crashing into those nearby. Bodies lay everywhere; some were struck down by the fallen beams, others from the smoke. A cry echoes from a deep pit at the back of the room, failing to catch the attention of the others. He repels down a few steps, bracing his feet against the wall. He swings, clearing the crowd, and releases the rope as it succumbs to the flames, landing near the pit. Below him, at the bottom of a cistern, stands an old woman, waist-deep in the water, clutching two crying babies against her breasts. Her legs buckle. She begins to falter. Arghan jumps in and breaks her fall.

"Creator be praised. My angel has arrived. I knew you'd come," she exclaims.

"What? How could you?" he asks, shouting above the roar of the flames, the choking, and the wailing.

"I foresaw this, and your face, in a dream, this day last week. I see now my work is done."

The woman hands him the babies and points below.

"There, sir, below the waterline, lies a hole. An underground channel connects to the well at the centre of the village square. You must pass through it if you're to save my grandsons."

"I'll come back for you," he says, stripping off his armour and outer clothing, preparing to dive.

"No you won't, Arghan. Save the boys. The rest is up to God."

"How on Earda do you know my name?" he asks, though no answer is given. He takes a deep breath and covers the babies' heads. He dives below the surface, kicking with all his might. Soon, the narrow passage gives way to a wider expanse. His head breaks the water to the sound of crying.

Relieved, Arghan shouts at the top of the well, "Braided lady! Anybody! Can you hear me? Help!"

A few moments later that same braided head he saw minutes before looks down at him from the top of the well.

"Orin! Nicah! My sons!"

"Let down the bucket," he says, bracing his legs against the walls of the shaft.

The woman hurries to unwind the line, then one by one he sends them up; tiny, writhing bodies cradled inside it. He follows, but halfway up the shaft his foot slips and his head strikes a stone. A flash of red fills his vision, then black.

And silence.

Arghan stirred when the morning bell tolled outside his window. It was the 7th hour of Midweek[1] morning, a full day past the dreadful events of the early hours of Tillingday[2]. He groaned and sat up, clutching the bandages where the arrow had pierced his shoulder. He slid out of bed, stumbled to the window, and opened the shutters. Across the courtyard, ash wafted from the charred remains of the library, carried by a gentle breeze.

He ambled to the mirror beside his cot. Even after the upheaval of the previous day, one of his faithful brothers had already laid out a basin of hot water and towels. He washed his face and stared into the mirror. The wolf-like calm of a predator's gaze looked back at him. How could so much be lost in so little time? He grabbed his razor, certain of what must

---

1. Midweek – Literally "Mid Week", the day at the middle of the seven day week according to the common calendar.
2. Tillingday – The second day of the week according to the common calendar, traditionally the day when farmers first till their fields for the season.

be done. Holding the long strands of his hair above his head, he sheared it close to his scalp working from his widow's peak back to his crown. The rest he shaved bald from his temples and over his ears, the back of his neck and head, and shortened the grizzled strands of his long beard by half.

A knock came from the door as he patted his face dry.

"Come."

"Master Arghan, forgive me for disturbing you."

"Reigh. What can I do for you?"

The youth stared at the floor, pale-faced and sullen. He held out a sealed letter similar to the one he had delivered to him in the vineyard. "She asked me to give this to you if— if anything happened to her."

Arghan approached him and took the parchment from his hand. "Thank you. I'm sorry for your loss, truly. You were a faithful servant to her."

Reigh nodded. He looked into Arghan's eyes. He opened his mouth as if to speak but his gaze fell back to the floor. He nodded again, turned, and hurried out of the room, sidestepping Pattron as he walked through the open doorway.

"Poor lad," said Pattron. "He's taking this hard. Perhaps some time here with us will help him sort this all out."

"Yes, indeed. You'll see to it he's cared for?"

Pattron closed the door behind him. "Of course."

"It's done then?"

"The Queen Mother has been laid to rest on Mount Trobus, as you ordered."

"Good, and Cybion and the others?"

"Locked up in the catacombs. How long do you expect us to keep them there?"

"They can die down there for all I care."

"You don't mean that—"

"Don't I? It's better than Cybion deserves."

"True, but—"

"But nothing. If just one of them escapes and makes their way to

Trianon, and tells the Archprelate what's transpired, Solstrus will surly write the Grand Prelate in Orbicon demanding an entire legion of Alpinian guardsmen — war or no war — be dispatched to raze this entire valley to ash, including this sacred place."

"But Cybion sends letters to Trianon each week. Without them won't suspicion arise regardless?"

"He'll still write his reports. In his own hand, by your dictation. I've seen to it. A militiaman will post them for you. Now that I've seized Cybion's treasury they'll cause you no more trouble. In fact, I predict they'll be most cooperative. They've seen what I can do to the Archprelate's knights. Greed and fear will keep them at bay."

Pattron stood silent as Arghan dressed, eyes darting as if deep in thought. "You've decided to break your vow, I see." He cocking his head, inspecting Arghan's haircut.

"I broke it the minute I touched the hilt of another sword," said Arghan, gesturing at his head. "This is just a formality."

"You'll be leaving us then? They'll kill you if you show your face in Trianon, you know that."

"They will try, but I can't abandon Cybella. I've got to find her; get her out of this mess she's in. The logical place to start is in the capitol."

Pattron's face grew sullen. He shook his head. "I'll miss you, brother." He opened his arms and the two embraced. "When do you depart?"

"After the midday meal. I hope to reach the falls by sunset."

"Come, there's something I have to show you." Pattron extended his arm toward the door.

Arghan nodded, grabbed his cloak, and followed. A few minutes later the pair stood outside the infirmary.

Arghan touched the door. "What's this about? Isn't this where—"

"You'll see." Pattron opened the door and stepped inside. Arghan followed.

A voice called from the sick bed at the centre of the room, "Master Arghan, you've come, praise His Name."

As Pattron moved out of view, Arghan's gaze fell on the captain who sat up in his bed and held out not one arm, but two.

Tears streamed down the captain's cheeks. "This saint of a friend of yours has made me see the error of my ways."

Arghan gasped, holding his hand against his mouth.

"He came in last night and prayed for me and look what happened!" He waved an arm that should not be there. "Veksire cut off my arm below the joint you broke, but overnight, I dreamt of an old woman, trapped in a well, with two infants held close to her breasts—"

Arghan's knees buckled and he fell to the floor, sobbing. "Depart from me, Lord! I am... I am... a sinful man, a sinful..."

"The Lord you call 'Yeshua' appeared to me and touched my elbow. When I awoke this morning I was whole. Forgive me for what I did to you. I renounce the guard. I renounce the Temple. I beg you to receive me as a Cantorvarian, sir. Let me join your order."

Arghan crawled out the door. He convulsed in the courtyard between the infirmary and the doors of the great hall. What was it that disarmed him so? Surely not only the words the captain spoke, not a miracle he hadn't even seen, though besides the captain few lived who could tell the tale except Arghan, who knew more than any other what damage he had done and could see for himself how it had dramatically been undone. No, it was a Presence, a Person — more thick and tangible than a mid-summer fog, only not as visible.

Pattron knelt by his friend's side. "Do you see now, brother, what I tried to tell you when the two of us were bound in that cage wagon?"

"But Silla, why didn't she... you spoke... and nothing, nothing..."

"No, brother, not nothing. In all my years treating men on the battlefield I've never seen anything like that. That arrow ought to have killed her the minute it pierced her heart, but it didn't. There's a power at work here beyond us all; Sovereign power, not to serve our will, but His."

Arghan nodded, looking back through the open door. He addressed the militiaman still guarding it, "Release him," he said, pointing back at the captain. "Treat this man as you would any of the brothers, that's an order."

Arghan inhaled the fresh mountain air and closed his eyes against the radiant sun. He exited the refectory and hurried up the steps to the courtyard.

Such a bittersweet gathering it had been. A final meal with the men he'd lived and laughed with for years. They all looked at him quite differently now, for obvious reasons, but their warmth remained. He would miss brother Eathid's roasted duck. Brother Holberht's songs. Brother Jadveer's tall tales. Brother Kavar's jokes.

He stared at the ground for a moment then looked toward the corner of the great hall. They'd found Kavar tied to a post inside, beaten to death. *What a hero.* Had he not had the foresight and courage to return here and ring that warning bell many more may have died. Though Rollo's violence meant to break him, his faithful friend refused to betray any of his brothers. What a saint he was. What saints they all were.

Men worth fighting for.

But they weren't the only ones to pay a price. He pulled Silla's letter from his breast pocket, summoning the courage to read it.

Dear Arghan,

If this letter reaches you, it means I am dead and there's nothing more I can do to help Cybella. It's up to you now. You must protect her using whatever powers you still possess.

I must warn you, the son who came home to me was not the one I had lost at the sea. He's detached. Vain. Dispassionate. He goes nowhere, does nothing, and says nothing without the man who rescued him by his side: the Liester of Luthargrad. I suspect the nobleman has some kind of power over him. In the time since Eriohn returned I've never been allowed to speak to him, let alone air my suspicions. The Liester is complicit in Cybella's disappearance, I'm sure of it; probably in league with that old buzzard Solstrus, whose motives are clearer; he never approved of women holding positions of power, let alone wearing the crown. He's been delaying Cybella's coronation since the moment the king died. He's never been a friend of Cortavian patriots either (as you know from the war), resenting the religious independence this kingdom enjoys in comparison to other Eskaran states.

As for us, some final words to settle things. I beg you to believe that your dear friend the late king Eriohn held you in the highest regard to his very last. It was he who allowed your escape from his dungeon after your trial, and he who saw to it the matter was covered up, for your sake.

As for how he and I came to be wed, it was my decision to seek annulment of our marriage after you were convicted, not his. I couldn't bear the stigma and shame of being the wife of a known war criminal, especially after discovering I was pregnant with your child.

While it's true Eriohn and I grew close while Queen Rose was dying of that awful illness (how could we not? He was her husband and I was her best friend), never once did he exhibit anything but pure intentions toward me and faithful friendship toward you. He loved you like a brother, so much so that he would have gone to war with the Grand Prelate for your sake, had I not persuaded him otherwise. He a widower with a young son; me a pregnant noblewoman with no prospects; the course seemed clear. He proposed marriage to protect my honour, and to safeguard what his dear friend could not. He was a wonderful father to Cybella and never failed to love her as his own. The fact that he left his kingdom to her when he thought his own son was dead proves that.

Perhaps someday you will find it in your heart to forgive me. Perhaps not. It doesn't matter. I did what I thought best for myself and our child. Now you must too. Save her Arghan. If it's your last act as an Erne Warder, you must save her.

Sincerely,

Silla

Arghan sighed. He sniffled and tightened the belt around his long overcoat. He threw his cloak over his shoulder, grabbed a satchel and backpack from the side of the well, and hastened into the stables near the main gate.

He stopped when he saw Gavek packing the saddlebags of a second horse. "What do you think you're doing?"

"I'm coming with you, that's what."

Arghan strode past him, secured his luggage to his horse then leaped into his saddle. "Out of the question, your place is here." He prodded the horse.

Gavek skidded in front of his path, holding up his hands. "No, hear me out."

"What's there to hear? I'll not have you following me on a fool's errand. There's a very good chance I'll get killed, and if I do, you might too. I can't ask you to take a risk like that." Arghan drove his horse forward.

Gavek raced ahead and dove in front of the door. "You can't do this without me. Has it occurred to you Cybella's disappearance might have something to do with the manuscripts Wardein has been smuggling to us? If something's happened to her how long do you think it'll be before something happens to him too? Our work recovering the lost Scriptures is too important for me to sit here doing nothing. I need to be sure they're safe. You can't read ancient Tzyani, or tell the difference between a forgery and the genuine article. I can."

Arghan dismounted and marched to where Gavek stood.

"I'll give it my best shot."

Gavek's face turned red, he stepped forward and screamed, "Do you have any idea how hard its been living here my whole life, the way I am? I'm not common like the others, you know that. I dream in numbers. I solve twelve riddles a day before most others get out of bed! Memorizing the volumes in the library was the only thing keeping me from going stark raving mad, the only thing! Now it's gone. Gone!"

"I know son, I know, but—"

"No, you don't know, Father Arthos, or Arghan, or whatever you're calling yourself now. In the past two days, I helped you escape, crawled through blackened catacombs, jumped out of a window, dangled over a cliff, warned you of an impending attack, and took a dive off a pier, all because of what's inside this!" He pointed at his forehead.

Arghan smiled and pointed at Gavek's chest. "No you didn't son, you did it because of what's in here, and I love you for it, but—"

"That's not what I mean, look." Gavek scampered back to his horse and retrieved some items out of one of the saddlebags. "I saved all of these from the library. This, the lexicon of ancient Tzyani words, the only one of its kind. This, the annuls of Saint Orctavius, founder of the Order of the Cantorvarians, keepers of the True Faith; and this, my translation of the Testament according to the prophet Gion, written in the coded shorthand I myself invented. These prove what Cantorvarians have known for centuries, that the Temple of Orbicon and all the Grand Prelates who've ruled there for as long as we can remember have been telling a lie! Their account of the Saviour's exploits on the Other World, out there in the heavens, isn't what Tzyani prophets revealed at all! There is hope in the Name of Yeshua, a name they themselves kept secret, and salvation is free for the asking, by faith! By faith, father! Not by the whims of the enlightened. By faith! Don't you see? Do you know what it says at the start?"

"I have a feeling you're about to tell me."

" 'In the beginning was the Word, and the Word was with God, and the Word was God!' The Word is Yeshua! I know now why my mother abandoned me here so many years ago, and why you must take me with you now. If Cybella is deposed, if the collection hidden below the Library of Trianon is lost or destroyed, what then? This truth is worth dying for if it comes to that! I beg you, take me with you. If you don't I'll go there alone."

Arghan searched Gavek's eyes. They gleamed like Pattron's had when he spoke about the miracle on the lakeshore, the same way captains did in the infirmary.

Arghan embraced him. "You're brighter than any of us, young Gavek. I can see there's no arguing with you. Finish packing and meet me in the courtyard. We'll leave after a final word with Pattron."

Arghan and Gavek rode into the courtyard toward the hitching post near the well, expecting to leave their horses there while Arghan went inside to speak to Pattron, but they slowed their pace when it came into view.

While they'd been inside the stable the Cantorvarians had formed two lines leading through the gate and across the bridge. Pattron stood near the well, along with Agape and a few of the brothers closest to Arghan. The inside line parted to allow the horses to pass.

Arghan dismounted and approached Pattron. "You didn't have to do this."

"Yes I did, brother. You deserve a proper send-off, and before you left I thought you'd like to meet the newest members of our order: may I present brother Theréon, the erstwhile captain of the guards."

Arghan bowed. "Welcome to our fellowship. I pray someday you may forgive me for—"

"It is I who begs your forgiveness, Master Arghan. Had it not been for your violence I never would have experienced the miracle that opened my eyes. I am forever in your debt. It appears we've been wrong about a great many things. I have a lot of thinking to do, and this seems like the right place to do it."

"It is indeed."

"Perhaps even Cybion will see the light, in time?"

Arghan studied Theréon's eyes. He drew close to him. "Perhaps. Until then he can stay right where he is, understood?"

"As you wish, Master Arghan." Theréon bowed and backed away, joining the line.

"Now, Pattron, you said 'members'. Where are the other new brothers?"

"Nowhere, brother. May I present to you *sister* Agape of the Lakeshore."

Arghan grinned and turned to face her.

"With your permission, of course, Prior," she said, bowing her knees. "I'm told there's not been a female member of your order for centuries. There's nothing else left for me in this world. I want what you all have, it's as simple as that."

"I think that's a splendid idea, sister Agape. I trust that in time you will have as much to teach us as we can teach you. But you don't need my permission, you need his." Arghan put his hand on Pattron's chest.

Pattron furrowed his brow. "What's that?"

"As I said earlier, I stopped being Prior of this monastery the minute my hands touched a sword again. I always knew my past would catch up to me eventually. I regret that it happened here. As far as I'm concerned, you were the obvious choice to succeed Ardwynn. He only appointed me his successor to honour tradition. I was his first disciple of this generation, but you've always been his best."

"I wouldn't say that, brother. He saw something in you. He believed in you, as do I. Go with God, and also with this." Pattron took a shiny metal object from his pocket and dropped it in Arghan's hand.

Arghan sighed. "Ardwynn's cross of sainthood. I cannot accept this."

"Yes, you can. When they were ransacking the Peak, one of the men under Rollo's command desecrated Ardwynn's sepulchre beyond repair. Until a new one can be built, I can think of no safer place to keep it than 'round your hairy neck."

The pair laughed for longer than the jest deserved. Perhaps it was the tension of the previous days finding its way out. An awkward silence followed. They embraced, finally parting with moistened eyes.

"Thank you for being my friend," said Arghan. He bowed to the others and then leaped into his saddle. He paused to look out over those assembled while his restless horse shuffled on the spot. "Brothers, please hear my last confession. I failed you as your Prior and I kept secrets from you as a brother, secrets that cost you dearly. But I swear to you, as much as it is within my power, I will set things right. I will protect you and the traditions of this sacred order with all that is within me, or die trying. For centuries we knew our Lord only as the Shepherd King, a truth passed down to us from the Tzyani prophets who first told the people of Earda about the Other World where the Saviour of the Universe came. But now we know His Name, Yeshua, and it is for that truth, for that Name I shall fight. Pray for me, brothers. Until we meet again, either here or in Paradise. Farewell." Arghan kneed his horse and sped across the bridge.

The stars spun across the sky, led by Jakav's monthly pursuit of Easa[3], otherwise known as the dance of the twin moons. At least that's how it seemed to Gavek. He'd observed the heavenly bodies often enough to know they moved, but not that fast. Was it the day's frantic ride through trails, winding up and down the hills along the Treighya river that dazed him? Or had the dramatic events of the preceding days finally caught up with him now that he was lying down? Perhaps he'd write a book about it someday if he ever finished the twelve others he had started to pen.

Arghan stirred on his bedroll on the other side of the campfire. Even the distant tumult of Ondolen Falls couldn't drown out his snoring. He sat up and threw off his blanket.

Gavek lifted his head. "What's wrong?"

"Nothing. Drank too much water. Go back to sleep. I'll return as soon as I've watered the ferns."

Gavek nodded and went back to counting the stars. Where had he left off? *Fascinating, I never forget.* No matter, he'd start over. Fatigue and dizziness really could dampen even the sharpest of minds. That would go in the book.

One minute turned into ten, then twenty. A wolf howled across the river. He sat up and stared, holding his wool blanket below his eyes. Blinking, he looked back up the steep slope near their campsite, opposite the river. "Arghan?"

He threw down his blanket and stumbled to his feet. He scurried away from the campfire, stopping to pet one of the horses. "Arghan?"

The darkness offered no reply except the song of nocturnal insectivores, busy culling the brush of bugs. High up the slope a torchlight ignited and glided at a steady pace through the trees. Gavek looked back at the campfire and then back up the hill. He dashed back to his bedroll to retrieve a dagger Arghan had given him and re-lit a miner's lantern he'd brought with him from his stay on Mount Trobus. He tiptoed through the forest to the foot of the hill and started climbing.

Several minutes later the slope leveled out. He leaned against a tree

---

3. Jakav and Easa – Earda's twin moons, named for the characters of Tzyani lore.

to catch his breath. In the distance, the torchlight had stopped moving and looked dimmer than before.

"Arghan?"

Another wolf howled, this time from higher up the mountain, followed by a growl, setting the hairs on the back of Gavek's neck on end. He quickened his pace, thrashing through the brush.

"Arghan?"

Gavek's lantern slipped from his fingers. He bolted toward the source of light at the bottom of what looked like a short slope. The ground gave way beneath him. He tumbled through a copse of vines and fell into a rocky crevice. Darkness gave way to torchlight the second before his body splashed into a pool. Water chilled his limbs. Thrashing against the murky pit he thrust his head into the air, gasping. He opened his eyes as a shadow appeared on the cave wall. He spun toward the source of light, only to recoil from the tip of a sword.

Gavek's gaze traced the blade from it's long, sharpened tip, up it's curved taper to where it broadened, set into a hilt adorned with cross guards shaped like the wings of a sea eagle.

"A 'Zwillingskralle',[4]" exclaimed Gavek, shivering, "a Twin Talon."

"There's no fooling you, is there?" Arghan rolled its hilt over his knuckles and whipped its blade into the scabbard hanging from his belt. It's twin hung below it. He pulled Gavek out of the water. "I thought I told you I'd be back shortly."

"And I thought you said you were only taking a whiz. There's wolves about, you know. I could have been eaten. What is this place?" Gavek wiped the water from his eyes. Arghan stepped aside, revealing a short passage leading into a chamber lit by torches. Inside it, a massive horde of gold coins, rubies, sapphires and emeralds sparkled and gleamed in the flickering firelight.

"Holy fire! What the—"

"War loot, seized by the Erne Warders from Zuelan forces during the war of 410." Arghan sauntered into the chamber, kicking aside a golden

---

4. Zwillingskralle – High late Gothan compound word for a "twin talon", the prized weapon of an Erne Warder.

lamp stand as he crouched amid the treasure. He dug through the coins as if to search for something. "The Zuelan Emperor loved to boast of his conquests, insisting captives and treasure be paraded behind his advancing forces; a sign of his invincibility, or so he thought. More like hubris, I should think. There's troves just like this all over Northwest Cortavia. Thulrek Von Terrack entrusted me with their locations just before he died after the siege of Kortova. He was our last Grand Master. I may be the only one left alive who knows where they all are. Ah, there it is!" He pulled a tanned leather sack out from under a pile of pearl necklaces.

"Why didn't you tell us about all this? We could have hired our own private army to protect the monastery with all—"

"Knowing this location could've gotten you all killed. Besides, I didn't come here for this," he said, kicking some Regalian[5] doubloons into the air. "I may be a butcher but I'm no thief. I came here for these." He tapped the pommel of one of his Talons. "And for this. This is mine."

He threw the sack at Gavek who buckled, slouching forward as he caught it.

Gavek peeked inside the bulky sack. Jewels as clear as ice sparkled near its brim. "Diamonds?"

"Diamonds. Some gold too. Enough to settle the debt of any bankrupt state I'm sure. Come. Make yourself useful. Grab a torch and follow me. There's a much easier way out of here than how you came." Arghan chuckled and slipped through a narrow channel at the back of the chamber.

"But... where did you get this? What—"

"That was my reward for saving the infant Eriohn's life. Not every problem can be overcome by force. Who knows where Cybella is? These may open doors my swords cannot."

"But what about—"

Arghan stopped and held up his hand. "Gavek, can you just give it a rest for the night? We have a long day of rowing ahead if we're to make one of the transports from Sigoe by Fastingday[6]. You can ask me all the

---

5. Costa Regalia is a nation on the south coast of the continent of Eskareon. See map section.
6. Fastingday – The sixth day of the week according to the common calendar.

questions you want then. Right now I want to get back to camp and get some sleep."

"Rowing? What about the horses?"

Arghan rolled his eyes and marched down the passageway.

CHAPTER EIGHT
Ghosts

Raindrops battered Gavek's forehead, awakening him from his slumber. He opened his eyes and blinked up at the cloudy sky. Wet grass and soaked leather aroused his nostrils. The canoe rocked, jerking him upright.

"Are we sinking?"

Arghan pulled the craft ashore. "We'll camp here for the night. Start setting up the tent. I'll be right back." He started inland.

Gavek stumbled onto the shore, kicking up pebbles. "Oh no you don't, not again. Where are you off to this time?"

Arghan continued to walk away. He pointed toward the stone ruins that stood on an outcropping high above the riverbank. "Fort Bohlin. Gotta pay my respects to an old friend. I'd ask you to come, but it's private."

Gavek followed. "I'll bet it is. Is there another treasure pit up there? A secret rendezvous, perhaps?"

Arghan sighed. "No."

The trail steepened. Gavek glanced back at the canoe. "You're just going to leave that there? It's not going to float away on us, I hope?"

"I've been rowing small craft for the past forty years, ten of those in the navy. No, it's not going to float away."

Gavek clutched his gurgling stomach. "Why did we have to trade in two perfectly good horses for that dreadful thing, anyway? The gorge was beautiful, mind you, but the rapids cleaned me out, it case you hadn't noticed me vomiting all afternoon."

"So that's what that was."

"I was thinking—"

"Were you, now."

They turned a corner. The trail narrowed.

"Yes. We're roughly two-thirds of the way between Ondolen Falls and the village of Kessa. I know you love your boats, but I'm clearly not cut out for whitewater navigation. Kessa's on our way. What say we get something proper to eat there, then trade that death trap back in for some new horses? That way we can save ourselves another two days of needless toil. We can cross into Trakalia and take the southeast road through the Ebon Valley to Ropa. From there it's nothing but gentle hills and quaint pastures all the way to Trianon."

"Out of the question."

"But—"

"I didn't ask you to come. You insisted, remember?"

"True, but—"

"I said no."

Gavek fumed. He ran his fingers over the tattered scarf around his neck. Kessa meant more to him than a proper meal and a comfortable ride. The old trading post near the Trakalian border may very well have been his birthplace. The distinctive embroidery on the swaddling blanket the old monks had found him in seemed to suggest it. He'd settle the matter of course, someday, when he got around to writing his book *Tapestries and Tassels of Eastern Eskareon*, probably after the 12 others he had on the go; perhaps sooner given he'd already settled on a title.

Arghan pointed. "We're almost there. Once inside, just give me a few minutes alone, will you?"

Gavek nodded. "Sure."

They passed the edge of a cliff and ascended a crumbling staircase. Below them lay the overgrown stone floor of the castle's chapel, bathed in feeble rays of light shining through a partly collapsed grand ogival window. They reached a landing. Arghan descended a staircase leading into the ruins, startling some pigeons nested inside crevices in the wall. He crossed the chapel floor and pressed his head against an old altar. After several moments of silence, he returned. Gavek stood on his toes and peered past his mentor's shoulder. Arghan moved to block his view.

"What are you hiding? Show me."

Arghan shook his head and grabbed Gavek's wrists. Gavek feigned resignation then bolted past him. Arghan winced, just missing Gavek's sleeve. He gripped his shoulder and staggered back. Gavek's gaze fell on the altar; a skeleton lay across it, arranged in anatomical order; the distinctive beak-shaped visor of an Erne Warder's sallet rested on its ribcage.

Gavek's mouth fell open.

Arghan hastened away. "Satisfied? There's no treasure buried here. Just bones. Bones of friends."

Gavek's dropped his chin against his chest. "I'm sorry, who was he?"

"Thulrek Von Terrack."

"The last Grand Master? I thought you said he died after the siege of Kortova?"

"He did, right here, making his last stand against the Alpinian guards sent to hunt us down."

"What happened?"

"After the Erne Warders' narrow victory over the Zuelan Horde at the siege of Kortova, while those who survived were weakened and wearied by the effort, the Alpinian Guard, who I believe deliberately delayed their arrival, turned against them, trapping most of them inside the castle. Von Terrack and I arrived late by ship and forced the remaining Zuelans to retreat, unaware of what the Alpinians were up to. By the time we discovered their betrayal, there was nothing we could do to help our comrades. Thulrek decided to regroup at Fort Bohlin. A Zuelan prisoner witnessed our escape and told the Alpinians. They pursued. We put up a brave fight but in the end, they overwhelmed us. Thulrek and I got separated during the struggle and I was captured; later forced to watch them run him through on this very spot."

Arghan stumbled back and collapsed on the altar. "I'm sorry, Thulrek! I failed you. I failed all of us! I could have fought harder. I should have fought harder."

Gavek stepped forward and touched his shoulder. In that moment, the closest thing he had to a father; the kind and sincere man he knew as 'Father Arthos' had completely vanished, replaced by the deeply flawed, broken man called Arghan of Danniker. Gavek knelt beside him. "It sounds to me like there's nothing you could have done. I'm sure Von Terrack would understand that. Whoever you are, whatever you've done, you're still the kindest, wisest man I've ever known."

"Am I?" said Arghan, jerking away. "Don't you see? After the terrible tragedy at Koerska, I became unable to wield my own swords, afraid of hurting another living soul. When the Alpinians stormed this place, I cowered in the next room over there, convinced I had no right to use them; that I deserved to die for what I had done." He covered his eyes. "All I could see were their faces, their innocent faces..."

"I don't understand... whose faces?"

"The women, the children, the old men... the Tzyani of Koerska, trapped inside the tower I was ordered to fire upon when we assaulted the town. I swear to you I didn't know they were inside, I didn't know."

Gavek glanced at the floor. "I read the accounts written by the Grand Prelate's inquisitors. I didn't for a minute believe what they said about you, or your comrades. They claimed the Erne Warders destroyed the Tzyani enclave deliberately, intent on stealing what they called 'esoteric secrets'."

"Lies. All lies. But it doesn't matter. In the end, it was my failure they used as a pretext to persecute and destroy us, and my inability to cope with what I had done that ultimately helped them finish the job. My failure to act that day, here at Bohlin, was all I could think of the night the Alpinians cornered us on the dock. I dared not hesitate again and ended up proving I really was the butcher they all claimed me to be." He looked at his twin swords. "I don't know what I was thinking going back for these. They've brought me nothing but trouble." Arghan stood up and unbuckled his belt, allowing his weapons to fall to the ground. He turned and started up the stairs. "We'll take the river. It's the fastest way to Trianon and there's no time to waste. I can only hope we get there in time."

Gavek watched Arghan disappear below the crest of the hill. He knelt there for a few moments, staring at the skeleton. Finally, he picked up Arghan's swords and carried them under his cloak.

Standing on Sigoe's pier, Arghan counted a handful of coins while he watched a pair of fur trappers paddle up the Onya river in their new canoe. "Happy now?"

"Quite," replied Gavek, "thought not as much as I would be if you'd just buy us another pair of horses. You're certain the river is faster? An Estates pony can cover—"

Arghan arched his eyebrows and shook his head.

Gavek held up his hands. "You can't blame me for trying."

Arghan chuckled. "Yes, I can. Quit stalling and get your things loaded." Arghan pointed up the dock toward a longship. "I've booked passage on that Ostergaardian freighter over there, the *Flussotter*. I paid quite handsomely for us to be her only passengers, so be on your best behaviour. Her captain's called Zigismundt. Tell him you're with me and he'll show you where can stow your things. I'm heading to the market for supplies. Come find me there when you're finished. But be quick about it, he sails at midday for Trianon. Here, don't forget this." Arghan bent down to grab Gavek's cloak. As he lifted it, his twin swords came tumbling out, clanging onto the dock.

"What are these doing here? I thought I made it clear at Bohlin I was through with them?"

"Well, you may be. I'm not."

"Is that so? You'd better hope nobody sees them. I should toss them in the Onya right now."

"Don't, they're mine now. Rights of salvage. Cortavian Common Code, section twelve, paragraph nine, 'Abandoned property falls under the ownership of whichever citizen claims it first after its original owner signals intent of disposal'. The Dockmaster is right over there, shall I call him and make a complaint?"

"Remind me why I let you tag along? What's gotten into you?"

"I could ask you the same thing. I saw the look on your face when we passed the ruins of Koerska this morning. If Pattron was here he'd tell you to let the past go. It doesn't matter what did or didn't happen there twenty years ago. What matters is the life you chose to live since, and what you do today. I know you've seen tragedies I have no experience of. What I do have experience of is the kind of man you've been my whole life. The truth is we might all be dead if it weren't for you. I don't think these swords ever failed you, I think your heart did, and you need to get it back somehow."

Arghan stepped back to avoid a man carrying a bag of grain. He furrowed his brow, watching the man throw his load onto a ship nearby.

Arghan's eyes moistened. He gazed at the plains across the river. "You sound just like old Ardwynn. He'd be proud of you I'm sure, as would Pattron." He took a few steps toward the landward side of the pier, then looked back and waved. "Perhaps you're right. Pack the swords, just be sure to hide them. If anybody sees you, you'll soon find out what trouble they'll cause. Then I will buy you a horse and send you home."

Gavek smiled and watched Arghan walk away.

Arghan strolled Sigoe's boardwalk, smiling for the first time in days. Nestled on the banks of the Onya river, the shipping hub had always managed to lift his spirit, even at the worst of times. It seemed little had changed in the years since he last walked its bustling streets. When the allied fleet docked there in 415 the port had only one harbour crane, now it had three. A few more pubs had appeared along the boardwalk, but the constant flow of bodies, boxes, barrels, and bovines remained just as he remembered it.

Gavek did sound just like old Ardwynn, he mused, his thoughts drawn back to his apprentice when he glimpsed a young man who resembled him. Arghan hadn't finished mourning his mentor's death when the perplexing events of the past week ignited the storm raging inside him. Had these circumstances which forced him to reconcile his past been guided by the unseen hand of the One whose true name he'd finally discovered?

He hastened through a stone archway leading into Sigoe's outdoor market, still watching one of the cranes behind him lift a load onto a ship. His body struck a wall of flesh and bone.

"Tenekt[1]!" shouted the husky foreigner, staring down at Arghan, spitting. He reached for a sabre hanging from a belt around his baggy red trousers.

Instinctively, Arghan also reached for his hip, the rattle of his coin purse reminding him his swords weren't there. His eyelids widened. He regained his footing and held out his hands in a conciliatory gesture. *Best to diffuse this.* He was sure he could take him down at least a dozen ways, but experience told him such a move would be considered a personal declaration of war on the Zuelan, not to mention all of his friends, and his kind always had friends — friends Arghan had yet to see or count. He grabbed a gold coin from his purse, touched it to his forehead and bowed, then held it out with his gaze fixed on the ground.

"Achad[2]", growled the man, batting Arghan's hand. The coin flew across the dock and into the river. He stormed away, muttering.

The predicted and hoped-for response. Thank the Maker.

A voice called from below the archway, "Now how on Earda did you know how to do that? I've seen other men lose a hand or an eye after an encounter with one of them."

Arghan looked over his shoulder to see a half-naked man leaning against the wall of the arch, holding out a wooden cup. "Well met, sir. Since when do Zuelan sailors walk freely in Sigoe, let alone Cortavia, anyway?"

The beggar offered a half-toothed smile through long white whiskers. "Ever since the young prince was crowned king a 'new policy of peace and understanding' has been implemented, according to the town crier's proclamation. You should've seen the long faces the Merchant's

---
1. Tenekt – Zuelan for "idiot / imbecile / contemptible fellow"
2. Achad – Zuelan for "away with you"

Guild wore while he read it — ha! That fellow and his friends have been buzzing about here all morning looking for something, seems to me. That's their vessel over there. More like a pirate ship than a trader I should think. We're supposed to give them free rein in the port and waterways now 'in the interest of trade', provided they follow the law. Crazy if you ask me, but then again most people call me crazy, so what do I know, I only lost a leg and half my wits fighting those bastards back in the day." The man unfurled a dusty blanket that had been covering his lower body, exposing a stump where his right leg had once been.

"Really, where?"

"Kortova. Pikeman, I was. One of them hacked my damn leg off with an axe before we turned the tide and sent them running. Surely you must have heard all about what happened up there." The old man pointed to the northwest with his thumb.

"Little bit, yes. Thanks for the information, friend. May the Father of Lights bless you." Arghan reached back into his purse and withdrew five silver coins and a small diamond, dropping them in the man's cup as he continued through the arch. "Let this be our little secret, okay?" Arghan interlocked his thumbs and spread his remaining fingers like wings against his chest, and bowed.

The beggar gasped. "The sign of the Erne!" He looked down into his cup and gasped again, wide-eyed and blinking. "By my brown britches, bless you, sir knight."

Arghan held a finger up to his lips while he patted the man on the shoulder before continuing through the arch.

In the distance behind him, the Zuelan had boarded his ship and was talking to some of his comrades, pointing at the spot where the two had collided.

G avek walked into the market, weaving his way through the crowd. *'Come find me there'* he says. *How could anyone in a place like this?* He stood on his toes and surveyed the sea of bodies and market stalls in the shadow of the half-timbered houses that surrounded the plaza. An auctioneer shouted prices somewhere behind him. A row of butchers dazzled onlookers to his right, cutting and packing orders faster than his eyes could follow. He passed an ox stall, then a florist. The stench of manure mixed with the sweet aroma of mountain flowers. He gagged and covered his mouth, eyes darting.

Salvation at last! Gavek squirmed past a pair of women tugging opposite ends of a scarf near a textile merchant's table and jumped on top of a low wall bordering the inner circuit of the plaza. He rolled his eyes when he spotted Arghan buying Horst[3]-grown apples at a stall near the same entrance he had used earlier. He jumped down again and pushed back through the crowd. Two men breezed in front of him, carrying a lumber beam; he dove under it and lurched against one of the apple crates.

Arghan took a bite from an apple. "There you are, I was wondering when you'd show up."

"Wondering... huff... when *I* would—"

A ruckus erupted in the midst of the crowd; it parted like a wave ahead of a large black mountain hound as it chased a ferret through the square.

A woman in a skirted hunting tunic almost as black as her long braided hair raced after the animals, longbow in hand.

A teen girl of similar appearance followed. "Rhodo! Halt! Heel, boy," she yelled as they tore off through the archway.

Three men carrying curved sabres pursued, dressed in the same foreign garb worn by the man Arghan had run into earlier.

Arghan threw a burlap sack full of supplies into Gavek's arms. "That can't end well. Here, take this." He snatched a man's walking staff, tossing him a coin in exchange, and sprinted through the archway after the pursuers.

"Wait!" Gavek threw the sack over his shoulder and ran after him.

Arghan skidded across the boardwalk behind a crowd of spectators gathered near the Zuelan ship. The dog now stood on its hind legs, bracing itself with its forepaws against the ship's main mast, barking at the

---

3. Horst – a hamlet on the road to Sigoe from Nova Engaric, known for its rich produce, including bright red apples bigger than a man's fist.

ferret which huddled inside ship's crow's nest, trembling.

"Get off our ship, mongrel," shouted one of the Zuelans, leaping onto the deck. He swung his sword at the dog, missing it by a hair. The dog retreated to the side of the deck, growling as the man closed in for another attack.

While the teen stayed behind, the braided woman rushed across the gang plank. "Leave him be!"

Another Zuelan jumped from the dock and landed in front of her. He waved his sword. "Stay back, woman. Your kind isn't welcome here."

"Please, I just want my dog. He's only doing what he's been trained to do. He's very... important to me. Let me board and I promise he'll trouble you no further."

"Our vessel, our rules, our dog now! It chases our master's pet and will learn obedience." He shouted over his shoulder, "Captain Zheyka, come at once."

Hearing this, Arghan raced unnoticed behind the crowd to the edge of the dock and slid into the water. He swam past the ship's bow and pulled himself by a mooring rope up the opposite side of the hull.

The Zuelan who had already taken a swipe at the dog chased it around the mast until man and animal stood on opposite sides of it, feigning starts to the right and left.

In a flash, the dark-haired huntress drew an arrow and fired it at the man, pinning him to the mast by his pant leg. The younger huntress drew an arrow and aimed it at him in the same time it took the woman to draw another and point it at the Zuelan blocking her on the ramp.

"I said, let me take my dog. Nobody needs to get hurt today."

As the two stared at each other across the plank, another Zuelan dressed in finer attire than the others, burst out of a cabin door holding a weighted fishing net and threw it over the dog. The Ostergaardian Shepherd snarled as he pulled the drawing cord, tightening it like a snare around the animal's body. He dragged it across the deck and hurled it overboard. "Off my ship, cur!"

"No!" cried the woman, firing at the same moment Arghan struck the Zuelan captain on the ankle, tripping him. The captain hit the deck before the arrow could strike his head. Still hidden behind the side of the hull, Arghan grabbed him by the collar and pulled him overboard, then dove into the water himself.

"Rhodo! Mother, do something! He'll drown!" cried the teen.

The woman advanced against the man who blocked her on the plank, offering him a target. He swung his sword and she dodged, spinning to kick him in the backside as she came up, sending her opponent splashing into the river. She ran onto the ship and leaned over the rail at the spot where the canine had gone over.

"Rhodo!" She threw off her quiver and dropped her bow, preparing to dive.

The man who she had pinned to the mast finally broke free and lunged at her with his sword.

A group of armoured soldiers ran toward the ship from the south end of the pier.

Leading them, the harbour master pointed his mace. "What's going on here? Drop your weapons. Stay where you are, all of you!" He and his men boarded the ship and encircled the group.

"This woman boarded our vessel, uttering threats against our captain."

"That's a lie. They threatened to kill my dog because it chased their master's pet ferret half way across town and ended up here."

"Is that true?" asked the harbour master.

"It's true," yelled one of the onlookers, "we all saw it."

"Who asked you?" said the harbour master. "Now tell me, foreigner, is it?"

"The beast boarded our vessel. What were we to do in the face of such disgrace? It's bad enough that demon cur defiled our noble vessel, but so did this Tzyani witch. She even fired at our captain." He spat on the deck in the woman's direction.

"I see neither a dog nor a ship's captain anywhere," said the harbour master. "I do see a loose ferret. Dogs are allowed in Sigoe. Those pests are not. Coax it back into a proper cage and you'll see no more trouble I'm sure, otherwise report to my office in the crane house yonder, to pay the fine. You all stay on your ship until you depart. That's an order. As for you," he said, pointing now at the woman, "get off their ship and stay off it."

"But—"

"Off!"

The Zuelan sneered, then turned toward the sound of his captain shouting at him from the river.

The woman gathered her bow and quiver and dashed back over the plank, fighting back tears. She embraced her daughter. "I'm sorry, Khloe. There's nothing we can do now. Rhodo's gone."

Gavek stopped nearby the women and spotted something stirring in the river. Arghan burst from the surface, spitting, clutching the dog against his chest. He rolled onto his back and swam toward a ladder beside the pier.

Gavek pointed at Arghan. "Excuse me, madam, look."

"Rhodo," cried Khloe, running to meet him. Her mother jumped beside her, followed by Gavek.

The woman dropped to her stomach and held her arms out over the ladder. "Rhodo! How?"

Holding the dog while it eagerly licked his face, Arghan glanced up at the braid dangling from the Tzyani mother's head, then looked into her dark brown eyes. Framed by eyelids bearing the hint of years, they stared back at him while he bobbed atop the waves. Both remained silent for what felt like an eternity as if searching for the words to say next.

"Well, uh, I believe this spry fellow is yours, is he not?" said Arghan, smiling.

She grinned. "Ah, yes, yes he is. Come on, boy."

Arghan pushed the dog up the ladder by its rump, squinting against the water dripping off its soggy fur. The woman pulled the canine up over her shoulder and onto the dock. It scampered past her, stopped in front of Khloe and Gavek, and shook its coat, spraying the two of them with water.

Still staring at each other, the woman and Arghan spoke nearly in unison, neither of them intelligible over the voice of the other. The two of them chuckled, blushing.

Gavek looked past the dog's wagging tail and smirked. *What's going on here now? Am I really seeing what I think I'm seeing?*

The woman held out her hand. "Here, let me help you, kind sir. I'm sorry, I don't know your name."

"That's because he hasn't told you yet," Gavek whispered.

Arghan grasped her hand, pulling himself up the ladder with his other. They rose to their feet together, still holding hands as Arghan stepped onto the dock, dripping.

"I am brother Arthos of Cairhn monastery, of the Cantorvarian order, but please, call me by my given name, Arghan. And you are?"

"Wrytha. Wrytha Pan-Deighgren," she said, still shaking his hand. As if suddenly conscious of it, she pulled her hand back and pointed to her right. "Oh, this is my daughter, Khloe."

Arghan bowed. "Mistress Khloe, a pleasure to make your acquaintance." As he lowered his head, a small river eel wiggled its way out of one of his coat pockets and landed on the dock.

The group erupted with laughter.

Watching his mentor and the huntress continue to stare at one another, Gavek blurted, "Arghan, aren't you forgetting something?"

"I'm sorry, what?"

Gavek arched an eyebrow and tilted his head.

"Oh, yes, forgive me. This is my apprentice, Gavek."

"Master Gavek, an honour," said Wrytha, nodding.

"Yes, honoured," said Khloe, curtsying, "and of course, you've both met Rhodo in the best way possible." She glanced at Arghan's waterlogged overcoat and Gavek's dripping face.

The group laughed again as Khloe tied the rope she'd been carrying over her shoulder around the hound's neck.

"Have you both had lunch?" interjected Arghan. "Perhaps there's a place we can all get dry and fed, and continue our conversation? I know a tavern with a massive hearth. My treat."

Wrytha smiled and bit the inside of her cheek. "That's a kind offer, sir, but sadly we must depart. We've engaged passage to sail for Trianon this afternoon." She looked up at the clock on top of the harbour archway. "Oh, no, no!"

Wrytha bolted down the dock. Arghan glanced at Gavek then ran after her, followed by the others.

Wrytha stood next to an empty mooring between two ships, watching a southbound flatboat drop its sail in the middle of the river. She paced the edge of the pier, holding the top of her head, then dropping to her knees and covering her eyes. "The scoundrels! They said they would wait for us."

Catching up soon enough to hear her, Arghan stopped and knelt beside her. "I don't understand."

"My twin sons — Khloe's only brothers..."

Arghan's cheeks flushed. He studied her face. *Twin sons?* Snippets of his nightly dreams flooded his imagination; the desperate swim through the black, chilly tunnel; the two infants he saved from the inferno his own ship had ignited. *What are the chances? Could she be —?*

Gavek watched Arghan stand up and hold his hand to his mouth, listening to Wrytha's reply.

"They ran away from our enclave on Lake Reva several weeks ago, on a fool's errand to the city. They've joined a dangerous group there that plans to... well, let's just say that boat out there was my last best hope of saving them."

Arghan dropped his hands and again knelt beside her. "Surely you can find another vessel bound for Trianon? I'm sure more than half of them docked here are heading that way."

"They are. I asked them all. That rat-infested, swine runner out there was the only one whose captain said would accept Khloe and I, and that was only after they'd pocketed most of my coin. The rest all spat at us on account of our braids."

"Your braids?" asked Gavek, looking at Khloe's hair.

Arghan glanced at Gavek, smirking. "You mean there's something I know that you don't, now there's a first." He looked down at Wrytha's head. "Tzyani women wear their hair over their right shoulder to commemorate their patriarch Jakav's vision of a rope let down from heaven on which angels descended from the throne of God." He lifted the tip of Wrytha's braid from her back and gently dropped it back over her right shoulder. "To touch it like this, is—"

"—A sign of faith in the promise," said Wrytha, completing his words, looking up at him.

"Gavek and I are engaged to sail for Trianon this afternoon on the wine runner the *Flussotter* as her only passengers. I'd be pleased to pay the fare for your passage, Khloe's and Rhodo's too. Would you do me the honour of accepting my invitation?"

"I couldn't, I mean, will they even take us? Their captain turned us down this morning. I'd assumed it was for the same reason all the others had."

"No, that was on account of me. I bought all the seats on her. I prefer to travel in private for my own reasons, but I'm happy to make an exception for someone like you."

"Will the *Flussotter* even wait for us?" interjected Gavek. "I thought you said her captain was in a hurry to bring his cargo to market."

He reached into his coin purse and flipped Gavek a double-headed Regalian doubloon. "They'll wait if I buy all the wine they're hauling. Go tell Zigismundt that's a deposit." He turned back to Wrytha. "There now Wrytha, daughter of Deighgren, does that allay your fears?"

Khloe stepped between them. She brought Rhodo to heel next to Arghan and the dog started licking his fingers. "Rhodo approves. We'd be happy to accept your kind invitation, won't we mother?"

Wrytha nodded and smiled, wiping tears from her eyes. "Yes, I think we will, thank you."

"Gavek, why don't you take Khloe to the ship with you to deliver my message to Zigismundt. If he doesn't listen, show him what else we've got packed."

Gavek leaned close to Arghan and whispered, "Are you taking about what's in the bag or hidden under my rain cloak?"

"Both."

Arghan held out his elbow to Wrytha. "Now, about that fireside meal?"

Wrytha looped her arm around his and he led her through the archway.

The last of the midday crowd exited the public house, shuffling past a few regulars huddled on stools behind the bar. Arghan and Wrytha remained seated in a cozy corner next to the fireplace. A barmaid finished drying a glass, threw a towel over her shoulder, and headed toward them.

Wrytha gripped the edge of the table and clutched her side, struggling to contain the laughter erupting from the back of her throat.

"...And there they were," said Arghan, waving his hands to frame a scene, "the four of them, riding the runaway barrique[4] down the river..."

Wrytha slapped the table and then gripped her mouth, shuddering and guffawing as tears streamed down her cheeks.

"...taking... taking turns..." Arghan's eyes moistened; he snorted, chortling between his words, "...at the tap..."

"Ha-ha-ha-ha... stop! Stop! I'll wet myself, I'll wet—"

"...trying to see who could salvage the most wine — by drinking it mind you..."

Wrytha howled, stomping her feet on the floor.

"...with barely enough time to jump off before the whole thing went crashing over the falls!"

Wrytha buried her face in her arms, convulsing in a fit of giggles. Arghan followed, reclining toward the ceiling.

A minstrel shook his guitar at them and shouted from the stage at the corner of the room, "Would you two keep it down over there? I've got to practice for this evening but I can't hear myself think, you fools!"

Arghan waved his hand in conciliation. "Apologies, friend." He raised his eyebrows and winked at Wrytha as the barmaid arrived at the table.

---

4. Barrique – an oversized barrel designed to hold large quantities of wine, commonly used in vineyards.

"Never mind 'im," said the barmaid, "takes 'is job far too serious. Can I get you anything else? Kitchen's already gearing up for the supper crowd."

Wrytha sighed. "My word, has it been that long?"

"I suppose it has," Arghan said, still looking at Wrytha, "but it'll be a few more hours before the *Flussotter* sails. Want to eat again before we leave?"

"Let's get something to take with us," she said, "I could use a walk after all that laughing."

Arghan nodded. They ordered a packed meal and soon found their way back to the boardwalk.

Neither of them spoke while they strolled amid the revelers along the quay, watching crews loading their ships for evening departures. She seemed as content as he was to take in the sights and sounds without commentary. This made him like her all the more.

His own joviality surprised him that afternoon. What was it about Wrytha that unlocked this dormant part of him? Perhaps it was his way of avoiding asking her the questions that he most wanted to ask, but was afraid to. He didn't dare spoil a single moment with her, enthralled by this beauty he had only just met. But he hadn't just met her, had he? She mentioned twin sons. What were the odds that the Tzyani woman whose infant twins he has saved so many years before and Wrytha Pan-Deighgren were one and the same? Were he to ask, this person he wanted so much to know might be replaced by the woman in his nightmares, and were she to learn the truth of his past, she may no longer see him as the kind monk from Precipice Peak who had saved her dog. He would become that reviled butcher who ordered his ship to fire on a tower full of civilians, her own kin. Yet, he had to tell her, somehow. Just not now.

"So, there it is," said Wrytha, breaking the silence as she caught a glimpse of the *Flussotter* in the distance. "You said she won't sail 'til six?"

"I did."

"So, we've got some more time to kill before then?"

"We do."

"Seems a shame to waste it waiting on the ship. Fancy a game of darts? I think I saw a stall back there."

"Only if you promise not to place a wager on the match," he said with a chuckle, "I couldn't hit the broad side of a cattle barn. You'd be robbing me blind, and then almost literally. My eyesight isn't what it used to be."

"Excuses, excuses," she said with a playful grin. "Come on, blind or not, I'll teach you."

Arghan's heart raced when she grabbed his hand. Beaming, she led him back up the boardwalk to the place she had seen.

"How much?" he asked the old man who tended the kiosk, nodding in the direction of the dartboard.

"Penny a dart, up to twelve darts a go. First to score a hundred wins the match and gets to pick any of these fine prizes here. Might want to rent the whole lot if you want to win a prize for the missus, there."

"Oh, she's not... I mean we're not..." Arghan blushed, glancing at Wrytha.

"You weren't kidding about your eyes, were you?" she said, giggling. "The prices are written on the sign over there, you know?"

"They are?" Arghan said, squinting.

She stood in front of him, resting her back against his chest. "He'll take twelve for the first match. Give me three. If I find out he's hustling me, he'll get less next time."

Wrytha took several paces back from the kiosk and fired the darts in rapid succession. Only one of them failed to hit the bullseye, and then only by a hair.

"Impressive," said Arghan, "who's hustling who?"

"Nobody. We're only playing for fun, remember?" She crossed in front of him, looking back over her shoulder. "Your turn."

Arghan smirked and took the same distance from the target. His first shot struck one of the carved wooden trinkets the vendor offered as prizes, knocking it off its shelf.

"Bought that one, I'm afraid," said the old man.

"Yes I did," said Arghan.

His second shot hit the edge of the target, deflecting to the table below. The next eight did no better. With two darts to go, Wrytha intervened.

"Ready for some tutoring?" she said.

"Please."

She skipped over, stood behind him, gripped his belt, and swung his hips. "Loosen up. Stand sideways, foot forward." She stood on her toes and rested her cheek against his. Looking at the target she pulled his hand into position in front of his face. "Look straight down the dart, cock your wrist, and let it fly." She guided his hand as he threw. This one hit the inner ring, two spaces from the bullseye.

"Ha, ha! There you go. You're on the board," she said before giving him a peck on the cheek.

He glanced at her, pausing as he made eye contact, surprised to see her face still inches from his own.

"Guess I just needed a little help from a qualified teacher."

"Guess so."

They lingered, looking into each other's eyes.

"Are you two lovebirds going to play or what?" interjected the vendor. "I've got other customers waiting, you know."

"We are. Six more for me. Three more for her." Arghan tossed a coin at the man without taking his eyes off Wrytha.

He took another shot, not as good as when she helped him, but close. She took another turn, firing her shots into the bullseye. He stepped up again for another go, cocking his hand for a shot.

"I'm curious, Arghan of Cairhn Monastery," she said seconds before he released the dart. "Are the Cantorvarians one of those orders who forbid their members to marry?"

The dart ricocheted off the side of the stall and burst a waxed-paper balloon at a nearby stall with a pop. Wrytha clapped, laughing.

"That's it. I'll give you a refund," said the vendor. "Got a reputation to keep with the neighbours."

"Cheater," said Arghan, taking her hand as the pair walked away. "Perhaps some more sightseeing then?"

They spent the rest of the afternoon meandering through the town, peeking into shops, chatting the day away without Arghan having ever answered the question she asked him at the darts game. Eventually, they circled back to the boardwalk and paused in front of the *Flussotter's* gangplank.

"Thank you, Arghan," Wrytha said.

"For what, letting you win that game of darts?"

"Ha! Fat chance. No, I mean for everything. For today. This afternoon. For helping me forget my worries for a while. I haven't had such a wonderful time in, well, I can't remember how long."

"Me neither. The pleasure was all mine. Think nothing of it." He turned to head up the gangplank.

She tugged his sleeve.

"No, that's just it. You have no idea. What you've done for me is far from 'nothing'. When you saved Rhodo, you saved my best hope of finding my sons. I know they're in Trianon but have no idea where they're staying, and neither Khloe nor I have ever been there ourselves. Rhodo's not only the best tracking hound in the mountains, he's known my boys since he was a pup. I'm counting on his keen sense of smell to lead me to them."

"I take it from the sound of your voice they're in some kind of trouble?"

"The worst kind. A few months ago, a radical named Teighthra Pan-Goron was banished from our clan for corrupting our youth with violent ideology. Recently, some of them decided to follow her to Trianon, including my twins. She's on a reckless crusade to exact revenge on our oppressors. I'm afraid whatever she's up to will get herself and her followers killed and invite the Alpinians' retribution on the rest of us."

Wrytha's eyes confirmed it. She had to be the mother of the infants he saved. She'd faced losing them once already, and seen her people massacred. She couldn't bear going through that again. He couldn't let her.

"Sounds troubling. Perhaps I could help." He took her hand and caressed it.

"No. I couldn't ask you to—"

"But you're not asking. I'm offering."

"What could you do? I couldn't ask you to put yourself in danger on my account. It's likely the Archprelate's entire contingent of Alpinian troops are on the hunt for my kin."

"You'd be surprised what I could do. Besides, I expect I may find myself at odds with them for my own reasons."

"Oh?"

"A wealthy patron of our monastery has gone missing from Trianon. That's why I'm headed there. I suspect the Alpinians' involvement. Solstrus hates us Cantorvarians almost as much as he hates Tzyani. He may have discovered her connection with us. Like you with your sons, I have no idea where she is, but I do possess a few articles of hers that carry her scent. If Rhodo is as good a tracker as you say, perhaps he could help me find who I am looking for as well. Were I able to find her, she could be of immense help to your people, including your sons."

"How?"

"Let's just say she holds a place of considerable influence in the Cortavian government."

Wrytha's eyelids widened. It was obvious he'd piqued her interest. She stared at him for several moments. How could her eyes have witnessed the horrors of Koerska and remained so radiant, so beautiful?

She pulled her hand away. "Can I think about it?"

"Of course," he said, blushing. "Let me show you to your quarters."

CHAPTER NINE
Voyage

The twin moons tracked across the northeast sky, reflecting off the teeming waters of the Onya as the *Flussotter* sped southeast toward Trianon.

"This is a much smoother ride than I expected," said Gavek, peeking over the hull as it cut through the water.

Khloe leaned over the rail beside him, patting Rhodo's head. "Boats really aren't your thing, are they?"

Gavek grinned and tightened his grip on the railing. "Not really. One of my phobias. Not sure how it started. We're making excellent time though, I must say."

"Well, it's the best time of year to sail, apparently."

"Is that so? I know next to nothing about sailing, for obvious reasons, I guess. Tell me more."

Gavek couldn't believe his own words. He didn't care to listen any time Arghan had tried to tell him about sailing. *What's gotten into you, anyway?*

"Oh, I don't either. It's just something mother said. I guess the late summer rains always get pretty heavy up river, overfilling the reservoir created by the dam; you know, the one the ancient Threicians built over Lake Kinnessarat? The mill-masters who run it let some of the extra go like every second day or something during Repose and Harvest, creating more current that makes all their ships go faster downstream when they want. Here, let me show you. Can I take one?" She pointed at a stack of blank pages Gavek had laid out to write on. "Sure."

Khloe ripped off the corner of a page and folded it into the shape of a boat. "And now this," she said, taking the mug Gavek held in his hand. She set the paper boat on top of the ship's rail and poured some water behind it, sending it sliding across the varnished surface until it fell off the edge where Gavek caught it.

Gavek clapped. "Ha! Well done. You'll make a fine teacher someday."

"I already am, sort of."

"Really? I assumed you were a huntress like your mother."

"I am, but in our culture, we all do something to help each other. Any one of us is a teacher or a student of someone else. Mother says there were so few of us left after the massacre at Koerska, we've had to do whatever it takes to survive. But I've only ever known the peace of our little village."

"Nova Elkahrn on Lake Reva?"

"Yeah, that's it. I was born there. Would you believe this is the farthest away I've ever been?"

"Yeah, I would actually."

"So I look that much like a country bumpkin, do I?" she said, swatting his arm, grinning.

"No," said Gavek, rubbing his tricep, "that's not what I mean at all, I—"

"I'm just messing with you. What were you gonna say?"

"Oh, okay. No, I mean it sounds a lot like me. This is the first time I've been outside the Lake Trieehd region. I grew up in the monastery there. That was a peaceful place too, but dreadfully boring, that is until recently."

"Really? What happened?"

Gavek hesitated. Was this really something he ought to be talking about? He'd overheard Arghan and Wrytha before they departed. If Arghan trusted Wrytha enough to tell her about Cybella's disappearance and their connection to her, it stood to reason Khloe could be trusted too. And besides, the details might impress her. *Wait, why does that suddenly matter to you anyway?* He leaned close to her. "Can you keep a secret?"

"Oh, I like secrets. The bigger the better. What is it? Are you on a secret mission or something?"

"What makes you say that?"

"I can just tell. We Tzyani are all like that, some more than others. Mother said my grandma who died before I was born had dreams about things before they happened."

"Really? Fascinating."

"You were going to tell me your secret."

"Oh, right. Well, the Cantorvarians '— that's our order; did I tell you?"

"Arghan did when we met on the dock."

"Right, well, though we've taken great pains to hide this, Cantorvarians have believed for centuries that the Tzyani Scriptures are the true basis of our faith and not the teachings of the Grand Prelate or the Temple. Until recently there was no way to prove our claims. That all changed when an old friend of Arghan's, a servant of Princess Cybella, the Royal Archivist Wardein found several ancient manuscripts, a complete set of your Scriptures, in a crypt under the Library of Trianon. We've been smuggling them out and I've been translating them one by one for a couple of months, but we were exposed last week and..."

Gavek continued to explain what had happened in Cairhn, focusing mostly on the conflict with Cybion and the Alpinian Guard, carefully glossing over the details of Arghan's past.

"Miracles? Amazing! And you've been translating these books all by yourself? You speak Tzyani, then?"

"Ancient and modern," he said, pulling at his lapels.

"Prove it."

"In divid pas quieskay, kobod-ka[1]?"

---

1. Translation: "In speaking <out loud> is my accent okay?"

"Anah, pos trevis[2], and you learned this all out of a book?"

"Several books, actually. We had the best library on ancient Tzyani in all Eskareon, at least until those monsters torched it. Now I hope to secure the original collection before Archprelate Solstrus finds it, but I'm quite worried because—"

Khloe jerked away. She stared out over the moonlit plains beyond the south bank of the river. At first her gaze appeared aimless, but then her eyes began to flicker, as though she was watching a spectacle unfold, tracing the swift movements of actors on a stage. "Because the Princess is in trouble. She was helping you, she's— she's Arghan's daughter! He's going there to find her. He dreams terrible dreams, of fire and water and death— and— Maker of us all! We've got to help you. I see it! We're supposed to help you."

"What? No, I didn't mean— how did you— how do you know? I've heard his screams at night. What does he remember? Khloe!"

"Sometimes I see things— like I'm having a dream all of a sudden, you know? Only I'm awake. Mother says its a gift, like Grandma-ma's. It's hard to explain. Come on," she said, yanking his hand, "we've got to talk to her."

Arghan knocked on the cabin door. He straightened his lapels and brushed some fibres off his tunic. He was about to tighten his belt when the door swung open.

"Oh, hi there," said Wrytha, standing at the threshold. "What's up?"

"Uh, nothing, just wondering how you're making out. Is the cabin satisfactory?"

Wrytha left the door ajar and waved him inside. "Exceedingly," she replied, chuckling. "It really wasn't necessary to ask the captain to give up his own quarters just for me. I'm used to roughing it; I've slept on the ground most of my life."

"All the more reason to enjoy some luxury. You deserve it after what you've been through, wouldn't you say? Besides, he's happy to sleep on

---

2. Translation: 'Yes, nice attempt.'

deck for a few extra coins."

"You have pretty deep pockets for a monk. How did you come into so much money anyway, if you don't mind me asking?"

Arghan watched Wrytha lift her bedroll off the floor and onto the captain's bed. It seemed she preferred the simplicity of what she knew. This attracted him all the more. He studied the shape of her eyes, the curve of her neck, the way she moved. He was certain she was the woman from the well; how could he ever find the words to tell her who he really was, especially in light of how she made him feel?

"I invested wisely in my youth," he replied. "After all, the Shepherd King doesn't disapprove of wealth, does He? Only its misuse."

"True, I suppose, but to lavish so much on one you know so little…"

"It's our way. We don't advertise it, but Cantorvarians hold Tzyani in great regard. Your people have suffered grave injustice for far too long. It's part of our mission to honour you and help when we see you in need."

"Yes," she said, standing with one hand on her hip. "Our Clan Father always speaks highly of your order, though I'd never actually met one of you until now. But even the kindest monks don't normally spend all afternoon entertaining their beneficiaries over no less than two meals, do they? I can't help feel there's more to your generosity than spiritual conviction."

Arghan's heart raced. Was she beginning to recognize him? "Perhaps there is, but… you're right, I have indulged far too much of your time. I should go. Forgive the intrusion." He walked back to the door.

"Arghan…" Wrytha took a few steps toward him. "You're not intruding. Please stay. I'm the one who should apologize. I must sound so ungrateful, grilling you like that. It's none of my business where got your money. I'm… that is, it's just been a long time since… I mean… I don't know how to…"

"How to… what?"

She pulled him toward her. "You called me 'daughter of Deighgren' on the dock after you offered to pay for our passage, so you evidently know enough of our language to recognize the 'Pan' in my surname means 'offspring of'. Were I married, 'Pen' would precede my husband's name as my surname. I'm a widow. My father's name is Deighgren. My husband's name was Wrikor. He died ten years ago in a landslide on Khloe's 8th birthday, returning across the mountains from a journey to Pella."

"I'm sorry to hear that, I—"

Wrytha reached behind his neck, pulled him close and kissed him on the lips.

"Wrytha, I—"

"I was right, wasn't I? Tell me you don't feel the same?"

"I do, yes. But... I must tell you something. I don't think this is the first time we've met. I—"

"Mother!" Khloe burst through the door, followed by Gavek. The two of them stopped and stared, each of them breaking into a grin as Arghan and Wrytha jerked away from each other.

Wrytha continued flattening her bedroll. "What is it, Khloe?"

Arghan's face turned red. He put his hands on his hips. "Gavek?"

Gavek eyelids widened. He shrugged his shoulders and pointed at Khloe, shaking his head.

"Well that's a first," quipped Arghan. "You, at a loss for words."

"Mother, Gavek and I were talking. We've got to help—"

All four of them lurched to the port side as the deck rocked below their feet.

"What was that?" said Wrytha, looking at Arghan. "Did we run aground?"

"No, something hit us."

A scream echoed from beyond the door. Arghan raced out onto the deck, followed by Gavek and Khloe. A Zuelan pirate withdrew his sabre from one of the ship's crewmen, dropping him overboard. Arghan glanced to the left. Another ship flanked the *Flussotter's* starboard side, keeping pace with it. Seven more Zuelan sailors jumped aboard and attacked the rest of the deck hands.

"Where is that Tzyani witch and her foul beast?" captain Zheyka screamed, holding one of the sailors at knife-point.

"There's the cur," cried another Zuelan, pointing at Rhodo, who stood up from where he had been sleeping, hunching his back, bearing his teeth, and growling as three Zuelans closed in on him.

Wrytha slid through the door on her knees and fired her bow, piercing the necks of the Zuelans nearest Rhodo with arrows.

"There!" Zheyka pointed toward the captain's cabin.

Ten more Zuelans leaped onboard and began terrorizing the crew.

"Gavek, fetch my swords, now!" commanded Arghan.

Gavek gripped the rail and raced up the stairs to the quarterdeck while the Zuelans closed in.

The *Flussotter's* captain came running up the stairs from the lower decks. "What's going on?"

"We're under attack," yelled Arghan. "If you've any weapons, fight man!"

The captain dropped below deck.

Wrytha released arrow after arrow while Gavek struggled with the ship's locker. Finally, reaching for another missile, her fingers touched the leather ring of her empty quiver. "Khloe, get your quiver, run!"

Gavek finally opened the lock, yanked out Arghan's swords, and threw them over the rail. Arghan caught each of them by their hilts and rolled them upright around his knuckles. He shouted and leaped over some of the crates, striking down two Zuelans as he landed.

Khloe ran to her mother's side and handed over her quiver. Wrytha emptied it and loaded the fingers of her bow hand with a bunch of arrows. She dove and rolled to Arghan's side, standing with her back to his. Arrows and swords flashed, dropping Zuelan pirates at every turn.

"I'm out again," said Wrytha as another Zuelan lunged at her. She dodged and kicked him in the hip.

"Here." Arghan tossed her one of his swords just as the Zuelan recovered his balance. The far-lander lunged again, this time falling to the deck when Wrytha struck his neck with the tip of Arghan's sword.

Wrytha stumbled against Arghan's back, panting. "Is that all of them?"

"I think so."

Khloe screamed. Arghan and Wrytha jerked toward the quarterdeck. Somehow in the fray, captain Zheyka had flanked them and was closing in on Khloe and Gavek. Gavek lunged at him, dodging a sword thrust. He grappled with him while Khloe jumped on Zheyka's back and choked him with her arm. Arghan bolted for the stairs. Wrytha sprinted to the opposite side. Zheyka screamed and kicked Gavek in the groin, sending him groaning to the deck. He threw Khloe over his shoulder, landing her on top of Gavek. He raised his sword for a final thrust.

"No," screamed Wrytha, leaping over the youths. She blocked his thrust as it came down, sending him reeling. Arghan threw his sword. The blade whirled through the air and plunged through the Zuelan's back. Zheyka dropped at Wrytha's feet.

Arghan and Wrytha stood staring at each other. Swaying, Wrytha mopped the sweat off her forehead and dropped to her knees.

"Are you okay?" said Arghan, rubbing one eye. He walked over to her and retrieved his weapon from their fallen foe.

Wrytha nodded, staring down at Arghan's other blade, still in her grasp.

Arghan stumbled back down the stairs.

"Are they still here?" said the Flussotter's captain, finally emerging from below deck.

"No, no thanks to you," growled Arghan as he passed by, headed for the starboard side. "Go check on your men; what's left of them at least."

Arghan grabbed several oil lamps from the masts of the *Flussotter* and leaped over to the pirate's ship. Grimacing, he threw each of them into far corners of the deck where they exploded, spreading flames in all directions.

As fire began to engulf the ship's deck a woman's voice cried out from beyond a cabin door, "Help! Please. Can anyone hear me?"

Arghan cocked his head toward the sound. He raced to the door to see a pair of eyes staring back at him through its tiny window. He grabbed the door handle, rattling the lock. "Stand back." Arghan spun his pelvis and broke the door open with his heel. A woman wearing a stained and tattered gown stumbled through the door and collapsed in his arms.

"Are you the only prisoner?"

"No," said the woman, gasping. She pointed downward.

"Wrytha!" yelled Arghan.

Wrytha looked up and saw Arghan waving. She leaped to her feet and ran to him.

"Take her," he said, putting the woman's arms over Wrytha's shoulders.

She headed back to the Flussotter. "Where are you going?"

"To get the others. You get to safety. Hurry." Arghan leaped over the growing flames and scrambled down the stairs to the lower deck. He called into the darkness, "Hello! Anyone?"

"Here," called a voice from the haze.

Arghan grabbed a lantern from a nearby post and ran toward the sound. Cages lined either side of the ship's hold. In each one of them stood women and children, as ragged and gaunt as the woman who had been held above.

"Father of Lights, why?" Arghan gritted his teeth and thrashed his sword, chopping the iron locks off the cages like they were made of straw. "Come with me, hurry." He lifted the smallest child into his arms while he hurried the others up the staircase.

Dodging the flames, the ragtag group of prisoners meandered their way across the deck and onto the *Flussotter* where its remaining crew helped them aboard. The last to leave, Arghan handed the child he carried to Wrytha, straddling the gap between the ships. He sprinted, balancing on the pirate ship's rail, and sliced each of the ropes the raiders had used to tie it to the *Flussotter*, then leaped back over as the Zuelan ship started to drift away.

Arghan collapsed onto the deck of the *Flussotter*, muttering, "I didn't know they were there. Yeshua, have mercy on me, I didn't know."

As he knelt there, looking down at the deck boards, Wrytha's boots came into view. He looked up at her, eyes reddened, face streaked with tears.

Wrytha turned away, tears pooling at the corner of her eyelids while she slowed her breathing. She turned the sword he had given her under the lantern light. "This hilt... the eagle... Arghan, this is an Erne Warder's sword. I recognize it because... because..."

"Because Erne Warders sacked your village, destroying everything you held dear. The sword is mine. Its twin also. But let me—"

Wrytha gasped, biting her quivering lips. She dropped open her mouth, panting and let the sword slip through her fingers to the floor.

Arghan reached out to touch her hand. "Wrytha, I—"

"Don't... don't touch me." She ran back into the captain's quarters and slammed the door.

Arghan picked up the swords and whipped off the blood left on their blades. He walked toward the stern and up the stairs to the quarterdeck where he handed them both back to Gavek.

"Told you so."

CHAPTER TEN
Trianon

Harbour seagulls cawed in the early morning sunshine. The *Flussotter* slid into its dock at Onya Landing on the western tip of Trianon's Merchant's Isle. Exempt from the Temple's edict forbidding commerce on Risenday, petty shopkeepers readied stalls along the quay to receive the daily flux of visitors. Ship captains stood among the piles of crates on the pier, haggling with agents. Along the waterfront, cranes unloaded everything from stone blocks hewn from the granite quarries of Roe to palette loads of textiles from Nova Engaric.

Gavek hurried onto the deck carrying his copy of Ontolorio's *Great Cities of Eastern Eskareon*, roused by the shouts of the crewmen who tied the vessel to the dock. He dropped his jaw when the city skyline came into view. *Trianon! Ontolorio's description pales by comparison.*

As far as the eye could see, half-timbered brick houses, shops, and offices, many as tall as three or four stories crowded the winding streets beyond the harbour wall. Above a forest of smoking chimneys, chapels, and bell towers, the distant parts of the city rose like a mountain of wood, stone, glass, and tile up to the plateau of the Doran Heights and Mount Tria. At the apex of Palace Rock stood the towering fortress from which the city got its name. A massive fog bank eclipsed it, spreading across the horizon like a mighty hand reaching to douse the flame of a giant candlestick.

Gavek doubled back to the table where he had left his papers and fetched his sketchbook and wadd stick[1]. He walked toward the port side of the ship for a better view of the cityscape, sketching as he went. His toe snagged something on the deck and he stumbled headlong onto a pile of bodies near the gangplank, recoiling at the sight of a hand sticking out below the tattered old sail the crew had used to cover them.

It wasn't a nightmare after all. He shuddered and backed away, turned, and plopped onto the ship's rail, allowing his feet to dangle over the side of the hull.

"Hoy, Gorrad!" bellowed the *Flussotter's* captain, flipping his crewman a coin. "Hire some gravediggers to come haul away this lot, you ought to find some 'cross King's Bridge in Onya Point. Tell 'em to hurry. I want us loaded and ready to sail out by noon."

"Aye, sir," said the grisly-faced river dog, dropping the coin into his pocket. He scampered across the gangplank.

Arghan emerged from below deck, followed by some of the rescued prisoners. "Captain Rosnick, Can I persuade you to take these people back to Sigoe with you? Most are river folk. I'll pay, of course."

"Keep your coin, Ostlander. You've spoiled me for passengers. Get the hell off my ship; you, the bookworm, and your Tzyani lady friends, too."

Arghan scowled. "Fine." He handed Rosnick a slip of parchment. "Make sure my wine is delivered to this address. All 48 barrels. Don't short me. I counted them. I know where you anchor and I know where you sail. Don't make me come find you."

"Easy... I thought you said you was a monk?"

Arghan pointed at the corpses under the sail. "Does that look like the work of a monk to you?"

Rosnick backed away, shook his head, and turned to direct his men.

Gavek watched his mentor's brow curl around a vacant and distant glare. Arghan beckoned the waiting refugees to follow him onto the gangplank.

---

1. Wadd stick – a late medieval form of a pencil

"Hey, where are you going?" Gavek jumped up and blocked his path.

"I've got to see these people taken care of. Go pack our things and meet me at that fishmonger's stand up there. I'll be back as soon as I can."

"You're not going to say goodbye to Wrytha and Khloe?"

Arghan brushed Gavek's arm aside and walked down the gangplank. "I don't think they want to hear it. Don't forget the swords, or the sack." Arghan descended into the crowd, followed by the destitute prisoners.

"You mean *my* swords, don't you?" Gavek took one last look at his unfinished drawing then tied the string around his sketchbook and headed for the quarterdeck. As he passed the captain's cabin, Wrytha opened the door and stepped outside, carrying her bow and backpack.

"Oh, Master Gavek, good morning," she said, scanning the deck.

"Good morning. If you're looking for Father Arghan he's already disembarked; said he needed to look after those poor folk from the ship right away. He bids you well."

She nodded, still looking away. "Please convey to him my sincere thanks."

"I will indeed. Farewell." Gavek smiled, then looked into the open doorway.

"Farewell." Wrytha called through the open door, " Khloe, come on, it's time to go." Shaking her head, she crossed the deck and paused at the gangplank to survey the crowd. Gavek noticed her head stop moving when she spotted Arghan in the distance.

Wrytha watched him for several moments then headed down the gangplank. "Khloe!"

Khloe sauntered out the door with Rhodo at her heel.

"You're all set with your trusty sidekick I see," quipped Gavek, blushing.

"Yes, I am. He obeys me more than he does mother, so I guess I'm stuck with him."

Gavek smiled and looked down, nodding. "Khloe, I—"

"Yes?" she said, stooping to make eye contact.

"I'm sorry how things turned out. It was so nice meeting you. You know... making a friend."

"Me too."

"Will I see you again?"

"I hope so. But mother—"

"I know." He nodded and looked down again. "I wish there was something I could do. I've known Father Arghan all my life. I've never seen him light up the way he did when he met Wrytha. It was good to see him so happy, even for a little while."

"I know what you mean. I've never seen mother quite so cheerful either, not since father died. But finding out who Arghan really was scared her. Why didn't he just tell her who he was from the start?"

"I think he was trying to do that when we barged in on them. I don't think he intended to deceive her. He carries a lot of guilt about what happened to your people, so it's hard for him to talk about. Based on what he's told me, I don't think he's guilty of the crimes people say he committed. But he can't seem to get past the fact that innocent people died anyway because of something he did. Whether he intended to or not makes no difference to him. I've seen him do things this past week that shocked me, but it was all to protect people he cares very deeply about. But violence takes a terrible toll on him. Anyway, listen to me. I'm sorry, you probably don't want to hear this, you've got to go."

"No, no. Tell me, quick. What do you mean by 'whether he intended to or not'? What did he tell you?"

"He said he'd never been to Koerska before that awful night, and then only in the dark. His commander told him the Tzyani had been evacuated and that Zuelan forces occupied the tower. He ordered Arghan to bombard it from his ship on the river. It was only after it caught ablaze that Arghan realized townsfolk were inside it. He desperately tried to save them, but he was too late. He did manage to get inside, but was only able to save two baby boys by swimming underground with them wrapped in his cloak."

"Wow!" Khloe fell against the door frame and covered her mouth with her hand.

"What?"

"Those were my older brothers."

"They were?!" Gavek's eyelids widened.

"Yeah. Mother told me the story often. Grandma-ma had a dream about it the week before it happened. She warned mother not to leave town that day to attend the annual hunt on lake Onkost. She didn't listen. She came back just in time to see the Erne Warders herding everyone inside the tower. They locked them inside it and covered the door with junk. This was after they killed everyone left alive in the town. Mother tried to remove the barriers but it was too much for her. She'd almost given up when a voice called out to her from a well. A man had somehow saved my brothers, just like Grandma-ma said happened in her dream."

"I can't believe it…"

"Don't you see, Gavek? There never were any Zuelans in Koerska. Arghan's commander lied to him."

"This changes everything," he said, pacing. "I gotta tell him! I gotta…"

"Khloe! Come on!" Wrytha called out again from the dock.

"This conversation isn't over. Have faith, Gavek." She held out her fist, prompting him to hold out his hand. She dropped a tiny, folded paper boat into his palm then kissed him on the cheek. "C'mon, Rhodo. Time to go."

Khloe took a few steps toward the gangplank.

"Khloe, wait." Gavek flipped open his copy of *Great Cities of Eastern Eskareon*, tore out a page, and circled a place on it with his wadd stick. "Here, take this."

"What is it?"

"It's a map of Trianon. If you want to find me, I'll be right there, at the library. It'll be the big domed building on the opposite tip of this island. At least that's what Ontolorio's book says."

"Who? Wait, don't you need this?"

"Nope. It's all up here now," he said, tapping his head. "Better get going."

Khloe nodded, smiling as she stuffed the page into her smock. She ran to the edge of the gangplank, turning back to smile again before disappearing down the ramp.

Khloe dashed through the crowd and headed up the stairs to Shore Street. "Mother, wait up."

Wrytha narrowed her eyelids. "Try to keep up."

"What's your hurry? It's only half past six. Why don't we get breakfast?"

"Do you forget why we came here, Khloe? Don't you care about your brothers? We've got leagues of ground to cover here. There's not time to waste." Wrytha let two carriages pass by then skipped across the street.

"How could I forget?" said Khloe, following with Rhodo. "If Orin and Nicah weren't so stupid I'd still be stalking bucks around the lake right now instead of chasing after them. If you ask me they deserve whatever trouble they get themselves into."

"Watch your tone. They're your older brothers and they're part of our family. That's all that matters."

"If you say so..."

"Khloe!"

They reached the opposite sidewalk.

Khloe halted. "Rhodo, heel. Stop."

"What are you doing?" Wrytha looked back with her hands on her hips.

"What's it look like I'm doing?"

"Don't play games, Khloe. I'm not in the mood. Give me that." Wrytha grabbed Rhodo's leash and started to walk away.

"Rhodo stay. Guard."

Wrytha fell backward, jerked by the leash.

Khloe scratched her nose. "Know what I think?"

"What's that?"

"I think you're running away from Arghan, not chasing the boys."

Wrytha looked past her as if watching something in the distance. "Preposterous."

Khloe looked over her shoulder and spied Arghan and Gavek crossing the street a block away. "Is it now? You fancy him, admit it."

"No."

"Mother—"

"Khloe, did you see what he did last night? Those swords of his... he's an Erne Warder, one of those bloodthirsty animals that massacred our people, including your grandmother. I can't believe I didn't put it together sooner. His accent, his age. He's *Arghan of Danniker*, Khloe. Didn't I tell you what he did to the people in Koerska's watchtower? I would have been one of them had I not gone hunting that day. What exactly is there to fancy about that?"

"That's what you were told after the fact. It wasn't like that at all. Gavek said—"

"Gavek said what, Khloe? He's Arghan's pupil. He'd probably tell you anything Arghan wanted him to. Don't be so naive."

"I'm not mother. You're only saying that because you've had years to brood over this. To resent what you *think* happened. You didn't witness all of it, and your heart tells a different story now that you've met the man, doesn't it?"

Wrytha stormed up the sidewalk. "I'm not listening to this. If you want to stay here with Rhodo I'll find the boys some other way."

"I saw his dreams last night; they flashed before my eyes," shouted Khloe. "He dreams of standing in a deep cistern with a blazing fire above him, an old woman and two infants. Of swimming underground, desperate to save them, and the lovely eyes of a young woman with dark braided hair..."

Wrytha halted in the middle of the street. She jumped away from a passing carriage and ambled back to where Khloe stood. She leaned over the youth and whispered, "Who told you that? I never—"

"Nobody, mother. I saw it. Don't you get it? Arghan's the man who saved Orin and Nicah that night. It isn't true what they say about him at all. He's been hated all his life for things he didn't mean to do. His commander told him Zuelans were in that tower, not *our* people. That's why his ship fired on it. If anyone's to blame it's that man, not Arghan."

Wrytha cupped her hand over her mouth. "He... came into the cabin last night to try and tell me something. Maybe it was...?" She shook her head. "No. Listen to me. What's done is done." She gripped Khloe's shoulders. "You may be right, but we've no time for this. Finding Orin and Nicah is our number one priority. Understand?"

Khloe nodded, looking down at her feet, and tugged Rhodo's leash. "C'mon, Rhodo, time to go to work." She stepped past Wrytha and led the dog up the street.

Wrytha took a few steps and then stopped. She bit her lip and looked back just in time to see Arghan and Gavek disappear past the corner of a street called Shippers Way.

A man in a violet cloak lowered his spyglass and pointed out the watchtower window. "Look, down there. Two of them. See the long braids over their shoulders? Tzyani. Huntresses of the woods from the looks of things. They came up the stairs from Onya Landing."

Another man in violet garb grabbed the telescope and held it to his face. He traced Wrytha and Khloe's progress eastward on Shore Street and dropped the instrument after they turned a corner. "Better hurry. I've lost them. Send Hascar and Jorvere after them. Tell one of them to report back if they discover the cell's hideout. Go alert the garrison. Tell them to assemble a force and keep them ready to deploy at a moment's notice. I'll keep watch here in case more of them arrive. Go!"

"Aye, Captain Raipheniel."

Gavek adjusted the load on his back, wincing. "So, what's the plan?"

Arghan rubbed his eyes, swaying. "We must... uh, first we go to the library, make contact with Wardein... he'll be able to tell us..."

"Tell us what?"

"Uh, he'll tell us..." Arghan braced himself against the side of a house. "He'll tell us exactly what's going on here. Before... before we do anything else."

Gavek watched Arghan stumble onto a narrow alley. Had he even slept the night before?

"You sure we're going the right way? Wouldn't it be quicker just to stay on Shippers Way 'till we reach Traitor's Circle?"

Arghan grunted and leaped over a puddle. "You read one book on Trianon and suddenly you're a travel guide, is that it?"

Gavek hugged the side of a nearby house, inching his way along the dry edge of the lane. "No, I just know the library is east and we're walking south. Where are you going?" He skipped back onto the cobblestones.

A woman hollered from a window above them. Arghan halted, holding out his arm to stop Gavek before the contents of a chamber pot splashed onto the alley in front of them.

Gavek recoiled. "Yuck!" He pulled the flap of his robe over his mouth. "I was wondering where that smell came from."

"I bet Ontolorio didn't mention things like that, did he?" Arghan sidestepped the mess and continued walking. "Trianon's an impressive place, but it's not quite the dreamland he made it out to be. Did you notice that watchtower we passed on our way off the dock?"

"No."

"Well, it's there. I saw the glint of a spyglass in one of its windows. It may have been a while since I was in the city, but I'd never known the harbour watch to be that attentive. There's somebody else up there. Cortavian troops or even Alpinian guards, possibly. They're watching the harbour for arrivals and that means they're on the lookout for someone. In the remote chance that happens to be us, I'd sooner avoid their view. Here, give me that book of yours." Arghan stopped and held out his hand.

"Why?" said Gavek, reaching into his bag.

"Just give it."

Gavek handed Arghan his copy of *Great Cities of Eastern Eskareon*.

"This was written in uh... 380, roughly?" He opened its cover.

"379."

"Close enough. Well, they built all sorts of towers across Merchant's Isle during the war of 410 you won't find on any map before that." Arghan opened the book and started flipping its pages. "Q, R... S..., T. There we are, Trianon." He flipped a few more pages ahead, then back, frowning when he saw the ripped edge where the page he was looking for should be. "That's funny. The map's missing."

"Are you sure?"

Arghan held out the book and flipped through it. "Rhone has a map. Riva has a map. Ropa has a map. Trianon, bigger than all of them, no map. You wouldn't have any idea why, would you?"

"Oh, yeah, now that you mention it, I uh, I tore it out…"

"You what?"

"I tore it out."

Arghan's nostrils flared. "By the black beard of Saint Keil why would you do such a thing?"

"I gave it to Khloe. They've never been here. Thought they would need it more than us. It's no big deal. It's all up here." Gavek tapped his forehead.

Arghan threw the book at him and smacked Gavek's forehead. "What about the catacomb tunnels I drew over top of it in invisible ink? Is that 'up there' too, genius?"

"Ow! What? Invisible ink?"

"That's right. You think the Library's the only place here with a hidden underground? How did you think I planned to get the Princess out of the city, let alone the manuscripts?"

"Well, I wouldn't know. You barely tell me anything anymore! It's a miracle you're even talking after…"

"After what?"

"Never mind."

"After what, Gavek?"

"Last night. You're heartsick over Wrytha. I saw the way the two of you looked at each other. But there's more to it than either of you realize, isn't there? You think she's the woman whose children you saved in Koerska, don't you? You're devastated now that she knows who you are. You think there's no chance she could ever forgive you for what you did."

Arghan flashed his teeth. "What? No, that's absurd. Mind your place. Give me my swords and the diamonds. Now. You're on your own. Go to the Library. Don't go to the library. I don't care. I've got to find my daughter."

"Tired of being your pack mule anyway, here." Gavek slipped the canvas sack off his back and threw it at Arghan.

Arghan swung it over his shoulder, wincing as it fell over his arrow wound. He stormed down the alley, splashing through a rain puddle as he neared the opening to an intersecting street.

"You've lost your mind lately, you know. What happened to the man who took me hiking when I was little? Who taught me how to read and memorize the nine virtues? Where's your Kahn-yodar[2] now?"

Arghan stomped back to where Gavek stood. "How dare you!"

"How dare I? You've acted like a boorish turd this entire trip!"

"Me? Did you ever stop daydreaming long enough to think maybe it's because of your incessant complaining? Who knew that getting you out from behind that desk would be the absolute best and absolute worst thing that ever happened to you, all at the same time?"

"And who knew it would take the events of the last two weeks to finally get your head out of your backside after 20 years! Can't you see there are greater forces at work here than your guilt-ridden ego?"

Arghan's face turned red. He screamed and pounded one of the wooden support posts of a nearby balcony, sending a flock of pigeons fluttering out from below the overhang. "Ah!" He spun backward and fell on top of a barrel, cradling his wounded shoulder.

"Give me some more bergaroot."

"No."

"What do you mean 'no', give it—"

"Pattron warned me not to if you got like this. You chew too much of it and you're not sleeping. It has a hold on you."

"Pattron... I knew it. Give me—"

Gavek yanked a tiny suede pouch out of his satchel and pitched it into one of the upper-storey windows of a nearby house.

"You little twit! What did you do that for?" Arghan screamed and bent over, clutching his shoulder.

"Sit up. Let me see that."

---

2. Ancient Tzyani words meaning "self control". See chapter 3: the trial.

Arghan slumped back and allowed Gavek to peel back the lapel of his tunic. Gavek unfolded the bandage over Arghan's wound, revealing reddened, pustular swelling where the arrow had pierced his skin.

"This looks bad. Pattron's sutures have torn out. He said to clean and change it daily. Have you?"

"Does it look like I have? I've had other things on my mind!"

"Okay. This is serious. We've got to get you to an inn where you can rest while I go see an apothecary. Pattron gave me a list of things that can treat something like this in case it happened."

"What, no. I'm fine. Cybella's in danger. Let's get—"

Arghan's legs wobbled and he fell into Gavek's arms.

"No, you're not. Look at you. Come on." Gavek pulled Arghan's arm over his shoulder and the pair continued onto a major street.

"Watch out for the towers..."

Once again, Arghan's best efforts to stay awake had proven futile. The moment Gavek had lain him down in bed in a place he knew not where, he surrendered to fatigue, and with it to the dreams that were bound to come. But for the first time in years, no nightmares plagued him. Instead, he found himself reliving the day he first believed...

Arghan takes a step closer to the falls. Spray from the chasm washes the blood from his head wound, streaming down his forehead and into his eyes. He glances back at the spot where he left his twin-swords near the riverbank, a few paces from the swirling torrent at his feet. He closes his eyes and lifts one foot, about to take his last step, and prays to a God he's quite sure isn't listening.

A voices calls from the riverbank. "Excuse me, are these yours?"

Arghan teeters back, looking over his shoulder. "Who? What did you say?"

"I said are these yours?" A grey-bearded man in a monk's cassock sets a fishing pole against a rock and stoops to lift one of Arghan's weapons from the ground. "Twin-swords. Very fine craftsmanship indeed. May I have them?"

"What?"

"May I take them? I mean, since you won't be needing them anymore where you're going."

"What do you mean 'where I'm going'?"

"It looks pretty obvious to me. You were about to kill yourself, weren't you? Well, get on with it then."

"What? No... I mean, I can't do it with you watching. Mind your own business, old man."

The monk wades into the water and hops up onto the rock beside him. "Old man? I'll have you know I'm not a day over 70. I'm just getting started. Now, may I or may I not have your swords?"

"No."

"Why not? You're going to die. What's the difference?"

"I..."

"What's the difference?"

"They're for honourable combat in defense of all that is sacred. They're not for common hands."

"Are you calling me common? I was a nobleman once upon a time, I'll have you know. Name's Ardwynn. Ardwynn of Castor. I was a Viscount-Mariner once upon a time before I found the Shepherd King and left it all behind."

"Is that so?"

"It is. Now about the swords."

"I said no."

"You're sure?"

"Positive."

"Oh, drat. Well, I shall have to end it all now too. Those are the finest swords I've ever seen. After having laid eyes on them, what else is there to live for?" The old man hops over to the rock beside him and grabs his hand. "Come on then, let's do it together."

"What? No! Surely you have more to live for than a pair of swords!"

"No. They're much too fine. If I can't have them I don't want to live either."

"That's crazy."

"Why?"

"Because..."

"Because why?"

"I see what you're trying to do. You don't understand. This isn't about the swords! I've done horrible things. Unspeakable things!"

"Like what? Confession time. I'm a priest. Let's hear it."

"I can't."

"Come on, you're an Erne Warder, am I right?"

"Yes..."

"So you're a brave, fearsome warrior then. I'm just a priest. Be brave. Tell it to me."

He looks into the man's eyes. Arghan might think him crazy if he weren't so... tranquil.

"Women and children — innocents — died at my order. After that, when my comrades needed me most, I couldn't bear to wield my swords again and now they're all dead. I'm a butcher and a coward. What have you done that comes close to that?"

"You'd be surprised. I had a man murdered once because I was sleeping with his wife and wanted her for myself. How's that for starters?"

"That's despicable."

"Utterly. But it's all gone, carried away by the only One who could lift it."

"Who's that?"

"The Shepherd King, praise His Name. So, let me ask you something. The women and children, did you mean it?"

"What do you mean 'did I mean it'?"

"To kill them all, deliberately."

"No, I didn't. Dear God, I didn't..."

"See, there you go. My shame is worse than yours. You can stop if you want to. Forget the swords. I think I'd better jump now. "

"No! You can't!"

"Why not?"

"Your eyes. There's no trace of guilt in them at all. I can spot a liar when I see one."

"No lie. My sin cost my son his life. The man's brother took revenge. He tried to stab me to death. My son, convinced of my innocence, stood in the way and took a poisoned dagger meant for me. In my grief, I gave the would-be-avenger my lands, and my treasures; buried my son, and joined a monastery. I've lived there ever since. If you don't believe me, come there, the brothers will all tell you."

The old man steps down from the rock and wades back to shore. He grabs his fishing rod and starts walking into the woods.

"That's it?" Arghan jumps down from the rock and kneels on the riverbed, allowing the rushing water to assail his body. His face barely above the surface of the water, he watches drips of blood disappear into the current. "How did you do it?"

"Do what?"

"Your son's death. The guilt… the shame… the sorrow… how did you bear it?"

"I didn't. He did. The Shepherd King did. Right after I took the first and biggest step."

"Which was?"

"I forgave myself."

"You forgave… yourself?"

"Yes. Follow me and I'll tell you all about it."

"Where are you going?"

"Down to the pool to catch some salmon for lunch. All this talking has made me hungry." The old monk disappears into the brush. Arghan sloshes his way out of the river and follows him into the woods.

"Don't forget your swords," Ardwynn bellows from beyond sight. "You never know, you may need them someday."

Arghan sprung up in bed. *High gable ceiling. Crackling fireplace.* Amber rays shone through an open window, illuminating the wall next to the bed. Chapel bells rang in the distance and a much louder bell clanged nearby.

Oh yeah, Trianon. The Mariner's Inn. But what time?

He slid out of bed, ambled to the window, and gazed up at the clock tower across Traitor's Circle. The Olde Man's hands pointed up and down.

The 6th hour. I've been asleep all day!

Footsteps creaked up the hall outside his room and paused before the door swung open behind him. He clenched his fists and scanned the room. Where were his swords?

"What are you doing up? Back to bed, doctor's orders." Gavek dropped his bag on a table near the door and pointed at the bed.

"I'm going, I'm going," moaned Arghan, closing his hand over his wounded shoulder. He strolled back to the bed and slipped under the covers, exhaling as he closed his eyes.

"I was only checking the time. Looks like I've been asleep all day. Have you been out this whole time?"

Gavek rifled through his satchel. "Yes, unfortunately." He pulled out several bottles, uncorked them, and poured a mixture into a cup on the table. "Took me all day to find an apothecary that would actually sell me something on Risenday. I was about to give up when I spotted a shopkeeper in the Old Town returning to his quarters above his store. He told me off, but when I whiffed the spirits on his breath I told him I was an Inquisitor and would report him if he didn't sell me what I wanted." Gavek walked to Arghan's bedside while he stirred the brew.

"Ha! Clever. Well done."

Gavek felt Arghan's forehead. "How do you feel?"

"Like sheep dung baking in the summer sun."

"That good, huh? Well, this ought to make it better in a hurry. Pattron's recipe. Drink up."

"What is it? It smells like a pig's arse."

Gavek chuckled. "You don't want to know. Just drink."

Arghan downed it in one gulp. "Ugh. Tastes the way it smells."

"It's supposed to. I'll make some more. You'll need two more of those before morning. I'll let you know when its time. Try and get some more rest. Okay?" Gavek walked back to the table and started mixing again.

"Gavek?"

"Yes?"

Arghan stared up at the ceiling. "I'm sorry. For the journey. For how I spoke to you this morning. You deserve better."

Gavek looked out the window. "I forgive you. You've not been yourself."

"No, that's just it. I have been, in a way. That's the problem. My old self I mean, not the new. The horrors of my past are a powerful foe. I've been fighting them all alone again and I realize now I don't have to. I'm grateful I have people in my life like you and Pattron and others to help me come to my senses when I'm losing my way. Bless you, son. I cherish your faithfulness and the effort you went to today."

Gavek's eyes moistened. He nodded and looked back down at what he was mixing. His voice cracked, "Wrytha has the same feelings for you as you do for her, you know. Still does, even after last night."

"Really? What makes you so sure?"

"The way she looked for you before she left the ship, and things Khloe said before they disembarked."

"Such as?"

Gavek got up from the table and slid his chair beside Arghan's bed. "It's all been a big misunderstanding. All of it. I don't want to get you worked up, but you deserve to know."

Arghan pushed himself up against the headboard. "Know what, Gavek?"

"First off, she is the woman whose children you saved that night—"

"I knew it."

"Wait, there's more. It may be hard for you to believe, but this is what Khloe said—"

"Out with it, Gavek!"

"She said Wrytha claims that when she returned to the village that night, it was Erne Warders who herded the townsfolk inside the tower and barricaded the entrance."

Arghan's face grew pale. "Oh dear God…"

"And before that, they killed everyone else in the town…"

Arghan sunk his head between his knees.

"And there never were any Zuelan forces there at all. Don't you see? It was all a big lie told to destroy the Erne Warders and to frame you. But who would do such a thing?"

Arghan threw his covers off and jumped out of bed. "Omhigaart Thurn."

"Who?" Gavek sprung from his chair and followed Arghan as he paced the room.

"My commanding officer. He's the one who told me when and where to fire. That snake! I remember seeing him talking to... Solstrus... he was in the room at our command post in Kortova when Thurn gave me my orders. He was only a priest back then, but a venomous zealot all the same, especially when it came to the Tzyani. It was him, it had to be! The two of them must have conspired. But why?"

Gavek grabbed Arghan's wrist. "Do evil men ever need a reason? Doesn't it all come down to the hate inside their hearts? Isn't that what Abba Ardwynn used to say? If you get caught up in asking 'why' you'll miss the blessing in it."

Arghan glared at Gavek. "Blessing? How can you call such betrayal a blessing?"

"I'm not. What I'm saying is the Father of Lights has known the truth all along. Do you really need to keep asking for forgiveness for something He never held against you in the first place? It's time to forgive yourself."

Arghan's lips quivered. "What did you say?"

"I said if the Father of Lights—"

"No, not that, the last bit."

"I said forgive yourself."

Arghan stared at a beam of sunlight on the floor. He looked up suddenly, patted Gavek on the shoulder, and returned to bed. "Bless you, Ardwynn," he whispered, closing his eyes.

CHAPTER ELEVEN
Pursuits

Wrytha scowled at the fletcher standing behind the stall. "Two Sovereigns. Not a penny more. Final offer."

The shopkeeper adjusted his cap and scratched his wiry whiskers. "Fine. Take them and get out of here before I change my mind." He handed her two bundles of arrows and turned away, muttering, "Tzyani witch…"

"Excuse me?"

"Nothing."

"That's what I thought. Pleasure doing business with you."

Wrytha tossed two coins onto the counter. She spun around and recoiled as a pedestrian whizzed by. She weaved her way through the writhing current of morning shoppers and stopped at the fountain at the centre of Traitor's Circle.

"Here, a dozen for each of us. Cost more than I'd liked. Use them sparingly." Wrytha drew a hunting knife from a sheath on her belt and cut the twine off one of the bundles then slid them into the quiver on Khloe's back.

Khloe rose from her perch on the edge of the fountain. "I usually do, don't I?" She held out a birch bark cup. "Got you a hot morning brew. Askhavahni trader who sold it to me says it'll perk you up. Looks like you could use it."

Wrytha rubbed her eyes. "You know what, after yesterday and then last night, you may be right." She took the cup, sniffed the steaming liquid, and reached down to pet Rhodo. "Smells promising. Now what about you, boy? Did Khloe get anything to perk you up or do we have to sell you to that Kyberian butcher over there?"

"Mother!"

"Just kidding." Wrytha held up a hand while she took a gulp of her beverage. "Mm, I could get used to this."

"It's not Rhodo's fault he hasn't caught their scent yet. It's not like the country. Look around, there's gotta be thousands of people in this city, and every strong smell you can imagine."

"Khloe, you don't have to defend him. I get it. It's just that we covered every dock and street on this island and the next. I never imagined it would be this hard. I'm beginning to wonder if we'll ever find the boys." Wrytha squinted. "Wait a second, what's that?"

Wrytha grabbed a blade of straw from Khloe's hair. *Must be from the stable we slept in last night,* she thought. Just then, Rhodo jerked Khloe away, pulling her through the crowd by his leash.

"Whoa! Mom— I think..."

"Khloe!" Wrytha dropped her drink and ran after her.

The dog quickened his pace, chasing a man in overalls who had passed by them moments before, carrying a set of tools. Leaping, Rhodo growled and latched onto something inside the smith's toolbox.

The smith glared over his spectacles. "Sweet juniper, let go of that you mutt! Dose is me tools!"

Khloe yanked the leash. "Rhodo! Cut that out!"

A ripping sound cut the air. A rag dangling from the man's toolbox gave way, half of it now in the dog's mouth, the other half still tied to the handle.

Rhodo dropped the tattered cloth on the ground and nuzzled into it, snorting.

Not another incident. Gotta defuse this. Wrytha caught up to where they were standing. "Sorry sir, it's his first time in the city. Country dog, you see—"

"Country dog, I'll say! More like a wolf if ya ask me. Keep 'im offa me or I'll call the watch." He pointed at an Alpinian guard who exited the doorway of The Olde Man. "I got a schedule ta keep. Now if you'll excuse me..." The man marched off and passed through the entrance of the clock tower.

"Mother, the rag, look!" Khloe knelt to pick it up.

"Tassels, it's a Khevet[1]." Wrytha took it and inspected the embroidery at its edge. "But not just any Khevet; I wove this, see the swirl? I think it's Nicah's."

"What would a clocksmith be doing with a piece of Nicah's Khevet?"

"I don't know, but I hope the Alpinians have nothing to do with it. Did you see that one come out of that clock tower as he entered?"

"Oh no, do you think they've been arrested maybe?"

"Hope not. But let's not jump to conclusions." Wrytha took a few steps and then turned her back to the door. "Let's assume the clocksmith came in contact with Nicah somewhere, or with his scarf at least. We're not about to run in there and ask him, not with that fellow watching us. Besides, if the boys were that close Rhodo would have noticed already. No, it's somewhere the smith's been before."

"Backtrack!"

"Exactly." Wrytha held the scarf to Rhodo's snout. "Rhodo, backtrack!"

The canine took a deep whiff, snorted, and took off with Khloe in tow, southward down The Meridian[2]. Wrytha sped after them, grinning. She drew her knife, sliced the cord from the second bundle of arrows, and tossed them into her quiver. She sheathed her knife and leaped over an apple cart in front of her path. *Now that's the Rhodo I was counting on!*

The trio raced down the street, dodging horses, carts, pedestrians, and other obstacles, spurning confused and angry rebukes as they went.

Rhodo took a hard left onto The Embankment. Khloe's shoulder

---

1. Khevet – a light scarf worn by Tzyani men as a symbol of their devotion to the Father of Lights.
2. The Meridian – a street running south from Traitor's Circle to the Ambertyne River embankment.

struck the corner of a house. She spun and fell onto the cobblestone, releasing the leash.

"Rhodo, wait! Mother! He's—"

Wrytha tapped Khloe on the shoulder as she bolted past. "It's alright, I've got eyes on him."

Khloe dusted herself off and scrambled to catch up.

Several minutes later Rhodo raced through the intersection at Oster's Reach, running under a carriage as it passed. Wrytha dove over another and watched the dog take another hard turn, this time to the right. It leaped over the retaining wall next to the muddy shoreline near the mouth of the Ambertyne River, somewhere between the Reach and the Library of Trianon. Wrytha skidded to a stop and leaned over the wall.

Khloe bounced beside her mother. "Is... huh... is he... did you lose him?"

"No. There. See him? On top of that dinghy next to the shore."

"How—"

"Stairs. There. Come on."

The pair scaled the wall and scampered down the steps behind a boat builder's shack. Rhodo leaped in and out of the dinghy several times, sniffing the wind. The dog paced back and forth at the shore, whining and panting as it looked out over the river.

Wrytha jumped into the boat and looked back at Khloe. "The clocksmith took this boat to the island." She looked up at the traffic passing over the Palace Bridge. "Probably to avoid the morning rush. But where did he launch from?"

Near the summit of Mount Tria, a harpist played a lilting melody in the hillside gardens of the Archprelate's estate. Solstrus sat under a shaded pavilion on the terrace behind his mansion at the top of the hill, gazing past cedars and bubbling cascades toward the distant skyline of the Old Town and Trianon Harbour. The melody ceased. The harpist turned a page and began to play another composition.

Solstrus wiped jam off the corner of his mouth with a napkin. "No, that won't do. The other one was quite lovely. Play it again."

The harpist glanced at the floor, blushing. She turned back the page and continued to play. Solstrus smiled while he sliced off another piece of roast ham and dipped it in his eggs. He lifted the morsel with a fork and opened his mouth. The music stopped again. He dropped his utensil and glared at the musician. Arching his eyebrows, he traced the direction of her stare and turned to see two men in violet cloaks descend the steps from his house.

The crow's feet surrounding his dark, sullen eyelids constricted. "You're a bit early, aren't you gentlemen?"

The new visitors strutted up to him and bowed.

"Your eminence," said the taller of the two, clicking his heels.

"Shouldn't you be out hunting subversives as directed, Raipheniel? Walk with me." The aged cleric threw his napkin on the table, got up, and passed between the two men, headed for the stairs. "I'm a busy man. I treasure the few moments of peace I get each day. What is it that can't wait until your afternoon report?"

The shorter Alpinian answered, glancing at Raipheniel, "Your eminence, we bring you alarming news. Our spies in the city centre have uncovered a cell of Tzyani assassins plotting your demise. Men under my command spotted reinforcements of theirs arriving at Onya Landing yesterday. We're here to take you to a secure location until we can track down all the conspirators."

"Is that so?" he said, entering the mansion. "Well, what sort of place do you have in mind that's more secure than my residence, Portaias?"

Raipheniel answered for his lieutenant, "Until we know the full nature of the threat we feel it best you not be seen in any place you frequent. The logical place to take you is the Palace of Trianon."

Solstrus tilted his head and shrugged his shoulders. "I'll not be intimidated by a rabble of heretic traitors. Double my guard if you have to, but I've no intention of following your advice. Do I make myself clear?"

"Yes, your eminence," said the knights, nearly in unison.

"Good."

Solstrus raised his eyebrows and held out his arms, signaling to a servant to bring his outer garment. An attendant rushed to his side with the golden cloak and helped him push his arms and head through it. He placed a cap on Solstrus' head and handed him a sceptre, bowing as he left.

"Now, since you've eaten up the last precious minutes I carved out for my breakfast you'll have to excuse me. I have an appointment with the Palace of Ministers."

"Feeling better?" Gavek closed the inn door and descended the steps to the street.

About ten paces ahead, Arghan stood at the edge of Traitor's Circle. He twirled his cloak over the protruding hilt of his Twin Talon.

"Like a new man, nearly." He closed his eyes toward the sun, allowing the morning rays to bathe his face. He massaged his wounded shoulder for a moment then gripped his belt and faced the centre of the circle.

Gavek stepped beside him, glimpsing Arghan's sword through the gap in his cloak. "Just the one today? Think you'll need it?"

One never knows. "The only time a Warder carries two at a time is when he's traveling, going into battle, or when he's still too wet behind the ears to know better, thinking he's got something to prove."

"How so?"

"Years ago, some of the men started wearing two at a time everywhere they went, making a big deal about never having to draw the second one to defeat an opponent. Using both smacked of weakness or desperation, they said. Foolish, if you ask me. Our numbers were decimated by the war at the time and a call went out to refill our ranks. Many men, fit in body but not in spirit, joined the order seeking fame and riches, caring little about the high calling of an Erne Warder."

"How could your Grand Master allow such a thing?"

"Enemy forces outnumbered us five to one. He did what he had to do, I suppose. Anyway, enough chit-chat. Let's get going." Arghan headed southeast toward the corner of Palace Street.

Gavek scampered close behind him, running his fingers across the splines of the books he carried, whispering the titles. His forehead bounced off of Arghan's back. "Why are you stopping?"

Arghan nodded to his right. "See that?"

Gavek looked through the sea of people and shop stalls that filled the plaza. "Can you be more specific?"

"There, past the fountain. The steps of the clock."

A man in dirty overalls stood at the entrance of the Olde Man, wiping his forehead with a rag and pointing in the direction of The Meridian. An Alpinian stood in front of him, nodding. The guard looked in the direction the man was pointing as five more Alpinians stepped through the doorway. The first one beckoned the others to follow and the troops took off down the street.

Gavek stood on his toes. "What are they doing?"

"Chasing somebody, from the looks of things. Did you see them pour out like that? They're at every tower in the city. Put your hood up. Stick close to the houses. We'll take the right side of the street past the corner."

The pair headed east down Palace Street. Several minutes later they neared the intersection of Oster's Reach.

Gavek slipped on a pebble, dropping one of his books. "Can you slow down a bit?"

Arghan turned back to help him. "The sooner we're off the streets the better. If you still had that map we'd have taken one of the tunnels and wouldn't have to worry about the Alpinians. Hopefully Wardein will have something similar in those archives of his, otherwise, my plan to get the manuscripts out of the city will require significant retooling."

"Not that again, and enough with the look, okay?"

"What look?"

"You know the look. The one you're making now."

Arghan smirked with a twinkle in his eye. "I'm just saying, it's not like you to tear out a page of a book for just anyone," he muttered. "And you say I'm the one with a crush."

"What?"

"Nothing."

They continued. As they neared Oster's Reach, Arghan spotted two carriages stopped at angles on the shoulder of the road at the western side of the roundabout. A collision? One vehicle was lying on its side. Two men stood in front of it, shouting at one another. One of them pointed northeast toward the Library and kicked stones onto the feet of the other. Gavek hurried past Arghan while he took in the spectacle. Arghan followed the sound of Gavek's footsteps, still watching the scene. Mentor and apprentice collided.

Arghan backed away. "Excuse me, sorry... Oh, you again."

Unfazed by the collision, Gavek stared down the street, slack-jawed and breathless. "Whoa..."

"Impressive, isn't it? They call it the eleventh wonder of the world."

In the distance, the Library of Trianon rose above the houses like a monolith amid a forest, the roof of its massive central dome gleaming in the sunlight. Four lesser towers marked the cardinal points around its circular facade, and four more, lesser than the others, marked ordinal directions, all of them interspersed with ornate columns, arches, and windows.

"The ancient Threicians were marvelous architects, weren't they?"

Gavek nodded. He whispered, "I never thought I'd ever... it's the most beautiful thing I've ever seen. It's everything Ontolorio said it was, and more."

Arghan put his arm around Gavek's shoulder and messed up his hair. "Oh, there's more. Want to see the inside? Come on. I'll make sure Wardein gives you the grand tour."

"Could've come from anywhere across the river," said Khloe, shading her eyes while she surveyed the opposite bank of the Ambertyne River and the docks of the Old Town to the east.

Wrytha faced the sea wall of The Embankment and Palace Bridge. "True, but considering the route he took, it seems unlikely he crossed the Ambertyne, otherwise why wouldn't he have landed nearer The Meridian and gone straight up it to that big clock tower he walked into? No, he landed here and walked up the Embankment for a reason."

Khloe faced the same direction. "Makes sense, but if he did take a boat to skip the traffic on the bridge, why didn't he row under it and land on the other side so he wouldn't have to walk through that awful intersection?" She traced the top of the bridge to where it connected to Merchant's Isle at Oster's Reach. "Wait! I know, look!" Khloe pointed and reached into her shoulder bag.

Wrytha walked toward her. "What?"

"See that clock at the end of the bridge?" She unfolded the page Gavek had given her and ran a finger across the map. "The Palace Bridge clock. Maybe he needed to go there first?"

"He did say he had a schedule to keep." Wrytha took the map. "Let me see... Palace Street would've been a straighter route to... the 'Olde Man' at Traitor's Circle. That's where we first saw him. But he took the Embankment because... you're right, look, another clock where it intersects with The Meridian."

Khloe grinned. She marched toward the shore and pointed across the harbour. "Maybe he started in the Old Town? Are there any clocks on that side?"

Wrytha held out the map. "The Harbour Clock, it's directly across from us."

"Great!" Khloe sauntered past her mother and led Rhodo farther up the beach toward the stairs. She broke into a sprint. "Last one there's a stuffed trout!"

Arghan rattled the handles of the Library's massive double doors and struck its iron knocker five times. The sound echoed from the lobby inside. He stepped back. "Somethings wrong."

Gavek ran his hand across the doors' gilded reliefs. "Strange isn't it, that it would be closed this time of day?"

"My thoughts exactly." Arghan sauntered across the marble floor of the Library's portico and stood at the edge of the stairway leading back down to the street. He scanned the crescent facade of the Ministry of Commerce building across the way, marking every figure along the sidewalk and checking every window, then surveyed its rooftop. For a moment, a glint of sunlight reflected from above the parapet directly opposite the Library's entrance.

"Put your hood back up. Follow me." Arghan skipped down the stairs.

"Where are we going?"

"Just keep up. You'll see soon enough."

Arghan led Gavek up the street, far past the Library, and turned left onto Shore Street at the north corner of the Commerce building. After they passed the offices of several shipping companies, Arghan glanced back at the rooftops. He grabbed the hem of Gavek's cloak and pulled him into a narrow alley. "Come. We must hurry now."

Arghan broke into a sprint. Gavek followed, huffing, fumbling with his books and the sword around his waist. Arghan turned at the end of the alley and followed the docks along the north shore of Merchant's Isle, slowing to allow Gavek to catch up. He stepped onto the fitted stones of the courtyard at the back of the Library and sprinted toward a circular mausoleum at its centre.

Gavek fell against the wall beside the door, panting. "The architect's mausoleum? What—"

"Yes. Everyone believes Picanes was laid to rest here; the interior tells a different story." Arghan rested his palm against one of the stones of the door frame and leaned into it, sliding it backward until it was flush with the rest of the wall. He repeated this on two others. The third one clicked and the door sprung open. Arghan beckoned Gavek inside and closed the door. He held a finger to his lips and scampered around the sarcophagus to the far wall and pushed three more stones. Metal clicked. Marble ground against marble. The lid of the sarcophagus popped open and a staircase inside it dropped like an accordion into a chamber below.

Gavek stared from the other side of the sarcophagus. "I thought you said you needed the map."

"To remember all of them, yes. Not this one. Saved my life once. Hard to forget. Come."

He pulled Ardwynn's cross from his neck and twisted it, revealing a magnesium-tipped match and flint striker. He grabbed a torch from a sconce inside the staircase and lit it.

"Watch your step." Arghan descended the stairs with Gavek close behind. Some fifty paces through a dank passageway he halted.

"Why are you stopping?" said Gavek, gasping. "Looks like it continues."

"It does, round a blind turn and straight into a spiked pit." Arghan stomped the edge of the floor and a door popped open. Peeking through it while he pushed it open, he stopped at the sound of something sliding against it on the opposite side. He doused his torch into a nearby receptacle and forced the door open, stumbling over something as he entered a room. He broke his fall against a huge mahogany desk while Gavek slid past him.

Gavek scanned the empty shelves along the chamber's high elliptical walls. "Wardein's office?" He crossed to the south side of the room, dodging books strewn across the floor, and stopped to look out one of three towering windows facing the harbour. He looked back at Arghan. "This place is a mess."

"Ransacked from the look of things. Wardein didn't do this. He's meticulous, like you. Somebody's looking for something."

"The ancient manuscripts?"

"No doubt. Stay here while I investigate the Library. And Gavek..."

"What?"

"Don't touch anything."

Gavek nodded and watched Arghan slip out the door. Several minutes passed, enough time to count the ships in the harbour five times over and estimate the height of nearly every building within view. He tapped the windowsill. His gaze fell to the floor where he spotted a first-edition copy of Heithenes' master treatise on geometry. He took a deep breath and looked back out the window. He glanced at the open book again and bent down to reach it. The office door swung open and Arghan scooted back inside.

"What are you doing?"

Gavek stared and puckered his jowl. "Nothing. Shoelace came untied.

Find out anything?"

"Place is deserted. Same state as this office." Arghan strode past the desk and opened the passage door. Gavek followed only to halt at the sight of Arghan's outstretched hand.

"No, you wait here in case Wardein returns. Keep quiet. Stay in the office. If anyone shows up, escape back out the passage. Wait for me in the alley we took off the street, otherwise stay put. I'll return as soon as I can."

"Where are you going?"

"Wardein's residence. Next logical place to look for him."

"How far is it?"

"A few blocks. Won't be long." Arghan slid out the secret doorway.

Gavek listened as the sound of Arghan's footsteps grew softer. He shook his head and folded his arms, sinking into the leather chair behind the desk. A gentle breeze blew in from one of the open windows and lifted the edge of a parchment lying on the desk. Gavek's eyes bulged. *Is that what I think it is?* He lifted the corner of the sheet.

The sound of footsteps stopped. Arghan's voice echoed through the passage, "I mean it Gavek. Don't. Touch. Anything."

Wrytha swung around the leg of a statue at the southeast corner of Palace Bridge and raced up the main thoroughfare of the Old Town, a street called The Parade. Khloe leaned against a building across the street from the Harbour Clock.

Threician design? Looks more like a lighthouse than a clock. Perhaps it once was?

Wrytha slowed to a stop a few paces short of where Khloe stood, placed her hands on her hips, and bent at her waist, panting. She righted herself and wiped the sweat from her brow. "Wipe that... stupid grin... off your face—"

Khloe wiggled her chin. "Ha, ha."

Rhodo strained against his leash, his head pointing toward the clock tower. Khloe tugged on the cord, attempting to reign him in. A bulky male figure carrying a sack over his shoulder crossed the street and descended a staircase at the back of the tower.

"Mother, look! That looks like Jeordri."

"Teighthra's son." Wrytha narrowed her eyelids and clenched her jaw. She marched to the edge of the sidewalk and stood with her hands on her hips. *Teighthra — the one to blame for all this. Teighthra the Zealot. Teighthra the 'inspiring' orator. Teighthra the son-stealer!*

"I need you to stand watch. Stay out of sight. Keep your hood up; hide your braid. There." She pointed to a warehouse behind a drydock that jutted inland beside the clock. "Think you could make it to that roof without being seen?"

"Are you kidding? 'Course I can. What are you gonna do?"

Wrytha grabbed Rhodo's leash. "I'm going in for a closer look. There, cross now."

Wrytha watched Khloe cross the road and sneak across the jetty to the side of the warehouse. The teen scaled a pile of crates and leaped, catching the overhang of the roof. Khloe's feet disappeared above the roofline.

Wrytha pulled up her hood and tugged on Rhodo's lead. "Rhodo, stalk."

The canine dropped its head and shoulders and crept beside Wrytha as she strode across the street. Wrytha paused at the top of the staircase and glanced over her shoulder, then crept down the staircase to the landing near the door. She nudged the latch.

Locked.

She unhooked a brooch from the lapel of her cloak, knelt in front of the door, and inserted the ornament's clasp into the keyhole.

"Come on. Come—"

The lock sprung open and she nudged the door far enough to see Jeordri sitting at a table with his back turned to the door, slurping.

Wrytha slipped through the doorway and whispered in Rhodo's ear, "Guard." She scanned the room. *He must be the only one here.* She tiptoed within a step of the young man and kicked his stool out from under him, sending him crashing to the floor.

"Ah!"

Wrytha grabbed the now wide-eyed twenty-something by one of his ears and lifted him to his feet.

"Where are the others? Where is Teighthra? Where are my sons? Tell me."

Jeordri spat out a piece of bacon, saliva dripping down his chin. "Clan Mother, w-what, h-how—"

"I'll ask the questions, young man!" She yanked on his ear and kicked him to the ground.

Jeordri shuffled onto his elbows, freezing at the sound of Rhodo's growl.

Wrytha straddled his body. "Talk, Jeordri, before I set Rhodo loose on you."

He held his palms out. "Okay! Okay! They're all on Merchant's Isle, buying supplies for tonight."

"What do you mean 'tonight', Jeordri? What's happening tonight?"

Jeordri closed his mouth and swallowed.

"Rhodo—"

"Wait! I don't know. Teighthra's got something big planned, that's all I know. She's supposed to tell us when they return."

"Which is when, exactly?"

"Should be any time now."

"And you weren't with them, why?"

"I was sent f-for the food. In the Old Town, they have excellent butchers in the—"

"Shut up! Rhodo, guard him." Wrytha walked back toward the table and looked up a stone staircase at the back of the room.

"Where's this go?"

"Main floor."

Wrytha bounded up the steps, opened the door, and peered inside. Stained glass windows flanked a single wooden door. Sunshine beamed through upper windows, illuminating a spiral staircase that ascended to a timber floor three flights above. Wrytha backed down the steps and returned to her captive. A shrill whistle sounded from beyond the exterior door.

Khloe. Someone must be coming, far enough away they can't yet hear her whistling.

"This is what we're going to do, Jeordri. You're going back to your table. I'm going to hide behind those crates over there, keeping Rhodo from making you his breakfast, provided you act like you have no idea I'm here. Think you can do that?"

"Y-yes. Yup. No problem."

Wrytha helped him to his feet.

Jeordri plopped back onto his stool. "Is it alright if I finish breakfast?"

Wrytha rolled her eyes and nodded.

Gavek paced in front of the windows of Wardein's office, looking out over the harbour.

Rooftops, counted. Ships, counted. Houses, counted. Birds, counted. Clouds, counted! Counted, counted, counted!

Another breeze blew in, lifting the same parchment Gavek had noticed earlier. The page took flight and rolled a few times before falling face-up on the floor.

Gavek bit his cheek and tapped his foot, looked down at the map, then out the window and back again. He walked over to it and gasped. "Ontolorio's map of the Ancient Threician Empire, limited edition print!"

He lifted it off the floor and studied the drawing, then scampered to the desk and sifted through the books and papers strewn over it. He glanced back at the entrance to the hidden passageway, then to the office door. He cleared his throat and took a step toward the latter, then another and another until he grabbed the door handle. He pulled it open, revealing a long corridor.

His footsteps echoed through the chamber. "Wow."

Columns lined either side of a vaulted corridor three stories high. Between each column and every floor stretched circular aisles lined with bookshelves, floor to ceiling. An archway at the end of the corridor opened into a massive sunlit room. Gavek scanned every direction, eyes bulging, as he dawdled along one side of the floor, running his hand across each column as he passed, bumping into one on the way. He reached the threshold of the reading room, a towering circular expanse at the heart of the structure. He looked out over concentric rows of reading tables to the opposite wall, where columns similar to those seen in the corridor lined every side of the interior facade, interspersed with arches. He accelerated to the service desk at the centre of the room, slowing as he neared it. He twirled, gawking at the frescoes painted on the domed ceiling. He batted the air behind his back until he touched the chair behind the desk.

"The Alpinians could kill me now and I'd die a happy man," he whispered, stumbling into the seat.

A light twinkled in Gavek's peripheral vision. Glancing down, he glimpsed a face reflected in the glass shroud of a reading lamp. His ears perked at the sound of flapping cloth behind him. Something whizzed past his head and he sprung from the chair, stumbling back against the desk.

A ginger-haired young woman in a scarlet robe pressed the empty spike of a candle stand against his chest like a spear. She growled and slid it toward his throat.

"Wait! Stop!" Gavek waved his hands and slid his backside along the edge of the desk. "Who are you? What—"

"Never mind who I am. Who are you? How did you get in here?"

"Um, ah, I'm Gavek... of the Monastery of, ah... Cairhn. You know, in the lake country up north? Trieehd to be—"

"I know where Cairhn is, you fool. Did Solstrus send you here? Are you another one of his agents?"

"Solstrus? No. Definitely, no. Why—"

"What are you doing here then, 'Gavek' of Cairhn?"

"I'm looking for Wardein; waiting for him, actually. I'm a friend of his. I mean sort of. We haven't actually ever met, technically, I mean we've corresponded endlessly, the man does have a talent for the quill."

The young woman relaxed her grip and let the candle stand rest against her hip. She stood it upright and turned away from Gavek. Smirking, she arched an eyebrow and narrowed her eyelids, irises hugging the corners of her eyes.

"Friend of Wardein you say?" She turned back again, tilting her head. She folded her arms. "Prove it. How did you get in here?"

"Um, a window. Came in through a window."

"All the windows are too high to reach from the street or the courtyard. Try again." She tipped the candle stand back and forth with her fingers.

Gavek swallowed. He watched her fingers for a moment then looked at her face.

"Tell me your name first," he said, straightening his back. "How do I know I can trust you? Tell me or I'm not saying another word."

She smiled again, revealing beautiful white teeth behind her moist, ruby-red lips. "I'm Sira, a student of Wardein's from the University of Trianon. I intern here at the Library."

"Okay, so why are you here all by yourself? Where's Wardein? Why did you try to kill me just now?"

"The Alpinian guards raided the Library a couple of weeks ago and have kept it locked ever since. They've been ransacking it daily, looking for the secret entrance to the catacombs. Today's the first day they haven't been inside for a while. Wardein hoped to use the opportunity to retrieve a document he left behind after he fled into hiding, one of great importance from his secret collection. He sent me here to fetch it for him. I'm sorry I frightened you. I thought you might be working with the Alpinians. It wouldn't do if I were captured either, especially on such an important errand, now would it?"

"No, I suppose not. But what's so important he can't do without it? Why is he willing to risk your life and not his?"

"I'm not permitted to say. He's quite mysterious, as you probably know, and strict. I dare not disobey him." She turned away, dropped her head, and sobbed, covering her mouth with her hand.

Gavek furrowed his brow, blinking. He took a step closer to her and touched her shoulder. "What's the matter?"

She sniffled and took out a handkerchief to wipe her eyes, smirking beyond his view. "I can't believe I could be so careless."

"Careless, how?" Gavek stepped in front of her and took her wrists.

Her sobbing intensified. Mascara streaked down her cheeks. "He told me how to get in undetected, and where to find the door to the catacombs, but I lost the instructions he wrote down for me of how to open it. I don't know what happened, I must have dropped it on the way over here. I tried and tried to solve it, I really did, but it's the most complicated puzzle I've ever seen! What am I to do? The Alpinians are bound to return any time. I can't leave without it."

A complicated puzzle? The most complicated one she's ever seen? Ha! We'll see about that.

"Fear not, Sira. The Father of Lights has led me to you. If ever there was a man born who could crack its code, it is I."

"Really? You think—"

"I know I can. Will you lead me to it?"

"Yes, it's this way."

CHAPTER TWELVE
Zealots

The bell of the temple at the corner of Gorion Circle chimed eleven. Arghan leaned against the granite wall outside Shipper's Bank and gulped the vial of medicine Gavek had given him. Revolting, but it was working.

He gagged and reached for his waterskin while he surveyed the front of a three-storey townhouse across the street. He took a swig of water and wiped the corner of his mouth as he stepped away from the bank. He meandered through traffic and crossed in front of the house, peering into the windows as he passed. He stopped at the corner and leaned against the wall, facing the street. He looked up and down the sidewalk then rolled around the corner and ducked into the alleyway. He raced to the back of the house and vaulted over a wall.

A garden teeming with all sorts of vegetables and herbs lay at the centre of the stone courtyard, enclosed by a low stone wall. A shed and greenhouse stood beyond it, its door ajar, the glass from its window shattered and strewn across the pavement.

What's this now?

Arghan walked over for a closer look. As he passed the corner of the garden he spotted a rake, broken in two. The tip of its handle leaned against the wall and the pronged end hung from a shrub in a planter box beside the shed. Dirt lay splattered over flattened vegetation surrounding a deep depression in the soil. Footprints cut through the centre of the garden, leaving a trail of earth up to Wardein's back door, which hung ajar.

Arghan opened his cloak and drew his sword. He scampered to the door. He pulled the handle and allowed the door to glide open before sticking his head inside. The footprints trailed across Wardein's kitchen and up a staircase adjacent to the wall. The floor above him creaked.

Arghan crept to the staircase. Faint rustling and the occasional thud reverberated above. He tightened his grip on his sword and ascended the steps to a landing. He watched a shadow move across the floor through an open doorway at the end of a hall. He tripped over a loose nail and the floorboards creaked when he landed. The rustling stopped and the door swung open. A man in a black gambeson charged him, wielding a sword. Arghan dodged it and booted his attacker in the back. He leaped over the railing and landed on the staircase below seconds before his attacker's blade struck the wall above his head. Steel clanged against steel. Arghan blocked a downward thrust with his Twin Talon.

The man pressed his attack, booting Arghan down the staircase and onto the floor. He leaped through the air. Arghan rolled backward, dodging the man's feet before he landed. Arghan raced out the door, leaped over the garden, and turned to face his assailant, whipping his hilt over his knuckles. He hated close-quarter combat; a Twin Talon wasn't built for it. But here, in the open air, there could be only one outcome.

You're good, but you're mine now.

The two combatants circled one another, the tips of their swords touching occasionally as they each looked for an opportunity to strike. Arghan studied his adversary now that he could get a better look at him in the sunlight. Blue eyes. Shaggy blonde hair and stubble. Rugged features, much the way he himself looked when he was in his thirties. Mud covered the front of the man's clothing.

"Took a dive coming in here I see," said Arghan. "Who are you? What were you up to in there?"

The man lunged at him again. Arghan parried his blow and twisted his hilt, locking the man's blade with his cross-guard. He charged and checked him into the courtyard wall.

"Answer me!"

The man's eyes focused on Arghan's hilt, now only inches from his face. "Eine Zwillingskralle!"

Gothan. Arghan's native tongue.

The man ducked, releasing his weapon enough to slip past Arghan. He dropped his blade and held out his palms. He spoke in Gothan again, bowing his head, "Wait! You are the famous Erne Warder they call Arghan of Danniker, are you not?"

Arghan responded, also in Gothan, "I am. How do you know that?"

"Wardein's been expecting you. Who else but a true member of the Order of the Sea Eagle could wield one of their blades as well as you do? Will you permit me?" He pointed at his sword.

Arghan nodded, still gripping his sword. The man picked up his weapon and slid it back into its sheath.

Arghan stared into the man's eyes for several moments before doing the same. "Who are you? How do you know Wardein? What are you doing here?"

"My name is Deighn Renzek. I am a knight in the service of his grace Weorthan, the Duke of Ostergaart."

"Renzek? Any relation to Danner Renzek, the Margrave of Remansk?"

"Yes, he's my father."

"I fought beside him in the battle of Borga Pass. An honourable, tenacious warrior."

"Yes, he told me stories about you. Fighting ten Zuelan warriors at a time? Quite a feat."

"Exaggerated, to be sure. They were tired. I was fresh. What's your mission here, young Renzek?"

"Officially, I am here as the Duke's representative to the royal court. Unofficially, my liege sent me to investigate the disappearance of his beloved, princess Cybella."

His 'beloved'? Arghan wondered. *How old is this fellow? She never men-*

tioned him in any of her letters.

Renzek continued, "In the course of my inquiries I met up with her trusted friend Wardein and have been working closely with him to solve the mystery ever since." He spotted a woman opening a window in the adjacent house. "Perhaps we should step back inside where we could discuss it further?"

"Agreed." Arghan beckoned Renzek to take the lead.

W*hat's taking them so long?* Wrytha massaged her thighs and dropped to her knees behind the crates inside the Harbour Clock's cellar. Rhodo's panting warmed her cheek. She stroked the shepherd's jowls and peered past the crates. Voices and footfalls echoed through the door. It creaked open and the footfalls grew louder.

"We're back. Anything interesting happen while we were gone?"
Teighthra's voice. The witch!

Jeordri's slurping was superseded by the sound of clinking plates and a stool sliding across the floor.

"No, mother. Not a thing."

Footfalls sounded throughout the room and up the stairs.

"Did you get everything I asked for?" Teighthra asked.

"Yup. What about you?"

A male voice answered, "Oh, we scored huge, big man."
Orin! My son!

Something heavy landed on the table, followed by the rickety sound of shafts of lightweight wood knocking into each other, a sound Wrytha knew only too well.

Arrows. A lot of them.

"Those, big guy, are the best bodkins money can buy. With the powerful new bows we bought in town, they'll pierce even the strongest armour, straight to the heart. With any luck, I'll land the killing shot myself—"

Wrytha dropped her head and closed her eyes.

Orin continued, "Solstrus won't even know what hit him!"

"You're right," interrupted Teighthra. "But it'll be me who takes him down. You fire faster than any of us, but you're not that accurate. The others will take out the guards while your covering fire gives me enough time to get close enough to him to finish the job. Understood?"

Wrytha stood up and shouted, "Okay, I've heard enough." She clenched her jaw, strode across the room, and stood opposite Teighthra, seething. She dug her index finger into Teighthra's chest while Orin, Jeordri, and two more Zealots of Pitha looked on, blinking, mouths gaping wide.

"Turns out I was right about you all along, wasn't I, you lying witch?! What sort of poison have you twisted these young minds with?" She addressed her son, "And you, Orin. You should be ashamed to say such things. I know I am to hear them! Get your things at once, and fetch your brother. We're getting out of here."

Orin gave Teighthra a questioning glance. He took a deep breath and looked back at his mother. "No."

Wrytha scowled. "No? What do you mean 'no'?"

Teighthra stepped in front of Orin. "He means he's found a true leader with the conviction to do what you refuse to do, which is to secure the safety of our tribe once and for all."

"Conviction? You call terrorism a 'conviction'? Pitha was a violent maniac who got thousands of our people killed and if you're not careful, you will too, spouting her destructive ideology. Get out of my way before I make you regret it!"

Teighthra reached for her dagger.

Wrytha grabbed her wrist before she could touch it and made a fist with her other hand, preparing to strike.

"Teighthra! Mother! Stop!" Orin pushed between the two women.

Rhodo's ears stood erect. He let out a deep growl and barked three times.

Wrytha's eyes met her son's. They spoke nearly in unison, "Intruders."

Screams bellowed from the upper floor, followed by the clamour of many voices and heavy footfalls. Wrytha let go of Teighthra's arm and the group looked up at the ceiling.

"Everyone, follow me," Teighthra shouted. She ran for the cellar door but stopped when it swung open.

An Alpinian guardsman stepped inside, sword drawn, followed by several others. "This is a raid! Give up, you're surrounded!"

Wrytha drew three arrows, nocked them together on her bowstring, and fired them simultaneously. One arrow struck the first man in the stomach and the second man above his collarbone. The third arrow ricocheted off the door frame and grazed another soldier's cheek.

"Upstairs! It's the only way!" Wrytha bolted up the staircase and the rest followed. They burst through the door and found several more Alpinian guards attacking the rest of Teighthra's followers.

"Where's your brother? Where's Nicah?" said Wrytha, scanning the chaos.

An Alpinian guard dragged a female zealot out the front door. She screamed, "He's upstairs! I saw them chasing him!"

Orin charged into a cluster of guards, tackling one to the floor. He snatched the man's sword from its sheath and slashed his throat with it. "See, mother, this is the only language these monsters understand!" He turned to face three more of them, thrashing the sword to keep them at bay.

What has become of my son? Orin, brave, foolish Orin! Wrytha raced past him and bolted up the stairs to the second floor. "Nicah!"

She sidestepped a trail of upended clutter and bounded up the next set of stairs to reach the third floor. Two Alpinians stood over a body resting in front of the turning gears of the clock mechanism.

One of them stepped aside, revealing Nicah's face. A pool of blood formed beneath Nicah's head. "Is he dead?"

"No, but nice work with your club. He's out cold. Why don't we save ourselves the trouble of processing and just finish him off? Nobody will know."

The guard lifted his club over his head. "Good idea."

Wrytha drew an arrow and fired it into his wrist. He dropped the club and screamed, clutching his arm. The second turned and lunged at her before she could nock another. He swung his sword, lodging it into a beam as Wrytha rolled out of the way.

The Alpinian chuckled, unable to dislodge his weapon. He drew a shorter blade from a second sheath on his belt. "Well aren't you feisty, beautiful one? We'll keep you nice and alive, you can be sure. Long enough to have some fun, anyway."

She reached for another arrow and wailed when the guard she had injured grabbed her wrist from behind. He punched her between the shoulder blades. Wrytha dropped to the floor, and clutched her throat, choking and gasping.

Wrytha's assailant flipped her on her back and leaped on top of her.

"On second thought," said the other guard, "I'll take this one to the wagon while you keep her down. Maybe she'll be a little more cooperative knowing we've got him and the others in custody. Stay put, I'll be back."

Wrytha strained against the hands that now held her wrists against the floor. She arched her neck and glared at the other guard, watching him drag Nicah toward the staircase.

Her assailant leaned over her and kissed her on the cheek. "You hear that? My friend is coming back and when he does—"

Wrytha inhaled. She thrust her hips upward, bridging his lower torso while she drove her hands in sweeping arcs along the floor down to her buttocks, knocking him to the ground. She rolled to her feet and stomped his groin, leaped across the room, and stumbled down the staircase.

"Nicah!"

A scream echoed from the bottom of the stairs. Wrytha braced herself against the wall and peered toward the floor below her, blinking. Rhodo stood on top of the guard who had dragged Nicah away, mauling the man's throat while Nicah lay unconscious to the side. Three more guards stormed the stairs. One of them took a swipe at the dog while the other two closed in on Wrytha.

"Halt!"

Wrytha doubled back and dashed across the room. She leaped over the groaning man on the floor. He caught her ankle, spinning her headlong toward a window at the other side of the room. Stained glass exploded into the air. Wrytha plummeted, flailing toward the drydock below.

Deighn Renzek peeked out a window overlooking Wardein's courtyard then closed the shutters. "One can never be too careful," he said, brushing some of the mud off his gambeson, his voice trailing off at the end, "especially when people leave rakes lying around." He faced Arghan, standing on the other side of a cutting table.

Arghan folded his arms. "What were you doing in the room upstairs? Did Wardein send you here to fetch something?"

"A map of some kind. Said it was crucial I find it for him."

The catacombs no doubt. If only Gavek hadn't given my copy away!

Arghan leaned over the counter. "You said the Duke sent you here after Cybella disappeared. What's his interest in this? He feels considerable affection for her, I gather?"

"Oh, he's absolutely smitten. He met her at a diplomatic function in Straskost a year ago. They've been corresponding ever since. That is... until her letters stopped. I'm his personal bodyguard, and that should attest to the value he places on her safety."

"It does," said Arghan. He strolled to the foot of the stairs and ran his finger along one of the nicks Renzek's blade left in the wall. "You're about thirty, I wager, Renzek? And the Duke—"

Renzek took off his gloves and dropped them on the counter. "Younger than me, sir," he replied, grinning. "Inherited the title from his father who died shortly before that same conference where he met the princess."

"I hadn't heard. News travels slowly where I live."

"So I gathered when the Queen Mother set off alone to find you. Did she travel back with you to Trianon?"

Arghan's gaze grew distant. "No. Silla's dead."

Renzek frowned. "Dead, how?"

"Alpinians attacked when I went to meet her. Silla got caught in the middle of it. It was foolish of her to travel unprotected. How did she get involved?"

Renzek dragged his fingers through his hair. "Wardein knew he had to get word to you somehow when Cybella disappeared. Her Majesty The Queen Mother got wind of his plans and insisted on going herself, despite his protests. She left in the middle of the night before he could talk her out of it. She didn't trust anyone at the Palace with the knowledge of your location and refused to wait until Wardein could find another courier willing to take a message to you after the first one failed him."

"Failed him, how?"

"Shortly after Cybella disappeared, Wardein became suspicious of his original messenger when the man didn't show up one day for a planned rendezvous. The courier later said he was detained by a family matter, but another person Wardein knows said he saw him elsewhere. Wardein met the courier again, gave him a bogus package to deliver, and had me follow him. He went straight to Solstrus. Who knows how long he'd been compromised, or how exactly. Shortly after Wardein fired the courier, Solstrus ordered a citywide manhunt for Wardein. The Alpinians raided the Library, locked it down, and have been ransacking it ever since, looking for Wardein's hidden treasures. Were it not for his secret passageways, he'd never have escaped."

"Hmm, that certainly explains the door, and the state his office was in."

"His office? Don't tell me you've been inside the Library?"

"Yes. Went there this morning with my apprentice Gavek." Arghan briefed Renzek on the morning's events.

"You're positive it was deserted when you left him there?"

"Well, I didn't have time to clear the whole building, but it seemed so, why?"

"Your apprentice may be in trouble. There's a student of Wardein's, a treacherous little nymph from Alpinia called Sira we're pretty sure is working for Solstrus. A few days after the raid Wardein sent me back to the Library to fetch him something, the same map I was looking for today, only it wasn't there. While inside I overheard her cooperating with the Alpinian guards. Their chatter sounded too intimate for her to have been coerced. She was one of Wardein's interns at the Library. Even when Solstrus' other agents aren't there, I'm sure she is."

"Schlika[1]..." Arghan withdrew from the table and paced the room, stroking his beard. "I've got to get him out of there. Will you come with me, then take me to see Wardein?" Arghan headed for the back door.

"As you wish, my lord. I am at your service."

"Lead on, then, and drop the "my lord" nonsense. 'Arghan' will do."

Renzek nodded and led Arghan across the courtyard, back to the shed.

"Cybella's disappearance is connected to the raid at the Library, no doubt," Arghan said after he closed the shed door. "Silla told me Solstrus claimed he had proof she was a heretic, by his definition, anyway; he said she fled the city to escape arrest. He must have discovered her connection to Wardein and intercepted her."

"That's what we believe."

Arghan studied Renzek's expression. "There's more to it though, isn't there? What aren't you telling me? You know where she is, don't you?"

"Not exactly, but we have our suspicions." Renzek pulled another door open at the back of the shed.

Arghan's nostrils flared. He pushed the door closed. "I swore on Silla's grave I would find Cybella and protect her. Do either you or Wardein know what happened to her or not?"

"We think so, but the rest is better coming from Wardein."

Gavek straddled the trap door, trying not to think about the long iron spikes at the bottom of the pit below. He blew his bangs aside and stared at the iron door beyond the open bookshelf.

Sira paced behind him. "I thought you said this would be easy for

---

1. Schlika (Shly-ka) - A Gothan interjection used to express surprise, anger, or extreme displeasure.

you?" She folded her arms and rested her head against the shelf beside him. "You wouldn't have said such a thing just to impress a girl, would you, Gavek of Cairhn?"

He glanced at her fiery red locks. "No." He reinspected the row of stone switches beside the iron barrier. "It's not my fault. I'm not exactly at my best today. I was up all night nursing a sick friend. At least I got this much right." He depressed one of the stones and the trap door sprung back into place.

"Good for you, but it only saved you from being skewered. You're no farther ahead than when we started."

"I know, I know." He stepped back and supported his chin with his thumbs. "What... does... this... mean?" He dropped his hands and read the engraving on the door for what felt like the hundredth time:

The combination right, you must do well, lest your soul be damned and burn in hell. First press one and then another. Get them wrong and be torn asunder.

"Not the wittiest verse I've ever read. Certainly not worthy of a place like this." He pushed one of the stones in again, then another, and then a third. "What gives? I tried every... conceivable... combination, and still nothing! What is it I'm not seeing?"

The trap sprung open again and he thrust his legs out to catch the edges of the floor. He gritted his teeth and punched the reset, landing back on the panel as it shut again.

"Ugh! What's the answer?" He took several steps back and fell against the shelves behind him, releasing a clicking sound as his shoulder touched one of the books. He gasped and looked at Sira. She leaped across the aisle and began rifling through the books near the place he stood. Every one of them she pulled made a clicking sound.

"No, wait," he said, spinning to catch her hand. "A wrong combination may spring another trap. Put them back. I think I know what I'm looking for."

"Well, get to it then," she said, pulling against his grip. "May I have my hand back now?"

"Yes, you may." He blushed, letting go. "The combination right, the combination right... ah, here it is! *The Combination of Right and Reason* by Gustav Langoe. A more boring treatise you'll never read. I used a copy of it to keep the window open nearby the desk back home." He pulled out the book and heard the clicking sound again, followed by a louder one from beyond the iron door. He peered inside the space it had occupied and saw a tiny spring-loaded switch at the back of the shelf, painted to match the wall. This was in addition to another switch below the book on the shelf itself, which was easier to see and matched the ones he saw in the gaps of the books Sira pulled out.

"The next one must be nearby, but where?" she said.

Gavek's gaze shot to the right. "There! *The Well of the Soul* by Annalynd Lamont." He grabbed the volume and another click sounded, releasing another lock in the door.

"Wait, how did you know to look there? How did you read the titles so fast?"

"I read pages at a time. It's a gift. As for where to look, I surmised 'the combination right' to be a literal pun, it's both the title of the first book and the direction to follow to the next, in this case, right."

"Brilliant. That means the next must be over here somewhere — and look, doesn't the spacing of the books from the first to the second match the metre of the verse?"

Clever. I really hadn't noticed. Gavek caught himself staring at her hair again.

"Gavek?"

"Uh, yes, good catch."

"So the next book must be the same distance right—"

"No, I don't think," he said, glancing over his shoulder.

"What?"

"Notice how new the inscription looks, and the mounting holes of the plaque. The plaque isn't as old as the door itself, meaning the combination lock was changed recently. Why then had the inscriber used archaic glyphs to write the message? Notice the one used to inscribe the 's' in 'lest', for example, how it's crossed and curled, looking much like an 'f' in today's letter forms?"

"Yes, then it's—"

"Done that way deliberately. So 'lest' indicates 'left'." Gavek scanned the shelf again.

"But how can it? Left following the same metre would take us back to the first book. It sounded like it released a lock, but the door remains closed, meaning there are others. I don't think the same switch triggers another lock." She reached between the books and flicked the switch with her finger.

"Correct, but read more of the verse, 'lest your soul be damned and burn in hell'. The second line is a clue also, meaning the first two books are on the same shelf in succession, 'first press one and then another'. But where is hell if not below us?"

"Aha. It's left on the next row down?"

"No, further than that." He stooped, reaching for the bottom shelf, and pulled out a book titled *The Soul's Inferno: Contemplations on the Many Levels of Damnation* by Dante Lattriaveri. The predicted click echoed, followed by a hissing sound and the clanking of metal. The iron door swung open and a cold breeze blew threw the opening. Inside it, a dim, flickering light glowed at the bottom of a descending passageway.

"You did it!" Sira leaped with her hands in the air. She embraced Gavek and kissed him, leaving the imprint of red lipstick on his cheek. She skipped across the aisle and scampered down the stone staircase beyond the iron door.

"Wait! The passage could be booby-trapped!" Gavek sprung after her, bounding off the tunnel walls as his feet skidded down the dusty stairs. He turned left through an open door at the bottom of the flight and slid into a vaulted, brick-lined chamber, stopping himself against a broad reading table at the centre of the room.

He looked up at the row of gas lamps connected to a long lead pipe running the length of the room. "Fascinating... the door's unlocking mechanism must also ignite these fixtures. Ingenious! But what sort of fuel is it?"

"Never mind the lights, look at the shelves, you idiot!" Sira stormed out of an open door at the far end of the chamber. "There's nothing here!"

Gavek scanned the room. Row upon row of diamond-shaped shelving designed to store scrolls stood empty around its perimeter.

Sira returned. "Nothing out there but a sewer teeming with rats, and this." She slammed a small marble bust onto the table and slapped down a handwritten card beside it.

"The playwright, Sorto."

"Never mind the bust. Read the card that was underneath it."

Gavek tilted it toward the light and read it aloud:

"My dear Solstrus, it will take a much cleverer man than you, and more than all the soldiers in the world to destroy or contain what I have found. God has picked a side in our quarrel and I assure you it isn't yours.

Sincerely,

Wardein"

"Ha! The old buzzard pulled a fast one on him! Brilliant." A shadow crossed the table. Pain exploded through his skull and his vision went black as he fell to the floor.

"Did you think I could miss if I really wanted to hit you?" Sira stepped over his limp body, marched over to the doorway, and shouted up the stairs, "Can I get some help down here?"

Two Alpinian guards descended the stairs.

"Take him to Solstrus. He may know something of value. Tell the others to come down here and start searching the sewers."

Khloe watched the Alpinian guards shove the last of the captive zealots into cages and drive them up the street toward Mount Tria. She leaped off the warehouse roof and scurried back down the stack of crates to the jetty. She rolled behind the drydock wall and peeked over it until the last soldier was out of sight. "It's clear, they're gone!"

Wrytha shook the water off her head and scrambled up a ladder inside the drydock. She rolled onto the jetty and collapsed. Was it Divine intervention? *Had to be.* Not because of the perfect way she cut the waterline after the four-storey drop. She'd pulled the same stunt off Reyad Falls plenty of times growing up. The water inside the drydock was the miracle. Had its operators drained it after the last high tide, or left a ship inside it, the fall would've killed her.

"Mother! Are you okay? That was—"

"Something I never want to go through again as long as I live." Wrytha wiped the blood from a cut on her forehead, sniffling. Her lips trembled. "Dear sweet Nicah... hotheaded Orin... what are we going to do about your brothers now, Khloe?" She rolled her head to the side and spotted a few pedestrians gathering at the corner across the street, pointing in their direction.

Wrytha pushed herself up. "Come on, let's get out of here." She zigzagged behind the Harbour Clock, heading east.

Khloe followed. "What happened in there?"

"I hid and waited for them. When they arrived I overheard them making plans to kill the Archprelate—"

"Are you kidding?"

"Like I've said before, Teighthra's a dangerous influence. Today she proved it. She and I got into it. The Alpinians surprised us. Orin fought the guards, Nicah was struck down, poor boy. I tried to save him, but... oh, and Rhodo... I don't know what became of Rhodo..."

"I can't believe how fast it all happened. I saw the others coming and tried to get their attention, but they were all so wrapped up in their conversations none of them could see or hear me over the noise of the harbour. They went inside and minutes later soldiers scurried out like rats from those buildings over there. Before I knew it you flew out of that window and—"

"It's okay, Khloe, you did your best, dear..." Wrytha stopped beside the tower, bracing herself against the wall.

"Seriously, Mom, are you—"

"I'm fine. Just a little dizzy. Did you see where the guards took your brothers? Were they okay?"

"Yes and no. Orin was shackled, struggling right up until they threw him inside a wagon. They carried Nicah. He didn't look good at all. They took everyone through that big gate, up the hill from the bridge." Khloe pointed.

Wrytha leaned against the corner of the clock tower and gazed past the rooftops of the Old Town toward the imposing fortress atop the cliffs of Palace Rock. *The big gate. Mount Tria. There's only one place political criminals go; they're taking my boys to the Palace dungeon!*

Continuing eastward, Wrytha took a deep breath, tightened her lips and straightened her back. She glanced down an alleyway and spotted one of the pedestrians she had seen before, standing next to a member of the Harbour Watch, pointing at her. Another watchman ran up behind the first and the two crossed the street, headed for the alleyway.

"Mother!"

"I see them. Come on!"

Wrytha grabbed Khloe's hand and dashed for one of the piers. They ducked behind some barrels and crept along the edge of the dock.

"There's got to be a ladder somewhere— there!" She pointed to a gap at the dock's edge. They hurried to it, slid down the ladder, and scrambled under the shelter of the pier.

Wrytha crouched at the base of one of the pylons. "I don't think they saw us. Tide's still out. We can rest here while we plot our next move—"

"Our next move? Listen to yourself, Mother. The people up there saw us — saw *you* fly through that window. Won't they go tell the Alpinians? They'll come after us for sure."

"We've got a little time, a little time is all—"

"You lost your bow and all your arrows, Mom—"

"I'll buy more, I—"

"With what, Mother? We slept in a stable last night and had half a pretzel each for breakfast!"

Wrytha glared at Khloe, tears gathering at the corners of her eyes. "What do you want from me, Khloe? Can you just shut up for a minute and let me think?"

Khloe dropped her jaw. Shedding a tear, she marched to another pylon and leaned against it. She bit her lip and scanned the harbour, listening to the waves lapping the shore. Another tear trickled down her cheek. Behind her, Wrytha sobbed. Khloe turned and watched her mother bury her face in her hands.

"I'm sorry, Khloe," said Wrytha between sobs. "You... you didn't deserve that. It's just, I—"

Khloe returned and crouched in front of her. "It's just that you've been carrying the weight of the world on your back for so long, you don't know how to ask for help, even when the Maker sends it right to you."

"That's not true."

"Okay, prove it then. Ask for help."

"From whom?"

"You *know* who—"

Wrytha rubbed her eyes then gazed out over the encroaching tide. "Saving us from river pirates is one thing, helping us with our current dilemma is another thing entirely. Besides, we don't even know where to find him. It's a big city. He could be anywhere."

"I know exactly where to find him, look." Khloe reached into her pouch and pulled out Gavek's map. "Gavek gave me this and said if I needed to find him, he'd be there, at the Library of Trianon. Find Gavek and we find Arghan." She stood up and pointed at the towering dome across from them, near the mouth of the Ambertyne River.

Wrytha took the map and squinted through her tears across the harbour.

"He'll help us," Khloe continued. "I know he will because he needs our help as much as we need his."

"Our help? Why?"

"He's here to find his missing daughter. He's desperate to find her."

"Sounds to me like he's got his own problems to worry about."

"Mother, his daughter is princess Cybella of Cortavia. You don't think if he finds her she can do something about Nicah and Orin's predicament?"

"What? Really?" She stood up, slapping the dirt off her backside. She took a few steps toward the shore and looked at the Library. "How?"

"I don't know how, I only know it's true."

"What do you mean you 'know it's true'?"

"Same way Grandma-ma knew to send you out of Koerska the night it was attacked years ago. The Maker showed me. He's intimately aware of everything that's happening, and despite how chaotic everything seems right now, He has a plan to see us through it. Give Him a chance. He'll show you."

Wrytha studied Khloe's face. *She can be stubborn, immature and downright childish sometimes, but when she gets like this... I see my own mother in her eyes.* She nodded. "Okay. Let's ask for help."

"What, really?" said Khloe, hopping beside Wrytha as she headed for the shoreline. Wrytha stopped at the water's edge and scanned the embankment. "We'll take a rowboat to avoid going back through the town. There's one we can borrow." They hastened to the vessel and pulled it into the water.

Barking interrupted the din of the waterway, followed by pattering, splashing footsteps coming from behind them.

"Rhodo!" Khloe jumped over the bow and landed in the shallow water on the other side just before Rhodo plowed into her, tail wagging.

Wrytha dropped to her knees and embraced their canine companion. "I thought I lost you, boy." She ran her hand across the dog's head, stopping when it whelped. "What's the matter?" She looked at her hand and saw it was streaked with blood. The dog's dark, wet fur had camouflaged a deep gash across its forehead. "Those monsters. Look what they did to you. You're going to need stitches."

Khloe nodded toward the quay. "Mom, look." The heads of two watchmen appeared above the stacks of cargo on top of one of the nearby docks.

"Okay, we'll fix him up later, we gotta go."

Asking Gavek to restrain his curiosity was like asking a bird not to fly. Arghan knew that. Did he really expect Gavek to resist exploring the Library when all he had to do was turn a doorknob? No, he only hoped to delay the inevitable. Gavek had what it took to avoid the likes of the Alpinian Guards were they to make an appearance, his escape from Precipice Peak proved that. But the wiles of a young vixen presented a singular threat Arghan wasn't sure Gavek could detect; he had only interacted with a handful of females his entire life, and seldom one his own age. Khloe had disarmed him easily enough, and she was sweet and innocent. The look on Renzek's face confirmed it: 'Sira' was anything but.

Arghan and Renzek snuck back to Picanes' mausoleum, following the same route he had taken that morning. He was about to unlock the door when a familiar voice called out to him.

"Arghan!"

Khloe Pan-Wrikor's long braid twirled as she leaped from the seawall stairs and ran onto the grand patio, trailing behind Rhodo, who pounced on Arghan's chest in a tail-wagging, tongue-slurping frenzy, knocking him to his knees.

"Who is this now?" asked Renzek, recoiling against the mausoleum, watching Arghan return Rhodo's jubilant greeting.

"An 'old' friend," said Arghan, smiling. "Don't tell me a tough guy like you is afraid of dogs, Renzek?"

Stiff against the wall, Renzek shook his head and swallowed.

Arghan chuckled.

Khloe approached him, the look in her eyes betraying her smile. "Hello, Arghan, I'm so happy we found you, we—"

"What's wrong, Khloe?"

Khloe looked at Rhodo. Arghan traced her gaze and spotted the gash on the dog's head. He examined his hands and saw it was blood, not seawater that wetted them. *Who or what did this?* He contemplated the answer until movement along the seawall caught his attention.

Wrytha stared at him from the stairs, wet and dishevelled. Arghan patted Khloe on the shoulder and walked past her, accelerating to where

Wrytha stood, slowing again as he approached and stopped in front of her.

Wrytha licked her lips and then bit them. She swept her fallen bangs to the side. Arghan closed the distance between them, reached behind Wrytha, and draped her braid back over her shoulder.

"Do you really believe in Jakav's promise?" she asked. "Or was that whole Cantorvarian monk identity just a cover story to protect yourself from the hangman?"

"I do believe. With all of my heart. That's why I'm here in Trianon, to preserve and defend the promise. I did not lie when I said I have lived the past 20 years as a Cantorvarian monk. Yes, it did afford me a hiding place. But it became much more than that. I grew to love my brothers and especially my late mentor, Ardwynn, who taught me everything I know about the faith. All monks take a new name when they commit to the order. Mine was Arthos. You are the first person outside a circle of close friends who I've ever told my real name, with the exception of those who figured it out for themselves, of course."

Wrytha took a few steps away and cast a questioning glance toward Khloe.

"As for this," he said, revealing the hilt of his Twin Talon, "I take no pleasure in the use of the sword. I wield it only to defend what I believe in and to protect those whom I love. I swear this to be true by my honour as both a monk and a knight, the Shepherd King as my witness."

Wrytha turned back and nodded, flexing the muscles of her jaw and biting her lip again as tears started to gather at the corners of her eyes.

He approached her and caressed the cut on her forehead with the back of his fingers. "What happened to you since we parted, Wrytha?"

Wrytha's voice cracked, "I found my sons. The situation was worse than I thought. A woman from my village, Teighthra Pan-Goron, who fashions herself some kind of zealot, seduced nearly all the young people in our tribe to follow her here on a fool's crusade. I found their hideout and overhead them planning to murder the Archprelate"

Solstrus. His campaign of hate was bound to garner such rage, eventually. "Did you have some kind of fight with her, or—"

She shook her head, flashing a smile while she pointed at her wound. "We argued, but no, this is the work of the Alpinians. They raided the place while I was still inside; attacked and arrested everyone there. I escaped by the skin of my teeth. Now my sons are locked away in the dungeon while the rest of Solstrus' minions scour the city looking for Khloe and me. I didn't know where else to turn, so I... I mean Khloe seems to think that you—" She gasped, staring at something past the southeast corner of the Library. "Maker help us, there comes some of them now!"

Arghan followed her gaze and spotted a squad of Alpinian Guards marching up the street toward the front entrance of the Library. He threw his cloak over her shoulder. "Come with me. I know a place to hide." He walked her to the mausoleum, where Khloe knelt, petting Rhodo and chatting with Renzek.

"Time to disappear," Arghan said. He nodded to Renzek. "Wrytha Pan-Deighgren meet my new friend Deighn Renzek, errand knight of his grace the Duke of Ostergaart."

Wrytha nodded. "Sir."

"My lady," said Renzek, bowing.

Arghan peeked past the mausoleum and then completed the unlocking sequence. The door sprung open, revealing the chamber inside.

Peering inside, Wrytha touched the tip of her braid. "You must know we're forbidden to desecrate the dead? We can't—"

"Fear not, this tomb's as empty as the Shepherd King's was after he rose from the dead on the Other World. But unlike His, this one never had a dead body in it to begin with." Arghan stepped inside and offered her his hand. Wrytha met a questioning glance from Khloe with a nod, then walked past the threshold and took Arghan's hand. Khloe followed with Rhodo at her heels. Renzek closed the door while the others fanned out around the room.

"It's best the two of you stay here while I go inside. I only came back to fetch Gavek. I'll be in and out before you can say 'metzvek[2].'" Arghan strode to the side of the room opposite the door.

---

2. Metzvek – A Tzyani word used during community footraces, roughly translated as "on your mark" as in "on your mark, get set, go!"

"Inside?" asked Wrytha, looking up at the shafts of light shining in through the vents at the top of the wall. "I thought we were inside?"

Arghan winked and activated the staircase hidden inside the sarcophagus.

Khloe skipped over and looked down the passage. "Cool! Does that go to the room where the secret collection is stored? Is Gavek inside, translating it?"

Arghan froze, blinking. He looked at Wrytha, then Khloe. "Not exactly, but how do you know that, about the collection I mean? Did Gavek tell you?"

Wrytha stepped between them, the expression on her face mirroring Arghan's. "Tell her what, exactly?" she said, glancing at both of them.

"He told me all about it on the riverboat," said Khloe, her eyes growing distant. "Then I had a vision of a young woman: blonde, dressed in a fine blue, satin gown studded with pearls. She was locked in a room. It was round; a tower, maybe? She's your daughter, isn't she? The princess Cybella?"

Renzek flashed his eyes. "Your daughter?"

Arghan nodded.

"What's she talking about, Arghan?" Wrytha said, taking his hand. "Is it true? Cybella is your daughter? What's this about a secret collection?"

Renzek walked the rim of the sarcophagus and folded his arms, looking over Khloe's shoulder.

Arghan addressed Wrytha, occasionally making eye contact with the others, "Several months ago, my old friend Wardein, master of the Royal Archives and trusted servant of the late King Eriohn I, followed a clue found by Gavek in a text stored in our monastery library. With it, he discovered another of the many hidden chambers below the Library of Trianon, one previously unknown to him. Inside it was multiple copies of a complete set of Tzyani Scriptures, stolen from your people by a Grand Prelate of ages past, rescued and hidden here by the Cantorvarians of the era. With Cybella's help, we've been smuggling them out one at a time; Gavek's been translating them. As you well know from how they've persecuted your people, Temple doctrine dictates that only members of the High Synod and the Grand Prelate himself may view and read the copies they hold in the Palace of Orbicon. But that's a lie, among the many other lies they've told throughout the centuries. The Scriptures reveal many truths they've concealed from the world in order to keep their grip on power, including the Name which is above every name, a Name the Shepherd King never hid from the Other World, and most certainly never chose to hide from this one."

Wrytha inhaled, glancing at Khloe. "I don't believe it…"

"I tried to tell you…" said the teen, arching an eyebrow.

Wrytha looked back at Arghan. "My people have kept our faith alive by oral tradition ever since the Great Persecution. Only we know His true Name. If you know it, tell it to me."

"Yeshua. The Shepherd King's name is Yeshua. Gavek says it means 'The Lord Saves'."

Wrytha tightened her grip on Arghan's hand, trembling. "When I was just a girl, my mother prophesied that a fallen knight, falsely accused just as our Saviour was, would someday expose the truth, and in so doing help deliver our people from exile. The villagers later scoffed at the memory of it, embittered by the horrors of Koerska. I discounted it myself for many years for the same reasons. But I always remembered something she told me privately. She said I would recognize him when he revealed the Saviour's Name."

Suddenly aware of his own heartbeat, Arghan stared at Wrytha, slack-jawed.

Shouts echoed through the soffit vents.

"I don't mean to interrupt," interjected Renzek, "but it appears the Alpinians have arrived and may already be inside."

Arghan listened for a moment. "Agreed. I'd recognize that snotty patrician accent anywhere." He kissed Wrytha's hand and stepped down the staircase. "Wait for me? You'll be safe here with Renzek while I drag Gavek out of there."

"No," she said, striking the air, fingers tensed. "I'm coming with you." She touched Renzek's arm. "Sir Renzek, can I trust you to guard Khloe for me?"

"Mother!" Khloe exclaimed.

Renzek clicked his heels. "With my own life if need be."

She nodded and held out her other hand. "Khloe, give me your bow and some arrows."

"Moth—"

"Now, dear."

Khloe complied, huffing. Wrytha threw the arrows into her quiver and followed Arghan down the stairs.

Arghan stood in the middle of Wardein's office. "Schlika, he's gone."

Wrytha emerged from the passage door and hastened to his side, looking down, distracted by the sound of shuffling papers beneath her feet. She nodded toward the door. "Inside?"

"Possibly." Arghan walked to the door and peeked through it, resting his hand on the hilt of his sword.

Wrytha skipped over a stack of books and crouched beside him. Boots clacked across the marble floor several rows down the massive corridor. A group of Alpinians Guards marched out from one of the aisles, dragging Gavek's limp body behind them. As they turned the corner, Gavek roused for a moment, eyes bulging when he noticed Arghan peering through the open door. He closed them again as a ginger-haired young woman in a blue and crimson robe pranced out from the aisle and turned to follow them.

"The little witch, she hooked him alright," muttered Arghan.

"What?" whispered Wrytha.

"Nothing. Come on," he said, beckoning her to follow.

Arghan and Wrytha crept down the corridor, watching the group take Gavek through the archway into the Library's central reading room until they disappeared around another corner. Beyond the threshold, an officer briefed another squad who stood in a circle.

Arghan made eye contact with Wrytha and held a finger to his lips. Together they crept further up the corridor and turned down the aisle the Alpinians had emerged from minutes before.

"Why don't we just get out of here; track the group taking Gavek?" whispered Wrytha. "There's fewer with him than there are here."

"True, but I want see whether they've found what they're looking for. That could change everything. I know where they're taking him; directly to Solstrus, no doubt."

Wrytha nodded and followed Arghan past the row of curved bookcases to the place where Gavek and Sira had unlocked the vault. She pointed. "Look, an open door between the shelves."

Arghan glanced back and nodded, then ran to the far side of the door and stood with his back to the shelves. She followed and stood on the nearer side of the opening.

Arghan peeked into the passage. "It's clear." He drew a dagger from a small sheath on his belt. "Stairwell's too narrow for a sword."

A few minutes later they entered the hidden chamber, stepping into the flickering gaslight. Voices murmured beyond the next room.

"It's empty," said Arghan. "Either they've seized the manuscripts or this wasn't where they were hidden."

"Neither, listen." Wrytha snatched Wardein's handwritten card off the table and read it to Arghan while he studied the marble bust of Sorto. She finished reading and tilted her head. "So what's our next move?"

"I think it's high time we had a talk with the man who wrote this."

CHAPTER THIRTEEN
Machinations

Wrytha dipped a chunk of bread in her stew, shouting over the raucous voices of the tavern crowd, "You're certain you can trust him? What's taking him so long?"

Arghan flagged a barmaid and tapped the edge of his stein. "Certain? No. But I'm confident he is who he says he is. As for Wardein, he's a cautious fellow. What Renzek said about him having to return to Wardein alone before he'll see us makes sense. It is pretty clever of Wardein to post lookouts to raise the alarm if even a trusted visitor arrives accompanied by another. Wish I'd thought of it."

Wrytha nodded and stared out the window.

Arghan squeezed her hand. "Hey, we will get your sons out of there. I promise."

Wrytha nodded and smiled, blushing as she looked into his eyes. "I wish I had your nerves. How can you be so calm? Aren't you worried about Gavek?"

"Concerned, yes. Worried? No. I can't explain it entirely. It's just... well, last night Gavek shared a few crucial details I never knew before about what happened in Koerska; things Khloe told him you said, that there never were any Zuelan forces there, for example. When I realized that I had been lied to I was able to see things in a different light. I doubt

I'll ever shake how sick I feel, having unknowingly caused the deaths of so many innocents, but the guilt was the heavy part. And now—"

"It's like a terrible weight has been lifted off you," Wrytha interjected. "So much so that other serious concerns feel lighter by comparison?"

"Yes, I suppose that's it. I didn't realize just how heavy a burden I was carrying until it was gone."

"I can relate. I blamed myself for Wrikor's disappearance. We argued bitterly the day he left for Pella. When winter passed and he failed to return, I thought my angry words had driven him away. But the next spring, boys from my village found his corpse deep in a crevice at the base of a scree slope, along with the remains of another person tied to a travois[1]. His diary revealed he'd come across a fallen traveller on his journey home. The man was too badly injured to move, so he stayed with him and nursed him back to health in a cabin in the mountains. He made his last entry that spring before setting off for the village, satisfied the man was well enough to travel. The rains were especially severe that year and its believed the two of them perished in a landslide. I regret how we left things between us, but knowing his disappearance wasn't my fault was a huge relief."

Arghan smiled, unaware he was touching her hand again until she glanced at it.

A jester on the stage in the corner of the room delivered another punchline and the inn's patrons erupted in laughter.

Arghan withdrew his hand and lifted his near-empty glass to his lips. "How's your head?"

"What?"

Arghan pointed at her forehead. "I said how's you're head?"

"Oh, Much better, thank you." She touched the bandage on her forehead and glanced a few aisles over at Khloe, who stood near the hearth, tossing morsels into Rhodo's mouth as the dog performed tricks. "The apothecary did a fine job. I was surprised he was willing to treat Rhodo too."

---

1. Travois – A frame slung between trailing poles and pulled by a dog or horse, used as a conveyance for goods, belongings or injured persons.

"Trianon is blessed to have some of the most learned physicians in all of Eskareon, thanks to the Library and the University. Neither campus is very fond of the Archprelate, and plenty of coin helps procure their silence, as well as their services."

Arghan stood when the barmaid reached their table. He held his hand over his glass. "Thank you, no more for me. Can you fetch some more stew and bread for my companions?"

"Where are you going?" asked Wrytha, pulling her hood a little further over her head.

"Ale's gone right through me. Back in a flash."

Arghan spun toward the side entrance at the same moment a man in a long, shaggy coat and knee-high boots stormed by the table, headed for the same place. Their bodies collided, each man recoiling.

"Watch where yer goin', ya big buffoon!" chided the man with a grizzly beard, through a set of jagged, yellow teeth. "Outta me way afore I cut yer nose off!" He stared at Arghan with one piercing blue eye, turning the one covered by a patch away.

"Forgive me, sir, my mistake." Arghan bowed and waved to the door.

"Ah, ya fairy. 'Fraid to face me? I'll cut ya ta fish bait faster than yer missus there cun twirl that braid 'o hers!" He drew a fencing rapier and pointed it at Arghan's chest.

Wrytha flashed her eyes and stuffed her braid inside her hood.

Arghan chuckled. "I advise against that, sir. You don't stand a chance, especially not with that toothpick." He pushed his cloak aside and rested his hand on the hilt of his Twin Talon.

The man hissed, and twirled the tip of his blade. "En garde!"

Arghan rolled his eyes, sighing. "Maybe we should get out of here, Wrytha? Shall we wait outside?" He extended his elbow.

She slid off the bench and took his arm. "Good idea."

They headed for the door.

"Oh, now I'm positive it's really you!" said the same voice, this time with much clearer syntax. The man threw off his hat. "You never were any fun at all, Arghan of Danniker, and still aren't now that you're an old stiff!"

Arghan and Wrytha stopped, exchanging smirks.

Arghan faced the man, grinning. "Wardein?"

"In the flesh," he said, yanking out a set of wooden teeth and twirling his hat as he bowed.

Wardein tossed his feathered hat onto a mannequin and plopped in front of a vanity inside one of the Continental Theatre's dressing rooms. Arghan brooded near the window, looking toward the public house where he and his companions had dined earlier.

Wardein ripped off his eye patch and hung it from a hook below a row of false noses, beards and other odd accessories. "So, what did you think of my performance?" He thrust his hands into a basin of soapy water on the table; scrubbed his face and dried it with a towel, leaving streaks of make-up on the cloth.

"I think it was a bit over the top."

"Ha! And how would you know? I'll wager you didn't even recognize my lines."

"Let me guess, they're from *The Three Swordsmen of Pereon?*"

"Of course, of course. Any fool could surmise that much. But to be exact, it was act two, scene two, third stanza. If guessing the play is the best you can do, I imagine it must have taken all day to find the last manuscript I sent you." He looked at Wrytha, waving his towel. "Can you believe it? It's like I never taught him anything."

Arghan rolled his eyes and ran his fingers across the scabs left on his face from the thorn bushes near the Oratory in Glenhava forest.

Wrytha gave Arghan a tinge of a smile.

Wardein looked in the mirror and teased his curly white hair into a pretentious mane. He waved his hands while he spoke to Wrytha, "That's the scene where the hero of the story, Dahn Torio defends the honour of his lady love from the uncouth brigandry of the pirate Rufus of Wyveren." Wardein leaned in and whispered, "Really, if he wasn't so daft he'd have seen I was trying to give him an opening to impress you." He faced the birdcage hanging next to the mirror. "Alas, there's no hope for him, is there, Pattie?"

"No hope," squawked the parrot.

Khloe giggled. "Whoa, a talking bird!"

Rhodo leaped from the floor beside the table and barked, pressing his forepaws against the wall below the cage.

Khloe tugged his leash. "Rhodo, no! Good bird. Pretty bird."

"Good bird, pretty bird," repeated the parrot.

Rhodo glanced at Khloe then sat, wagging his tail and moving his head in time with the swaying bird.

Arghan batted the shutters closed. "That's enough, Wardein. Cybella's missing. This woman's sons have both been arrested; Gavek also. So if you don't mind, please stop playing games and tell me everything you know."

"He has a point, old man," interjected Renzek, "I could have told him everything, but I bit my lip. You owe him an explanation."

"Don't 'old man' me, Deighn. You'd have nothing to report to your Duke, if it weren't for me."

"Really?" said Renzek, resting his hands on his hips. "You're sure it's not the other way around?"

"Don't flatter yourself. You're fit, but I tell you where to go and when."

"Enough!" Arghan crossed the room and grabbed Wardein's shoulders. "Quit messing around."

Wardein broke away, beating his chest, and waved at the various costumes hanging on the walls. "You think this is all fun and games for me, Arghan? It's a matter of life and death! I lost my map of the catacombs so using them is out of the question. Wearing a disguise is the only way I can travel without being arrested. The Alpinians are everywhere! You of all people know what that's like." He looked at Wrytha again. "Did he tell you he spent the better part of two decades pretending to be a monk to save his neck?"

"She's heard the story," said Arghan, glancing at Wrytha. "And I wasn't pretending; my conversion was real. Do you think I would've gotten mixed up in this trouble otherwise? I brought my own map of the catacombs, so that solves one problem. Khloe, if you're finished with it would you give it to him, please?"

"Oh, sure, here." Khloe handed Wardein the map.

"Splendid, I'll make copies for each of us." Wardein examined the page. "Citrus ink, I presume?"

Arghan nodded.

Wardein frowned. "Such vandalism! It looks like it's been torn from a copy of Ontolorio's—"

"Never mind that. Tell me about the manuscripts. Are they secure?"

"Oh, the scrolls!" Wardein touched Khloe's arm the way a grandfather might when telling a story. "Imagine what a chore they were for me, dressed up as a Library custodian, smuggling them all over here, one at a time, right under their noses. That's 66 volumes, and there's an average of five copies each in the collection. So much for Silla's opinion that I'm too old for all this! I may not be able to see more than ten paces in front of me but my wits are sharp as ever. Be sure to tell Silla that next time you see her. I presume you traveled back with her?"

Arghan sighed. "Silla's dead, Wardein."

The old professor froze. He inhaled through his teeth, his jaw quivering. He gave Wrytha a questioning glance before looking back at Arghan, searching. He stumbled back onto his stool and rubbed his thighs while he stared at the floor.

Wrytha approached Arghan. "You never mentioned this person before. You don't mean Silla Raventhern, the—"

"Queen Mother? Yes," replied Arghan. "She also happened to be Wardein's niece." Arghan looked at Wardein. "You introduced us, remember?"

Wardein closed his eyes, allowing his head to sink closer to his lap.

Arghan continued, "She and I married shortly before the assault on Koerska. When I was falsely convicted of war crimes because of what happened there, she lied to the Archprelate in order to have our marriage annulled, claiming we had never consummated our union when indeed we had, once, on our wedding night. She married King Eriohn I soon after that. Eight and a half months later the product of our one night together was born princess Cybella of Cortavia."

"I tried to warn Silla to stay out of this," interjected Wardein in a sorrowful tone. "I tried to stop her, but she just wouldn't listen. What happened? Was it Solstrus' men? Did they follow her to Lake Trieehd, or was it the Liester's?"

"The Liester's? No, it was neither," said Arghan. He went on to relate the chain of events that led to Silla's death. "Silla did mention her suspicions about this fellow called the Liester of Luthargrad. What do you two know about him? What makes you think men working for him may have killed Silla?"

Wardein looked at Renzek, his eyes now glassy and bloodshot. He faced the mirror and reached for a bottle of spirits sitting on the vanity. He popped its cork with his teeth and took a swig. "It's all my fault, Arghan," he said, shaking his head. "Cybion being sent to Lake Trieehd; Cybella's peril, the kingdom under threat from within and without; all my fault."

"Renzek told me what happened with your courier," said Arghan, taking the bottle off the table, "I'm not here to assign blame, Wardein, only to make things right. What do you mean the kingdom is under threat? What's this 'Liester' up to? Silla told me about his sudden arrival with Eriohn II shortly after Cybella's audience with the King, her subsequent departure, and her disappearance. Clearly, you both believe the two events are connected."

Wardein rubbed his eyes then nodded at the young knight via the mirror. "Renzek?"

"We do," answered the Ostergaardian. "Shortly after my arrival and contact with Wardein, he asked me to sneak aboard the Liester's vessel, the *Estria*, where I found evidence that suggested the princess had been on board."

Arghan gripped the hilt of his sword. "Evidence, what evidence?"

"I found her royal seal on the Liester's desk, the same one used to sign all her letters. Beside it was a comb belonging to her; I recognized it because it bore her royal monogram. His ship also showed signs of recent violence. I surmise he and his privateers intercepted and attacked the royal yacht en route, perhaps even sunk it before taking her prisoner."

"So she's here then, in Trianon, somewhere?"

"Quite likely," answered Wardein.

"The palace. Traitor's Tower?"

"Possibly, though I've also followed the Liester to the Archprelate's mansion on more than one occasion and seen both men talking to members of the Palace of Ministers. Solstrus may be the one who commissioned her capture and if so, may be holding her at his estate, scheming some sort of parliamentary coup."

"Well it seems the Liester would know where Cybella is in either case." Arghan tightened his belt and headed for the door. "Where do I find his ship?"

Wardein leaped from his chair and blocked the door. "Arghan don't! That's what he wants."

"What who wants? Explain."

"The man calling himself the Liester of Luthargrad."

"What do you mean 'calling himself'?"

"Cybella came to me before she departed; showed me a letter of ransom and blackmail sent to the king from the Liester, wherein he claimed to be holding the once-thought-dead prince hostage. Only I knew it wasn't the Liester who wrote it."

"How?"

"Several years ago, the Liester sent a signed copy of his memoirs to the Library, along with a personal note to me in thanks for a donation of books I made to the Maritime College of Luthargrad. My work with ancient texts over the years has made me something of a handwriting expert, having long ago learned to spot forgeries. The man who wrote the letter wasn't the same man who wrote the King."

"A secretary then, in either case, taking dictation?"

"No. Though wealthy and cultured, the Liester's a flamboyant buccaneer who revels in boasting of his exploits, including how he taught himself both to read and write. He'd never have dictated to another what he could write himself. He said as much when he lamented over the invention of the printing press in his letter to me, saying how much 'an affront to the art of script' he believed it was."

"Okay, you've convinced me. What's that got to do with anything?"

"It has to do with everything, let me assure you," said Wardein. "He demanded the King tell him where you were hiding and to supply him with a map of the hidden caches of loot the Erne Warders took from the Zuelans during the war. If the King failed to comply, he threatened to not only kill the prince but to lay waste to the entire country with the help of an army of Zuelan mercenaries under his command."

"He could do it, too, if his claim is true," said Renzek. "Nearly the whole Cortavian army is off supporting the Gothans in their war against the Lyracians because of a pledge the late King made to help them. Duke Weorthan's forces are leagues away, held up at the border of the Duchy because of treaty obligations with the Crown not to cross it. All of this would have changed had Cybella reached Straskost as planned and made an official plea for assistance."

Arghan's gaze darted between the two men. "As planned, what do you mean?"

"The dying King ignored the Liester's demands, not believing his son was alive," Wardein inserted. "He sent Cybella to ask the Duke for help. In order to throw disloyal courtiers off the scent, he commanded Cybella to sail north to Ropa, where she was to caravan cross country, first to warn you in Cairhn and then take you with her the rest of the way to Straskost. Little did he know the Liester was in league with the Archprelate, whose spies likely tipped him off about Cybella's mission."

Arghan turned and opened the door. "All the more reason to pay him a visit."

Wardein grabbed the hem of Arghan's cloak. "Arghan, don't you see, whoever he is, he knows everything about you. He wanted you to come. You dare not fall into his hands. He can't be allowed to know you're here."

"You underestimate me, Wardein. I have no intention of falling into his hands. He'd do well not to fall into mine. Let him know what he knows. He'll know the tip of my blade soon enough. Now get out of the way."

"I'm coming with you," said Renzek.

"No. Stay here. Protect Wardein and the others."

"Arghan," interrupted Wrytha, taking him by the arm, "I asked you for help, not protection. If you think confronting this man will lead you to Cybella and that she can secure my sons' freedom, I'm with you."

"Of course. Forgive me, I didn't mean to—"

"I know what you meant," she said, taking his hand. "Perhaps though it would be better if we waited 'till nightfall?"

"Yes it would, you're right," replied Arghan. "Good idea."

Khloe rolled her eyes, smirking.

"Professor Wardein," Wrytha continued, "is there someplace we might all sit and get to know each other better until then?"

Wardein looked at her, pop-eyed, then glanced at Arghan and Renzek. "Of course, right this way."

Two doormen bowed and opened the gilded doors of the Archprelate's mansion. Solstrus strutted inside and stopped at the centre of the vestibule, holding out his arms while his attendant removed his golden robe and cap.

Solstrus tossed him his sceptre. "Is he here?"

"On the terrace waiting for you, your eminence. Under the pavilion."

"Good, and you dismissed the harpist?"

"Yes, your eminence."

"Excellent. See to it we're not disturbed."

Solstrus traversed the vestibule and passed through the doors leading to the terrace while another pair of servants held them open. He descended the steps and approached a solitary figure who leaned against one of the columns of the pavilion, looking out over the harbour.

"Greetings 'your lordship'," said Solstrus, grinning. "I trust your presence here means the matter has been resolved satisfactorily?"

The man stroked his long grey beard. "Indeed it has." He removed his wide-brimmed, feathered hat and massaged his bald scalp. "Now, about the gold you promised me."

Solstrus' eyes flashed, drawn to the large gold earring in his visitor's left ear.

"You're really throwing yourself into the role of 'Liester of Luthargrad', aren't you, 'captain'?"

The man sneered and took off his leather gloves. "Well, somebody has to. The real Liester can't exactly exploit his fame from the bottom of the Cortavian Sea now can he? But don't change the subject." He waved his gloves in Solstrus' face. "I took care of the elder Eriohn for you, and the princess. Now I've proven Eriohn the younger will do whatever I tell him to do, and as I said, each little errand I send him on will cost you. So, about the gold, Solstrus?"

Solstrus shrugged his shoulders and stepped away. "I suppose he is much more cooperative than his father. But dealing with his troublesome sister is one thing. Reversing his father's policies is another. The Palace of Ministers are every bit as resistant as the first Eriohn was to conform to the Grand Prelate's will like the rest of Eskareon. They're adamant to maintain the Tzyani's refuge."

Solstrus' visitor grinned. "That will change once the younger is in power. With the bulk of the army wasting away in the Ugrarian Republic fighting the Lyracians, The Palace of Ministers are rapidly losing support. The people will demand the return of an absolute ruler. You'll see, and when it happens, we'll finally wipe out the Tzyani, once and for all. Imagine the Grand Prelate's pleasure when you make a triumphant entrance into the synod with the head of the last Tzyani heretic on a platter. Ostros will surely make you a Patriarch of the Temple for that. Who knows, with that kind of glory you may even have a shot at becoming Grand Prelate yourself someday. Sounds to me like you owe me a lot more than what I'm asking for."

Solstrus looked out of the corners of his eyes. "And to me, it sounds too good to be true, old friend. You're sure all you want out of this is the gold?"

"That's right."

"Fine. I'll arrange for half of it to be delivered to your ship."

The imposter's piercing blue eyes flashed; he reached for his cutlass.

"Half? Don't test me, old man."

Unshaken, Solstrus held up his hands and smirked, dropping his eyelids over his pupils. "Old man? You're no whelp yourself. Now put that away. There's still the matter of Danniker. You've yet to deliver him; I'm beginning to doubt he's alive."

The imposter left his cutlass sheathed. "He'll come to us, It's only a matter of time."

"Well, when he does you'll get the rest. Until then, half is all you're getting."

The two men studied each other's eyes, neither one willing to betray their secrets.

"Fine." The imposter put his hat back on, marched to the corner of the terrace, and disappeared down a staircase.

A moment later Captain Raipheniel came up it. "We've locked the prisoner in your wine cellar as ordered, your eminence. You may question him at your convenience."

"Splendid, captain. Tell the guards I'll be down after dinner."

Bathed in the amber glow of sunset, the *Estria* floated peacefully at its dock north of Trianon's Old Town district. Roughly seventy paces down the quay, two silhouettes topped a ladder along the southwest side of the King's Pier and crossed the deck, hidden by the shadow of the watchtower at the end of the dock.

Arghan peered around the corner of the tower. "This is perfect, follow me." Ducking to hide their ascent, he and Wrytha bounded up the stone staircase to a landing next to the door.

Wrytha whispered, "You're sure it's empty?"

"Royal yacht's out; there's nothing to guard. Step back." Arghan kicked the door in, sending the lock bouncing across the wooden floor inside.

They scurried to a loophole in the tower's hoarding and knelt below it.

Arghan took out his spyglass. "Excellent. Broad view of the whole dock, including the ship, and look, there's Renzek, watching it from the other side."

Wrytha grabbed the telescope and looked through it, resting her head against Arghan's cheek.

"You could take a shot from here if you had to, yes?" he said, side-eyed.

"With my eyes closed." She lowered the telescope and inhaled, suddenly realizing how close he was.

"Well, just in case, keep them... open." Arghan met her gaze. He glanced at her lips, leaned in, and kissed her. "Wrytha, I—"

"Shh," she said, holding a finger to his lips. "Later. Better get going." She straightened the knot on his cloak. "And be careful."

He winked, pulled his hood over his head, and headed for the exit. Several minutes later he joined a stream of pedestrians, reaching the corner of the dock where the *Estria* was moored. He leaned against a lamp post within view of the ship and slid into a seated position, withdrawing a copper flask from his satchel. He took a sip, wincing to pretend the brew was something stronger than apple cider, and surveyed the vessel.

Not a soul on her deck... must all be ashore, or below?

Arghan took another swig of cider and casually turned his gaze toward the inland side of the quay, freezing when he spotted a menacing figure walking toward the ship. Flanked by a rabble of mariners, the man bore the regalia of a captain of the high seas: a broad-brimmed hat sporting no less than two feathers; a long, black, buttoned overcoat, and a gold silk sash tied around the waist. A sailor's cutlass, adorned with the Arms of Luthargrad hung from his belt. But it was neither the man's appearance nor his entourage that chilled Arghan's veins. It was his swaggering gait; his piercing, sunken eyes, and then, his voice, a voice he'd heard many times before.

"Duty stations!" called the Liester, waving his hand at his crew. "I want you all looking alive for our guests. They'll be here any minute now." He removed his hat and dashed up the plank.

Duty stations. A privateer captain from Voldovia would have said 'man your posts'. 'Duty stations' was the order of a naval officer, particularly one accustomed to commanding elite marines. This was the order of an Erne Warder; this was the voice of Omhigaart Thurn.

Arghan took another sip from his flask and pretended to stumble to his feet. He zigzagged back toward the guard tower and disappeared behind it, then bolted for the ladder and descended it to the dinghy he and Wrytha had left at the water's edge. He grabbed the oars and rowed the small vessel toward the port side of the *Estria*, hugging the quay below the wooden docks to conceal his approach. He secured the boat to one of the trestles between the piers of the *Estria's* dock; took another rope and lassoed it to the quarter gallery railing and used it to scale the hull of the ship. He jumped onto a narrow balcony and knelt below an open window.

O mhigaart Thurn stood behind the elegant window of the *Estria's* captain's quarters, admiring the spectacular view from the ship's coveted anchorage next to The King's Pier, where the royal yacht once moored.

A fitting reward for the 'Liester'. He did 'rescue' the late king's lost heir, after all.

He picked up a telescope from a nearby table and spied through it to the southeast, where the mighty Palace of Trianon stood on Palace Rock, an ancient volcanic mound that towered above the crowded houses and maze-like streets of the city's original settlement. He traced its walls westward, following the line of its narrow drawbridge across the jagged gorge to the walled plateau of Mount Tria. The tops of opulent mansions and stately public buildings peeked above the battlements of its massive perimeter wall, bathed in the same dusky light that beamed onto the windowsill.

Young Eriohn has done his chores I see. Not a single defensive catapult remained pointed at the harbour. What could stop his plans now? Thurn glanced at the clock ticking next to him. He crossed the room and reclined in a plush leather chair, crossing his feet on top of the Liester's desk. He traced its polished mahogany surface, recollecting the time he'd strangled the Liester to death on top of it.

How could he forget that day six months before, when the pirates under his command had discovered the famous privateer run aground near the coast of Eskhasia? They took the stranded captain and his crew prisoner, intent on looting the ship and ransoming the nobleman to his kin in Voldovia, but the moment they presented him to Thurn he realized the Liester was worth more to him dead. Even Thurn's own men could see how much he and the stranded nobleman looked alike. It didn't take much convincing for them to go along with his plan to assume the Liester's identity and use it to slip back into the country that wanted him dead. There he would exploit his relationship with the Kaighan's[2] prized captive, the young shipwrecked prince of Cortavia, and exact his revenge on a world too small for him.

A knock came from the cabin door, rousing Thurn from his thoughts.

"Captain, the young king has arrived."

Ah, that must be him now, right on time. Just as he was told.

Thurn leaped to his feet, humming a foreign tune while he ascended the stairs. The young king hurried down the dock toward the *Estria*, followed by a group of Cortavian soldiers.

Eriohn stepped onto the gangplank and threw his cloak over his shoulder. "Permission to come aboard?"

"Of course your Majesty, be my guest." Thurn bowed and pointed toward the captain's quarters. He allowed Eriohn to step onto the deck but halted the guards halfway across the gangplank "You may leave. The king's life is safe with me and my crew, I assure you."

The soldiers exchanged questioning looks. Then the one closest to Thurn leaned past him, addressing Eriohn, "Your Majesty?"

"Do as he says. What do I need to fear from the man who saved my life?"

"He's not the one we fear, your Majesty."

Thurn smiled, crossing his arms. "We've got plenty of swords here,

---

2. Kaighan (pronounced Kai-gun) - the title given any number of major territorial warlords of the Zuelan Horde.

and men who know how to use them. Worry not, Sergeant at Arms."

Some of Thurn's men gathered at the edge of the deck, an assortment of ruffians from all over the known world. Nearly all of them folded their arms along with him and stared at the Cortavians. One of them, a bulky Trenegalian spoke with a booming voice, "Yeah, that's right. He's safer with us than your lot."

Eriohn nodded in agreement. The sergeant's face reddened as he backed down the gangplank and led the soldiers away.

"Thank you, I thought I'd never be rid of them," said Eriohn as he walked beside Thurn. "Have the Kaighan's men arrived yet?"

"Not yet, but I expect them by sundown," said Thurn, opening the door to the captain's quarters. "How goes it in the palace?"

Eriohn's countenance changed once he stepped inside the cabin. He furrowed his brow and tightened his jaw. His breathing sharpened and his lips settled somewhere between a pout and a sneer. "I've done all that you told me to do. Cybella's taken care of and I've arranged a meeting with the First Minister in the morning to discuss the legislation the Archprelate wants brought forward, but—"

"But...what?"

"It's just... all this pretending... this subterfuge... the Kaighan taught me Zuel[3] was the god of might, the god of force, the god who subdues all infidels with the sword. Does it really serve him to slink about like weaklings? Wouldn't it be better to cut them all down? You said yourself that when the streets run red with blood they'll finally know the error of their ways." Eriohn's face reddened with rage. He began pacing the floor, bouncing his gaze in various directions as if incensed by the taunting voices of unseen witnesses.

Thurn opened a cabinet behind his desk and pulled out a tall, crimson, spiral-shaped bottle. "There, there, lad, it appears you're losing perspective again. You needn't fret. Is your calling as the prophesied emissary of Zuel not simply to obey the voice of his prophets and take your place in history? You'll see his will unfold swiftly enough. Remember, it's

---

3. Zuel – the supposed deity worshipped by Earda's Eastern Hemisphere, especially by the Zuelan Horde from whom they derive their name.

your destiny to bring enlightenment to this wayward continent. That is the very reason I summoned you here tonight. You have a pivotal role to play in the destiny of nations, remember that. Here now, take the Elixir of Knowing to clear your head, and recite the oath before our visitors arrive."

Eriohn flashed his eyes. "Yes, my prophet." He opened his mouth and yanked the bottle from Thurn's hand, sending the lid bouncing across the desk. He cocked his head and guzzled its contents until the vessel was empty, then set it down again on the edge of Thurn's desk, almost missing the tabletop. His eyelids drooped and fluttered. "I am the emissary of Zuel, sent back to my land to subdue it in his name; I devote my life to his service."

Thurn snatched both bottle and lid and reconnected them before shoving them back inside the cabinet.

"That's it," said Thurn, pulling out a chair while he looked out the window. "Here now, take a seat. I see our visitors have arrived."

Two silhouettes passed by the window. Heavy footsteps creaked across the deck. The cabin door rattled when an unseen hand pounded it with something heavy and hard.

Thurn struck a confident pose, standing with his hip against the desk, the fingers of his right hand outstretched on its surface. "Enter."

Two menacing figures, each wearing long, thick, studded coats and fur-brimmed, pointed helmets came and stood inside the cabin, curling their noses as they each surveyed the room, their right hands resting on the hilts of their broad, curved swords.

The one with a black pointed beard locked eyes with Thurn. "You are the one my master calls 'Encani[4]', I presume?"

"Kapash[5]," answered Thurn, bowing. "My true name is Omhigaart Thurn. But here you must call me 'Liester'. This is Cortavia's new king, Eriohn II."

Eriohn nodded, then rested his head back against the chair.

Thurn's visitors looked at each other with eyebrows raised, then back

---
4. Encani – Zuelan dialect meaning "indentured one"
5. Kapash – Zuelan dialect meaning an assertive, assuring "yes".

at him.

"I know, it all gets confusing sometimes, even for me. And you are?"

"I am called T'kuk. This is Zeng," he said, after which the younger man nodded. "The Kaighan said you were his best trickster. Do you have my master's gold?"

"Yes, there it is." Thurn pointed to a large chest near the wall.

T'kuk strode to it and opened the lid, exposing a gleaming pile of gold coins, bars, brooches, and tableware. "Impressive, but this cannot be all of it," he said with his sharp, guttural accent. "We'll come back when you're prepared to honour your agreement with the Kaighan." He wrapped his fingers around the hilt of his sword and kicked the chest closed, then beckoned Zeng to grab hold of one of its handles.

Thurn rushed to his visitors, holding out his palms. "Honourable warriors, please, no need for haste. All is well. Allow me to explain. "

T'kuk tilted his head, resting his foot on top of the chest. "We're listening."

Thurn was no novice when it came to Zuelan culture. He could tell the men didn't care whether the treasure fell short of what he had promised the Kaighan. It was all part of the dance. They were waiting to hear what was in it for them.

"Gentlemen, if you please, come near the desk. I've something to show you." Thurn reached into a cabinet and retrieved a large parchment which he unrolled onto the table, revealing a detailed map of Cortavia. He withdrew two massive, blue carbuncles from his lapel and dropped them on specific points of the map.

"These are yours to take. Would you believe there are thousands more like these buried in troves all across this country, seized by the Erne Warders from the late Kaighan during the last war? I'm one of two men left alive who know where they all are, though the secret of how to unlock them was entrusted to my counterpart. His delay is why I failed to extort the rest of your Kaighan's payment; but I shall soon rectify this deficiency if you'll honour me by accepting these gifts and by taking this deposit back top your master. I've never failed to deliver what he wants, the young king's efforts prove that. The city's defenses are down and nearly two-thirds of the Cortavian army is off helping the Gothans fight Lyrance. So, what say you?"

T'kuk smiled and grabbed one of the gems. "We shall return to our Kaighan and do as you say, Encani. He has great faith in you. Do not disappoint him. His fleet stands ready, massed in Metacartha harbour."

"Splendid. He need only wait a few more days for my signal fire and then his invasion can begin. Hail Zuel!"

"Hail Zuel!" they echoed as they carried the chest out the door.

Arghan topped the ladder behind the watchtower and dashed to the stairs.

Wrytha jumped the last few steps and landed in front of him. " I saw everything. What happened? I thought you were going to confront him? What did you hear at that window that made you row back here with such haste?"

"Bad news, for all of us." Arghan pulled her toward the ladder. "Come on, we've got to get back to the theatre and come up with a plan."

"A plan? Wait, Arghan—"

Arghan held her elbows. "Did you see that strutting peacock, the one in black, barking out all the orders?"

"Yes, that's the Liester, I presume."

"Oh, he'd like everyone to believe that, and from the looks of things they do." Arghan stepped down the ladder. "I was warned that he exerts an unnatural influence over the prince, now I've seen it in action; he's bending his will with some kind of potion."

"Who is he then?" she asked, following.

Arghan jumped into the dinghy and untied the line. "A dead man. Quite possibly the most ruthless and dangerous one in all of Eskareon."

"Dead man? You're not making any sense."

"He's an Erne Warder, Omhigaart Thurn, former Warder-General and once my commanding officer, the man who ordered the attack on Koerska. I saw him hanged for it with my own eyes, at least I thought I did."

Wrytha looked toward the *Estria* and scowled. "I saw it too."

Arghan set down the oars. "You did?"

"King Eriohn invited a delegation of Tzyani survivors to witness the event. When a community is decimated as much as ours was, new leaders are selected from the young. I was one of them. How do you suppose he managed to escape?"

"By never being under the rope to begin with, I suppose. A disguise, a double, maybe? He's pretending to be someone else now, maybe that's what he did then too." Arghan picked up the oars and started rowing.

"Hey," cried a voice from above, "forget something?" Deighn Renzek shimmied down the ladder and jumped into the boat. "I take it you spotted the Zuelans?"

"Saw and heard," replied Arghan. "Thurn's plotting another invasion with them. Here, you take the oars. My shoulder needs a rest."

"Thurn? Invasion? What, who—"

"The Liester's not who he appears to be," said Wrytha, still glaring at the *Estria*.

"We've got to get back to Wardein," said Arghan, taking a seat next to Wrytha. "I'll explain the rest on the way. Suffice it to say I'm positive Cybella's locked up in the Palace. It's crucial we get her and the Tzyani prisoners out of Trianon as soon as possible."

H as it really been thirty days? Cybella pushed aside her breakfast tray and ran her fingers across the rough sandstone of the windowsill inside her cell, counting the grooves she had etched in it each day of her captivity.

Thirty days in the tower without a single word from a living soul.

Thirty days of the wind.

The gulls.

The rattle of that same silver tray as it slipped onto the shelf through the slot in the door each time she was given her rations for the day.

She sighed and pounded the tray with her fists, flipping over the fine plates and silverware on top of it. She shoved the tray out of the window and watched it twirl through the air until it ricocheted off the cliff below and disappeared into the sea.

Sliding to her knees, she braced herself against the cold edge of the windowsill and dropped her chin on top of her wrists, gazing past her long golden bangs across the Strait of Cortavia. The view was the only thing that made a stay in the Tower bearable. The circular room's massive arched window had no bars. Were a prisoner to jump from this height they'd be doing the palace jailer a favour, saving them the trouble of escorting them to where they'd be tried, hanged, or axed. But she wouldn't jump; she'd get out another way, the opportunity simply hadn't arisen yet.

Though the distant coastline of Eskhasia remained shrouded, the morning sun had just banished the last of the fog on the Cortavian side of the channel, when a ship made a turn toward the harbour between the mainland and the Isle of Woe, passing two others as they sailed out. In the distance above its masts, the lighthouse atop the Isle's jagged rocks, once the graveyard of countless wrecks, came into view and cast a long shadow across the waves, pointing at her like the outstretched finger of an accuser.

She marveled at how aptly named that craggy rock was, now that she realized it had nothing to do with shipwrecks or ghostly legends. It was the last part of the world a prisoner locked inside the Traitor's Tower would ever see.

But at least she had a view. Aribond, Renir, Bortrandt, Caeli, Rosa; what had become of her friends? Were all her royal attendants under suspicion too, locked away and questioned elsewhere, all because of her?

She closed her eyes and folded her hands. "Father of Lights, hear my plea. Will you forget me here? Shepherd King, rush to my aid. Your lamb is caught in a thicket; wolves surround me. Nonetheless, if it's Your will that I am to die here, grant at least the manuscripts are saved, and dear old Wardein escapes Solstrus' inquisitors, and my father, my..."

Had her last letter ever reached him? More importantly, had the scroll?

She pushed off the windowsill and rose to her feet. At the same moment, footsteps sounded across the bridge beyond the door. Keys rattled; six locks clinked in rapid succession. The heavy door creaked open, revealing two lines of soldiers on either side of the bridge. Two violet-cloaked Alpinian guardsmen strode inside, taking positions left and right of the doorway.

A wiry figure of average height, wearing a fine suit of green, white and gold crossed over the span, entered the room, swaggering between them to stand at the centre of the spiral motif on the floor. "Hello sister, are you ready to talk?"

Cybella thrust back her shoulders. "Eriohn." She marched to within reach of him and struck his face.

A guard drew his gladius.

Eriohn brushed it aside. "Put that away. She'll get what's coming to her soon enough."

Cybella leaned in and pointed. "I'll get what's coming to *me* soon enough? How dare you keep me locked up in here all this time! I demand an audience with the Lords of the High Court. If you have a charge against me, lay it publicly, so that I will be tried and proven guilty according to Cortavian law. Otherwise, elder prince or not, you've no right to—"

"I have every right!" He held out his right hand and made a fist, displaying the Crown Ring. "I'm the rightful heir; I'll be crowned king, you'll see!"

Cybella scowled, looking at the green sapphire encased in Eriohn's golden band. "You have no right to wear that. That violates every legal procedure of succession. So what if you're alive after all, and the eldest? None of that matters after father's will was read. Cortavian law—"

"Cortavian law doesn't defend traitors, or heretics and it certainly doesn't extend the rights of succession to half-bloods by writs of forgery! Bring her in!" Eriohn beckoned his soldiers. Two men dragged a woman inside and threw her on the floor in front of Cybella.

Cybella burst into tears and fell beside her. "Caeli?"

Her friend's once beautiful brown curls were all but gone, shorn to a bleeding and bruised scalp.

"What have you done to her, you monster?"

Eriohn waved again. "Bring it in."

One of the soldiers who had carried Caeli marched to the door and received an ornate wooden box from one of the others. He trod back to where they stood.

Caeli lifted her face toward Cybella, revealing her swollen, purple eyelids. "I'm so sorry, my lady," she stammered, "I held out as best I could, but when they threatened my nephew, sweet little Jorast, I just, I... forgive me, my lady." She fell onto Cybella's breasts, sobbing. Cybella cradled her, looking up at Eriohn, nostrils flaring.

"What happened to you on that God-forsaken coast, Eriohn? What happened to the brother who sang me songs, pulled my hair, chasing me around the Tree of Life in the palace garden?"

Eriohn stared down at her over an upturned nose. "I grew up, that's what. I'm no brother of yours and you know it!" He reached for the box and turned the tiny key inside the lock, opened the lid and grabbed the papers inside it.

"Now let's clarify what we're talking about, shall we?" He opened one of the letters and read it aloud, nodding toward one of the Alpinian guards, " 'My dearest daughter Cybella, imagine what joy I felt the day your letter arrived. Will you forgive me for all these years not even knowing you were mine?' " Eriohn held the parchment in front of Cybella's face. "See here where it is signed? Do you deny that is the hand of the convicted criminal, Arghan of Danniker? Do you deny you were conceived by his seed, and not by my father Eriohn's?"

Cybella said nothing, dropping her gaze to the floor.

"And what about... this one?" He shuffled the papers and unfolded another. " 'My dear lady Cybella, how often I have thought of our all too brief dinner atop my terrace overlooking Kinnessarat[6]. Weren't the twin moons ever so enchanting that evening? Though I must confess, not

---

6. Kinnessarat – The mountain lake that forms the source of the Onya river in the Duchy of Ostergaart, a semi-autonomous region of Cortavian ever since the war of 410.

quite as enchanting as your lovely eyes, bluer and purer than a mountain spring. How soon may we meet again, that I may profess my love to you in person, without leagues of country and political complexities forming a wall between us?'"

Eriohn held out the second letter. "Is this not signed by Weorthan, Duke of Ostergaart? Is he not content to hold half the country? Is his father's reward for winning the war not enough for him that he conspires with you to sit on my father's throne as well?"

"That's not true! You wouldn't even have a throne were it not for the Ostergaardians and their champions the Erne Warders! Weorthan is a kind and honourable ruler, more honourable than—"

Eriohn threw the letter at Cybella. "Silence!"

The parchment fluttered to the floor while he picked another.

He shook his head. "Ah, here is the most damning one of all. 'Fear not, my future queen. I have every reason to believe the texts I've found prove your rights and the true nature of the faith we share. Though not even I can decipher them, there is one who can, a student of my old comrade and friend at the monastery of Cairhn. Leave them to me. Soon we will learn their secrets. May I be so bold as to say how delighted I am to see my prayers answered, that a young woman of your insight and gifts should finally recognize what a treasure the Library is, and should stand poised to take the throne. You're called not only to heal our weary land, but to champion a great reformation that will change the world. Your humble servant, Wardein.' "

Cybella tightened her eyelids and hugged Caeli. She felt another parchment fall on top of her hair.

"The High Lords have already heard the evidence against you and found you wanting. Their verdict will be read in the Palace of Ministers on the Feast of Alpinia, this time next week, from where you will be paraded through the streets to Traitor's Circle on Merchants Isle and hanged along with all the other enemies of the state, including your friends."

"No, don't do this Eriohn. Listen to the Spirit. Solstrus has twisted your mind with his hate. Father taught us—"

"*My* father was a fool deceived by a seductress. Yours is a butcher who slaughtered innocent women and children."

"He saved your life when you were still a babe!"

"Enough of this, take her away." Eriohn pointed to Caeli. Two soldiers came and yanked her from Cybella's grasp. Cybella struggled with one of them, only to be pushed across the room and thrust down upon her modest bed. The Cortavian watchman straddled her chest, holding her wrists against the bedposts.

"That's good, restrain her while we depart." Eriohn stooped to retrieve Cybella's letters then stormed out the door, followed by the Alpinian guards.

The native Cortavian soldier loosened his grip on Cybella's wrists the moment the others crossed the threshold. He leaned closer and whispered, "Forgive my aggressiveness, your highness. A few of us are not with him, though we pretend so. Long live Eriohn the First." The soldier released her, holding a finger to his lips, and scurried out the door.

CHAPTER FOURTEEN
Audacity

Ammonia fumes flooded Gavek's nostrils. He wrinkled his nose and opened his eyes, blinking in the flickering light.

He gasped, shielding himself as a burning torch swung close to his face.

"Where—"

A voice boomed from beyond the flame, "The Archprelate will speak to you now."

The torchlight receded into the dark. A door opened, revealing a violet-tinged silhouette. The figure walked away, leaving the door ajar.

Where am I? Gavek rubbed a swollen welt at the back of his skull, wincing when his fingers touched it. He pushed himself off of the crude, straw-lined cot he was lying on, stumbled to the door and leaned against the frame. He squinted, looking around the chamber.

Vaulted stone ceiling. Oil lamps on every column. Cool, humid air. Racks along every wall; some in the middle of the room; the blurry image of sparkling glass reflecting from each of them. A wine cellar?

Gavek lumbered to the middle of the chamber and peered down the centre aisle. Daylight from above bathed a steep staircase at the end of the room. Two guards descended it and stood on either side of the base of the stairs. A long shadow moved down the steps.

Conical cap. Layers of cloth. Gleaming jewels. The Archprelate! Think fast, Gavek. What did Arghan say to do if this happened?

"Your eminence," Gavek said, kneeling, "I come on an urgent mission from your nephew, Abbot Cybion. Did you catch the culprit who attacked me? I have news to report."

Solstrus cocked his head and held out a ringed hand. Gavek took it and kissed his jewelled finger.

"Is that so? Why don't I recognize you if you're one of Cybion's men? Who are you?"

"I am Gavek, of the monastery of Cairhn, your eminence. I'm their librarian. Several months ago, one of the brothers alerted me that contraband manuscripts had been delivered to the monastery from Trianon without my knowledge. I reported this to the Abbot and he ordered me to cooperate in his investigation to root out the culprits. Our efforts flushed out a deceiver in our midst, the war criminal called Arghan of Danniker—"

Solstrus stirred at the mention of the name. "Danniker, you say? Go on."

"Yes, your eminence. As I was about to say, we discovered this man had been hiding among us under an assumed identity for many years. Cybion attempted to capture him but the heretic escaped. He ordered his Alpinian troops to chase him, thinking he headed for the port of Ostergaart on the shores of Lake Vedehed. Cybion sent me here to report this to you and to ask for reinforcements to help with their pursuit. If you don't believe me, check my belongings. Cybion gave me a letter that will prove this to you."

"It's true," said one of the guards, approaching with Gavek's satchel. He took a parchment out of it and handed it to Solstrus. "Here, look."

Solstrus squinted, skimming the page. "Hmm. This appears to be Cybion's own hand and seal." He rubbed his whiskers. "So, brother Gavek of Cairhn, why then did you not come straight to me and report this when you arrived in the city? What were you doing milling about the Library?"

Gavek bowed his head. "My vanity got the better of me, I must confess, your eminence. Please grant me absolution."

"What are you babbling about?"

"I fancy myself a bit of a puzzle breaker. I deduced that Wardein, Master of the Library of Trianon, was the person who sent the manuscripts. I thought that if I could expose him before coming to see you I would get credit for his capture. That's why I helped one of his students open Wardein's secret vault; I felt if I won her trust she would lead me to him. Imagine my chagrin when the red-headed wench knocked me out!"

Solstrus chuckled, clapping his hands. "Ha! Quite ambitious, aren't you? And clever indeed, as Sira herself has attested."

"What? She has? I thought she was working for Wardein? Did you apprehend her too? Force her to confess?"

Solstrus chucked again, wiping the corner of an eye. "Oh, Gavek of Cairhn, you are an amusing fellow indeed. Come. We'll reward your efforts soon enough." Solstrus took Gavek's hand and led him up the stairs.

"You will? Really?"

Solstrus put his arm over Gavek's shoulder. "Sira says you did a pretty fine job deciphering the locking mechanism on that door. Think you could put your keen wits to work finding where that cunning weasel Wardein moved his little trove of secrets?"

"Yes your eminence. I know I can!"

"Splendid. Please forgive my lack of hospitality. One cannot be too careful these days with all the subversives running about. I commend you for your initiative. We'll make sure you're cleaned up and fed and put to work. How does that sound?"

"Thank you, your eminence," said Gavek as they exited the cellar, shuddering at the ingratiating tone of his own words. *That felt a little too easy.* Would his ruse buy him the time he needed to escape or was Solstrus up to something?

Deighn Renzek threw his gloves on the table. "Rescue them all at once? You can't be serious?" Candelabra flames danced in his wake as he paced the floor of the catacomb.

Applause and laughter echoed down through the street grate outside the Continental Theatre, interrupting the gentle dripping coming from outside the chamber.

"It's our only chance," said Arghan, standing behind a table in the middle the room. He unrolled a map of the Palace of Trianon. "An attack is imminent. Audacity is the only option we've got."

Wardein reclined in his chair. "I know it sounds dangerous, as all rescue attempts are. But I'm curious, Sir Renzek, what troubles you most about the idea?"

"Everything," he said, waving. "For starters, we don't know for sure Cybella's in the Traitor's Tower; but if she is, that's a very tough spot to get her out of even if we had a team of knights at our disposal, which we don't. I don't want her getting killed in the attempt. Do you, Danniker?"

Arghan glared, leaning over the table. "What kind of question is that? Of course I don't. This is my own daughter we're talking about, remember? I have very good reasons to believe she's there and I'm aware of the obstacles. This will be a stealth mission, not a castle assault. We're not looking to provoke a fight. No doubt it'll be a challenge, but my knowledge of the tunnels below the Palace give us an advantage. Once inside, I'll create a ruckus to divert the guards, giving you an opening to make your move."

Renzek folded his arms. "How can you be certain they'll take the bait, though?"

"Look, if there's one thing I'm sure of, its how much Solstrus hates Tzyani, not to mention how arrogant the Alpinians are. When the Archprelate and his men get wind that their prized captive 'heretics' have escaped they'll devote whatever forces they can to their pursuit. That will leave only the Cortavians to deal with."

"Go through it again please, Arghan," said Wrytha, resting her elbows on the map. "I trust you, but if we're going to use my kin as bait I want to be absolutely sure of every detail."

"Certainly." He waved over the table. "Renzek, take heed." Arghan pointed at a spot on the map. "Wrytha and I will enter the palace dungeon here, via the tunnels Eriohn the elder showed me when I escaped years ago. These lead directly to the detention block. While Wrytha frees her people and leads them out, I will rouse the Alpinians. When you see them leaving their posts, you must act swiftly. It's a short walk from the courtyard well to the curtain wall stairs. Those will take you directly to the catwalk to the Traitor's Tower. Afterward, there ought to be no more than four guards between you and the cell door—"

"This is where the Alpinian uniform I had our wardrobe department make for you will help the most," inserted Wardein, winking. "Just be sure to act the part, and don't forget to have Cybella put on that nun's habit I'm sending with you before you leave the tower."

Renzek rolled his eyes. "I'd really sooner cut them all down than play charades."

"You're a talented swordsman, I'll give you that," said Arghan. "But subterfuge is preferable to engagement. As you pointed out, Cybella's life is at stake and you'll still be outnumbered. I'll be there to support you once I'm sure Wrytha's group is safely away."

"That's the part that concerns me, Arghan," said Wrytha, pointing at the map. "If you want the Alpinians to chase us, what's to keep them from actually catching us? How can you be sure they won't find the tunnel entrance leading out of the dungeon or perhaps already know it exists? After all, it has been twenty years since you used it."

"If the tunnel's been discovered they'll have sealed it off and we'll be blocked anyway. Renzek won't get the signal and we'll abort. But I'm quite certain they haven't found it—"

"And the reason for that is... ?" interrupted Renzek, raising his eyebrows.

"That tunnel is known only by Cortavian kings. Prion VI had it constructed after he was restored to the throne. He was held prisoner there during the Nobles' Rebellion of 212 and was determined that should he ever be deposed and imprisoned again he'd have a means of escape. As for the Alpinians finding it after Wrytha's exit, I certainly hope they do. In fact, I'm counting on it."

"I don't understand," said Wrytha, pushing away from the table. "If it's so secret how can you be sure they'll find it?"

"Because you're going to leave the door wide open behind you."
Renzek returned to the table. "What?"

"Listen," sung Wardein, "I sense a surprise coming."

"The passage has two exterior entrances, but only one exit out of the dungeon, on the lowest level of the prison, a place reserved for enemies of the state; where I was once held and where Wrytha's kin will be. But here," he said, pointing at another place on the map, "here it diverges into five branches. Only one of them, this one, affords safe passage, the others are laden with deadly traps. The king's passage contains a door that can be barred from behind in the event of an escape. When the Alpinians pursue, they'll split their forces, dooming the majority and confining the rest. Satisfied?"

"Sounds ideal to me," Wardein said, squinting. "If it was good enough for a king it ought to do nicely, I should think. What a delightful caper it shall be. Makes me wish I was younger."

Arghan touched Wrytha's arm. "I know I'm asking a lot of you. Are you with me?"

Wrytha nodded and smiled, caressing his hand.

"Renzek?"

Renzek sighed. "It better work, for your sake. Now, about the most important detail of all: our final escape. Duke Weorthan ordered me to hire a ship and keep it on standby in case Cybella needed an escape. Wardein made the arrangements days ago; said he hired a captain of your mutual acquaintance, a fellow named 'Boskan' as I recall?"

Arghan's eyes sparkled. "Boskan? Excellent! I didn't realize that old sock was still on the foot. That's good news if ever I heard it. You spoke to him recently I trust, Wardein?"

"Yes, indeed. Boskan's schooner will anchor offshore here, near the curtain wall's southernmost tower, where the drainage canal empties into the sea. He'll have a launch waiting to pick you up on the beach. From there you and Cybella will sail for Ropa."

"And the two of you trust this man enough to carry the princess and I to safety?" said Renzek, giving them each a questioning glance.

Wardein answered, "Arghan's old chum Boskan made a mint running arms and supplies for the Erne Warders during the war. He was furious when that all dried up after the Temple eradicated the Order. He's been working as a smuggler ever since. So he's no friend of the Temple or the state."

"Not to mention I saved his life once," Arghan continued, "and will pay him enough for this job to retire a wealthy man. Boskan may be a scoundrel, but he's a loyal one. I trust him."

"It's settled then," said Wardein, clapping his hands. "Best get some rest if you're heading out at midnight."

Renzek snatched his gloves from the table and marched out of the room.

"A bit touchy, isn't he?" said Wardein.

"I think he assumed he'd be calling the shots," said Arghan, rolling up the map. "Now that there's real stakes involved I think he's even less impressed that I'm making all the decisions. I can't blame him. I was the same way at his age."

"He was worse," said Wardein, winking at Wrytha as he left the room. "It would seem years living as a monk served your spirit well. It's so good to see you, old friend, despite all that's happened. I'm off to my bunk."

Arghan smiled and bowed. He rolled up the map and turned toward the door to see Wrytha waiting for him.

"I think it's safe to go outside now that the sun is down," she said, holding out her hand. "Join me for a walk?"

"I just want to fetch my cloak, Arghan." Wrytha skipped inside the Master Dramatist's study and snatched her garment from a hook near the door. She returned a moment later and peered across the room. "Hey, everything okay?"

Khloe sat on a rug next to Rhodo in front of a fireplace, resting her chin on her knees.

"Khloe? Did you hear me?" Wrytha crossed the room, knelt by her daughter's side and stroked her hair. "Khlo', what's wrong?"

Khloe sniffled, petting Rhodo's head. "I'm worried. About everything."

"I know things look pretty grim, but you're usually the optimist. What about all the things you've foreseen? Weren't you the one telling me to have faith a few hours ago? You heard Arghan say the Name. If he's the one the seers foretold, what's there to be worried about?"

"That's just it, mom. He is the one. I should have lots of reasons to believe everything's going to be okay, but with everything going on now, suddenly nothing make any sense. I have no idea what's gonna happen between now and the end, or what's it going to cost to get there."

"You're thinking too much. You just need to get some rest—"

"No!" Khloe batted Wrytha's hand away.

"You had another vision, didn't you?"

"A dream this time, actually. I took a nap on that couch over there while the rest of you were downstairs. I still don't know why you left me out of that, by the way—"

"We discussed this, the less you—"

"I know, I know, the less I know the better. That's easy for you to say. You get to do something while I sit here and wait. Do you have any idea how frustrating that is? You don't even know what other people are thinking half the time. I do, and it's killing me feeling I can't do anything about what's going on."

"I'm sorry, Khloe. I can only imagine what it's like for you. You get your prophetic gifts from your grandmother. They're not something I've ever experienced. I know you're frustrated, but it's better than being locked in a dungeon right now like your brothers. I can't put you at risk helping to save them. Be patient. Please tell me, what did you dream?"

"Promise me you'll tell him; warn him."

"Warn who?"

"Arghan. He's in danger."

Harbour buoys chimed in the distance while waves lapped the piers below Palace Bridge. Two figures emerged from a secret door, hidden behind a crevice in the abutment.

"I wish I'd known this was here a few hours ago," said Wrytha, stepping into the moonlight on the shore of the Ambertyne river.

"And I wish I'd been there to help you," said Arghan, closing the hatch.

Wrytha led him down the ladder to the beach. They walked along the base of the seawall in the narrowing gap between it and the incoming tide.

They began to speak almost simultaneously, laughing at themselves afterwards.

"You first," said Arghan, bowing.

"I wanted to talk to you about what happened on the *Flussotter*..."

"I was hoping you would. I—"

"Wait, let me finish. I'm sorry I shunned you after the pirates' attack. You've been nothing but good to me since the moment we met. I simply couldn't reconcile what I felt in my heart with what I saw with my eyes. I could have given you the benefit of the doubt; a chance to explain yourself. It's just... I've never felt so—"

"Vulnerable?"

"Yes."

Arghan stopped and faced her. "Wrytha, I came to Trianon to rescue my daughter, but since we met I haven't been able to stop thinking about you. I think I fell in love with you the minute you pulled me up that ladder in Sigoe. How's that for vulnerable? To me you're a rose growing in a forest ravaged by fire; a ray of sunshine through clouds of black. I swear to you, I'll give my own life if that's what it takes to save Orin and Nicah, because they're your sons and mean so much to you."

Wrytha gasped, tears moistening her thick black eyelashes. She grabbed his hand and kissed it. "That's what I was afraid of; what I wanted to talk to you about. I have feelings for you too, but—"

"But?"

"Whatever is going on between us, I think it's best if we put it aside and focus on the task at hand. I'm worried for my sons. Terrified, actually. I'm not sure I can handle being worried about you too. I beg you, trade places with Renzek. Send him with me to the dungeon, draw us a map or something, we'll manage, we—"

Arghan leaned close to her. "How could I do that? I won't leave you. We'll get through this together. What's wrong? What's causing you to say such things?"

"Something Khloe said to me on the way out of the theatre. She had a dream; saw you shackled in irons, a prisoner again."

Arghan took a step back, glancing at the surf hitting his boots. "No. I'll never be a prisoner again."

"But—"

"Hear me out. I've been set free from the only prison that ever truly held me, a prison of the heart. I've forgiven myself and Yeshua has forgiven me too. His love has healed me. So has yours. What could happen now that would deprive me of that freedom? I must do what I must do. The chance to right my wrongs compels me; fills me with hope. I've escaped chains before and I can do it again. Just watch me."

Wrytha pulled him closer. She held his cheeks and kissed him, unconscious of the fact they now stood ankle-deep in the river.

"Careful, you'll get soaked," he said, twirling her back onto the pebbled shore.

"Oh, I'm already in over my head," she said, kissing him again. "We make quite a pair, don't we? Dare we be so indulgent under the circumstances, Arghan?"

"I think we both deserve to be, if only for a moment. Why let the darkness take anything more from us than it already has?" He took off Ardwynn's cross and placed it around her neck. "If we survive this I promise you I'll spend the rest of my days making your life a happy one, if you'll have me."

Wrytha embraced him. "You know I will."

Orin Pan-Wrikor wheezed through blood crusted nostrils as a black hood was thrust over his head. Vice-like hands seized his arms and dragged him out of his cell.

"You're coming with us," snarled a voice. "The Archprelate wants a word with you."

The young Tzyani twisted and slammed his shoulder into one of the heavy bodies beside him. His captor's grip loosened. Pain exploded below his solar plexus. He collapsed, vomiting inside his shroud.

"Try that again and we'll kill you on the spot," screamed the same voice. "Believe me, there's no shortage of us who would like an excuse to cut your limbs off and let you bleed. Now behave yourself!"

The same hands lifted him from the ground, dragged him across the floor and up a flight of stairs. The air chilled. A door creaked and the hands lifted him from the ground and hurled him into a waiting carriage.

"Archprelate's estate," said the commanding voice, followed by a thud. Horseshoes clacked and the vehicle lurched into motion. Around a bend and down a hill, a third of an hour, or perhaps a half, and then it stopped...

Solstrus certainly seemed eager to ingratiate himself with Gavek. Why else had he fed him like a king then quartered him here for the night? But Gavek wasn't falling for it. He wasn't about to fall asleep either. He bided his time, analyzing the intricate fresco painted on the ceiling above his bed until the clock on mount Tria Cathedral chimed twelve.

Gavek waited for the guard outside his room to pass the door, then grabbed the pillows behind his back and stuffed them under the covers, arranging them in a line the same length as his own body. He slipped out of bed, tiptoed across the floor and leaned against the wall beside the window. He watched the guard pass again, unlatched the pane and stepped onto the ledge outside.

The layout of the place had been a matter of simple deduction, based on all the books he'd read about Threician renaissance architecture. So far, Creitane's treatise on the subject had proven invaluable. As predicted, the ledge overlooked the portico and ran the length of the rear facade. The basic layout of the second floor would be a near duplicate of the first, which he'd studied after being escorted to his room that morning. Seeing Solstrus' penchant for his view of the city, evidenced by the well maintained garden pavilion where he'd dined three times that day, the semi-circular protuberance and collonade some sixty paces to the east of him most likely was the balcony outside the Archprelate's private suite.

He scrambled up a lattice beside his window and carefully traversed the roof. He was about to descend another onto the porch when he noticed the back gates of the estate swing open and a carriage drive in. It stopped in front of the entrance of the lower courtyard's carriage house and wine cellar. Alpinian guards jumped out of the wagon, dragging a pair of struggling captives inside the building. *Fresh prisoners for Solstrus' expanding inquisition?* With no time to ponder, Gavek finished his descent and dropped several paces behind a guard who stood along the collonade, looking out over the back estate.

They obviously expect break-ins from without, not within.

Gavek touched the handle of one of the double doors that led inside. It squeaked, causing him to leap behind a nearby planter box full of shrubs. He peered past it to see the guard still looking out over the railing.

Is he deaf? Just in case he isn't...

Gavek grabbed a rock from inside the planter and threw it past the guard. It landed with a rattle somewhere in the courtyard below.

The guard leaned over the rail and called out to another, "Hey, did you hear that?"

Gavek didn't wait for the response. He jumped up, turned the latch and skipped inside the darkened room. As his eyes adjusted, the outline of a large, leather chair and desk emerged, and beyond it bookshelves flanked a closed door. To the left was another door, closed, and to the right another one hung open, through which shone an amber glow from the adjacent room.

Solstrus' study!

Gavek wasted no time admiring the decor. He slipped behind the desk and scoured the papers across its surface.

Too dark. Can't read any of them!

Footsteps approached from the source of the light, which grew brighter as the footsteps grew louder. Gavek dove under the desk as the light grew brighter still, followed by the sound of voices.

"Don't believe me? It would seem your feminine wiles succeeded where my persuasive arguments fell short, my dear."

Solstrus. Who could mistake his reptilian slither?

"Well done, I must say, in spite of all the help our new king and his handler failed to offer, I might add. Bravo. Bravo indeed. Would you care to read it?"

"I would. Show it to me."

Gavek rubbed the welt on the back of his head. *Sira! You little witch...* Something dropped on top of the table.

Candelabra?

Solstrus slid into his chair and thrust his bare legs and feet into the space below the desk. Gavek recoiled, hugging the inside front panel, grateful that the tabletop shadowed Solstrus below the waist.

Solstrus bumped the side of the desk with his knee, releasing a spring-loaded door. He pulled something out of it; from the sound, it had to be parchment. Lighter steps circled the desk, followed by the same flapping sound.

"Ha, ha! He did it! The First Minister signed it," said Sira.

"Must have been right after you bedded him, I should think."

Gavek shuddered.

"Anything for a righteous cause, your eminence," she said, giggling. "Now we need only secure the evidence you seek and all your problems will be solved."

"About that. You've excelled in every task I've given you except that one. I want you to head out early. Go back to the Library. Take that monk Gavek with you and—"

"What? No! You can't possibly trust him?"

"Of course I don't trust him, my dear. But it's no longer a matter of trust but of expediency. He accomplished in less than an hour what your team failed to do in weeks. I suspect he's lying about something, but it doesn't matter. What matters is he wants to help us. So let him. He may well be able to track down Wardein in time for the execution. If and when he does, he'll have served his purpose. Have the guards kill him then and only then if that is what you want. But we need Wardein. If we can capture him and force him to confess their misdeeds publicly, that'll be cause enough to take Cybella's head. Then, once we've recovered the manuscripts and proven her father's complicity, the legitimacy of the entire house of Eriohn will fall, and with it, that young whelp's claim to the throne. Then, with the Palace of Ministers' cooperation, the kingdom will finally be mine to do with as I see fit."

"Starting with a purge of those filthy Tzyani?"

"Exactly."

She leaped into his lap. Gavek shut his eyes at the sight of her bare legs, and wretched at the sound of smacking lips.

"Mm, no. It's too chilly here," said Solstrus. "Let's put this important paper away and carry on next door, shall we?"

"As you wish, your eminence," she replied, giggling again.

The light faded away along with their footsteps. A door slammed and the room went dark, save for the moonlight coming in from the double doors and windows.

Take Cybella's head? Have the guards kill him? We'll see about that!

Gavek pressed the desk panel to release it. He snatched the parchment, stuffed it inside his robe, and shut the panel again. He scampered out from under the desk and paused at the doors to the balcony, glancing back toward Solstrus' bedchamber door, grimacing at the sounds coming from behind it. He pulled the latch and tiptoed past the planter, headed back to the lattice. He glanced at where the guard had been and froze when he realized he had moved. Still scanning the grounds, the guard approached from the portico, directly in Gavek's path. Gavek jumped behind the corner of the porch seconds before the guard looked ahead and passed it. He let out his breath, turned the corner, and shimmied up the lattice.

Moments later he slipped back into his bedchamber and slid onto the floor below the window. He yanked out the parchment and read it in the moonlight, clutching his robe and, at times, beating his chest. There it was in black and white: government support for a royal coup and plans for genocide. A Tzyani genocide.

CHAPTER FIFTEEN
Infiltration

Arghan landed in shallow surf at the edge of the Narrows and held out his arms to catch Wrytha by the waist. He extended his hand toward the cave opening. "Feel that?"

"A breeze, coming from inside."

"Must still be open. Come on. We'll wait 'till we're deeper inside to light the torches."

They zigzagged through a narrow passageway, descending under Palace Rock.

Arghan stopped after a turn. "Okay, we're hidden now. Will you do the honours?"

"Clockwise, right?" said Wrytha.

"Yes."

Wrytha twisted Ardwynn's cross and struck the magnesium match hidden inside it. She lit both torches and then extinguished the match by reassembling the pieces. She smiled, holding the ornament up to her eyes. "Hmm. Romantic and practical."

Arghan winked. They rounded another turn and entered a cavern.

Arghan raised his torch, surveying the shadowy, rustling forms among the dripping stalactites overhead. "Might want to pull your hood up," he said, donning his own.

She covered her head. "Why?"

"Bats."

Wrytha shuddered. They continued through the chamber, treading up an incline until the terrain leveled again in front of five wooden doors built into the rock.

"That door is the safe route," said Arghan, pointing, "the others have traps, but they cross each other on the way and at the opposite end, the exit is the second door from the left." Arghan opened it, releasing a gust of air.

"That's quite a breeze," said Wrytha, watching their torch flames dance.

"Yes. It is. More that I expected." He gripped the handle of his sword and whispered, "Look," pointing at a light shining from an opening up the tunnel.

"Have we reached the dungeon?"

"No. The entrance isn't for another few hundred paces." He pointed to a pair of empty sconces mounted to the wall. "Let's leave our torches here and follow the wall by hand."

They crept forward through the darkness and approached the glow.

Wrytha tugged Arghan's cloak. "Wait, do you hear that?"

"Yes. Voices."

"I can't understand what they're saying, but they sound—"

"I can understand them." Arghan unsheathed his sword and peered past the corner.

A hole in the side of the tunnel revealed another large cavern lit by a series of oil lamps hanging from the walls. A team of barefoot men clad in tattered garb arranged a pile of barrels around one of the cave's natural columns while another stacked more of them along the walls, all under the watchful eyes of seven Zuelan warriors who paced behind them. Toward the back of the chamber, a third team of slaves hoisted another barrel through a hole in the ground.

"What are they doing?" said Wrytha, drawing an arrow from her quiver.

"Nothing good."

"Can we sneak past them?"

"Yes, but if they're doing what I think they're doing, we can't afford to. Watch my back?"

Arghan bolted through the opening in the wall and landed in the midst of the group, severing the sword-hand of the Zuelan warrior beside him with a slash.

A labourer dropped the barrel he was carrying and screamed, "Kalar![1] Kalar!" then stumbled past the others and jumped down the hole in the floor. The rest followed.

The remaining Zuelans drew their swords and lunged toward Arghan.

He grabbed one of the lamps from the wall and shook it over the pile of barrels, screaming, "Kaped! Kurs kal orsk delach lah, nomed! Nomed! Ur commish vosk ondrevar!"

One Zuelan held up his hand and clenched his fist, signaling the others, then shouted at Arghan, sneering. The others spat on the ground and dropped their swords before scrambling down the ladder. Arghan ran to the edge of the shaft and watched the last of them jump off it into a chamber below. He jumped to the other side of the hole and kicked one of the barrels into it, then another and another, sending them crashing down the shaft until the entire opening was blocked.

He scrambled back up the slope to the tunnel opening, meeting Wrytha before she could slide down to meet him. "We've got to hurry. No telling how much time we have until they come back."

She followed Arghan back into the tunnel. "Arghan, wait a second. What were they doing? What did you say to them to make them run off like that?"

Arghan raced ahead. "During the war, Gothan spies reported that Zuelan alchemists had discovered an ancient recipe for a deadly substance while traveling through one of their conquered lands and were trying to recreate it: a black powder capable of great destructive force when ignited. I saw a crude form of it once, on a ship we raided. Whatever is in those barrels smells exactly like it. I think they were planning

---

1. Kalar – Zuelan word for a demon of the nether world.

to use it to undermine the Palace foundation before their attack."

Her eyes bulged. "So you threatened to ignite it, then and there?"

"Precisely."

They skidded around a corner. Jagged rock gave way to smooth stone and they slid, splashing into a pool of water at the bottom of a sharp incline, dousing their torches.

"Whoa! You didn't tell me we'd have to swim part of the way," said Wrytha, shaking the wet from her hair, "is the rest of the passage flooded, I wonder?" She sniffed her fingers, then tasted them. "It's seawater."

Arghan backed against the wall. "I was afraid of this. We're below sea level. Shoreline erosion must have bored the channel and flooded it, either that or the Zuelan intrusions cut a swath to the shore."

"How far is it?"

Arghan didn't answer. His breathing deepened and accelerated.

"Hey, what's wrong?" She groped the dark to find him.

He took a couple more deep breaths, then spoke, gasping between his words, "It's... it's the underground... the dark... it's like... it's like..."

"The well. When you saved Orin and Nicah?"

"Yes." He swallowed. "Just give me a—"

"How far is it, Arghan?"

"Only... fifty paces or so on foot..."

Arghan felt Wrytha's breath flow over his beard, followed by the sweet taste of raspberries as she pressed her lips against his.

"Moh avid lieachtah, Arghaneh," she whispered.

He founds her braid with his fingers. "What's that mean?"

"It means 'I am with you, Arghan'." She squeezed his hand. "Let me take the lead. Come."

Wrytha tugged his hand and dove into the water. Arghan snorted, recalling the Warder's oath he recited for young Reigh that day in the Vineyard. He dove in after her, kicking through the dark, counting the seconds with each stroke. A minute passed, then another as he rounded the deepest part of the tunnel. His lungs started to burn. Dizziness swirled between his temples. How far was it now? He widened his eyelids, probing the darkness. His pulse quickened when a blurry glow ignited above the waterline. He breached the surface, splashing and coughing as Wrytha grabbed his hand.

"I've got you," she said, pulling him onto a platform behind a stone door. "Looks like we're here."

Arghan, pushed himself to his feet, teetering into Wrytha's arms. "That's... the last time I ever want to do that. Just... give me a minute..."

Voices came through the door. Wrytha glanced at Arghan. He nodded and crouched behind her as she pushed it open.

Wrytha Pan-Deighgren watched the helmeted figure who stood under a flickering torch near the end of the passageway. Arghan leaped from the shadows and hooked his arm around the man's throat, leveraging it against his other hand until the guard fell limp. He waved Wrytha onward, pointing down a divergent corridor while he proceeded up another.

Moments later Wrytha approached a large cell. Several figures huddled on the floor inside it.

She whispered to those nearest, "Dannika? Korin? Is that you?"

"Clan Mother," exclaimed the teenage girl. "We thought you were dead. Everyone, it's Wrytha! She's—"

"Shh!" said Wrytha, holding a finger to her lips. She surveyed the others' faces. "Where's Teighthra, Orin, and Nicah?"

The crowd parted, revealing a young woman cradling Nicah's head in her lap.

"Auria?" said Wrytha, gasping. She grimaced when she spotted Nicah's bloodied face.

"He's been like this since they dragged us in here," said the young woman. "We did our best to bandage him up. I don't know what else to do for him."

"Where are Teighthra and Orin?"

"The Alpinians stormed in a while ago," answered one of the boys. "Took them away with them."

Wrytha's nostrils flared.

Arghan scampered to her side, dangling a set of iron keys in front of her. "I've taken out as many guards as I could without attracting suspicion. But we don't have much time."

Wrytha grabbed the keys and opened the lock. She bolted inside and knelt in front of her son.

"Nicah? It's mother, can you hear me?"

"M-mother? I-I can't... I can't see..."

Wrytha stroked his hair and pressed her forehead against his. "It's okay, Ni, we're getting you out of here."

Arghan glanced down the corridor and then dashed in after her. "What's the matter?"

"My son, Nicah. The Alpinians hit him pretty hard. What are we going to do? We could carry him out, but he's barely breathing. He'll never make it through the flooded passage."

Arghan rested his hand on her shoulder and knelt beside her. He scanned the room while the others gathered around. Fresh young faces stared back at him — mostly teens, none older than their early twenties, all expressing various levels of dread.

"Your other son, is he here?" he asked Wrytha.

"No," said the girl named Dannika. "The Alpinians took him. Teighthra too."

"How long ago?"

"I can't tell. A couple of hours, maybe?"

Arghan inhaled through his nostrils and exchanged looks with Wrytha.

"I'll take Nicah with me," he said. "You lead the others back through the tunnel. Meet me in the cave of five doors."

"What are you going to do?" Wrytha said, standing, motioning for the others to follow while Arghan carried Nicah through the door.

"Just trust me. There's no time to explain. Everyone be as quiet as you can."

Wrytha nodded. She kissed Nicah on the forehead and looked Arghan in the eyes before running off with the others.

Arghan's only hope of escape now hinged on a twenty-year-old memory. He'd memorized the layout of the Palace dungeon when he was a prisoner. The tunnels remained. Would the rest be the same?

He propped Nicah against a nearby wall. "Rest here a minute while I scout ahead. I'll be back for you."

"Ah... o-okay... w-who are—?"

Arghan took a few steps and peered around the corner toward the staircase he believed led to the level above. As he recalled, the subterranean complex consisted of three floors. It appeared political prisoners were still kept on the deepest level; that's where they had found Wrytha's clan folk. The cells on the rest of the floor were deserted.

While Wrytha had made contact with the others, he'd gone ahead and disabled all the guards on the lowest level. But he expected a patrol to appear on the staircase at any moment. As he recalled they typically traveled in pairs, checking each level as they went. With any sign of trouble, one man would retreat to alert the others while his partner engaged the threat. He'd have to take them out two at a time if he had any hope of escaping undetected.

He leaned against the cold stone wall and watched the stairs, praying the others would succeed. He glanced back at Nicah, marking the youth's sorry state.

Kid must have been unconscious for hours. Blindness, brought on by the trauma to his head? If only Pattron were here to look at him.

An iron latch rattled. Hinges squeaked. Arghan looked back at the staircase. Two guards appeared, as predicted. When they neared the foot of the staircase he crouched like a leopard, ready to pounce.

They can't be allowed to free their comrades.

Arghan sprung from the corner, grabbed their helmets, and slammed their heads against the floor.

There was no choice now but to carry on. With the patrol immobilized, their absence would soon be noticed by the posted guards on the floors above. He grabbed a set of keys from the belt of one of the fallen men and used it to open an adjacent cell and dragged the men inside. He left Nicah where he was and bolted up the stairs, stopping just short of the doorway to peer outside. A pair of guards stood near an intersection ahead. He held two fingers to his lips and released a piercing whistle. "Help! A prisoner escaped! Get the others!"

A row of dirty faces suddenly pressed between the bars, leering at the door, while the guards sprung into action. One ran to alert the others while his partner charged toward the doorway. Arghan jumped behind the opening, tripping him as he passed and sending him hurling down the stairs. The guard struck his head on the floor below and collapsed, unconscious. At the same moment, reinforcements arrived. Arghan repeated the manoeuvre on the next man; he too fell unconscious from the fall. By now, all the prisoners cheered and hollered at every move Arghan made. The remaining guards skidded short of the doorway. Arghan screamed and lunged toward them. He tackled the first and struck the man on the side of the neck, dropping him cold. The other three drew their swords. Arghan kicked the next man's wrist, knocking his weapon to the floor. Another lunged with his sword. Arghan ducked and punched the man in the armpit, releasing his weapon seconds after it found its mark in his comrade's head. Arghan threw him over his shoulder, knocking him breathless. He stepped over the choking man. The last remaining guard tossed his sword to the side and dropped to his knees.

"Give me your restraints," Arghan shouted.

Within minutes, Arghan had all the surviving guards cuffed and thrown inside the empty cell on the bottom level, along with the dead.

Militiamen? Cortavian regulars or Alpinian Guards would have put up a better fight.

He raced past a row of cells and the groping, outstretched hands that thrust out from each set of bars, ignoring the pleas of the prisoner as they clawed at the hem of his cloak. He jumped back down the stairs to retrieve Nicah and carried him onto the middle floor, stopping at the threshold of the next staircase. Turning back, he threw the prison keys down the corridor, bouncing them across the floor until they slid behind the bars of the last cell on the left. He glimpsed a pair of withered hands snatch them before he bounded up the stairs.

Staring back into the dark tunnel, Wrytha stopped inside the chamber of five doors and pushed the last of the escaping youths past her. Arghan had said to wait for him. How long would he be? How would he possibly make it out?

Eyes darting, she cocked her head, listening for any sound coming from the tunnel.

Nothing.

She tightened her quiver strap and reached over it to count her arrows. She was about to step back inside the tunnel when the hinges of another door moaned like the strings of an out-of-tune cello.

"Arghan!" she cried, smiling. She sprung to his side and pulled Nicah's arm over her shoulder.

"Can you manage him the rest of the way?" he said, already moving back into the tunnel.

"I think so, but, hey, wait! How did you get here? I thought you said those tunnels were full of traps?"

"They are," he said, picking a few darts out of his cloak and throwing them to the cavern floor. "But they're easier to avoid when you know where they are and how they work."

"But there's only one exit from the dungeon, right after that the flooded passage, how—"

"One of the other tunnels passes under the well outside the royal stables. The guards were so busy rounding up the prisoners I freed that they didn't notice me going the other way, deeper inside the castle, down the well, and back to you."

"The prisoners you freed?"

"I'll explain later. I've got to get going," he said, stepping back through the doorway.

"Wait, Arghan, you can't go back in now," she said, eyes bulging, "won't the Alpinians be swarming the castle?"

"Maybe. Maybe not. I was surprised not to see any in the dungeon. Regardless, I don't see any other option. This may be my only chance to rescue Cybella. Renzek's likely already inside. If we don't make a play right now, they'll realize what's going on, tighten security or possibly even move her, or worse. Then there's the matter of locating Orin and your kinswoman."

Wrytha exhaled and wiped her forehead with her wrist, staring at the floor. "Okay."

He skipped back to where she stood and kissed her forehead. She grabbed the back of his neck, pulled him close, and kissed him on the mouth.

"Don't wait for me," he said, gasping as they finally released. He jumped inside the tunnel and started to run. His voice echoed back from the cave, "Lead the others to safety, 'Clan Mother'. You've got a clear path back to Wardein's lair. I'll meet you there when I'm done."

Wrytha glanced at her son's face, then glared at the tunnel entrance, her eyelids narrowing. "Be careful, Arghan."

"I'll do my best," he said as he disappeared into the darkness.

Deighn Renzek slipped through a doorway and stood outside the easternmost tower of the Palace fortress. So far, Arghan's directions had proven reliable; he stood less than forty paces from his goal. He inhaled the moist sea breeze that blew up from the cliffs and peered through the thickening fog toward the two gas lamps that marked the location of the bridge that connected the curtain wall to Traitor's Tower. It was time to play his ruse. He adjusted his violet cloak and cleared his throat as he approached the corner, only to halt as soon as he turned it. He glanced from side to side, then spun around to scan battlements.

No guards stood at the corners below the lamps and the others were nowhere in sight. Had Arghan's diversion really drawn that many troops away?

He scowled and drew his sword. He crept across the bridge and approached the door.

"Your Royal Highness, are you in there?" he spoke between the narrow bars of a window. "Hello?"

He reached for the latch. As he touched it the door swung inward, carried by the swirling breeze. He pushed it further and stepped inside.

"Cybella?"

A wave of clomping footfalls came from behind. Renzek's eyes flashed. Roughly forty soldiers poured in from either side of the curtain wall and hustled down the bridge. He hurried to the window and looked out at the cliffs and crashing surf below.

No escape.

He threw off his cloak and whipped his sword around his wrist seconds before Cortavian troops invaded the room.

CHAPTER SIXTEEN
Trapped

Arghan emerged from the dark shaft at the centre of the Palace courtyard, gulping the fresh night air. He peered over the damp wall, blinking, and surveyed the perimeter. Though night still shrouded the Palace facade, it shone by comparison to the tunnel's interior, bathed in moonlight and the glow from sconces along its three tiers of galleries. Arghan marked the absence of lanterns carried by patrolling watchmen and cocked his head toward the ruckus coming from the drawbridge.

Confident that the palace guards were busy containing the escapees at the gates, he heaved himself over the wall, halting when agonized cries echoed from the shaft below.

Some of the guards must have searched the dungeon and found the escape tunnel. Now they're making history; the first and only victims of traps laid centuries ago.

He looked East, then North. The straightest route to the Traitor's Tower was through the royal greenhouse and up the aqueduct to the twin towers of the Palace reservoir, but it normally got sealed during alert protocols, as did the exit to the Palace gardens, where Renzek had made his entrance. He gambled on a riskier route; one that would remain open while others were not: North. He raced toward the main entrance of the Palace, stopped out of range of the torchlight, and drew his sword.

"Halt! Who goes there?" cried a voice from one of the alcoves beside the doors.

"We need help," Arghan shouted. "The mob pushed the captain over the drawbridge."

Carrying a torch, the watchman sprung from the alcove and rushed toward him. "What is this?" the man said once his light hit Arghan's figure.

Arghan sidestepped the sentry, grabbed his wrist, and clubbed the side of his neck with the pommel of his sword, dropping him with a thud to the cobblestone pavement. Arghan pulled off the man's surcoat and helmet and put them on, and snatched a ring of keys from his belt. He dragged him to the well and threw him inside.

Where is his partner? Why didn't he come?

Arghan ran to check the opposite alcove but found it empty.

Just one guard at the door?

He unlocked the inside door and peeked inside. Two other guards flanked the entrance to a vaulted corridor that looked like a cathedral nave, with rows of columns on either side. The red carpet on the floor indicated it led to the throne room. Outside it, hidden at the back of one of the side aisles, a sunken staircase led to subterranean tunnels soldiers used to access various parts of the complex. This was Arghan's objective. But how would he cross the sprawling gallery without the guards seeing him?

He searched the booth behind the alcove. A wooden lunch box and mug sat on a little table against the wall.

Perfect.

Arghan whipped the mug down the gallery, knocking a porcelain statue off its pedestal, and shattering it against the marble floor.

"What the devil was that?" exclaimed the guard closest to the noise. "Who goes there?" He took a defensive stance and held out his halberd.

"Check it out," said the one at the far side of the red carpet.

As the first sentry passed by, Arghan grabbed the lunch box and threw it over his head, down the corridor in the opposite direction. The box crashed open and slid down the floor, attracting the second sentry's gaze. The first man glanced back, then continued toward the fallen statue while the second set off in the direction of the box. Arghan sprinted across the corridor and kicked the first man in the inside of one leg, dropping him to his knees. He smashed his head against the corridor wall, threw him into an adjacent ballroom, and jumped inside it in the time it took for the second one to spin around.

"Deihglus? What the hell—" exclaimed the second sentry. He rushed toward the ballroom door, glancing back cautiously in the direction of the phantom threat he'd first gone after. As he stepped through the door, Arghan smashed him in the face with the pole-end of the other man's halberd. He pulled a rope from a nearby curtain and tied the two sentries together, then raced back out and sprinted up the red carpet.

Arghan raced eastward along the battlements, slowing to walking speed each time he neared one of the lookouts. The disguise he'd stolen from the courtyard watchman seemed to be doing its job, but a bit too well for his liking. Even with the war, how could the capitol fortress have so few defenders? Defensive ballistae and mangonels lay disassembled and abandoned at each one of the towers he passed. Why? The mystery vexed him almost as much as the throbbing in his shoulder.

The curtain wall curved southward. A gust of salty air blew in from the sea. He leaned into the wind to keep his course while clouds rumbled overhead. Lightning flashed, illuminating the dense, low clouds over the Strait of Cortavia and the distant spire of the Traitor's Tower. Soon he was within sight of the narrow bridge that led to its door. The daughter he'd only spoken to in letters was only paces away. He would free her and tell her everything he had longed to say since the moment he learned she existed.

As he bounded around the corner his foot snagged something heavy lying across his path and he tripped, arms flailing before he hit the surface of the bridge. He spit dirt and groaned, dragging his elbows across the stones and pushing his chest away from the floor. Dizzy from the fall, he staggered backward and squinted through the darkness to inspect the obstacle. He gasped and dropped to his knees when his gaze fell on Deighn Renzek's bloody, mangled corpse.

A voice cried from the door of the Traitor's Tower, "Now!"

Just like when Renzek had been cornered, Cortavian troops poured in from the adjacent towers of the curtain wall, led by Eriohn the younger and men he recognized from his reconnaissance of the *Estria*: the Liester of Luthargrad's crew, or so they pretended to be. In truth, they obeyed the command of the man he knew as…

"Omhigaart Thurn," Arghan whispered through clenched teeth. He whipped his Talon from its sheath.

"Hello, Arghan," said the same voice who had shouted the command that sprung the trap. "My, it's been such a long time, hasn't it? I must say, you haven't changed a bit, except for the grey hair." Thurn stepped through the tower door and sauntered toward Arghan, followed by more swordsmen and other members of his crew.

Arghan pointed his sword above his head with both hands and turned parallel to the bridge, dropping into a stance resembling a horseman standing in stirrups.

"Where's Cybella? What have you done with her?"

"Oh, she's perfectly fine, and will remain so, provided you do as you're told."

Arghan thrust out his knees, looking to either side as the soldiers closed in.

"You lying snake. I've taken you at your word before and it cost me dearly. Never again."

Adrenaline flooded Arghan's veins. He stepped in the direction of the curtain wall and swung his blade. Three men screamed and fell behind their comrades, suddenly deprived of their hands. The others rushed past them. Thurn lifted his arm and gestured with his fingers. Eriohn nodded and waved at a group of archers. Thurn withdrew among his men as they passed him and closed in on Arghan from the other side. Steel flashed and clanged as Arghan cut down each furious wave of men who attacked him. The line of archers aimed high and released a volley of blunted arrows tipped with stones, which fell like hail into the melee. One found its mark on Arghan's temple. He buckled and staggered. A barrage of wooden clubs joined the rain beating down on him from the sky. Arghan's vision faded to black.

Khloe Pan-Wrikor sprung from her bunk, gasping, throwing off her covers, and stumbled to the window, awakening Rhodo at the foot of her straw-packed mattress. She leaned on the sill and peered through the watery streaks behind the glass, beholding the amber reflections of gas lanterns across the rain-drenched roundabout at Oster's Reach. The clock on Palace Bridge chimed five, attracting her gaze toward Mount Tria, the place that haunted her thoughts.

I can't take this anymore. Gotta know what's going on.

Every time she closed her eyes she saw him, and it terrified her.

I can't lie here doing nothing; I've got to do something, even if it's just to stand and watch.

Khloe snatched her clothes from a chair and threw them on while Rhodo paced in front of the door.

She slid her dagger in and out of its sheath and donned her hooded cloak. "C'mon, Rhodo. We're taking a walk."

The shepherd followed at her heels. She nudged the door open, glancing down the hall inside the Continental Theatre's living quarters toward Wardein's bedchamber. The dim glow of a waning fire and the lilting cadence of snoring signaled his unawareness.

She tiptoed down the hall and descended the stairs. Within minutes she braced herself against the rain and hurried across the circle toward Palace Bridge, with Rhodo following in earnest.

Flanked by cavaliers, two carriages rode into the early morning darkness and prevailing fog, exiting the rear gate of Solstrus' estate.

Gavek, roused from his quarters a short time before, sat beside Sira inside the second vehicle. *A twelve-rider escort? How can I escape them?*

Who's in the second carriage?

Mindful of Sira's watchful eyes, he let his head fall against the window moulding and shook it as if startled. He pushed himself back into his seat, blinking. He looked back out the window, watching the street lanterns whizzing by as the vehicle made its way westward down Palace Street toward the bridge to Merchant's Isle.

"You're sure you're up to this, Gavek of Cairhn?" she said, pulling at the cuffs of her blue velvet gloves. "I won't have to knock you over the head again just to keep your eyes open, will I?"

Gavek wondered how she could be so chipper, knowing what she'd been up to that night, but he wasn't about to ask her. It was enough that she might believe him incapable of duplicity.

"I'm not used to getting up this early. I'll be fine," he said, rubbing his eyes to perpetuate his ruse. He looked ahead and then back out the window, still refusing to make eye contact with her.

"I thought all monks got up before sunrise?"

"Not me. I prefer to work late. Now, do you mind if we skip the small talk? His eminence gave me a map of the Library to use in our search. I'd like to study it a bit more before we get there." He pulled out a parchment from under his cloak, careful not to dislodge the one beside it: the agreement he'd stolen from the Archprelate's office. He unfolded the map and held it close to the window. He wasn't at all interested in helping Sira find the manuscripts, of course. That was his ploy to get out from under Solstrus' thumb. So far, the ploy was working. No, he wanted to study it in light of the subterranean tunnels he was already aware of. There had to be another way out of the Library. If he could deduce its location before they got there, he'd have a better chance of escaping.

Sira smirked and looked at him side-eyed. "Come now, you're not still sore about what I did to you, are you?"

He nodded without taking his eyes off the parchment. "Literally? Yes. Yes, I am, actually. My head feels twice its normal size, thanks to you."

"What was I to think? You could have been working for Wardein, leading me into a trap."

"Please. I think it's pretty clear who was trapping who, don't you think?"

"I promise it won't happen again."

"Sure. Let's just forget it; focus on finding what the heretics are hiding, shall we?"

"Fine."

Khloe and Rhodo passed the statue of St. Dahved at the midpoint of Palace Bridge only to scurry back again behind its pedestal when a pair of white horses cantered out of the fog at the end of the crossing.

White horses. Alpinians.

She peered past the corner and watched their numbers grow as they emerged from the mist. As the cavalcade passed the statue she glimpsed a familiar face behind the window of one of the carriages.

Gavek! What?

She ran into the middle of the bridge immediately after the last pair of horsemen passed, looking up the hill toward the Palace and then back again at the procession. She watched the group split in two as they passed the clock on the island side. Half of them, including the lead carriage, turned left and headed southwest down the Embankment. The rear carriage, transporting Gavek, turned right.

Khloe looked up at the fog-shrouded silhouette of the massive dome in the distance.

Gavek's carriage is headed to the Library. But where are the others going? She could only follow one. But which?

She slapped her thighs. "Stalk, Rhodo. Track at heel!" she said, skipping back in the direction she had come from and accelerated after the travellers.

Arghan moaned, lifted his head, and gazed bleary-eyed through the dim light of a chamber toward the sound of a soft, sweet voice. Beyond rows of columned arches, flames flickered on two iron candle stands on either end of a marble sarcophagus. Mounted below a life-size figure carved into the vessel's lid, a plaque read: 'Eriohn I'.

On its opposite side, a female figure knelt with her forehead pressed against the lid, muttering a verse, "The Shepherd King supplies my every need. He lays me to rest amid verdant meadows, slumbering sweetly beside tranquil pools. He restores my soul, leading me in the way of His righteousness for the sake of His Name—"

"Hello?" Arghan huffed, trying to stand, rattling the chains he suddenly realized shackled him between two pillars.

"Father?" She rose from behind the sarcophagus and rushed to Arghan's side. "Is it true? Is it you?"

Arghan blinked, opening his eyelids wider this time. "Grace?"

"What? No, it's me, Cybella. Are you Arghan of Danniker?"

"I am. What's the... what did Wardein say to t-ell—"

"Two swords are better than one," she said, holding his face.

"But a true Warder's weapons are the hands that wield them," he replied.

She fell on his neck and embraced him, kissing his cheek. "I knew you'd come."

"So did others, unfortunately. I fear I've failed you, your Majesty."

"We've all failed the Kingdom at some point or another, haven't we father? What matters is now, and seeing you here, my hope is renewed."

"Seeing me... in chains?"

Voices echoed from the top of the staircase at the side of the room.

"Listen, we don't have much time." She plucked the sapphire that hung from a silver chain around her neck and twisted the stone's setting, revealing a tiny vial. "Here, drink this."

"Jewel's hollow," he said, seeing it change colour after he drained it. "Tastes like... bergaroot extract?"

"Among other things to set you right again, and to neutralize the root's addictive power."

"Clever girl."

"Don't credit me. It was Wardein's idea, with a little help from the Royal Alchemist and the propmaster at the Continental Theatre.

Wardein figured you'd make a rescue attempt, and if you failed—"

"I might have taken more than a few lumps in the process."

"Exactly."

"Where are we? The crypt below the palace chapel?"

"Yes."

The sound of voices intensified.

"Listen, Thurn thinks he has the upper hand—"

"You know him? How?"

"He told me, the arrogant serpent. He thinks he can hide us here from Solstrus; get what he wants from us; use us as leverage against each other. The royal bodyguard remains loyal to me, though he's corrupted the rest of the palace soldiers with promises of riches. He exerts total control over my brother; how I cannot explain. My allies believe he's working with Solstrus to take over the kingdom but has obvious plans to betray him."

"He has no intentions of taking it over. He wants to destroy it."

"Destroy it?"

"I spied on his vessel two nights ago; overheard him plotting with Zuelan mercenaries to attack Trianon. The castle's practically defenseless. Coastal artillery has all been dismantled. I believe there's an invasion fleet sailing for the city as we speak."

Cybella took a deep breath. "You've got to get out of here. Find Wardein. The manuscripts are all that matter now. Take them to Ostergaart. Tell Weorthan to send his forces across the border, with haste. Our treaty means nothing if Cortavia ceases to exist."

"I wouldn't leave you even if I could get free. Cybella, there's something I must tell you, your—"

"You will and you must, father. This I order you as your Queen. My spies have sent word of Thurn's plans and our location to the Alpinians. I expect them to intervene soon."

"And do what?"

"Solstrus wants me dead; thinks he has the proof and backing to make it happen. He plans to execute me at Traitor's Circle at high noon on the feast of Alpinia, along with some Tzyani prisoners he claims are terrorists."

"What? No! I won't let him."

"Save your strength, father. I am not afraid to die for what I believe. God will prevail. Solstrus has no evidence compelling enough to warrant his actions. I have faith in the citizens of Trianon. Once they see me paraded in shackles, they'll see Solstrus for the monster he is and put an end to his reign of terror once and for all, I'm sure of it."

"Not if the Zuelans strike first."

A door burst open at the top of the stairs, releasing a ray of light from the floor above. Long shadows preceded clomping footfalls. Several members of the *Estria* crew invaded the room, followed by Omhigaart Thurn and Eriohn the younger.

"That's enough. Take her away," said Thurn, snapping his fingers.

Cybella maintained eye contact with Arghan as two men each grabbed one of her arms. "The last manuscript... tell me, did Gavek—"

"Yeshua," hollered Arghan as the men dragged her up the stairs, "the Shepherd King's name is Yeshua."

Thurn obscured his view. "Hello, Arghan. Nice to see you awake again at last." He nodded to another soldier who handed him a small wooden chair. He placed it on the floor, sat on it backward facing Arghan, and rested his forearms on the headrest. "We've got so much to talk about, you and I."

Cybella's elixir started coursing through Arghan's veins. He straightened his back and scowled at Thurn. "What could I possibly want to talk to you about?"

"Well, I imagine you have all sorts of questions like 'where have you been all these years?' and 'I thought you were dead' and 'how did you fool me', those sorts of things."

"I couldn't care less. You're a liar, a snake, and a traitor—"

"The Order betrayed me!" Thurn screamed, kicking his chair across the room.

"How do you figure?" Arghan said. "Seems to me it was the other way around. Your actions at Koerska brought the Alpinians down on our heads. You certainly lied to me; I nearly felt the axe for it. There never were any Zuelans in that village, were there? You made it all up, why?"

"The Alpinians made me a better offer."

"The Alpinians? A better—"

"That's right! I sacrificed everything for the Order; poured my own blood out in the war; stole countless piles of loot from the Zuelans. And for what? Veknir's reward? He told me on his deathbed he planned to give it all back! I lost four sons fighting for him, and then, on top of that insult he had the gall to name Von Terrack his successor instead of me?"

"Von Terrack had honour. You had none. It was as simple as that."

Thurn struck Arghan with the back of his hand. "You're lucky I need you alive or you'd get worse. Von Terrack's honour came by birthright; mine came by wielding my Twin Talons. You tell me, which one is legitimate?"

"What do you want, Omhigaart? This discussion is pointless," said Arghan, spitting blood. "Do want to punish me for the sins of others? Is that it?"

"No, I plan to use you to get what is rightfully mine." He beckoned one of his men, who signalled another upstairs. Two men carried down a small table. Another handed Thurn a rolled up piece of linen. Thurn unravelled it on the tabletop, revealing a map of Cortavia.

"I know that Von Terrack hid the Zuelan treasures in caches across the country and told you all about them."

Arghan glanced at the map, then looked back up at Thurn. "I haven't got a clue what you're talking about."

"Don't insult my intelligence, Arghan. You know this is Von Terrack's map. I stole it from his study right before the Alpinians reduced Erne Rock to ashes."

"If you say so."

"I know so. Do you know how I know?"

"No. Enlighten me."

"Well, after leaving you to take the fall for Koerska I scoured the countryside, this map in hand, in search of those treasures." He addressed the bystanders as one might speak to a jury, "And to think, I actually thought I was doing myself a favour by helping destroy the Order. The treasure vaults should have been easy pickings with no Warders left around to defend them, right?"

Arghan rolled his eyes. Thurn hadn't changed; he still relished being the centre of attention.

"Wrong," Thurn continued, "Von Terrack was too clever for that. He made secret arrangements with Eriohn to seize the assets and deliver them back to their rightful owners in the event of his death. All but two of them had been picked clean by the time I arrived." He pointed to the map. "The others were tough nuts to crack; all of them were full of ingenious and deadly traps as you well know, but I did manage to recover the loot from two of the sites between the time I escaped execution and when I fled the continent, despite the efforts of those treacherous Alpinians and their empty promises."

"Sounds to me you should have cut your losses," Arghan said with a grin. "Surely there was enough gold in those two sites alone to live the rest of your days in luxury?"

"There would have been, Arghan, had I not lost them to the Eskhasian Trench, trying to escape."

Arghan laughed. "Ha, that sounds about right."

Thurn threw a punch deep in Arghan's stomach. He landed two more before Arghan's knees buckled and he collapsed, groaning, hanging from his chains.

Thurn shouted in Arghan's ear, "I spent twenty years as a mercenary slave for the Zuelan Horde after I washed ashore! Victory or death was my creed. Do you have any idea what that does to your mind, Arghan? Day in, day out, slaughter or be slaughtered?"

"I saw my share of that in the war. We all suffered from it."

"Not like this. The Zuelans forced me to commit unspeakable atrocities. I had almost given up hope for justice in this life, that was until that fool the Liester of Luthargrad got shipwrecked near my enclave. That was when I made plans to return to Cortavia."

"To do what, exactly? I still don't know what you want."

Thurn beckoned the young prince, "Tell him, Eriohn."

Eriohn strolled behind Arghan. "Father told me Von Terrack's secrets, things he shared with him and nobody else, except you, that is. Things like the location of other troves he never marked on the map. Like yours, near Ondolen Falls, for example."

Arghan flashed his eyes.

Eriohn circled him and pointed at the map. "And this location, in particular, deep in the Ondar River Gorge at the west end of Lake Trieehd. That is why you lived there all these years, isn't it, to guard it? He called it the greatest treasure of them all, greater than all the other troves combined. He said Von Terrack protected it like no others, with sophisticated machines powered by the falls: locks and doors, traps and snares designed by Helvetia's master clockmakers. Impregnable. But not to one who knows their secrets. Not for you."

Thurn interjected, "Imagine my surprise and jubilation when the prince told me you were very much alive and could be of use to us in this regard."

Arghan shook his head. "And here I thought all you wanted was to see Cortavia burn."

"Oh, it'll burn, Arghan. It'll burn," replied Thurn. "See, I told the Kaighan the troves remain full for the taking. He thinks I'm only here to dismantle Cortavia's defences, which I've already done. When he invades, he'll reduce Cortavia to ash looking for them, which will be perfect for me. By the time he realizes he's been had, he'll be locked in battle with the Duke of Ostergaart — because let's face it, Cortavia's defences don't stand a chance — and you and I will be way ahead of them, free to get to the bottom of things in Ondar Gorge."

"Over my dead body. Why would I ever help you?"

"Well, let's just say if you don't, it'll be over Cybella's dead body. But not all at once. No. I'll keep you locked up here, sending you pieces of her until you comply or there's nothing left but her head."

Arghan dropped his chin against his chest. Thurn feigned cooperation with Solstrus as a means to an end: a way to arrange her arrest, confinement and coercion. It had all been an effort to get to Arghan, and had succeeded.

"I'll do it," he said after a long pause, "but only when I'm satisfied the princess has been delivered safely to Weorthan. If so much as a hair on her head is touched I won't cooperate. I'll cut out my own tongue before I tell you how to breach that vault."

Thurn winked at Eriohn. "I sincerely hope it doesn't come to that. I always enjoyed our little chats. I will personally vouch for her safety and deliver her to the Duke at the proper time, provided you cooperate."

Arghan regained his footing. "Let me see her. If she's out of my sight I have no reason to believe you."

Thurn arched an eyebrow, looking first at Eriohn. "As you wish. But it'll be under guard." He addressed Eriohn, "Tell the Cortavians to bring her back down. Assign some guards to watch them until I return."

"Where are you going?" asked Eriohn.

"To the *Estria*. I've got a few loose ends to tie up before we sail in the morning." He sauntered past Eriohn and ascended the stairs, followed by his crewmen. "I'm so looking forward to working with you again, Arghan, truly."

Eriohn glanced at Arghan before heading to the staircase himself.

"What happened to you, Eriohn?" said Arghan, stopping Eriohn in his tracks.

Eriohn marched back. "I beg your pardon?"

"I saved your life when you were just a babe. That's got to be worth something. Hear me out."

Eriohn spit in Arghan's face. "You won't sway me with your blasphemous lies, infidel."

Arghan searched Eriohn's eyes. They seemed clouded by an impenetrable darkness. "Even so, I will pray for you."

Eriohn spit again. "Guards!" he shouted and stormed up the stairs.

Arghan jerked his chains. Though his stomach ached with the sting of Thurn's blows, the adrenaline summoned by the encounter left him itching for a fight. Every fibre of his being rebelled against confinement. But what could he do except sit and wait? He grunted, tugging his restraints one more time before closing his eyes. *Useless. Don't waste energy. Plot your next move should the opportunity to escape arise.*

As soon as he shut his eyes, the sound of a creaking door and footsteps signalled the arrival of another visitor. Were the Cortavians returning with Cybella, as ordered?

A white-bearded soldier wearing the colours of the royal bodyguard rushed toward him, sweating and wide-eyed. "I've little time. Are you the Erne Warder, Arghan of Danniker?"

"Yes," he answered with an incredulous look, "and you are?"

"Kohlin, son of Erebald." He produced a key from inside his sleeve, continuing to speak as he unlocked Arghan's fetters, "You look different with that grey beard of yours. I met you once, when old King Eriohn pinned a medal on your chest for saving the prince. Bet you regret that now, don't you?"

"Regret what? The beard or saving young Eriohn?" Arghan asked, rubbing his wrists.

"Saving the prince, of course. The beard suits you."

Arghan chuckled. "Cybella sent you?"

"Sort of. Told me weeks ago to help you out if you showed up. There's a few loyalists left in the royal court, including me. You must do what you can to save her."

"That's the plan, Kohlin."

Shouts echoed outside the door, as did the sound of crashing metal and stomping footsteps.

Arghan marched to the base of the stairs. "What's going on up there?"

"The Alpinians arrived in force soon after the Liester left the chapel and confronted Eriohn the younger, demanding Her Majesty be handed over. They're fighting over her now inside the chapel. That's how I managed to slip away."

"How many?"

"At least forty Alpinians. There's only eighteen of us. I'm the only loyalist who got assigned the chapel."

"Got a sword?"

"No," said Kohlin, showing him the empty scabbard at his hip. "I was on the door. Alpinians took it from me straight away; too eager to waste time on an old coot like me. Yours is still here, though."

"It is? How do you know?"

"You don't forget a sword like that, son. They laid it in on the priest's desk in his study, behind the altar, when they dragged you in here. Must've forgot all about it."

"Okay. Well done. Eriohn the elder would've been proud." He patted the old man on the shoulder and sprung up the stairs, pausing at the threshold to peek through the door.

Surrounded by toppled pews and dead bodies, a crowd of Cortavian soldiers and Alpinian Guardsmen filled the transept between the crypt door and the altar, locking swords. The casualties told Arghan the Cortavians were losing the fight; less than ten remained, pressed hard by the Alpinians against the steps of the apse. He watched as a small group of Cortavians, separated from the main group, pushed young Eriohn through a window seconds before another group of Alpinians burst through the vestry door behind the altar, pushing the remaining Cortavian troops into a circle in the middle of the transept. A female voice screamed from inside the vestry.

Cybella. They must have kept her there while Thurn interrogated me. The Alpinians have come to take her.

Arghan sprinted from the crypt door, kicking one of the Alpinians in the back as he leaped around the others, then scooted past the altar.

"Look! It's Danniker!" shouted one of the Alpinians at the back.

The Cortavians landed a few stabs at the Alpinians thanks to the distraction, only to collapse under an intensified push from their foes.

"Finish them! I've got Danniker. You two, follow me." Shouted an Alpinian wearing a decorated collar.

He and two others rushed after Arghan as he dove through the vestry doorway. With seconds to spare, Arghan kicked the door shut and turned a key left in the lock. He wiped the sweat from his eyes and scanned the room while the Alpinians pounded the door.

Open window with a chair below it. Tattered shreds of embroidered silk caught at the edge of the pane. Cybella was here; that's where they took her.

He spied a glint of polished metal at the back of the room. He slid across the priest's desk as one of the Alpinians slammed his shoulder against the door. The door frame creaked and splintered. An axe blade shattered the wood surrounding the doorknob, sending the handle clanging across the floor.

Arghan grabbed his Twin Talon from beside a bookshelf. The three Alpinians stormed the room. He leaped onto the desk, kicking the first in the jaw. He jumped the blade of the second, returning the thrust with one of his own, purchasing a corner of his opponent's shoulder. He scored another strike against the third when he landed on the floor.

More Alpinians rushed through the door. Arghan jumped past the desk and pulling the top of a nearby bookshelf, collapsed it in front of their path. He bounded up the chair below the window and dove through the open pane, landing in a rose bush outside. Thorns raked his face and hands as he rolled out onto a nearby path.

"Cursed weed!" he said, tugging his cloak free, reminded of his misadventures in the forest of Glenhava.

An Alpinian paused on the windowsill, preparing to descend a ladder which Arghan only now noticed was leaning against the wall below it. Arghan wiped blood from his brow and glanced at his hand, shaking his head. He dashed behind some trees and sprinted down a gravel path that led to the palace gardens. With the Alpinians in hot pursuit, now led by the officer whose face he had kicked, Arghan leaped a rail beside the path, rolled down a grassy hill and bolted into a hedge maze.

He led the Alpinians around several turns then dove behind a fountain in a circular area at the terminus of a dead end. The Alpinian officer halted as he turned the corner, causing his men to stack up behind him.

One of the knights batted the hedges with his sword. "Where'd he go?" He circled the fountain and looked back at the officer. "Captain Raipheniel?"

"I don't know," he shouted. "I don't know."

CHAPTER SEVENTEEN
Aftermath

Wrytha pointed toward an open door inside Wardein's cellar. "Keep him warm 'till I return. You'll find everything you need in the next room: food, medicine, blankets, cots; even a nice warm stove." She watched the weary escapees shuffle past her then headed for the spiral staircase at the corner of the chamber and gripped the rail.

"Clan Mother?"

Wrytha turned back. The girl named Auria approached her. *Sweet girl. How did she get mixed up in this?* No more than a year or two older than Khloe, she and Nicah had long been sweethearts.

"Yes dear, what is it?"

She fell on Wrytha's shoulder and burst into tears. "Thank you, sincerely, for everything you've done for us. We had no idea what we were getting into. None of us did. I'm so sorry about Nicah and Orin. I'm so sorry for everything. We should have listened to you. We should have—"

"Hush now, child. Think nothing of it. All of us make mistakes, especially in our youth. You're only human. Go join the others. I'm sure you're starving after that trek of ours."

Auria smiled and nodded, wiping away her tears.

Wrytha took a few steps up the staircase.

"Wrytha?"

"Yes?"

"What do you think is going to happen to Orin and Teighthra? Do you think they're okay?"

"I pray so, dear. I pray so. Go be with the others. I'll be back as soon as I can."

Wrytha bounded up the steps and slowed near the top, tiptoeing to the back side of a secret door leading into the theatre's living quarters. She breezed through it and closed what looked like a bookshelf inside the scriptorium. Several moments later she passed the door to the room Arghan and Renzek had been assigned and stopped to look inside. The empty bunks against the wall showed neither had returned. She gazed out the window, looking in the direction of Palace Rock and closed her eyes for a moment while she counted the loops on her braid, praying for their safe return. She continued down the hall toward Wardein's quarters. As she passed Khloe's room she stopped mid-stride, spotting the covers left on the floor.

"Khloe?" she said, springing into the room. She looked at the bed, then the empty chair and ran back into the hall. "Khloe? Rhodo?" She sprinted for Wardein's door and opened it without knocking. The old man lay snoring in a leather chair in front of the fireplace, clutching a bottle of Cortavian whiskey.

"Wardein!" said Wrytha, kicking his foot. "Where's Khloe?"

Wardein shook his head, blinking over bloodshot eyes, searching for the vector of Wrytha's voice. "She's not in her bedroom?"

"No, she's not. I left her here with you. You were supposed to be waiting up for us." She grabbed the bottle from his hands and threw it into the fireplace, shattering it.

"I'm sorry, I—"

"Yes you are sorry. Send somebody to fetch that apothecary of yours. Use all the cash in Arghan's purse if you have to, just get someone down there who can attend to my son." Wrytha pulled her bow up over her shoulder, tightened her grip on the handle, and stormed down the hall.

The cavalcade stopped at the curb outside the Library of Trianon, dwarfed by the pillars of the plaza's curved portico. Khloe and Rhodo huddled at the corner of the south tower, watching Gavek and Sira disembark from the coach.

Khloe eyed Sira's short red hair and scarlet robe. "What do you suppose Gavek is up to, travelling around with that saucy wench, Rhodo?"

In the short time she'd known her inquisitive friend, Gavek had never been at a loss for words. The way he shunned Sira's gaze suggested he was not at ease, as if the scary brutes at his heels weren't reason enough. She watched the Alpinian cavaliers dismount, form two lines behind them, and march them inside.

When the last one disappeared behind the closing door, she bolted across the plaza, watching it swing and latch seconds before she could catch it. She huffed and waited a moment before she tried the latch.

Frog spit! Locked.

She took a few steps to the left and peeked through a window. The soldiers paused to light lanterns, then continued to lead them down the main corridor toward the building's domed interior. She arched an eyebrow and bit her upper lip, thinking.

"Wait a minute," she whispered, "I know."

She pushed away from the windowsill and raced counter-clockwise around the portico, headed for the mausoleum at the back of the building. She'd watched Arghan get inside that way. How hard could it be?

Sira stood with her hands on her hips, a few paces behind Gavek in the empty vault where they had discovered Wardein's taunting note two days before. "Well, genius, see anything we might have missed, like a symbol or a code; anything that might lead us to Wardein?"

Gavek paced the walls with a lantern, pretending to search for markings. "No, I don't. Not here." He faced her. "This room is a dead end. But don't worry, I managed to uncover other secrets you didn't find, elsewhere in the Library."

"Is that so?" said Sira, looking at one of the Alpinian troops. "We tore this place apart for weeks. You only found this chamber because I led you to the door, remember?"

"But he opened it, didn't he?" said the Alpinian, rolling his eyes, "Solstrus wants to indulge him. I'm getting tired of the place. Let's see what he's got."

Sira closed her eyes for a moment, then pinched her lips. "Lead on, Gavek of Cairhn. Show us your great discovery."

"Right this way," he said, smirking as he marched up the stairs. He patted his abdomen, checking that the hidden parchment he'd stolen from Solstrus' study hadn't moved. This was his chance. Would his plan succeed? All he had to go on were a few casual words spoken by Arghan the day they'd snuck inside the Library. The rest was a gamble, a mystery, an unknown.

He loved it.

Khloe descended the staircase below Picanes' sarcophagus and felt her way through the darkness. Retracing Arghan's steps had helped her open the tunnel, but now she was on her own. *Should have brought a lantern. Where does this go?*

She reached for the rope hanging from her belt and groped the darkness until she touched a furry head. "Rhodo," she whispered, tying the cord around his neck. "Lead. Escape." She felt a tug and followed the canine deeper into the tunnel. Rhodo paused, sniffing a breeze that wafted in from the darkness ahead, then turned sharply and quickened his pace. Eventually, he stopped and scratched a spot where a sliver of light penetrated the wall.

"Here?" Khloe felt the outline of a door. *Where's the latch?*

Muffled voices came from beyond the crease. She held her ear to it.

"I told you, we searched here already."

The vixen?

"Did you now? Watch this."

Gavek!

Something pounded the floor beyond the door. A latch clicked and it swung open, flooding the tunnel with light.

Yikes!

Khloe yanked Rhodo's leash and scampered back into the dark. Gavek ducked through the door and turned straight toward her. She froze when the light from his lantern illuminated her form. His eyes bulged. She held a finger to her lips and crept backward while Gavek watched, mouth gaping.

"What's the matter? Why did you stop?" said Sira, unable to see past him.

"Uh, thought I saw a trap or something. Just making sure its safe." He nodded at Khloe and she motioned for him to follow.

As she made the turn toward the exit, Gavek broke hard left, running in the opposite direction until he disappeared beyond another turn.

"Hey!" yelled one of the Alpinians, "where's he going? Get back here!" He and the man behind him squeezed past Sira and dashed after him. Moments later, their screams echoed from beyond the corner and Gavek sprinted back toward Khloe, alone. Another Alpinian stepped in the gap at the intersection of the two tunnels, intercepting him before he could reach her.

Khloe pulled the rope off Rhodo's neck. "Rhodo, attack!"

The shepherd snarled, leaped down the corridor, and sunk his teeth into the back of the knight's neck, pulling him to the floor. The knight screamed, writhing in the animal's grip.

Gavek stumbled over them both and scrambled to his feet near Khloe. "How?"

"Never mind. C'mon, mausoleum is this way. Rhodo, come."

"Mausoleum?" whispered Sira, smirking. She waved to the remaining troops. "You three, after them!" She clung to the wall while they squeezed by, then darted back into Wardein's office.

Gavek gripped Khloe's hand. They bolted through the mausoleum door into the early morning mist, skidded across the paving stones and sprinted along the southeast wing of the Library. One of their pursuers drew a club from his belt and threw it at Gavek. It struck him between his shoulder blades and he collapsed, howling.

"Gavek!" Khloe yelled, hearing him fall. "Rhodo?" she called, rushing to Gavek's side.

The canine lunged at the man in the lead, knocking him on his back; mauling his face and neck while the others passed, drawing their swords. They closed in on Khloe while she struggled to lift Gavek from the pavement. Something whizzed over Khloe's head, then another. The two swordsmen collapsed onto plaza, each with an arrow protruding from their faces.

Wrytha dropped from the seawall and nocked another arrow. She rushed to stand between Khloe, Gavek and their pursuers.

"Mother!"

"You okay, Khloe?" she shouted, aiming at the mausoleum door.

"Yes. I'm fine. Gavek needs help."

Wrytha glance at Rhodo, who was still gorging the Alpinian's limp body. "That's enough, boy. Guard Khloe." The canine scampered to Khloe's side while Wrytha crept toward her.

Wrytha lowered her bow and knelt beside them. She touched Gavek's chest. "Can you stand, master Gavek?"

Gavek coughed, rolled over and vomited.

"Yuck," exclaimed Khloe.

"Yeah, I'm okay," answered Gavek, gasping and stammering. "Give me a second. Cursed thing knocked the wind clean out of me." He huffed, pushing his upper body away from the ground. Khloe pulled his arm over her shoulder and helped him to his feet.

"What the blazes were you thinking, going out like that?" Wrytha said, pointing at Khloe.

"I was worried. I—"

"Never mind," Wrytha interrupted. "Let's get him back to the theatre. There are people there who need our help. Wardein may not have crawled out of his bottle in time to do something about it."

Gavek, patted the front of his robe. "I've got something you're going to want to see; Wardein too, I'll wager, and Arghan most of all."

"Well, it'll have to wait."

"Where is Arghan, anyway?" said Gavek, exchanging looks with the two women.

"He... he hasn't returned," answered Wrytha.

"Hasn't returned? Did he go somewhere?"

Wrytha took Gavek's other arm. "Later, Gavek. Let's go."

With Rhodo in tow, the trio passed the southeast corner of the Library, oblivious to the presence of a shadowed figure who stood behind an open window directly above them.

Sira Beihan watched them walk out onto the sidewalk and head southwest down the Embankment. "The Continental Theatre," she whispered. "So Wardein's been under our noses the whole time, holed up with his thespian friends." She strutted away from the window and headed for the stairs. "Well, not for much longer, dear professor."

"He's coming around, your eminence."

A blurry silhouette came into Orin's view. The man held a riding crop above his head as if poised to strike. He lowered it to his side and turned away from a battered and unconscious female figure who hung from shackles against the wall.

"You animals! What have you done to her? Teighthra, can you hear me?"

"Silence!"

Orin's vision flickered with stars; pain shot through his scalp.

"My men say you tried to kill them," said Solstrus, "is that true?"

"I..."

"Speak up!"

Throbbing spread through Orin's cheekbone.

"Ugh... I... I'd do it again. G-give me a sword and I'll show you — show all of you."

Laughter filled the shadowy chamber.

"I told you, your eminence. Let us have our revenge."

"No, I think not."

"But—"

His voice cut short at the sound of a slap.

"But nothing. Kill him now and you'll make him a martyr for his kin. No, you and the others will draw and quarter him in Traitor's Circle for all to see, especially that Tzyani-loving heretic princess of ours, right after we behead her and hang the rest. Isn't that right, my dear?"

Footsteps. Orin watched Solstrus cross the room and stand over a young woman in a shimmering gown. Kneeling, gagged and bound at the wrists, she struggled against Solstrus' grip while he pinched her cheek.

Who is she?

Orin's vision faded to black before he could think of an answer.

The *Estria's* first officer burst into the captain's quarters. "Captain," he hollered, straightening his bloodied jacket, "we have a problem. A big one."

Omhigaart Thurn looked up from the chart on his desk and glared at the swarthy Regalian. "What the devil happened, Torrento?"

"The Alpinians," he said, catching his breath, "not long after you and the others left they surrounded the chapel and attacked us."

Thurn sprung from his seat and tramped past the desk. "The princess?" he demanded, taking the man's lapels. "Tell me Eriohn got her out of there?"

"No, sir. Eriohn himself escaped only in the nick of time. They outnumbered us more than two to one, and Solstrus sent his best. They seized the princess and killed the others. I'd have died too, but Solstrus needed me to deliver a message." He handed Thurn a scroll.

> *I'm disappointed, old friend, but not surprised. Perhaps you planned to extort me for more gold by taking such action, but a deal is a deal, you know where I stand in such matters.*
>
> *It would seem the grip you had over the Palace has waned. One of Eriohn's own men alerted me of your indiscretion. I've taken Cy-*

bella from you to ensure you keep your end of the bargain. Bring me Danniker as promised to collect the balance of what I owe you and we'll call it even.

No hard feelings. Don't test me though or I will respond in force. I hold all the cards now. The Palace of Ministers is on my side. Consider your continued freedom a sign of my patience and gratitude for the invaluable contribution you've made. I await you at my estate.'

"Curse him!" Thurn growled, crumpling the parchment in his fist. He grabbed a model ship off the desk and threw it, smashing it to pieces against the wall. He threw his belt around his waist and screamed, "Take me to Danniker!"

"I can't, captain. I saw him escape during the ruckus in the chapel."

"You did nothing to stop him?" Thurn's face turned red. He stomped across the room and drew his sabre from its scabbard. He grabbed the back of Torrento's head and slid the blade across his neck. Torrento collapsed, gurgling and clutching his throat.

He yelled out the door, "Dreighton! Get in here!"

"Yes, captain?" said the greasy-haired crewman, eyes bulging when his gaze fell on his crew mate writhing the floor.

"You're promoted to first officer. Salerio will be second. Tell the crew we'll sail for Metacartha within the hour."

"Yes sir!" He clicked his heels and turned to leave.

Thurn arrested him. "Wait, one more thing." He breezed back around the desk and reached into the cabinet behind it. He retrieved another spiral-shaped bottle like the one he had given Eriohn before, then paused at the desk to scrawl a message on a slip of paper. He returned to Dreighton and handed him the items. "Send these by courier to the prince before we sail. You have your orders, now snap to it."

"Yes sir. But—"

"Spit it out Mr. Dreighton."

"What about the Kaighan's gold?"

"Fill a chest with rocks and cover the top with coins and jewels we skimmed from the first one. Zuelkar's had enough time to inspect the bogus map I gave him and count the loot we already sent. He'll have no reason to suspect trickery. When I tell him what Solstrus has done, his greed and ambition will compel him to order the invasion." He marched up the stairs and onto the deck. Dreighton followed. "By the time he figures out I've cheated him it'll be too late. Meanwhile, I'll have my revenge on Solstrus, Danniker, and the rest of this miserable country. This is by no means over, you'll see!"

Prince Eriohn stood in his dressing gown on the balcony outside his royal suite. Sweaty and trembling, he cast a vacant gaze toward the Narrows and watched the *Estria* sail through it and turn south past the Isle of Woe where it soon disappeared into the fog. Licking red nectar from his lips, he crumpled Thurn's note and let the crimson bottle fall from his fingers and crash into pieces on the polished marble floor. He jumped onto the guardrail and teetered for a moment, then spread his arms and whispered, "As Zuel wills it, so it is done." He slipped off the rail and plummeted toward the cliffs below.

CHAPTER EIGHTEEN
Confrontations

Daylight beamed through the grate above the catacomb and sounds of the day's first traffic echoed down from the street.

Gavek walked out of the chamber where the Tzyani zealots now slumbered and crouched beside Wrytha, who sat on the floor, leaning against the wall.

"I think he's going to be okay," he said, wiping the sweat from his drooping eyelids.

"What?" Wrytha stammered, awakening.

"Nicah. I gave him some herbs for the swelling and some fresh bandages. That's all I can do for him until we get him to a proper doctor."

"Oh," she said, exhaling. She rubbed her eyes. "Thank you, Gavek. I'm sure you did your best."

"His skills are most impressive," said Wardein, handing her a cup of water, "I'm sure the great Threician healer Androcles could've done no better."

Wrytha took the drink but avoided Wardein's gaze.

"Not really," said Gavek, "the techniques I used are more in line with those of Sophoclus."

"I dare say you're correct," said Wardein, winking. "As I recall his biographer Terrenean covered such matters in volume five of his memoirs."

"Volume six, to be precise."

"Right you are, young Gavek, well done." Wardein beamed, holding his lapels.

"At any rate," continued Gavek, oblivious that Wardein was testing him, "it's nothing I haven't watched Pattron do."

"I can tell you hold him in high regard," Wrytha said, closing her eyes again before she swallowed a gulp of water. "Was he your teacher at the monastery?"

"All the elders were. But I didn't get along with many of them; they were too slow for me. Pattron was the only one who could hold my interest, and Arghan of course. He was always willing to listen to my ramblings. I'd have gone mad otherwise."

Wrytha grew silent at the mention of Arghan's name. She closed her eyes, curling her brows downward while her chin began to quiver.

"I'm sure he'll turn up," said Wardein, "Arghan's been through worse."

Wrytha sprung from the floor and turned her back to Wardein. She paced the room, looking up at the sunlight coming through the grate.

"He's right, Wrytha," Gavek said.

Wrytha wiped away a tear and nodded. "I hope so."

The sound of footsteps reverberated from the spiral stairs. Wrytha spun to face it. She turned away again when she heard the clacking of Rhodo's claws.

"No sign of him upstairs," said Khloe, entering the room after Rhodo. She sat down beside Gavek, suppressing a nervous giggle as Rhodo set upon him, licking his face.

"Hey, cut that out," said Gavek.

Splashes sounded from the tunnel at the end of the chamber. Wrytha grabbed her bow and aimed an arrow in the time it took Gavek to open his eyes. A deep voice groaned behind the corner.

"Arghan!" cried Wrytha as he stumbled into the room. She dropped her bow and threw her arms around him, gripped his face and kissed his lips.

"Huh... nice to see you too," he said, breathlessly. He threw his sword and scabbard on the table. "Gavek!" he exclaimed, spotting him, "how did you—"

Gavek sprung up, followed by Khloe. The pair surrounded and embraced him.

"It's good to see you safe and sound, Gav," Arghan said.

"You too," said Gavek, patting Arghan's shoulder. "You look exhausted. Let me get you some water."

"I'll get it," interjected Wardein, "you've got things to discuss. Good to see you back in one piece, Arghan."

"Glad to be in one piece, old friend. Thank you. Fetch my duffel too, would you please?"

Wardein nodded, misty-eyed. He offered Wrytha an apologetic glance before scampering up the stairs.

"What happened?" asked Khloe. "I feared the worst; I dreamt you were chained in a dank cellar, and—"

"You did?" Arghan said, arching an eyebrow.

"What about the princess?" said Wrytha, tugging his arm while she inspected the slashes on his face. "Did you find her? Did you find out anything about where they took Orin? And where's Renzek?"

Arghan's expression grew sullen. "Renzek's dead."

Khloe gasped and covered her mouth.

"I found his corpse on the bridge to the tower, shortly before I was ambushed myself."

"Ambushed, by whom?" said Gavek, tightening his brow.

"Omhigaart Thurn. He was waiting for me; somehow anticipated what I would do, and when."

Gavek seized Arghan's lapel. "You mean *the* Omhigaart Thurn — your former commander? How—"

"When we found Wardein after you were captured, he and Renzek briefed us about their efforts to find Cybella. They told me they had evidence the Liester of Luthargrad was responsible for her disappearance, so I decided to reconnoitre his vessel the other night. It was then I discovered he and Thurn were the same man." He looked at Wrytha.

"Warder captains used to post sentries onshore to guard their ships while in port. One of his must have spotted us. Our presence came as no surprise to Thurn; he anticipated I would try to rescue Cybella. That's why he kidnapped her, to lure me to Trianon."

"Lure you?" Wrytha asked. "Why?"

Arghan told her about the treasure troves and the remaining vault under Ondar Falls.

"You mean he's done all this for money?" Khloe asked. "Unbelievable... "

"He's planned all this in detail, I'm sure. What he didn't count on was Solstrus finding out what he was really up to. Had the Alpinians not intervened I doubt I'd have escaped so soon."

"The Alpinians?" asked Gavek.

Arghan briefed the group about the rest of his experiences since they had separated, including the Alpinian's raid and Cybella's capture. They in turn did the same.

"That was a gutsy move," said Wrytha. "Cybella must think she had a better chance with Solstrus than Thurn."

"Indeed," Arghan remarked, "though I fail to see how. She was only ever a pawn to Thurn, but Solstrus plans to execute her."

"So where is he keeping her," asked Wrytha, "at his estate?"

"No. After I eluded the Alpinians, I doubled back to the chapel and overheard the officer they call 'Raipheniel' tell his men to rendezvous 'on the Isle' to guard her and the other 'political prisoners.'"

"There were prisoners at the estate, briefly, I'm sure of it," said Gavek. "I saw the Alpinians drag two people into Solstrus' wine cellar while I was sneaking around the place. But I'm pretty sure they transferred them later."

"What makes you say that?" asked Wrytha.

"When they took me to the Library this morning there was another carriage ahead of mine. I think they were in it. It was gone when I arrived and only six Alpinians remained to escort us inside."

"I think he's right, mother," interjected Khloe, looking at Gavek, "I saw half the group break away after the bridge. They headed somewhere onto the Isle, but I couldn't tell where exactly because of the fog. But I did notice the windows of the carriage were shuttered and locked, unlike Gavek's."

Arghan stood up. "The Isle is a better place to hide them, for obvious reasons. They could be anywhere." He circled the table, looking at the map on top of it. "We have less than 30 hours to find them before the execution."

"He'll want to shorten his route to the execution site," said Wrytha, pointing at the map. "He's afraid of ambush."

"Precisely," said Arghan. "It's clear Thurn and Solstrus were using one another to achieve competing goals. Solstrus must fear Thurn's retribution, and if he's that concerned—"

"He'd want to keep them in a secure location, as close as possible to the execution site at Traitor's Circle," said Gavek, tracing his finger over the map. "But not in any of the Alpinian's watchtowers, that would be an obvious place to look. What is the most secure location on Merchant's Isle aside from those?"

"Shipper's bank?" said Arghan.

"Shipper's bank," echoed Gavek, nodding as he tapped the place on the map.

"One way to be sure," said Wrytha. "Khloe, think Rhodo might be up for a run after dark?"

Arghan and Wrytha led Rhodo down the cobblestone path of Garden Row, weaving through a throng of revellers, heading westward toward Shipper's Bank.

"What a spectacle," said Wrytha, looking up at the festival lanterns hanging over the street. "Do Trianonians always go to such trouble on the eve of a feast day?"

"As long as I can remember," answered Arghan. "Makes me wish we were here under better circumstances; it's quite the party, except for the executions, of course. Can't say I enjoy that part, let alone understand it."

"Same here. For such a cultured city they certainly have a perverse fascination with settling scores."

"Indeed. There's the bank. May I do the honours?"

"Sure." Wrytha handed him the leash and knelt at the side of the road, holding a piece of Orin's clothing under Rhodo's nose. "Rhodo. Track. Find Orin."

Rhodo took a few steps up and down the street, sniffing the wind while Arghan followed.

"Is that what he normally does?" he asked.

"Only when he can't catch the scent right away," said Wrytha.

"Shall we circle the building then?"

"Worth a try."

The trio wove through the marble columns that lined each of the building's four sides.

Wrytha frowned when they neared the end and cast Arghan a sideways glance. "It's not looking good. What made you and Gavek certain they'd be here?"

"Shipper's Bank has a sordid history with the Palace of Orbicon. The Cantorvarians believe the bank has laundered funds for the Grand Prelate for centuries, converting cash from tainted sources such as war loot and the proceeds of crime seized by the Alpinians into sanctified 'donations'. If Solstrus wanted a secure location to make an off record 'deposit', this is the logical place to look."

"Well, crooked bankers or not," said Wrytha as they completed the circuit, "I don't think they're here. Rhodo would have caught something by now. Is it possible the Alpinians used a subterranean entrance?"

"It's possible." Arghan handed her the leash and reached into his satchel to retrieve one of the duplicate maps Wardein had made. "There's a hidden entrance at the back of that alley there," he said, pointing. "Let's check it out."

They ducked behind the crowd and took off down the alley. Moments later they descended a staircase and entered a tunnel.

"Look there," said Wrytha, shivering. She retrieved a lantern from her pack and lit it. "Are those carts of some kind?" She pointed toward a set of tracks leading to and from an opening in the tunnel wall.

"Trolleys. The kind used for moving gold. That's got to be the bank's foundation."

Rhodo jerked his leash and accelerated when they drew closer to the feature, then whined and barked, tugging in the direction of another, northbound tunnel.

"He's caught something now," said Wrytha, "but the trail leads away from the bank."

"Perhaps they only passed through here on the way to somewhere else," said Arghan. "Let him off. See where he goes."

Rhodo charged up the northbound tunnel, splashing through the puddles on the passage floor.

Wrytha dashed ahead. "We dare not lose him; he's faster than both of us."

They charged after the dog, following the sound of his paws crunching the debris that littered the path. Eventually, the faint tolling of a harbour buoy echoed from an opening in front of them. Myriad points of light pierced the darkness beyond it, bobbing as though floating on the waves.

"Ship's lanterns," Arghan whispered before emerging from the exit. He crouched and inhaled the salty air, surveying the scene while Wrytha caught up to him. A motley fleet of vessels anchored throughout Queen's Passage, the channel between Merchant's Isle and the distant shoreline of the smaller island called Onan's Landing.

Wrytha scanned the waterfront. "Where's Rhodo?"

Arghan pointed. "There."

Rhodo paced at the end of a nearby dock.

Arghan whipped a pebble into the water. "Schlika. Solstrus is even more clever than I thought. He's thinking like an Erne Warder. He's hid them on a ship. We don't have time to search the entire harbour and there's no telling where they'll land."

Wrytha scanned the harbour. "So it's impossible to know which route they'll take to the execution site."

"Right. We'd better get back; plan the only move we have left to make."

"Which is?"

"We've got to stop the execution before it happens."

Gavek huffed and slid a wooden crate onto the back of a wagon in the alley behind the Continental Theatre. "That's the last of them." He secured the gate and leaned against it, wiping his brow.

"Well done," said Khloe, handing him a cup of water.

"No thanks to you," he said, winking before taking a gulp.

Khloe swatted his arm, causing him to spill some of his drink.

"Hey, I was just kidding—"

"I've been busy packing," she said, crossing her arms. "I got fed up listening to you and Wardein argue about which way to pack the manuscripts. As if what order they go in matters right now." She kicked a pebble. "What's taking them so long? Why couldn't mother just let me go with them?"

"She is a little overprotective," said Gavek, "but can you blame her after what happened last night?"

"We would've made it."

"Would you, now?" said Wardein, chuckling as he exited the theatre.

Khloe rolled her eyes and went back inside while Wardein approached the wagon.

"Fiery lass," he said, handing Gavek a sealed parchment. "Here's the manifest. Be sure to check it when these are loaded and unloaded from Boskan's schooner. He may be tempted to keep some scrolls as souvenirs, even though he's been paid handsomely enough. We both know how important this cargo is."

"You can trust me, Master Wardein. I'll see to it."

"I know you will, and I know I can, which is why I want you to have this as well." Wardein handed him a folio and another parchment.

"What is this?" said Gavek. He tucked the folio under his arm and unfolded the sheet.

"The folio contains all my important documents, including detailed notes of recent plans I've made. The parchment is a letter to the princess."

Gavek's eyes bulged while he scanned the letter.

"Professor, no... I don't deserve—"

"Yes you do," he said, resting his hand on Gavek's shoulder. "More than any man I know. If anything should happen to me, there are explicit instructions enclosed to the Library's governors to honour my recommendation you be made Master of Her Majesty's Royal Archive and Chief Librarian of Trianon, pending her royal ascent, of course."

Gavek's eyes moistened; his voice cracked. "Of course... I... I don't know what to say, Master Wardein." He secured the folio and papers inside his satchel.

A crash thundered from inside the theatre, followed by a scream beyond the door. Gavek and Wardein spun toward it as it burst open, pushed by one of the young thespians Gavek had met earlier that day.

"Master Wardein," shrieked the slender young man, "soldiers are breaking down the front door!"

"The Alpinians?" said Gavek, his mouth gaping, meeting Wardein's frenzied gaze with one of his own. "How?"

Wardein swallowed, trembling as he gripped the young actor's shoulders. "Get out of here, Fynn. Run to the tavern. Tell the others not to return."

"But professor—"

"Go!" said Wardein, pointing down the alley. He pushed the young man's shoulder as he ran past. He pointed to the reins hitched to the side of the wagon. "Gavek, drive to the docks. Go now."

Gavek followed close behind him as he scurried to the door. "Wait, no! Khloe's in there."

"Do you hear me, son? Get the manuscripts out of here!" said Wardein, catching his breath. "Tell Boskan's men to load the crates as quickly as possible. You must set sail immediately after they're secured. Wait for no one. Leave Khloe to me." He pushed Gavek away, opened the door and ran inside.

"No!" said Gavek, running after him.

Gavek paused inside a curved corridor, panting. Shouts came from directly ahead. He looked down a short hallway, past the double doors which stood open to the stage. Alpinian troops stormed the outdoor spectator's court, carrying torches. Sira strutted in behind them, her signature crimson robe contrasted against the sea of violet cloaks streaming in from behind. She met his gaze and grinned, nodded, and pointed in his direction.

Gavek bolted up the staircase to the theatre's dormitory. "Wardein! Khloe!" He raced down the hall, glancing into the rooms as footsteps thundered up the staircase behind him. He reached the end of the actors' block and kicked open the door leading to Wardein's suite, reeling at what he saw. An Alpinian soldier marched out of a room carrying Khloe over his shoulder, struggling to maintain his grip while she kicked and screamed.

"Let go of me you vile oaf!" she yelled, elbowing him in the ear.

"You heard the girl," said Wardein, charging out the door after them, carrying a prop cane. "Let her go!" He struck the knight on the head, causing him to stumble.

The knight growled and threw Khloe against the wall. "You'll pay for that," he snarled, drawing his sword. He dodged Wardein's second swing and thrust his blade through the professor's torso.

"No!" screamed Gavek, sprinting down the hall.

Khloe scrambled to her hands and knees behind the knight's legs just as Gavek dove through the air, tackling him to the floor. Khloe crawled to Wardein's side while Gavek straddled the Alpinian's shoulders, pummelling his face.

"Get out... you've got to escape... get to the clock," said Wardein, gurgling blood, as Khloe cradled his head in her lap, "pull the lever before you go below."

The Alpinian fell limp. Gavek pushed him away and grabbed Khloe's hand as a squad burst into the hall, followed by Sira.

"After them," she screamed.

Gavek tugged Khloe's arm and the pair raced around another corner with the squad in close pursuit.

Wardein stared at the ceiling and quoted one of Sorto's verses, "Here we are at the curtain call, I pray you've seen I've done my all, to right this world of its woes and rid Your Kingdom of its foes."

"How touching, professor, a poet to your last breath," said Sira, smirking as she stopped and stood over him. "It seems I've finally won. We found your wagon. Thanks for packing the manuscripts so well. Solstrus will appreciate that when he takes possession of them."

"You've f-f—"

"I'm sorry, what? Speak up professor." She knelt down to hold her ear near his mouth.

"You've failed."

Sira chuckled. "Is that so?"

Wardein gripped her scarf. "Yes. God knows all about Solstrus' misdeeds, and so does Arghan of Danniker." His hand fell to the floor.

A member of the Alpinian squad hurried back around the corner. "Mistress Sira, they've vanished."

"Have none of you learned a thing from your experience at the Library? Nobody just vanishes. Did you search everywhere?"

She marched around the corner and stopped in front of a clock at a dead end. She glanced behind it, then felt its side. She triggered a switch and the clock swung open like a door on a hinge, releasing a cloud of dust. She coughed, batting the air as a pile of bricks became visible behind the opening.

"Wardein..." she whispered, scowling.

Another member of the squad exited one of the doors behind her. "What do we do now?"

"We have what we came for. If they want to hide, let them. We'll burn them out."

With Rhodo at their heels, Wrytha and Arghan turned the corner of Grayfriars Lane and Garden Row, two blocks away from the Continental Theatre.

Wrytha studied the layout of Traitor's Circle drawn on the back of her copy of the map of the catacombs. "I'm sure I can make a shot from anywhere around the perimeter. But how will we get through security to begin with? Won't they have all six streets blocked off, checking for weapons as people enter?"

"Two ways," replied Arghan, "Gavek and I will return to our suite at the Mariner's Inn and spend the night there. Its front door opens into the circle. That covers us. You, Khloe, and the others will come by way of... can you flip the page?"

Wrytha turned the sheet right side up, revealing the map of the catacombs.

"Here," Arghan continued, "there's a passage into the basement of the Olde Man. The clock tower should provide an excellent firing angle. We'll use it to escape once we free the prisoners."

Wrytha stopped and gripped Arghan's arm above the elbow. "The last time I saw the Olde Man it was crawling with Alpinian soldiers. What if it still is?" She lifted his wrists, wincing when she saw the abrasions left by the shackles he'd worn in the Palace chapel. She squeezed his hands. "Be honest with me, Arghan. Do you really think we stand a chance of succeeding tomorrow?"

Arghan gazed into her eyes. "Failure isn't an option for me. Do you remember what I told you during our walk under the bridge?"

"I do, but I sincerely hope it doesn't come to that. Orin's life is precious to me, but I'm not sure I could live with losing either one of you. I can't see any of us coming out of that plaza alive, can you?"

Arghan frowned. "There is another way. One that would give us a distinct advantage over all these obstacles. But you'd like it even less than this plan."

"Tell me."

A wave of screaming pedestrians suddenly filled the street.

"Help!" cried a woman wearing a sleeping cap, carrying an infant. "Somebody help! My house! My house!"

"What's this now?" said Wrytha, dodging the bodies bustling past them. She sniffed the air. "Do you smell... smoke?"

Arghan gasped when he looked in the direction the crowd was running from. Smoke billowed over the rooftops surrounding Oster's

Reach, set aglow by a wall of flames.

"Arghan, the theatre — it's on fire!" Wrytha dropped Rhodo's lead and bolted down the street.

"Wrytha, wait!"

Arghan snatched the dog's leash and charged after her. Heat radiated across his face when he caught up to Wrytha, who stood trembling only steps away from the edifice, transfixed by the blaze. A beam from the upper floor cracked, releasing what sounded like a moan before it spun and fell, careening toward the street.

"Wrytha!" he cried, snatching her away seconds before the blazon member splinted into pieces where she had stood. "Come on!" He led her into the same alley where the others had loaded the wagon. "The wagon's gone. Their work is done. We told them to wait in Wardein's underground hideout when they finished, remember?"

Wrytha glanced at him, dazed and blinking, then traced the line of muddy tracks leading out of the alley. "Yes, that's right…"

Guilt burned through Arghan's heart, hotter than any inferno. The sight of flames still traumatized her because of what he did in Koerska. He clenched his jaw. "No, it was Thurn's fault," he whispered, responding to his own thoughts. "Come, we'll take the back way in, under the bridge." He led her across the paved circle of Oster's Reach, pausing midway to glare at a procession of mounted Alpinians crossing the bridge. He looked toward the Library and saw another, smaller contingent watching the blaze from across the street. "Come," he said again, hastening down the steps to the river.

Several moments later they raced up the underground passage, splashing through the puddles outside Wardein's lair. Wrytha broke away, racing ahead. She skidded into the chamber and slowed, covering her mouth when her gaze fell on the pair huddled behind the table in the middle of the room. Tears sprouted from her eyelids. "Oh, thank God, Khloe!"

"Mother?" said the teen, lifting her head from Gavek's chest. She sprung from the bench where they sat. She ran to Wrytha and embraced her as Arghan and Rhodo entered the room.

Arghan stormed past Wrytha and Khloe. "Is everyone okay, Gavek? What happened?"

Gavek shook his head and dropped his chin against his chest, weeping. "Wardein..."

"What?" said Arghan, gripping Gavek's shoulder.

"He's dead," answered Khloe, red-faced, looking into Wrytha's eyes, "he... he died trying to save me."

Wrytha sobbed. She embraced Khloe and looked at Arghan. "I was so angry with him. I could have forgiven him, I should have—"

Arghan tensed his jaw and inhaled sharply through his nostrils. "The Alpinians lit the fire, didn't they?" he asked Gavek. "I saw some outside. How did they find you?"

"I wish I knew..." Gavek wept audibly, handing Arghan the parchment Wardein had given him. Arghan scanned the page. A single tear escaped the corner of his eye before he refolded it and handed it back to Gavek.

"It's as if he knew it was going to happen," said Gavek, staring at the opposite wall. He shook his head as if to rouse himself from his thoughts. "Arghan, I'm pretty sure the Alpinians seized the manuscripts. We had them all loaded on the wagon before they attacked. I snuck out after we eluded them and checked. The wagon's gone."

Arghan patted him on the shoulder. "You did your best, son. Put that letter in the lock box I gave you, along with the agreement you stole from Solstrus. Change into some trousers and a doublet. Bring the map of the catacombs. You're coming with me." Arghan threw off his grey cloak and pulled off his travelling garb. He grabbed the duffel Wardein had retrieved for him earlier and dumped it out on the table. Among the items were his second Twin Talon and a short-sleeved, navy blue gambeson embroidered with the emblem of the sea eagle. He pulled the garment on and hitched his second sword and scabbard to his arming belt.

"Where do you think you're going?" said Wrytha, drawing near to him as Gavek went off to change.

"If Solstrus wants a war, I'll give him a bloody war."

"All by yourself? Arghan, no! That's suicide. You said earlier Solstrus was thinking like an Erne Warder. Are you certain you are?"

Arghan stared at her with a mournful expression until Gavek interrupted.

"Ready," Gavek said.

Arghan nodded toward the tunnel exit. Gavek started for it and he followed.

"Arghan?" said Wrytha, running after him.

He turned back and took her hand. "Remember when I told you back on the street that I had another option in mind, one that you wouldn't like? Well, Solstrus holds all the cards now. It's time to level the field. Trust me, love. It's our best hope."

Wrytha bit her lip, searching his eyes. Eventually she squeezed his hand. "Okay. What do you need me to do?"

"Stay here, take command of the zealots." He handed her his treasure purse. "Get up early. Hide your braid under your hood. Go to the market. Buy bows, arrows and swords for all the Tzyani who can wield them. The blades are a last resort. It's covering fire I'll need. Use the tunnels as I told you to reach the Circle. Take up positions in the upper stories of the Olde Man. You'll know what to do when you see me."

Gavek and Arghan crouched in the shadows across the street from the Archprelate's estate, below a towering oak in a park called 'the Green'.

Arghan scowled. "This place will do; tie them up and wait for my signal." He dashed off, leaving Gavek to tend to their stolen horses.

Arghan's face simmered just like it did after Silla was slain. It turned Gavek's stomach to imagine what he might do next, considering what happened after they left Wardein's lair. The Alpinian cavaliers he ambushed on the Embankment never knew what hit them. Gavek finished securing the horses and whispered a prayer, thanking God that Arghan was on his side.

Arghan crouched against the estate wall and beckoned him to follow. Gavek cleared his throat and made the sign of the Three-in-One. He grabbed a burlap sack from the back of one of the horses and sprinted across the street.

"You're positive you memorized the route of every guard you saw?" asked Arghan, unravelling a rope when Gavek dropped down beside him. "There's no turning back now."

"Positive. Eight in the front. Eight in the back. Split equally between the grounds and the portico."

"Good." Arghan swung the rope over his head, latching a grapple to the top of the wall.

Moments later they knelt behind a hedge on the opposite side while Arghan surveyed the scene. "Okay. Give me half of those," he said, reaching.

Gavek groped inside the burlap sack, counting the lanterns and torches they'd collected from the Alpinian horsemen. Were these the tools they used to set the theatre ablaze?

"Stick close to the wall," Arghan whispered. "Stay low. Follow it to the trellis on the side of the house. I'll do the same on the opposite side. Wait until you're against the wall to light your lanterns and torches. Throw them after you hear me throw mine, then get to the second floor as fast as you can. We'll meet outside Solstrus' quarters. I'll go first."

"Got it."

Gavek watched Arghan creep behind the hedge up to the driveway and pause to gather some of the pebbles that covered its path. Arghan whipped one of them over his head, striking the fountain in the centre of the courtyard.

"What was that?" said one of the guards, turning toward the sound when the stone ricocheted off the statue's copper exterior. Arghan scampered across the driveway and disappeared behind some shrubs.

Gavek followed a hedge that ran perpendicular to the house's facade, and headed for the mansion's eastern wall. Before he could reach it, a figure walked through an archway only steps ahead of him. The lightly armoured soldier glanced back past the arch and proceeded to loosen his trousers. The sound of spattering liquid and the smell of warm ammonia intensified as the man turned in an arc in front of Gavek's face.

"What the—" exclaimed the man, spotting him. He fumbled for his weapon.

"Schlika!" exclaimed Gavek.

Gavek threw a swift uppercut. The guard howled and collapsed, clutching his groin. Next, he grabbed one of the heavy stones beside the hedge and swung it like a hammer, clanging against the soldier's nose guard. The guard fell limp. Gavek scanned the darkness around him, bug-eyed and panting.

"You okay over there?" shouted another guard from the lower terrace.

"Schlika," Gavek whispered. He closed his eyes, imagining the layout of the grounds as he had seen them in daylight. He slid off the fallen guard's helmet, put it on and stood up from behind the hedge. "Sorry," he said in the Gothan language, lowering his voice, "cursed gardener left his rake out. Tripped over it. Think I sprained my ankle."

"Schlika," said the terrace watchman. "I'll watch out for it. Go down to the barracks. I'll cover for you."

Gavek waved, then walked as swiftly as he could while pretending to limp. He passed the corner of the house then jumped over the hedge and raced for the outside wall.

A faint crash came from the other wing of the mansion, followed by another. Arghan had begun his assault. With only seconds now to act, Gavek dumped out the contents of the sack and lit each one of the lanterns, using the last one to ignite his torches. He threw the first lantern, missing an upper-floor window by a hand's breadth and watched it explode against the wall.

"So much for that idea." He ran the length of the house, hurling the rest of them into the windows of the ground floor. He paused at the end to watch the glow intensify as flames spread throughout each room. "That's more like it."

A bell rang from the second floor, followed by cries of alarm. Gavek hastened back to the trellis and scaled it, huffing as he reached the side portico in front of the door leading inside. He began to open it but jerked it nearly closed again as an Alpinian guardsman raced down the corridor toward the centre of the house, bellowing. Gavek peered past the door, listening.

"Come with me," said a voice unlike the first, "we must evacuate his eminence at once."

Gavek waited until the clanging footfalls subsided. He scooted inside, blinking when a thickening cloud of smoke floated across his eyes. He held his cloak to his face and dashed down the hall. Metal clashed against metal. Screams and thuds reverberated from deep inside the house. Gavek raced toward the agreed rendezvous point, leaping over the bodies of several fallen Alpinians until he skidded to a stop just short of an open door outside Solstrus' bedchamber.

Arghan stomped out, flinging blood off his sword. "Not here. He's in the wind."

Gavek dashed past him, scanning the room while Arghan followed. He scrambled to one of the night stands beside the bed and doused the lantern on top of it. He dropped to the floor and inspected the baseboards.

"There!" Gavek leaped up and ran toward a sliver of light along the floor. He ran his fingers over every object on the wall above it until he reached a candle sconce. He twisted it until it clicked. A section of the wall popped open, revealing a lit passage.

"Gavek you singular genius!" muttering Arghan, striding toward it.

"No, I'll go," Gavek said, pulling his dagger from its sheath. "I'd wager this leads to the wine cellar and back stables. If you hurry, you might catch them on the way out while I follow them from behind."

"Done," said Arghan, nodding. He raced out of the room.

Gavek sprinted down the passage, which led him to a narrow, spiral staircase; first of wood, then of metal and finally of rock, as though it had been hewn from the mount itself. The choking dryness of smoke gave way to dank, musty air. He reached a long, narrow, bricked tunnel and splashed through a series of puddles until he slammed into a wooden door.

He grabbed the latch and rattled it. "No! No you don't!"

He backed up several paces then sprinted, slamming his shoulder against the barrier. The door's hinges flew through the air, clinking across the floor at the same time he stumbled headlong onto it. Faint shouts, grunts and clanking steel came from beyond the cellar door. He spit dust and shook his head, looking up at a barefoot figure in a fine silk nightshirt.

Solstrus withdrew a dagger from a jewel encrusted sheath. "Sira said she put an end to you!" He growled and lunged at Gavek.

Gavek rolled. Solstrus' blade struck stone. Gavek kicked a wine rack over Solstrus, breaking at least a dozen bottles over his head. Solstrus writhed under the weight of the shelf, his white shirt now stained red.

Gavek leaped on top of Solstrus and pummelled his face until it grew swollen and bloodied. "You... had... Master... Wardein... murdered!"

"Gavek! Stop! We need him alive!" Arghan stood at the foot of the cellar stairs. He flung the blood off his blades and whipped them into their scabbards before running to Gavek's side.

Gavek withdrew, sobbing. "What has become of me?"

Arghan knelt beside Solstrus and held two fingers to his jugular. "Don't worry, he's alive. We've got to get out of here. Help me move him."

"The princess who would be queen," said Sira, sipping a glass of wine as she clenched Cybella's cheeks. "Well we'll see which one of us is wearing a crown come tomorrow."

Cybella pulled away, growling through her gag.

Sira held a hand to her ear. "What's that? I don't understand; speak up, wench." She giggled and snapped her fingers.

An Alpinian loosened Cybella's restraint.

"Untie me and we'll see which one of us is worthy of it, witch," Cybella taunted, bearing her teeth.

"Ha, she's feisty, isn't she?" said the Alpinian in the Gothan tongue.

"For now, Sergeant Horst," answered Sira, smirking, winking at Cybella. "Pity this one expired, isn't it?" She pointed at Teighthra's lifeless body tied to a post next to Cybella. "I would sooner have watched her burn at the stake. If you must torture the prisoners, try and keep them alive. Killing them too soon takes all the fun out of it."

The Alpinians cackled.

Orin thrashed his chains, yowling through an eyeless, black hood.

"Is there no end to your perverse abuses, you hypocrites?" said Cybella. "Haven't the Tzyani suffered enough? I'll see you all tried and hanged for this if its the last thing I do."

Sira and Hurst chuckled.

Footfalls clomped down the steep staircase behind them.

"Mistress Sira," said the courier, bowing as he removed his feathered cap. "Forgive the intrusion. I've got urgent news from Captain Raipheniel." He handed her a sealed scroll.

'Initiate Sira: Estate attacked. Mansion ablaze. Several knights slain. His eminence missing. Likely kidnapped by the criminal Arghan of Danniker. My forces occupied fighting the blaze. Your orders: weigh anchor and set sail for Encharra immediately with the prisoners pending Danniker's capture and arrest.'

Sira's grin vanished, replaced by a sullen glare.

"What's it say?" asked Horst, leaning over the page.

Sira crumpled the dispatch and tossed it out an open port hole. "Nothing. Just last-minute changes to our route. We're to dock near Knight's Bridge and take them by way of Tribune's March."

"Really? That's a bit predictable don't you think?"

Sira pushed him aside. "Solstrus demands expedition; it's the shortest route. We're to arrive at noon sharp and execute them without delay." She finished her wine with a gulp and stormed up the stairs.

Cybella glanced at the open port hole then watched Horst follow Sira up the stairs, and smiled.

CHAPTER NINETEEN
Execution

Khloe pointed at a recess in the catacomb wall. "Should be right here," she said, glancing at the page in her hand.

"Okay everyone," said Wrytha, nocking an arrow, "follow me. Stay alert."

Rearmed, each of the sixteen Tzyani zealots readied their bows and followed her into the narrow passage and up a winding staircase, covering each other at every landing until they reached a wooden door. Faint whirls, clunks and knocks came from behind it.

"What's that sound?" whispered Khloe, kneeling with an ear to the keyhole.

"The Olde Man's clockworks," answered Wrytha. "We're in the right place. Rhodo, scout."

The shepherd ran his nose along the bottom of the barrier, snorting. He sat and gently scratched the door.

"It's clear," said Khloe.

Wrytha nodded. "So far." She tugged the handle and entered. Dank, musty air filled her nostrils. "Ugh," she groaned, scrunching her nose. She crossed a gloomy chamber, headed for another staircase, and stopped suddenly when something snagged her toe. She recoiled, aiming her bow by instinct. "Khloe, the lantern, there."

Khloe scooted beside her and held up their only light source, revealing a withered corpse chained to the wall. "Eww."

One of the young men hustled to where they stood. "Forgotten prisoner — from an interrogation gone wrong, maybe? The Grand Prelate's soldiers have done deeds like this all over this city. Look, tassels." He relaxed his bowstring and used the tip of his arrow to probe a tattered kerchief hanging from the corpse's neck. "He's wearing a Khevet."

"One of our own," said the teen girl called Dannika, stepping forward. "When I get my hands on one of those fair-haired fiends I'll make them sorry they crossed us."

"You'll do no such thing," said Wrytha, moving between the girl and the young man. "That goes for you too, Zedekael. All of you, listen to me. We're here for justice, not revenge. The Shepherd King reserves the right to avenge, remember?"

"But Teighthra told us—"

"Teighthra is a misguided fool who nearly got you all killed. I am your Clan Mother! If anyone plans to disobey me, get out now and find your own way home. Otherwise, fall in. End of discussion."

Wrytha pivoted and headed for the stairs. Khloe followed, leading Rhodo.

Dannika passed Zedekael, giving him a knowing look. Zedekael rolled his eyes and joined the others. They proceeded to the main floor.

Wrytha crouched at the top of the stairs, looking out over the dusty stone floor. Particles swirled in the air, lit by golden sunbeams shining through the stained glass windows that flanked the tower's enormous pointed door. A staircase built into the outside wall rose from a landing opposite the cellar stairs, continuing its orbit around the tower's square interior until it terminated at a landing four flights above.

Wrytha repeated her last command to Rhodo. The dog bounded up the staircase, sniffing and wagging its tail. Several moments later it dashed down again, reporting with a single bark.

"Thank the Maker, it's clear," said Wrytha. "We'll tripwire the stairs just to be safe. Jeordri, Matticai, take care of it, then join us at the top. The rest of you, with me."

They passed through the two-story room that housed the clock's four faces and mechanism, ascending the chamber by way of a spiral staircase to another room of even greater height, which housed an array of cast iron bells of various sizes. They reached the top and fanned out inside the observation gallery.

Wrytha, Khloe, Dannika, and Zedekael knelt behind the stone parapet overlooking Traitor's Circle while the others divided into teams of two to occupy each of the tower's bartizans and other three walls. A gust whirled through the gallery.

"Not that I'm complaining," said Khloe, shivering, noticing the lines of colourful pennants flapping above their heads, "but where are the Alpinians?" She traced the cords from where they were anchored above them, down to the rooftops of the lower structures around the circle. "You can see the whole world from up here."

Wrytha scanned the plaza like a hawk scopes a field. A stream of pedestrians poured in from each of the six streets that fed the circle, joining the throng already throwing rotten produce at the common criminals tied to chopping blocks around a platform at the centre of the forum. Beside each one, a hooded axeman stood ready to relieve them of their heads. Behind the executioners, heavy stakes stood on pyres in the middle of the stage. Between the platform and the Mariner's Inn, spectators in colourful attire sat on bleachers overlooking the scene. A drum rattled and a mountain pipe began to wail amid shouts bellowing from the north. Wrytha's nostrils flared when she glimpsed a procession of violet cloaks enter the plaza from the terminus of Tribune's March, escorting two carriages.

"It's them," Wrytha said, lifting her bow over the parapet, "get ready!"

A pair of hooded Alpinians stepped out of the lead carriage, carrying amphoras,[1] followed by two more who carried what looked like a body wrapped inside a burlap sack. The amphora-bearers marched onto the platform and smashed their vessels over the firewood at the bases of the stakes, dousing them with a dark, sticky liquid, then ignited a nearby

---

1. Amphora – an earthenware vessel used to transport either dry or liquid commodities by ship.

brazier and stood at attention at either side of it. The other two threw their load between the pyres and then joined the others. A red-headed figure in a crimson robe emerged next and strutted to the centre of the stage.

Khloe nocked an arrow. "That's the witch that nearly killed Gavek and me — Sira!"

Wrytha touched Khloe's bow hand. "Wait." Eyes darting, she scanned the crowd again, then cast her gaze across the windows and rooftops around the circle. "Where is he? Come on, Arghan—"

The pipes and drumming stopped. A hush fell over the spectators. The door of the second carriage opened, re-awakening frantic murmurs from the crowd when a blonde female figure in a flowing satin gown stepped out, followed by a hooded male in a tattered tunic and trousers. A nearby guard yanked off the eyeless sack. The ruddy young man blinked and squinted.

"Orin!" said Wrytha, almost breathless. She whipped her braid behind her head, stood up, and drew her bowstring, steadying herself with one foot on top of the parapet, following the body of the guard who prodded the prisoners toward the stage. "I've got the one behind them. Everyone, pick a target. Khloe, track the one next to the blonde. That must be Cybella."

Rhodo's ears cocked on end. A crash resounded from one of the floors below.

"Someone's sprung one of the traps," cried Jeordri.

Wrytha nodded without taking her eyes off her target. "You, Matticai, and Jaren, go! Rhodo, guard. Everyone else, fall in beside me!"

"Captain Raipheniel!" yelled a courier, leaping over a pile of smouldering debris inside the ruins of Solstrus' mansion.

"What is is?" said the swarthy Regalian, wiping his soot-stained brow.

"Sentries at Knight's Bridge report Sira's party docked the *Waverunner*."

"What?" He smashed a bottle of spirits on the floor. "I gave her orders to sail."

"Last report indicates she's leading a procession down Tribune's March."

"The witch! She's going ahead with it! She may be bedding the Archprelate but that's the last time she crosses me!" He flung his belt around his waist and slid his sword into its scabbard. "Sergeant," he yelled to the man standing beside the pavilion where Solstrus had eaten breakfast days before, "any word from Lieutenant Portaias?"

"No sir; last time I checked, his team was still searching for his eminence."

"Curse that meddling Danniker," he muttered, "everything was under control until he showed up." He stomped over the wreckage. "Assemble the men; we ride for Traitor's Circle at once!"

The crowd buzzed like a beehive, jostling for a better view as the jailers marched Cybella and Orin toward the stage.

"Who ya s'pose that pretty young woman is, Gustof?" asked an old woman, frowning as they passed by. "What's she done?"

"Don't know, mum," said a soot-faced man standing beside her with a broom over his shoulder. "Hey, what are you lot up to, anyway? Ya run outta crooks so now yer snatchin' fair maids off the streets?"

One of the Alpinian knights whipped his blade short of the man's face, forcing everyone nearby to recoil. "Shove off, peasant."

"Leave them be, you insolent oaf," cried Cybella, twisting her shackles, "I'll not have you treat my subjects that way!"

The knight snorted. "Yeah, and what are you going to do about it, your highness?" He shoved her, causing Cybella to stumble to her knees.

"Hey!" Orin yelled. He halted, closing the gap with the Alpinian who prodded him from behind. He thrust his elbow into the man's solar plexus and then, using the slack gained by his deliberate misstep, flung the chain that joined him to the knight's belt around the neck of the guard ahead of him, choking him to the ground. He kicked him in the face for good measure then offered Cybella a hand. "Is it true?" he said, lifting her to her feet, "you're princess Cybella, heir to the throne?"

"Yes, for what it's worth," she said, brushing her bangs aside, "and you are?"

"Orin Pan—"

An Alpinian's club struck his back. Two more soldiers joined the fray, raining down blows until he fell limp on the pavement.

"Orin," cried Cybella as they dragged him by. "Orin?!"

"Those devils!" shouted Wrytha, straining against her bowstring. "I can't get a shot."

"I can't either," said Zedekael, adjusting his aim, "too many people in the way."

Khloe skipped toward the stairs. "I'll go down, see if I can—"

"No, you don't! Get back here." Wrytha lowered her bow and shook her fingers.

"We've got to do something," said Khloe.

Wrytha wiped the sweat from her brow and bit her lip. She threw off her cloak and ran to the door. "If they try to light the pyres, fire at will."

"Where are you going?" said Dannika.

"To get a better angle."

Wrytha's forehead throbbed in tune with her quickening pulse. She scrambled down the stairs and raced across the floor of the bell chamber.

Matticai topped the stairs coming up from the level below. "Clan Mother?"

She replied without looking at him, "We heard the commotion; everything all right?"

"Yeah," he said, puffing out his chest, "couple of purple-cloaks with crossbows barged in here a few minutes ago. Me n' my boy Jeordri turned 'em into pin cushions. Shoulda' seen it, it was—"

"Another time, Matticai," she said, huffing. "Help me up?" She held out a foot and reached for the ledge of one of the tall open windows.

"Sure," he said, running to her side. He folded his fingers and stooped, allowing Wrytha to use his hands like a stirrup. He grunted and lifted her over his head until she could grip the sill, leering up at her as she scrambled over it. "Anything else, Wrytha?"

Wrytha looked at him out of the corner of her eye. "Get back to Jeordri; keep watching in case more arrive."

"Sure," he said with a wink, skipping away.

"And Matticai?"

"Yeah?"

"Mind your eyes or I'll tell your mother."

"Uh, okay, Wrytha, whatever—"

"Clan Mother."

"Uh, okay, Clan Mother." He nodded, blushing and hustled down the stairs.

Wrytha shook her head and clung to a nearby column as she inched her toes out onto the ledge outside the opening. *Where are you Arghan?* She scanned the crowd one more time before letting go of the wall and crept out onto the back of one of the stone gargoyles on the corner of the ledge. She aimed an arrow at Sira. "Now that's more like it."

Sira Beihan paced behind the hooded executioners while three squads of Alpinian guards fanned out around the circumference of the platform. When finished taking their posts, Sira nodded and the prisoners were dragged onto the pyres and lashed to the stakes. She circled behind them in order to address those sitting in the bleachers.

"First Minister, ladies and lords, palatial ministers and magistrates, I am the Archprelate's initiate, Sira Beihan of Alpinia. Solstrus regrets that neither he nor the captain of his guard are able to officiate today's proceedings, having been attacked by ruthless criminals working with the Tzyani zealots." Sira bowed toward a man who wore a jewelled necklace over a fur-trimmed cloak. "First Minister, have the Lords of the House heard the charges against these commoners and found them wanting?"

"Indeed we have," he said.

The axemen raised their weapons in unison.

Sira raised her hand. "Does it please the House for his eminence to exact the people's vengeance?"

"It does."

She dropped her arm in a chopping action. Axes fell. A dozen heads rolled off the stage and onto the plaza. The crowd cheered. A white streak flashed across her peripheral vision. Horse hooves thundered up Palace Street. A commotion erupted among the spectators and she looked toward the sound.

"Curse you, Raipheniel," she muttered, "you won't stop this." She bellowed to the executioners beside the brazier, "Light your torches!"

"But you've not read the charges," called the First Minister, rising to his feet.

The torch-bearers gave each other a questioning glance.

"Just do it!" screamed Sira.

An arrow whizzed past Sira's head, slicing her cheek.

"Agh!" she screamed, wiping a streak of blood from her face.

"Shields!" commanded Sergeant Horst, lifting his own. "Close ranks!"

The troops constricted around the pyres under a hail of arrows.

Raipheniel traced their origin. "Get in there!" he hollered, pointing at the clock tower. His contingent drew their swords and raced through the crowd.

Someone shouted from high above the bleachers, "Stop! All of you, or the Archprelate swings!"

The crowd suspired with awe at the sight of two men standing on the roof of the Mariner's Inn. One stood nearer the edge in a silk dressing gown, soiled, ragged and trembling; his hair standing on end. The other poked him with the tip of a sword; seething, muscular, sombre and keen, clad in the eagle-embroidered navy blue arming doublet of an Erne Warder.

Arghan tightened a noose around Solstrus' neck and booted him toward the end of a banner mast. "Let the condemned go or so help me

God he'll fly like a kite!"

Solstrus screamed, spitting flying from his foaming lips, "Do as he says, you imbeciles!" A stream of urine trickled down his leg.

"My word, is that Solstrus, the Archprelate?" squawked the First Minister's wife, fanning her face. "Who does that ruffian think he is?"

"Arghan of Danniker," muttered Raipheniel as he hurried past. "Do it! All of you, stand down, that's an order."

"No!" screamed Sira, contorting her ruby lips, scrambling over the piles of chopped wood. She grabbed one of the executioners' torches and lit it off the brazier.

"Sergeant!" snapped Raipheniel, pointing.

Horst drew his sword and lunged at Sira. An arrow shot past his shoulder, beating his blade to her heart. Sira collapsed on the pyre, clutching the arrow shaft protruding from her chest. Horst grabbed her torch and whipped it away from the woodpile, throwing it over his shoulder. He stumbled to the top and untied Cybella and Orin.

"Who's that?" said Orin, straining to look over his shoulder as Cybella took his hand and led him off of the pyre.

"My father," answered Cybella, grinning.

"Your father—"

"What now, Danniker?" called Raipheniel.

"Cut them a path to the door of the Olde Man. Let them enter then close it up. Not one of you is to set a foot inside, understood?"

Raipheniel nodded and gestured to Horst, who called his men to form two lines, parting the spectators from the stage to the door of the tower. Cybella and Orin rushed to it, ignoring the jeers of the groping crowd.

"They're gone. Please, let me go," said Solstrus, teetering, attempting to turn back on the mast.

"Shut up," said Arghan, jabbing with his sword. "You're worse than your nephew. Tell me where the manuscripts are and I'll think about it."

Solstrus gritted his teeth, eyes tightly closed. He opened them again, swaying, groping for the mast at the sight of the street below. He loosed his bowels. The discharge oozed down his leg and plummeted three stories, finally splattering on the head of the governor of Shipper's Bank. "Mount Tria," he stammered, "caretaker's shed... south of the... Cathedral... of Trianon."

Arghan grinned and sheathed his sword. "See, now was that so hard?"

"Danniker?" called Raipheniel.

"Now we wait," Arghan said, watching the long hand on the Olde Man's clock face hit a minute to noon. He estimated the Tzyani would need at least fifteen minutes to make it back into the catacombs, that was if Gavek had reached them in time to give them the message.

"Do you really think you've any hope of escaping, Danniker?" said Raipheniel, pacing.

He turned away and looked at Hurst, who nodded slightly, indicating a point of interest with his eyes. Raipheniel smirked when he spotted lieutenant Portaias leading a squad down an alley near the back of the inn.

"I'm done running, Raipheniel," Arghan replied, oblivious to the impending threat. "This ends here and now."

The Olde Man's bells gonged the first notes of their noontime toll. Portaias and his men kicked open a set of dormer windows and rushed toward him from either side.

Cybella tore the lace trim off her cuff and tied her golden locks into a ponytail while she peeped through the Olde Man's door. "I can't believe it. What's he doing?"

"Don't know, but whatever it is, I approve," Orin said, groaning, running his fingers over the lump on his scalp. "I thought the king was your dad?"

"It's complicated," she said, rushing to his side. "You're bleeding. Here, let me—" She caressed the purple flesh beside his swollen right eye.

"Ow," he said, hunching his shoulders, batting her hand away, "I'll live."

"Orin, bro, who's the babe?" said Matticai, thumping down the stairs with Jeordri close behind. Rhodo raced past them and leaped on Orin, tail wagging and licked his face.

"Hey buddy, nice to see you too," Orin said between the slurps. "Watch your tongue, Matticai. This 'babe's' royalty."

"Oh Schlika, really? My bad." He made a clumsy attempt at a bow. "Your royalness."

Orin rolled his eyes.

"Cybella will do."

Matticai kissed her hand. "Whatever you like 'Bella. Your wish is my command."

"Um, perhaps this isn't the time for long introductions," she said, pulling away. "We've got to get out of here."

"Agreed," said Orin. His grin vanished, replaced by a sombre stare at the sight of Wrytha running down the stairs.

Wrytha slowed as she neared the floor. Her gaze fixed on her son, she dashed toward Orin and slapped him across the cheek.

"Ow!" he cried, "that hurts!"

"You're in a lot of trouble when this is over," she said, throwing her arms around his neck, kissing him. "For now, let's get you to safety. Jeordri, Matticai, call the others down."

"Yes, ma'am," they said.

Cybella, stepping forward. "I'm sorry, you are?"

"Forgive me, your highness," Wrytha said, bowing. "My name is Wrytha Pan-Deighgren. I'm the Clan Mother of the Tzyani enclave of Nova Elkahrn on Lake Riva. This impetuous fool," she swatted Orin's shoulder, "came from my own womb, though you'd never know it by the way he behaves."

Footsteps came up the basement stairs. In a flash, Wrytha aimed an arrow at the landing. "Gavek!" she exclaimed, lowering her weapon.

"Gavek?" said Cybella, hastening to greet him. "The librarian, of the monastery of Cairhn?"

Gavek leaned against the pony wall next to the stairs, panting. "Yes, that's right. Pleased to finally meet you, your highness." He tried to bow but only managed to drop his head a little. "I'd — wait a second, excuse me." He forced himself the rest of the way. "I'd have arrived sooner but I forgot to take a torch and got lost."

"You... got lost?" said Khloe, giggling as she scampered down the steps ahead of the others. "I thought you said you have an eidetic memory?"

"It's dreadfully dark down there and its been a very long night."

"Tell me you know how we're getting out of this," said Wrytha, hands on her hips.

"Boskan's ready to sail at Onya Landing, near the place the *Flussotter* dropped us. His ship is the *Duskrider*. Nicah and Auria are already there. Arghan sent me to lead the rest of you to it."

"What about him?" said Wrytha, licking her upper lip, glancing back through the window.

Gavek looked at the floor and bit his tongue.

"What about Arghan, Gavek? Look at me." She studied his eyes when he finally looked up. "He's not coming," she said, realizing the answer, "never planned to. He's going to get himself killed so we can all escape?"

"The last true Erne Warder," whispered Cybella.

"Something like that," Gavek finally admitted.

Wrytha leered through the window. "Not if I can help it. Gavek, take Cybella and the others to the rendezvous. If we don't make the pier within the hour, sail without us. That's an order. All of you, obey the princess. You must make sure she is delivered safely to Duke Weorthan of Ostergaart. Gavek will lead you there. I'll do my best to catch up, perhaps in Sigoe if we're lucky."

"Sigoe?" Cybella queried, "won't the Alpinians anticipate that? Wouldn't it be shrewd to sail to Ropa and take the Ebon valley to Straskost, by way of Cairhn?"

"It would, your highness," answered Gavek, "but Arghan believes an invasion from the sea is imminent."

"Invasion?" exclaimed Cybella, "what—"

"A Zuelan armada," Wrytha responded. "Thurn's masterstroke. Gavek will explain later."

"What are you going to do, mother?" said Orin, "we can't just leave you."

"Why not?" she said, touching his chest, "you did once already. There are bigger things at stake now, Orin. Your brother was injured badly when you were arrested. He needs your protection, so does Cybella. It's crucial she succeed in her mission, for all our sake. Others have already given their lives trying to save her. It must not be in vain. It's time your learned how to use those muscles of yours to protect people, instead of avenging them."

"Your mother's right, Orin," said Cybella. "Yeshua's already smiled on us today; He can deliver the Erne Warder and your mother too."

"Yeshua... how do you know—"

Something banged the door, rattling the hinges.

"Go, all of you, now!" Wrytha pointed toward the cellar exit then bolted back up the tower stairs.

With Arghan distracted and the throng turning into an angry mob — some of them forming a human barrier between the execution stage and the Olde Man — Raipheniel ordered Horst's contingent into the inn, hoping to exploit the advantage while it remained. "Where the blazes are my crossbowmen?" he asked Horst, meeting him behind the bleachers. "They'd make easy work of this were they here."

"They're still in the watchtowers," answered Horst as they rushed through the inn door, "as Solstrus ordered."

"Solstrus, curse him; he should've left military decisions to me. The Grand Prelate will have our heads if he goes down. To the roof!"

Meanwhile on the ledge, Portaias and his men pressed their attack from both sides, forcing Arghan to draw his second Talon. While parrying a thrust from his left, Arghan dodged another from his right and sidestepped, dropping his weight as he swung his blade in a feigned attack, landing its heavy pommel at the joint of the man's wrist, disarming him. He kicked him off the roof while ducking yet another strike.

"Thugs, all of you," he taunted, dispatching another to the street. "Never fought a proper war in your lives!"

The next attacker swung low.

Arghan leaped over the blade, swinging both swords in an inward, arm-over-arm draw, whipping them outward again as he landed, striking both the low-swinger and the Alpinian to his right. "A perfect eagle! Von Terrack would've been proud!"

Portaias grabbed something from behind his waffenrock. "Eagle this, you arrogant son of a she-dog!" He bounded off the steep roof, flanking his own men, and flung a handful of iron pellets in Arghan's face.

Arghan skidded off the ledge. One of his Talons slipped through his fingers, tumbling through the air until it landed somewhere on the street below. He caught the mast with his free hand inches away from Solstrus' ankle and dangled there like a cat hanging from a tree. Solstrus drove his heel onto Arghan's knuckles. Arghan grunted and batted him with the flat of his remaining sword, dislodging Solstrus from his own tenuous perch. He kicked his legs up and around the mast while Solstrus fell. Arghan released his hand grip, dropped his torso and hung upside down to see Solstrus now clinging to the mast with both hands, kicking and screaming in the wind.

"You're mine now, Danniker!" Portaias hollered, with a devilish grin. "They'll sing songs about me: the knight who slew the last Erne Warder!" He raised his sword above his head, preparing to strike.

An arrow sliced through the air like a beam of light and struck Portaias in the eye. A second flew, then a third, striking the last of his men in their hearts while he was still upright. The three bodies tumbled off the roof, crashing onto the bleachers amid the shouts and screams of those forced to evacuate them.

Still hanging upside down, Arghan looked past Solstrus' writhing body and caught Wrytha's gaze, gaping. She dangled over the centre of the plaza, with her legs twisted around one of the pennant cords that was anchored between the tower and the inn's roof, her raven-hued braid twirling in the wind. She swung herself upright and threw her bow over the cord, using it to zip the rest of the way down it until she rolled on the roof in front of the mast.

"Give me your hand," she shouted.

Arghan flexed his stomach muscles and swung up to take her grip. Wrytha pressed her heels against the mast bracket and grunted, falling onto her rump as she pulled him upright.

Arghan straddled the mast and sheathed his Talon, sweat dripping from his beard. "This will make a great story at the wedding, don't you think?"

Wrytha scooted forward and slapped his cheek. "Don't you ever do that again, Arghan of Danniker or so help me God I'll—"

Arghan crawled onto the roof and kissed her.

"Mm, later, you handsome fool. More Alpinians are on their way." She pushed him aside and stood up, aiming another arrow at the window she'd seen the others use to reach the roof. "We need to escape."

Footfalls thundered through the open pane.

"Right. Give me a second, cover the window." He sprung onto the mast and pulled Solstrus up.

"What are you doing?"

Arghan pushed Solstrus face down onto the roof, cut the rope below the noose and retied it around his ankles.

"No, don't!" squealed Solstrus, kicking.

Arghan dragged him by the ankles and pushed him over the ledge. Solstrus plummeted, wailing, until the rope jerked taught and he fainted, swaying inches above the bleachers.

"That's better," Arghan said, gripping Wrytha's elbow, "let's go."

CHAPTER TWENTY
Flight

Arghan and Wrytha scrambled onto a balcony on the south side of the inn.

"Wait," said Wrytha, "we're going the wrong way. Boskan's ship is docked at Onya Landing."

"We're not going there," said Arghan, monitoring the footfalls stomping across the roof behind them. He leaped to the next balcony and climbed onto the back side of the roof.

"We're not?" said Wrytha, following.

"I'll explain later; let's lose these goons first." He steadied himself with his hands outstretched, then sprinted along the ledge, vaulted across the alley, and landed on the adjacent rooftop.

Wrytha jumped without a head start and landed ahead of him.

Arghan snickered. "Show off."

They raced across the rooftop toward the northwest corner of the townhouse. Arghan glanced back to gauge their pursuers progress and stopped, squinting. "What are they doing?" Rather than following, the Alpinians were stacked up at the edge of the inn's roof, shouting at each other.

"And here I thought that game of darts in Sigoe was just an act," said Wrytha, looking in the same direction. "They're all pointing at something in the harbour. Wait, their captain just arrived. He's waving them back."

A great boom cracked through the cloudless sky like the sound of thunder, followed by what she could only imagine was the sound of a warrior angel in flight. The spire of the Palace of Trianon exploded in the distance, collapsing in a hail of stone and mortar onto the rooftops of the Old Town.

Wrytha opened her mouth and shuddered. "Father of Lights have mercy on us!"

"Tell me what you see," said Arghan, gripping her shoulders, squinting at the blurry shapes in the distance.

"Black sails as far as the eye can see, emblazoned with golden, fanged skulls; the harbour's full of them!"

"It's begun; the Zuelan fleet has arrived. There's no time to waste. We must hurry."

"Hurry where?"

"Mount Tria. The cathedral cemetery. Solstrus told me where they hid the manuscripts."

"Are you crazy? That's across the river; we'll never make it in time."

"We won't make it to the landing now either. With the Zuelans in the harbour, Boskan will waste no time disembarking once the others make it aboard, that's if they haven't sailed already. Those may be the last surviving copies of the lost Scriptures. I owe it to Cybella — to the world — to try to save them. I've done my duty as an Erne Warder, now I must do my duty as as a Cantorvarian. We stole some horses from the Alpinians last night and hitched them in the alley behind the theatre. It's only a few blocks."

Flashes of fire and puffs of smoke cascaded across the fleet, each accompanied by a thunderous crack. A hail of projectiles wailed through the air like dread wraiths, blasting into several buildings across the city, including the roof of the Mariner's Inn which exploded in a spray of splinters.

Wrytha screamed and said, "Lead the way."

Horst secured the door of the Olde Man. "It's no use, sir, the citizens are going berserk out there. I'd wager the *Waverunner* is already hemmed in by the Zuelan fleet. Everyone's fleeing south across the Ambertyne. By all accounts, Zuelan raiders have already made it ashore."

"Blast it!" boomed Raipheniel, throwing off his cloak. "Where did they all come from? How did they get past coastal artillery? What the blazes are the Cortavians doing, sitting on their halberds?"

"What Cortavians? Take away the palace guards and practically all you have left are the caretakers and gardeners. The rest are off fighting the Lyracians, remember?"

"Of course, the bloody war. If only the First Legion wasn't wrapped up in it too. Danniker wouldn't have gotten away with any of this if they were here. But that's wishful thinking; it's down to us. We've got to get the Archprelate to safety. Nobody saw the prisoners leave, which means there's got to be a way out of here."

Horst glanced at Solstrus.

The Archprelate sat on the wooden floor with his arms wrapped around his knees, rocking back and forth, staring at the wall and muttering, the noose still tied around his neck. "Danniker... the manuscripts... he's... he's going to get them back... ruin us all..."

Horst nodded and directed his gaze toward the cellar steps. "Captain... a word?"

Raipheniel nodded and the two men headed for the stairs.

"Keep watch 'till we return," he said to the other knights in the room.

The men reached the cellar.

Horst crossed the floor and opened the door leading to the catacombs. "This is where they went, I'm sure of it. Probably how they came in too. You can be sure it leads to the same network of catacombs we used to transport the princess and the zealots from the bank to the docks."

"That's excellent, Horst! How did you—"

He pointed to the corpse against the wall. "We interrogated a suspect here last week. Clocksmith heard the screams and discovered what we were up to. I let him go in exchange for a few 'trade secrets', which included the location of this door and at least a half dozen others across the Isle."

"Capital. Let's round up the others and get going."

"That's the other thing I wanted to discuss, captain," said Horst, gripping Raipheniel's arm. He leaned closer and whispered, "You said we've got to get the Archprelate to safety. But do we?"

"What?" said Raipheniel, pulling his arm away. "It's our duty."

"Hear me out, captain. You saw the old man; he's lost his wits. He soiled himself up there, by the Temple! He got what he deserves if you ask me, and what did our brothers in arms get, including the good lieutenant? Kicked off the roof — an inglorious death! Maybe it was our duty to save Solstrus before, but now there's a Horde running amok through the city and you want us to risk our necks rescuing that filthy tyrant? Who's to say we're all liars if we tell the Grand Prelate he perished in this invasion? I say we string him up, head back to the Cathedral, grab whatever gold we can — possibly even settle the score with Danniker — and then get the blazes out of the city while the getting is good."

Raipheniel studied the veteran's weary eyes. If anyone would get away with speaking his mind to the ambitious younger captain from time to time, it was Horst. But had he gone too far? Screams came from beyond the Olde Man's rattling door. Raipheniel looked at the crest on his violet waffenrock then peered up at the stairs. "No rope. We'll carry him down to the catacombs. Bring some oil and a torch. His body can never be found."

Fires raged all over Merchant's Isle, filling the streets with clouds smoke and ash. Under cover from artillery fire, Zuelan mercenaries stormed the quay and soon rampaged through the streets, driving a mob of frantic civilians southward through Traitor's Circle. Though clad in mismatched armour looted from fallen foes from across the known world, refinished with black lacquer, each man's armoured mask bore the same contorted visage of an angry demon; their helmeted foreheads crowned with a single, up-swept horn.

"Take their heads!" screamed their Dai-Kaighan[1], his curved blade oozing with blood. "You are harbingers of doom in the service of Zuel!"

A group of invaders split off from the rest and finished routing the hapless denizens of Trianon from the plaza then hurried to the execution stage and fanned out around the circle.

"We're too late," one said in their native tongue, kicking a piece of wood at the bottom of the pyre.

"How can we be?" hissed another. "Look, the fire was never lit."

A figure emerged through the black smoke at the circle's edge. Omhigaart Thurn — his Liester disguise discarded for a simple black gambeson and his grizzly beard shorn to a fine white stubble — marched across the plaza and bounded up the empty bleachers. He slowed when he reached the place where Arghan's fallen Talon had embedded itself in one of the seats.

"Danniker," he sneered, constricting the deep creases of his well-worn face. He snatched the blade by the hilt and whipped it through the air a few times before sliding it under his heavy leather belt. His piercing blue eyes surveyed the remnants of the rope dangling from the mast above, then traced the one wire stripped of lanterns to where it anchored to the Olde Man's tower. A further glance at the debris around it's door — more dense than anywhere else in the plaza — told him the rest of the story.

"Search the tower!" He barked, descending the bleachers. "Use the hounds."

A Zuelan warrior held a piece of tattered silk to the snouts of two dogs he controlled by a twin-corded, studded leash. Muscles rippled below sleek coats of black and amber. The animals bounded up the wood pile to the place where Cybella had been lashed. They darted around it, snorting, then bolted down it again and raced to the Olde Man. Mouths foaming, they cocked their cropped ears and paced in front of the door.

"See?" cried Thurn, hustling to it. "Good lads," he said, dropping pieces of jerky at the canines' feet. "Break it down!" he hollered.

Several minutes later Thurn, accompanied by a few members of his

---
1. Dai-Kaighan – Literally 'half' or inferior Kaighan, an officer subservient to their warlord.

crew, stepped into the darkened passage of the catacombs, drawn to the sight of coals glowing from a nearby alcove.

"Someone get me a torch, a lantern, anything," he said, waving his fingers when he spied a glint of gold on the constricted finger of the smouldering corpse. He took out a kerchief and shook it while a crewman handed him his lantern. He gripped the ring with the cloth, slid it off the dead man's finger and held it to the light.

"Still hot," he said, grinning as he turned it in front of his eyes.

"Look at the engraving," said the man with the eye patch who had fetched the lantern. "Isn't that—"

"The Archprelate's seal?" Thurn said, chuckling. He rolled the kerchief around the ring and stuffed it in his pocket while he spat on Solstrus' charred remains. "Fiercely done, Arghan," he said, kicking the head he surmised had been severed prior to the burning. "I didn't think you had it in you."

The hounds sprung into the tunnel and bounded down the passage, bellowing.

"After them," cried Thurn, snapping his fingers and pointing. "We'll catch him yet."

"Looks clear," said Zedekael, spying through the grate, overlooking Onya Landing. "The ship's anchored offshore. There's a man waiting on the pier next to a launch."

Gavek pulled up his hood. "That's got to be him. Let's go." He hurried up a staircase and ducked through a doorway to reach the alley above.

Khloe crouched behind him and surveyed the trail of abandoned vehicles littering Shore Street. "Creepy; it's deserted."

"Just because it looks that way, doesn't mean it is, Khlo'," quipped Orin in a snide tone. He ran past them and ducked behind one of the abandoned carts. He peered over it and waved them on.

Khloe stuck out her tongue at him, shaking her head. "Arrogant jerk. Who's he think he is?"

"Never mind him, come on," Gavek said, tugging her elbow. "Khloe and I will go first, in case anyone's watching." He made eye contact with Cybella, who nodded her agreement.

They scurried across the street and down the stairs to the quay. When they neared the berth they signaled the others.

Gavek called out to the portly fellow who stood on the dock. "Boskan?"

"Aye, lad, an' ye must be Gavvock," he answered, extending a hand while he scratched his stubbly cheek with the other. "It's about time. Me men 're eager to get the 'ell out of 'ere with what's brewin' o'er yonder."

"It's *Gavek*, actually," he said, grimacing at the touch of the man's vice-like grip.

"Whatever. We're ready ta' sail." He looked over Gavek's shoulder, watching the rest of the group approach. "Crikey! This is yer party? Wardein said nothin' o' this many, let alone the dog. Rozghow," he called to the man at the oars, "we'll hafta make two trips." He turned back to Gavek. "Me launch only holds a dozen, don't ya know? You an' yer girlfriend can go first if ya like."

Gavek blushed. He looked back, fiddling with his satchel strap while he watched the others progress across the landing. "Schlika," he exclaimed.

Thurn's black hounds burst over the wall and raced down the steps, snarling as they leaped onto Cybella's back, pushing her to the ground.

"Princess!" cried Orin, turning back at the sound of her scream.

Rhodo growled and broke from Khloe's grip.

"Rhodo!" she yelled, too late to stop him.

The shepherd bolted past Orin and leaped through the air, catching the throat of one of the Zuelan hounds as he landed. Orin grabbed Cybella's arm and pulled her to her feet, ripping her skirt from the jaws of the second beast. "Run," he shouted, pushing her ahead. He glimpsed Thurn and his men drawing their swords as they topped the stairs. "Archers, cover us!" He grabbed Cybella's hand and they sprinted for the dock.

Scattered midway across the landing, the Tzyani zealots dropped behind cover and released a volley of arrows, killing two of Thurn's men.

"Take cover!" yelled Thurn, ducking behind a crate.

"I don't see Danniker. Who are they? Not Cortavians?" the man in the eye patch said, dropping behind him.

"Does it matter, Crowe? Give them a taste of Zuelan fire. The princess is with them. She's getting away."

Crowe grinned and snatched a ceramic sphere from his belt. He unfastened the lid of Thurn's lantern and used it to ignite a short rope dangling from the strange ball. He threw it in the midst of the archers and it exploded, spraying shards of hot metal, killing those nearest the blast.

"No!" cried Cybella, watching them fall.

"Get out of there, fall back," cried Orin, waving to the others.

The rest of the zealots retreated to the dock, firing along the way.

"What the devil was that?" exclaimed Gavek as the zealots dropped behind the barrier bordering the embankment and continued to fire.

"In the boat, all o' you," said Boskan, wild-eyed as he too ducked behind cover. "Now I see why Wardein paid so much." He waved a red cloth in the air, signalling the *Duskrider* to weigh anchor. "Rozghow, you take the princess with the first lot. The rest o' you, follow me to that skiff over there. 'Er owner can't mind if we take 'er at a time like this."

"What about Rhodo?" Khloe implored Gavek. "We can't just leave him. Rhodo, come! Rhodo!"

Still locked in feral combat with the Zuelan hounds, Rhodo ignored her cries. The shepherd ravaged the throat of one of the mongrels, crushing it while the other mauled his hind leg. He sprung from under his dispatched foe and attacked the other, gouging out its eyes. The hound whimpered away while Rhodo stumbled toward the shore, swaying until he collapsed just short of the wall.

"No," screamed Khloe, her face awash with tears as Rozghow paddled the launch away, "Rhodo!"

"Khloe, no. It's too late," her brother said, restraining her.

Unable to overpower Orin, she wailed and fell on Gavek's chest, sobbing.

Cybella slid close to Khloe and stroked her hair. "I'm so terribly sorry."

Thurn stopped at the edge of the dock and stared at Gavek as the boats pulled away.

Crowe slid to a stop beside him. "I'll throw another. They're still close enough."

"No!" commanded Thurn, grabbing Crowe's hand before he could touch his belt. "You'd kill them all. I need the princess alive to control Danniker."

"But where is he? Commanding the ship?"

"Unlikely. He'd have come ashore to meet them." He scanned the hills of the city south of the Ambertyne. "Is he tied up with the Alpinians somewhere, perhaps? Planning a rendezvous upriver? That's got to be it." He rushed to the stairs. "If we can catch that schooner and take the princess back we'll have him. He'll come running like he did before. The crew and I will hasten back to the *Estria* and signal the fleet to pursue. As for you, I've got a special mission."

"Name it," said Crowe, following him up the stairs.

Thurn put his arm over Crowe's shoulder. "Take the Zuelan raiders who came with us and search the city. Tell them there's a special reward in store, which at least is partially true. Stop at the blacksmith's shop this side of Knight's Bridge and steal some horses. You must outrace the Horde to Mount Tria and fetch Solstrus' treasure before they take it. I want what he owes me, and while you're at it, keep lookout for any sign of Danniker."

Wrytha's mare had barely landed behind the cathedral wall when another terrible crack echoed from the harbour and a great, unseen projectile whizzed through the air. Twisted by fright, the mare landed off-balance, sending Wrytha tumbling across the lawn. Seconds later, the dome of the Palace of Ministers exploded, propelling shards of copper sheeting as far away as The Green while its noble spire toppled over its facade.

"Wrytha!" Arghan shouted, sliding off his mount. He ran to her side.

"I'm okay," she said, brushing herself off. "What is that dreadful thing? It sounds like the wrath of God! Look." Her jaw dropped when she spotted the fallen spire and the Palace's burning towers in the distance.

Arghan hurried back to his horse. "Remember when we stumbled upon those sappers in the cavern and I told you about the black powder Zuelan alchemists had invented?"

"Yes."

"We captured one of their magicians once; I watched him ignite some of it. Sounded just like that, only this is much worse. My guess is they made a weapon out of it somehow, capable of hurling projectiles."

"Like a trebuchet..."

"Exactly, only far more powerful. Von Thulrek dreaded this day. That's why he kept it a secret. He shuddered to think the ambitious warlords of central Eskareon might get the same idea." He took his saddle and steered his horse toward the cemetery.

Wrytha pointed at her animal's front legs. "Arghan, wait, the mare is done. I think she rolled her ankle in the fall."

Arghan held out his hand. Wrytha ran and took it, leaping onto the saddle behind him.

Moments later they passed from under the shadow of the great cathedral and descended the hill toward the cemetery, oblivious to a group of men who carried a chest out its front door while they passed by.

Arghan scanned the field of monuments, headstones, and mausoleums. "Solstrus told me the cart was hidden in the caretaker's shed, but it's all a blur to me. You'll have to—"

"There," said Wrytha, spotting a tall door ajar near the crossroads of two paths. "Some shed — looks more like a carriage house."

They rode up to it, hitched their horse near the door, and crept inside.

Arghan kicked the straw at his feet. "Schlika. That lying toad, there's nothing here!"

"No, but there was," said Wrytha, stooping to survey the floor. "There's a set of fresh tracks leading outside, and look—"

"What? I don't see it."

"No, silly me, of course you don't."

"What can I say, I never liked carrots. What is it?"

"The front set of wheels are slightly narrower than the back, forming two parallel lines, and it looks like the front right has a crack in it by the impression it leaves after every rotation."

"So?"

"So I noticed the same thing in the alley the night of the fire. I thought nothing of it, until now."

"The wagon was here," Arghan said, "but where did it—"

Something rattled behind a workbench at the back of the room. A metal pail fell with a clang and rolled out onto the floor.

"Who goes there," Arghan belted, gripping the hilt of his sword.

"I don't want any trouble," said the ashen-haired man who emerged, wearing an apron. "I thought you was one o' them murderers people say are runnin' amok in the city."

"Who are you?" Arghan asked, taking his hand away from his weapon.

"I'm the caretaker."

"Why haven't you fled?" asked Wrytha.

"I'm waitin' for me missus. The priest 'ill kill 'er if she leaves the cathedral less than spotless."

Arghan and Wrytha exchanged glances, each of them shaking their heads.

"The wagon that was here. Where is it now?" Arghan asked.

"Alpinians took it, right around noon. Afore that thunderous racket started."

"Say where they were going?" Wrytha asked.

"No, but they were in a mad hurry, let me tell you. Said they had to catch a ship. I watched them go, all the way down through the Ovens."

"The Ovens?" Wrytha said, glancing at Arghan.

"There are so many bakeries in the south quarter they call it the 'Ovens'" he explained. He addressed the caretaker again, "You're positive they went that way?"

"Oh yeah," he said, "I was so miffed at 'em fer stealin' me lunch I stood out there, fumin' n' cursin' at 'em while they drove through the city and out the south gate. You can see quite a lot from up here."

Wrytha smirked at Arghan. "Well, some of us can."

Arghan rolled his eyes. "Come on, we'll catch them when they stop for the night. The road to Encharra's a two day ride by wagon."

"Encharra?"

"It's the only other deepwater port on the coast. They're probably planning to ship the manuscripts back to the Temple State by way of the Inward Sea route to Endrata to throw us off the scent, thinking we'd be looking for them here, in Trianon."

"Clever man. I knew you were good for something."

"Have to be when you can't see anything past twenty paces," he said with a wink and headed for the door.

"Going somewhere, Danniker?" a now familiar voice called.

The caretaker gulped and ducked back behind the workbench.

"Raipheniel." Arghan sighed, cracking the joints in his neck.

Arghan watched eight silhouettes form a line, flanking their captain, who stood holding a claymore at the centre of the opening. Gone were the Alpinians' violet cloaks and embroidered waffenrocks, replaced by suits of gleaming plate armour.

"You know what else I'm good at?" he said, winking at Wrytha again. He bellowed and charged at Raipheniel.

Raipheniel parried, catching Arghan's blade inches from his helmet. Two men at the flanks rushed at Wrytha, who scored a glancing shot before they closed the distance. The arrow deflected and struck the dirt.

"Need a bodkin point to pierce this, darling," said the knight swinging his sword.

Wrytha grabbed a rafter above her head and dodged his thrust, batting the pair of them in the face of their helmets with her heels. She scrambled into the loft and drew three arrows at once and fired them at close range. The knight howled, clutching his chest after the tight cluster of points drove through his breastplate and into his shoulder.

"You were saying?" Wrytha snapped, drawing three more.

"Watch out!" cried the second knight, fleeing.

Arghan dodged Raipheniel's heavy blade, drawing the group into the crossroads. He vaulted onto a nearby sarcophagus, baiting another blow. Raipheniel swung again. Arghan leaped, kicking the captain's wrists as they passed over the lid, crushing the joints with a crack against the carved stone figure on top of it.

Raipheniel dropped his claymore and staggered back, screaming.

"Armour's only good if you know how to use it, lads. Who's next?"

Two more lunged at him. He rolled, ducking, and came up behind his attacker's blade in time to roll the man's body over his back, sending him crashing to the ground. He blocked a slash, then another and kicked the next between the legs. The man dropped with a groan.

"Don't forget your codpiece next time, son!"

"Stop attacking one at a time you imbeciles!" yelled Horst from behind a cone-faced helm. "Surround him!" He charged at Arghan, joined by three others while the fifth man ran past the corner of the barn and stopped to cock a crossbow.

Wrytha scrambled to the edge of the roof as he took aim and swayed, trying to line up a shot.

"No you don't," she said, releasing an arrow seconds before he squeezed the trigger, slicing his bowstring before the hook dropped.

"What?" he said, flipping up his visor to inspect his weapon moments before Wrytha's weight drove him face-first into the ground.

Arghan weaved among the remaining five, looking for a moment to strike. One man thrust far. Arghan took his arm at the elbow. Two rushed him from either side. He dropped and rolled, causing them to collide with a crash. He kicked the side of their knees. The men collapsed, shuddering with agonized cries. The tip of Horst's blade grazed Arghan's shoulder blade. Arghan dropped his Talon, staggering. Horst raised his sword, winding up a killing blow. An arrow pierced his exposed neck and he collapsed, gurgling at Arghan's side.

Arghan huffed, wiping the sweat from his pulsing, reddened brow as Wrytha helped him to his feet. "Marry me when this is done," he said, reaching for his waterskin. He took a gulp of water.

"You fool," she said, playfully. "You know in my heart I already have.

But couldn't you have picked a more romantic place than a graveyard next to a pile of fresh corpses to ask me out loud?"

"They aren't all dead," he said, pointing at the writhing wounded.

Wrytha crossed her arms and arched an eyebrow.

"Wait a minute," Arghan added, "the walk by the river counts as the first, doesn't it?"

"No it doesn't. You didn't say the exact words then."

"I'll make it up to you."

"Yes, you will."

"You promised us treasure," sneered one of Crowe's Zuelan companions, smashing the cathedral's offertory box across the checkered vestibule.

Crowe kicked the coins away and strutted out the door. "Be patient, Gaikahn," he said, descending the steps, returning to his stolen horse.

The other mercenaries followed him and prepared to ride.

Gaikahn watched Crowe jump into his saddle. "I'm beginning to think you don't know where it is, one-eyed-bird-man."

"I don't care what you think. How could I have known the Archprelate's estate would be burnt to a cinder? The Alpinians must have cleaned it out. We've more places to search, so shut your mouth or the Kaighan will hear of it." He squeezed his knees and his mount galloped off.

Gaikahn spat on the ground where Crowe's horse had been and mounted his own. "Racchad-ni[2]!"

Crowe was headed for the stately mansions along the south bank of Mount Tria when a glint of light caught his eye. He peered down the slope below the cathedral and spotted the armoured figures of the fallen Alpinians strewn about the cemetery crossroads, near the shed where Arghan and Wrytha had defeated them less than an hour before.

"What's this now?" He made a fist in the air. "Hold! This way."

A short time later Crowe and his entourage dismounted near the carriage house. He passed a row of white destriers tied to a fence near

---

2. Racchad-ni – Zuelan, meaning "Insolent fellow"

the shed, touching their violet caparisons as he went, noting how each horse's saddlebags hung tight against their bodies.

He strained to lift one of the satchels and opened it. "There it is," he said, running his fingers through the Regalian doubloons inside. He closed it again and turned his back to it, watching the others. "Check out those bodies," he said, pointing at the fallen Alpinians.

The group reached the front and discovered Raipheniel leaning against the tip of his sword, straddling the corner of a sarcophagus with his elbows.

He tried to slide it under his breastplate but it deflected off his armour. He kicked it away, cursing. "Pathetic, Raipheniel. Can't even manage to kill yourself..."

"Well, well, what happened here?" quipped Crowe, announcing his presence.

"What?" asked Raipheniel, startled. "I've seen you, you're one of the Liester's men. Danniker happened, that's what. He and his Tzyani witch did this." He looked down at his dangling gauntlets.

"Danniker was here?"

"I just said that, didn't I?"

"Why?"

"If I tell you, promise me you'll put me and my men out of our misery, then go kill that son of a she-dog."

"Count on it."

Wearing an expression of retrained disgust, Raipheniel surveyed the faces of the Zuelan warriors and then looked at Crowe. "He's after a wagon filled to the brim with scrolls. He places great value on them for some reason. So did Solstrus, but he's no longer a problem since we took care of him, and so I could care less what happens to them now."

"Oh, that was you. Thurn thought Danniker did it."

"Danniker? No. He's a deadly fighter, but he clings to the Warder's code."

"Where was the wagon headed?"

"I ordered two of my men to take it down the coast road to Encharra. They were supposed to meet our ship there but that plan's botched, along with the rest. They'll have to stop for the night. Danniker knows this. If you hurry you may catch him before he finds them, or not. Rest assured he'll turn up. The mongrel always does. Satisfied?"

Crowe nodded.

"Now, about our agreement..." Raipheniel dropped his head over the edge of the sarcophagus. "Make it clean."

Gavek leaned against the *Duskrider's* taffrail, brooding over the shimmering reflections in its foaming wake. Beyond the distant lights of Rivenrach, the lanterns of a hundred ships crowded the river from one bank to the other, mirroring the starry sky. By his calculation, nearly the entire Zuelan fleet that had attacked Trianon now pursued them, and though they lagged behind by several leagues, one of the lights appeared brighter than the rest. Was it the *Estria*, like the *Duskrider*, also renowned for her speed? Had Thurn's crew made it back in time to spearhead the chase? He closed his eyes and prayed Rivenrach's watchmen had received Boskan's warning signal.

"Couldn't sleep either, I see?" Cybella leaned beside him, offering a reassuring smile.

"No, your highness," he said, straightening up.

"We're alone. Call me 'Bella', Gavek; all my friends do, at least the ones I give permission to." She chuckled and winked.

Gavek offered a feeble smile. "Uh, nice outfit," he said, still processing her request.

"Isn't it lovely?" she said, looking it over. "One of the Tzyani girls lent it to me. Much better for travelling in than a tattered evening gown, I should think."

"Indeed," he said, nodding. He went back to staring over the stern.

"You're worried about them, aren't you?" She said, sitting beside him.

"Of course, aren't you?"

"Yes and no."

"What do you mean?"

"The unknown stirs my fears, as it does for us all, but even so, I have faith Yeshua is watching over us — Arghan and Wrytha too. I sense His Presence."

"You sound like Khloe, on a good day I mean. How is she, by the way?"

"Poor dear, cried herself to sleep after Boskan gave her a glass of spirits to calm her nerves."

"She loved Rhodo very much. It's got to be killing her. Doesn't help that she has no idea where her mother is."

"No, I suppose not. Rest assured, that noble beast will never be forgotten. When this is over, I'll build a statue of him on the very spot he fell."

"Do you really think there will be anything left of Trianon to go back to?" He dropped his head and pulled out the letter Wardein had given him.

"What's that?" she said.

"A letter. Wardein gave it to me to deliver to you. For what good it does now."

Cybella took the parchment and skimmed the message, smiling.

"That's excellent, Gavek. I'm glad to see Wardein and I were of the same mind on the issue. Having this guarantees it. Congratulations, I can think of no better man for the post."

"Do you honestly believe any of that matters now?" Gavek asked, raising his voice. He turned to look at her, his eyes gaunt and sullen. "Will you even have a kingdom to rule? For all we know, the raiders left in the city have reduced the Library to ash by now. Look at them, Bella!" He pointed at the Zuelan fleet in the distance. "They're not going to stop until we're all dead and the country lies in ruins."

"Not if the Erne Warder has anything to say about it."

"Oh that's ox manure and you know it," he said, throwing Wardein's letter at her feet. He turned away, walked a few paces and slung his arm over the ropes of a Jakav's ladder and started to sob.

"Did Arghan ever tell you why Tzyani women wear their hair in braids?"

"Yeah," he said, sniffling and wiping his nose, "he said it symbolized

Jakav's revelation of a rope let down from heaven on which angels ascended and descended."

"Do you realize the ladder on which you're hanging is called after that very same thing?"

"It is?" He said, "I mean, yes, of course I knew..."

Cybella grinned. "Sure you did. Wardein never lied to his future Queen and neither should you."

"You're right, sorry. Sorry for snapping at you too. I've not had a proper night's sleep in ages."

"Perhaps you should go below deck and try and get some now. I'm sure Boskan has some spirits left. We're not out of harm's reach yet as you've pointed out. I'll need my new royal adviser as sharp as he can be if we're to get through this."

"Right you are, your highness. Thank you." He bowed and headed for the hatch.

Cybella looked downriver and called back to him, "Gavek, do you recall when you translated Pollos' epistle to the Tzyani; how you rendered the 11th chapter, first stanza?"

Gavek surveyed the horizon before he spoke, "Now faith is the substance of things hoped for, the conviction of things not seen." He smiled and rubbed his eyes. "Good one."

"Have faith, Gavek."

Gavek bowed again and disappeared below deck.

Cybella dropped to her knees, facing the Zuelan fleet. She rested her forehead on top of her folded hands. "Father of Lights in the heavenly realm, revered be your Name, Your Kingdom be manifest, Your good pleasure be done, on Earda as it is above..."

CHAPTER TWENTY-ONE
The Horde

Wrytha peered through Arghan's spyglass, watching the tavern window across the road. "Looks like they're ordering another pint."

Arghan sighed. "Thank the Living-Light-Father, we needed a break like this. I'm done fighting for the day. Keep watch here? I'll get the wagon and meet you up the road?"

"Sure."

Arghan crept across the moonlit road and knelt below the steps of the lonely seaside inn, pausing to the sniff the salty air blowing in from the beach. He closed his eyes for a moment, savouring the sound of gentle waves. He glanced through the window then unhitched the team's reins.

The door burst open and he retreated below the porch. A couple, latched in a lingering kiss, stumbled down the stairs, giggling and walked toward the dunes.

Ah, Tolpa, no wonder the bards sing of your shores. He re-emerged, loosened the reins and jumped into the driver's seat. *Thankfully, the Alpinians have heard the song about your ale.* He nudged the horses forward and the wagon dawdled away, quickening when he passed through the archway marking the entrance of the village.

Several minutes later he spotted Wrytha by the roadside, slumped over the neck of her horse, her braid dangling over its white mane. She stirred at the sound of the rattling wheels and fumbled with her bow in a feeble attempt to aim it.

"Looks like I'm not the only one who's tired," said Arghan, hopping down from his seat. He picked up her bow and offered her a hand. "Why don't you ride in the wagon with me? There's some room in the back if you'd like to sleep."

"That's tempting," she said, "but you look like I feel." She rubbed her eyes and nodded northward. "I spotted a barn in an abandoned vineyard just over the hill. We'll be no help to our loved ones if you run us off a cliff. Let's get a little sleep, shall we?"

"Gladly," he breathed, "lead the way."

Boskan shooed his passengers toward a rope ladder while he scanned the river with his telescope. "Hurry, no tellin' 'ow much time y' have. Curse this fog, I'd sooner not've stopped at all."

"Noted," said Cybella, scowling. "And watch your tone, sailor; don't forget who I am."

"You'll be the queen o' nothin' if they catch us 'ere," Boskan whispered, snapping the spyglass closed.

Cybella gripped her hips and squinted. "What's that?"

Two Tzyani boys carried Nicah in a blanket behind her while some of their comrades followed.

"Careful," said Gavek, directing them toward the *Duskrider's* port side.

Auria walked close beside them, holding Nicah's hand. "Hang on, Nicah, we're taking you to someone who can help."

Sigoe's harbour horn sounded through the early morning fog. Nicah's carriers lowered him down to the others waiting aboard Boskan's launch.

On the way to join them Orin clutched Gavek's shoulder. "Doesn't feel right, splitting the group like this; you're sure you know what you're doing? Our enclave is only a day away. You really want to waste time taking him up to Lake Trieehd?"

"It's not a waste," he said, straightening his back, "if anyone can help him now, it's Pattron."

Cybella called down to the launch, "You'll be safe there, all of you." She faced Orin. "The Zuelan fleet's delay can only mean one thing: they've stopped to sack Rivenrach. If so, it's likely they'll land troops to secure the south bank to protect their fleet's advance, cutting off the route to your village."

"And what about the rest of you?" Orin implored. "It's two days more to reach Straskost." He met Boskan's gaze. "You really think you can outrun them that long?"

Boskan looked away.

"We need only reach the Fortress of Kortova," Cybella answered. "Count Vernik's men will see us the rest of the way. Your best shooters are still with us and your cousin Sibia has volunteered to lead them." She touched the arm of the tall girl who stood nearby.

"Not all of them," Orin said, watching Khloe emerge from the deck hatch. "Khloe's coming with me." He beckoned her to follow him down the rope ladder.

Gavek's face flushed. "I'll miss you."

Khloe turned to face him, her chin quivering. "Me too," she said with an air of resignation. "It's for the best. I've... got to stay with my brothers."

Gavek searched her eyes for the sparkle that was no longer there. He stepped forward, held her face and kissed her on the lips.

Matticai whooped from the launch. "Gavek, the ladies man!"

Khloe giggled, pulling back. "I'll miss you too," she said, sniffling as a tear escaped her eye. "Until we meet again?" She dropped a folded parchment ship into his palm.

Gavek smiled.

Boskan's ears cocked. He glanced over his shoulder, eyes bulging when he glimpsed a black hulk speeding toward them out of the fog. "Mother of a... brace yourselves!"

Waves frothed. The *Estria's* bow collided with the *Duskrider's* starboard side. Timbers creaked and moaned. Splinters flew. The *Duskrider* lurched, jolting those who stood on her deck.

Boskan pointed toward shore as he caught himself at the ship's rail. "Rozghow, row!"

A roped harpoon shot into the *Duskrider's* main mast.

"Pull up beside her!" cried a coarse voice from the *Estria's* deck.

"Come on!" shouted Gavek, grabbing Khloe's hand. He booted Cybella overboard then pulled Khloe over the rail with him.

"Archers!" cried Sibia. The zealots still on the deck scurried for cover and took aim at the *Estria*.

A voice screamed from the *Estria*, "Fire!"

Deafening booms split the air; flames flashed and smoke billowed in a rolling cascade from open hatches along her starboard side, blasting holes through both sides of the *Duskrider's* hull.

"Abandon ship!" yelled Boskan, stumbling from the attack.

"What was that?" cried Cybella, splashing through the waterline. "Threician fire?"

"Worse!" answered Gavek, treading water beside Khloe. "Swim for the shore!"

Voices bellowed and a bell rang from the shoreline, followed by the sound of pounding footfalls.

Zuelan raiders leaped onto the *Duskrider*, flashing their sabres. Arrows whizzed, cutting down half their number. Another wave followed. More fell, and still more, until they swarmed the ship, slashing Boskan's men as they went. Boskan drew his short sword only to have it batted from his hand by the same blade that soon ran him through.

"It's no use, there's too many of them!" yelled Sibia. "To the water!"

The zealots dove into the river moments before the raiders overran their positions. A Zuelan archer took aim with his recurve bow and fired. The arrow whistled through the air, causing one of the Tzyani girls to turn toward the sound moments before impact.

"Andriel!" Khloe cried, watching the girl slip below the waves.

"Stop!" commanded the *Estria's* second officer, Salerio. He grabbed the archer's wrist before he took another arrow. "One of them could be the princess!" He beckoned the others, "Search the ship. She may still be here."

Salerio strutted to where Boskan lay bleeding, muttering under his breath. "Where is she?" he demanded. "Where is Cybella?"

Boskan waved him down, too weak to speak. When Salerio stooped to listen, Boskan thrust his dagger between his ribs.

"You'll ne'er know," he said as Salerio collapsed beside him. He closed his eyes. "God help ye, Arghan, wherever ye are."

Rozghow and the others from the launch pulled the survivors onto Sigoe's wharf while the grey silhouette of the *Duskrider* disappeared below the waves of the Onya.

The Harbour Master came running, leading a squad of watchmen. "What the blazes happened out there?" He inspected the remains of a wooden pier decimated by the *Estria's* volley. "What was that terrible noise?" He waved to a group of archers and they formed a firing line at the edge of the dock.

"The Zuelans happened, that's what," said Gavek, helping Khloe to her feet.

"More pirates? That's just what we need. Sergeant! Call out the garrison. We'll put an end to these devils once and for all."

"No!" insisted Cybella, "you must evacuate the town. Head for the fortress. Summon the Reeve."

"Summon the Reeve?" snapped the Harbour Master. "Who do you think you are?"

"She's the queen apparent, you imbecile, I'd listen to her if I were you," said Orin, clenching his teeth.

The *Estria* fired another volley. The missiles zoomed over their heads, blasting through a row of shops along the boardwalk.

"Princess Cybella?" scoffed the Harbour Master. "She's missing. Young Eriohn's returned. He's to be crowned."

"News travels slow here," said Gavek, rolling his eyes.

"Listen to me your provincial oaf," said Cybella, gripping the man's waffenrock, "I am very much alive, though soon may not be if you insist on playing games. Call the Reeve now, or I promise you'll regret it."

Riders galloped their horses onto the boardwalk. A puffy-eyed, greying gentleman with a curled moustache dismounted his horse, followed by a contingent of guards.

"What seems to be the problem, Danvig?" said the old man, unusually calm.

"Pirates, Lord Garecht. They attacked these people offshore. This one claims she's the queen apparent if you can believe such a thing."

The old man squinted, studying her features until he spotted the birthmark on her right cheek. "I do believe it, Danvig. Show some respect."

"Uh, yes m' lord. Forgive my ignorance, your highness," he said, bowing to Cybella.

Cybella nodded and smiled as Garecht took her hand and turned his back to Danvig.

"Little Bella? My, how you've grown! You sat on my knee once, during the royal visit of '21. I suppose you don't remember?"

"Sorry, no," she said, blushing. She scanned the river, looking for a sign of another attack. "Reeve Garecht, I implore you to evacuate Sigoe. These are no ordinary pirates! A whole fleet of Zuelan raiders is after us! They laid siege to Trianon, then Rivenrach, and soon they—"

Another salvo blasted out of the *Estria*, this time blowing the top deck of the harbour crane to splinters.

"Light the fires!" bellowed Garecht, waving his arms as he ran back to his horse. "Sound the bells! Evacuate the citizens! Come, Bella," he called, holding out his hand, "ride with me!" He cried to one of his cavaliers, "Captain, collect her friends. To the Guildhall!"

"Now that's a welcome sight," said Gavek, spotting a troop of halberdiers marching toward the riverfront as he and the others rode into the Guildhall's courtyard.

"Captain," shouted Garecht, "I want your best men here in twenty minutes. You will escort the princess and her entourage to the fortress."

"At your command, m' lord. I shall return with dispatch." The captain nodded and sped off on his horse.

"This way, your highness," said Garecht, dismounting. "You and your friends may wait in the council chamber, it's the securest place here."

The group dismounted and gathered at the entrance.

Cybella followed the Reeve. "Thank you, Lord Garecht. I wonder if we might impose one more thing upon you?"

"Name it, your highness," he said, taking her hand.

"One of my companions needs care, urgently. We planned to send him to the monastery of Cairhn, they have a monk there who—"

"Pattron the Hospitaller? Yes, I've heard of him. Your mother asked if I knew him on her way there herself, the week before last I think it was."

"Wait, my mother — she was here?"

"Yes, she stayed one night at my estate; said she had urgent business on Lake Trieehd. I assumed it was a matter of health when she asked about him. How is she?"

"I... I don't know. I thought she was, that is—"

"Reeve Garecht," interrupted an attendant, "the Exchequer requires your signature. He cannot approve evacuation of the treasury without it."

"Forgive me, your highness, duty calls. After I'm finished with my affairs here I must see to my family's safety as well. Whatever you need, I am sure the captain can accommodate you." He bowed and hastened through the portico.

Gavek watched the Reeve depart. "Wait for me here?" he asked Khloe.

She nodded and he left her with her kin.

Cybella frowned and rested her chin on her fist, sitting on the steps to the Guildhall council chamber.

"Everything okay?" said Gavek, taking a seat beside her.

"Yes. The Reeve's providing us escort to Kortova, thankfully. They should be here soon. Once we're safe inside the fortress I'll ask them to take the others to Cairhn as planned."

"Sounds good. What's troubling you then?"

"The Reeve said my mother passed through here last week on her way to Cairhn."

Gavek took a deep breath and looked away.

"Gavek?"

"I'm very sorry to have to tell you this. Your mother is dead."

Cybella gasped. She covered her mouth as tears welled up in her eyes. "How?"

Gavek continued, "An Alpinian archer shot her."

"Shot her? Why? What was she even doing there?"

"She came there to find Arghan and sent him a letter he believed came from you, imploring him to meet her on Cairhn's wharf one night. There, she blamed him for your disappearance and demanded he intervene. Sadly, her visit came in the midst of Abbot Cybion's violent crackdown against the monastery after he uncovered Arghan's true identity. There was a confrontation; she got caught in the crossfire."

"He tried to tell me... in the crypt of the Palace chapel," she mused, staring.

"He cherished your mother's life, despite their differences. Seeing her fall awakened his rage; there wasn't an Alpinian left alive by the time he was through. He's ashamed of what happened that night. We rushed her to Pattron, but it was too late."

Cybella shuddered, struggling to contain her sobs.

Gavek slowly put his hand over her shoulder and patted it. She fell on his chest, weeping.

At the same moment, a commotion broke out among the Tzyani zealots.

"Let go of me!" shouted Khloe, pulling her wrist away from Orin's grip. "Mother would not approve!"

Cybella dried her eyes with her sleeve. "You'd better see what that's about."

"Yes..." Gavek jumped down the stairs and hastened to where they stood. "What's the matter?"

Khloe pointed. "Orin wants to abandon the princess; said we should go back and defend our enclave."

"Is that true?" said Gavek, with a look of disbelief. "What about your brother?"

"He knew the risks when he signed up for the cause."

"Knew the risks?" said Gavek, his mouth gaping. "You're going to leave your twin brother to his fate while you run off and get yourself killed? For what?"

"Pitha would have," Orin said. "We must be prepared to make sacrifices. Running and hiding is for cowards; its all we've done for twenty years! Teighthra taught us—"

"Teighthra?" Khloe fumed. "I can't believe what I'm hearing."

"I don't care if you believe it. Your place is with us, Khloe. Mother may be stupid enough to become the butcher of Koerska's whore, but—"

Khloe slapped his cheek. "Orin! Shame on you. He saved your life twice over! Once when you were a babe and then—"

"Save it, Khlo, we're getting out of here, end of discussion." Orin yanked her away.

Her toe caught a loose stone and she stumbled to the ground.

"Hey!" cried Gavek. "That's enough! Leave her be."

Orin shoved him away. "This doesn't concern you, Goyani[1]!"

Gavek grabbed Orin's sleeve. Orin punched Gavek in the cheekbone with the other hand. The pair tussled, falling to the ground in a flurry of fists and gnashing teeth.

"Stop it! Both of you!" cried Cybella, leaping on top of them. She pried them apart and pushed each of them away. "This is no time for that kind of foolishness!"

"You're right, your highness, I'm sorry," said Gavek, wiping blood from his lips with his wrist.

Cybella glared at Orin. "If you want to go, go. But force your sister or anyone else to follow you and I promise you, you'll spend the rest of you days an outlaw in my kingdom."

"Whatever!" Orin, sneered. He looked around to the others. "Who's with me? Come now if you want to prove yourselves."

---

1. Goyani – a Tzyani word referring to anyone who isn't Tzyani.

After a few moments exchanging questioning looks among the group, Dannika and Zedekael broke away and stood behind Orin.

"Dannika? No." said Khloe.

Dannika shook her head, avoiding Khloe's gaze. She took Orin's hand. "Let's go."

The Zuelan fleet emerged from the fog and began to form a crescent-shaped blockade around Sigoe's waterfront. A three-masted vessel with an inscription on its hull that read, *'The Leviathan'* took centre stage.

An ominous figure in heavy armour covered in black bear skin sat on a platform aboard the flagship; shifting his weight on a simple folding stool, he clutched his knees and surveyed the shore with his coal-black eyes. He commanded the warrior who peered through a telescope at his side, "Haracht-Wan, report."

"Just like the last one, my Kaighan," answered the wiry man with a pointed beard. "A few pitiful defenders occupy towers along the shore. The rest flee to the north."

The Kaighan licked his teeth, then stood up and kicked his stool away. "Is there no one in this cursed country man enough to face me? Thurn promised me treasure! I don't think these infidels have any, otherwise, they would fight for it! If they prefer to die without honour, so be it." He descended a set of stairs, smacking the rail with a riding crop. "Bombard the settlement. Burn it to the ground. Land the rest of the raiders. Drive them into their precious fortress; Kortova won't save them. Her walls defied us once, but this time..." he ran his ring-covered fingers over the ornamental reliefs on a hulking, cast-iron cylinder set on a massive carriage. It spanned the height of three men from head to foot. He stopped near its mouth: a gaping orifice as wide as the distance from a man's elbow to the tip of his fingers. "This time they will taste the Dragon's breath!"

Having risen before dawn and with leagues of winding roads now behind them, the haggard couple drove their vehicle over the crest of a hill overlooking the Onya's bifurcation east of Rivenrach and headed for a ferry crossing that would take them to the north bank.

"Fog's as thick as chowder down there. I'm glad you know where you're going," said Wrytha, surveying the valley below.

"Even so, you'd better take the reins if it's that bad," said Arghan, handing them to her.

She sniffed the air as they started down the hill. "Do you smell that?"

"Smoke..." said Arghan, inhaling.

"It's getting worse," Wrytha said, coughing. She pulled her scarf over her face and pointed across the road. "Arghan, there's a glow on the horizon; it looks like the source of the fire."

He took out his spyglass. "Father of Lights—"

"What?"

"Rivenrach's ablaze. I expected the Zuelans would be sacking Trianon for days, but it seems they headed upriver and laid siege to the town."

"Arghan — they're chasing the *Duskrider*, what do we—"

"Turn here. Head for the bridge."

"But you said—"

"I know, but it's our only chance now; there won't be a ferry in the water from here to the Kinnessarat dam."

A grim scene greeted them when they reached the bridge: abandoned vehicles cluttered the deck as far as the fog would reveal. They weaved their way through them, passing over each of the bridge's ascending Threician arches until they neared the top and emerged from the fog. Wrytha gasped and yanked the reins, halting between twin towers at the bridge's apex.

Arghan lurched forward. "What's wrong?"

"Look!" Wrytha said, jumping down from the wagon. She took a few steps and stopped.

Arghan followed. A gust of air blew up from the river, answering his question before he could reach her.

"Schlika," he exclaimed, surveying the chasm where the crest of the bridge used to be. He sighed, and traced the remaining curve of the obliterated arch from the base of another pair of towers across the gap down to where it disappeared into the mist.

A pebble fell from one of the towers.

Wrytha reached for her bow. "Arghan!"

A hail of arrows rained down, striking the horses and piercing Arghan's left forearm. He grunted. The horses whinnied and bustled, causing one of them to lose its footing. Wrytha dodged it and rolled into the doorway of one of the towers. The horse's hind leg slipped off the ledge and it fell, dangling from its harness. The wagon skidded forward and tipped on its side, spilling the crates of scrolls across the roadway. Arghan dove behind it. He bellowed, snapped off the bloodied arrowhead, and moaned as he pulled the feathered end out of the top of his arm.

"End of the road, Erne Warder!" cried a voice from one of the towers. The distinct patter of padded leather boots, unmistakable to Arghan's ears, closed in on him from either side of the bridge. "Give it up! You're surrounded."

Panting, Arghan tore off his scarf and wrapped it around his forearm. "Come get me if you dare, you motherless dogs," he yelled, staggering to his feet. "Wrytha? Can you hear me? Where are you?"

He drew his Talon and peered past the side of the wagon. Zuelan warriors formed a line spanning the bridge and edged their way closer. A light sparked in his peripheral vision; he turned his head to see a cluster of flaming ceramic balls roll out from the tower.

"Schlika!" He exclaimed, ducking behind the cart.

The grenades exploded in a ball of flame, instantly igniting the precious cargo and knocking the cart against his head, dropping him to the ground. The other horse reared away from the spreading flames and fell off the bridge with the other, dragging the flaming carriage over with him. The Zuelans whooped and rushed Arghan's position. One of them kicked Arghan's Talon off the bridge and clutched him by the throat while the others took turns kicking him.

"That's enough! We need him alive!" cried the voice from before.

Arghan rolled onto his stomach, groaning. The Zuelans yanked him to his feet. Blinking, he watched a figure in a black coat and eye patch push Wrytha out the tower door, holding a dagger to her throat.

"Easy, now, Danniker, behave yourself or you'll never hear the soft sweet voice of your pretty lady friend again."

"Yeshua," he whispered, glancing between Wrytha and the flaming cart, "how could you let this happen?" He looked at Wrytha, marking the fury in her eyes. "You must be one of Thurn's dogs. I can smell the stench of hell from here."

"The name's Crowe, I'm surprised you don't remember me. We fought together in the war; I was only a lowly helmsman then."

"My eyesight isn't what it used to be. Come closer so I can get a good look at you."

"Ha! There's that dry wit I remember. Do you take me for a fool?" He looked at one of the Zuelans. "Tie him up. We've got an appointment to keep with the *Estria*. Treasure awaits, my friends."

A Zuelan pulled out a rope. Wrytha thrust her elbow into Crowe's solar plexus and twisted her torso, knocking them both off the bridge.

"Wrytha!" Arghan screamed, watching her fall out of sight. He dropped his weight and twisted his forearms, repelling the two Zuelans who were gripping his wrists. Another lunged. He ducked and threw him over the edge, pulling the warrior's sword from its sheath as he fell. Another swung his blade, and then another, each man's attempt met with unbridled fury as he dodged and weaved between their ranks, hacking them down until the last of them fell to the wayside.

He threw the sword off the bridge and staggered to the broken ledge. He peered down into the opaque mist; seeing only the blurry silhouettes of flying birds, hearing them caw as they flew back and forth through the expanse. He closed his eyes and fell face down, sobbing on the road. "Wrytha... dear, sweet Wrytha... no..."

Something clanged across the deck. Arghan opened his eyes to see his Talon resting near the edge. A hand appeared, followed by another, then a raven-black head of hair.

"Are you going to lie there moaning all day or come help me up?"

"Wrytha!" he cried. He scrambled over and pulled her onto the bridge. "How—"

"The arch broke away at an angle, leaving a jagged ledge below the road. I saw it when Crowe pushed me out the door. I made sure his smelly head broke my fall. He's still down there somewhere, out cold."

Arghan chuckled and embraced her.

"How's that?" said Wrytha, turning his arm.

"Ow!" he exclaimed, wincing. "Can't move my fingers. Hurts when I try to make a fist."

"Don't then. Here, sit down." She tore off a section of her skirt and tied it like a sling around his arm.

"You're pretty good at that," he said, watching her.

"One learns a few things raising two adventurous boys."

Their eyes met, then they both looked upriver. The view remained shrouded in fog.

"What now?" she said, glancing at the burning crates.

Arghan sighed, closing his eyes while he shook his head. He slid over to pick up his sword, then stumbled to his feet and sheathed it. "We keep going; find our friends before Thurn does and help them escape."

"It would be nice to know what Thurn has up his sleeve," she said, "I'll bet one-eye knows."

"Read my mind, love; let's pull him up and ask him." He stooped to grab the rope the Zuelan was going to bind him with. "I have an idea how to make him talk."

CHAPTER TWENTY-TWO
Kortova

Sigoe's housecarls cleared the treeline, galloping their horses up the winding mountain path overlooking the Onya, northwest of Sigoe. Cybella's heart surged with hope. Kortova's mighty walls loomed in the distance, bathed in sunlight at the summit of the green mountain from which the fortress got its name. There she would order the signal fires lit, alerting Duke Weorthan's forces to come to Cortavia's aid.

A watchman cried from Kortova's gatehouse, "The Reeve of Sigoe flies the red banner, open the gate."

Kortova's massive portcullis creaked open, revealing a darkened passageway leading to the castle's interior. The riders sped through it and emerged inside a broad courtyard.

A man wearing a fine doublet descended a grand staircase outside the castle's central keep, flanked by an entourage.

Cybella dismounted and addressed him as he approached, "Count Vernik, I presume?"

"I am," he said, taking her hand, "and who might you be?" He looked at Reeve Garecht as if to pose the question to him too.

Garecht cleared his throat. "Her Royal Highness Cybella, Crown Princess of Cortavia."

Vernik flashed his eyes and knelt along with his entourage. "Forgive me, your highness; reports of your disappearance, and your attire—"

"I was kidnapped and held hostage by a conspiracy to usurp the throne. We need your help, Count Vernik. Zuelan forces have invaded the country. My friends and I are en route to the Duchy to beg Duke Weorthan's intervention."

"It's true, m' lord," said Garecht's captain, "a scout ship attached Sigoe's wharf this morning. More are on the way."

"Light the signal fire," Cybella insisted. "Alert Straskost. Open the border. Per the Treaty of Roe, the Ostergaardians are hereby granted royal authority to enter crown territory at the Duke's discretion."

One of Vernik's attendants, a greying, lanky man wearing a beret leaned toward the count's ear. "She can't do that, your grace, only the Monarch can. She's not been crowned."

"What's that?" said Cybella, arching her eyebrows. "Speak up, man. Who are you?"

"Your highness," he answered, bowing, "Doran Pel of Nova Engaric, the count's solicitor."

"The count's solicitor—"

"Really, Vernik," said Garecht, shaking his head, "you're going to lawyer up at a time like this? Will you never cease being petty? My port's being sacked as we speak."

"No disrespect, your highness," Vernik said, avoiding Garecht's gaze, "but the southern barons pay their bills. The crown of late has not."

Gavek stepped forward and touched Cybella's shoulder. "Excuse me, your highness? May I?"

Cybella nodded.

"And who are you sir?" asked Pel, looking down his long nose.

Cybella answered for him, "This is my special adviser, Gavek of Cairhn, Master of the Royal Archive."

"Master of—" Pel said, smirking. "Isn't that Wardein—"

"Wardein was murdered. I took his place," Gavek interrupted. "Here's the deal: section nine, paragraph sixteen of the Treaty of Roe grants the King's heirs, representatives, and appointed delegates the power, in the circumstance of immediate and deadly peril, to enact the mechanism of border incursion for a period of two weeks, pending royal approval or veto—"

"You really think she'll be crowned by then?" Pel quipped.

"I think there's a chance there won't be a Kingdom by then," Gavek answered, pointing at Pel's chest, "but my opinion is moot, as is yours. The Treaty makes no demand the Monarch be alive in order for his heir's powers to be in effect. It does, however, prescribe stiff penalties for failing to comply; something to do with offenders being deprived of their hands and feet as I recall, oh, yes, and forfeiture of lands and titles — nearly forgot that bit—"

"Here, now," said Vernik, holding out his palms, "it's clear our introductions have gotten off on the wrong foot—"

"That's an understatement," Khloe whispered.

"I'm at your service," Vernik continued, "I simply want to make sure I'm not taken to task by the barons. You know how jealously they guard their estates. They've never been happy about the Treaty. They felt the King gave the Ostergaardians too much in exchange for saving the country. They fear that if allowed to cross the border the foreigners will never leave—"

"Foreigners?" Cybella exclaimed. "There's at least two thousand Zuelans heading upriver — with powerful new weapons I might add. They'll reduce Kortova to sand."

The Count chuckled. "Really, your highness. I respect your station, but you're hardly qualified when it comes to military matters. Kortova's walls have never failed. Its garrison is the only force of any consequence in Cortavia at present, outside Trianon. I'll put the garrison on alert, but if you want me to summon the Ostergaardians, I'm afraid you'll have to put your order in writing." His gaze turned to Pel as he concluded.

"Paperwork will take a few hours to draft — the afternoon at least," Pel offered. He turned to Cybella. "Your adviser may supervise if you wish?"

"Paperwork?" quipped Garecht, "you sound like my exchequer!"

"Fine," Cybella said, sighing, "but expedite your efforts, Mr. Pel." She addressed the count, "In the meantime, my companions and I could use a hot bath and some food, as could the Reeve and his men."

"Certainly," Vernik replied, snapping his fingers. "My staff will see to your every need. It would be my great pleasure to host you and your advisors in my private dining room for dinner, as a conciliatory gesture. I'm sure there is something elegant in my late wife's dressing room you could wear for the occasion. At the sixth hour, shall we say?"

Gavek and Cybella exchanged glances. Gavek shrugged his shoulders. Cybella rolled her eyes.

"As you wish, Count," she said, "but we're leaving for the border as soon as that order's signed."

"Bloodthirsty predators," Arghan fumed, scanning Sigoe's smouldering wharf from one of the hills overlooking the town. He spotted two Zuelan support vessels lingered offshore.

"The Zuelan fleet has come and gone," he said, shaking his head as he snapped his spyglass closed. "All that are left are the looters. Looks like the rest are massing upriver. They'll hit Kortova next. I hope her defenders are better prepared than Trianon's were." He jumped down from the rocky outcropping he'd been standing on and remounted Crowe's horse.

"Any sign of the Duskrider?" Wrytha asked, saddled in another.

"I didn't see it."

Wrytha shaded her forehead and peered northward. "So its possible the others made it ashore ahead of the attack, or perhaps even landed farther upriver? Isn't there a landing at Roe?"

"A small one. Kortova has one too, where the mountain meets the shoreline. I can't see them sailing as far as the Kinnessarat Dam, but its possible. Either way, they'd be playing right into Thurn's hands, if what Crowe told us is true."

"You think he'd lie after being hung by his ankles from a bridge? Didn't you see his face when the torch burned through the rope?"

"I did. Too bad he fainted before he could see how I double-tied it. They're usually even more talkative after falling that first time only to be caught by the second knot."

"Can I see that?" Wrytha asked, holding out her hand.

Arghan handed her his spyglass.

Wrytha held the lens to her eye. "I thought the road looked a bit colourful. There's a massive caravan heading up the mountain to the fortress. Hundreds, maybe thousands of people. If the others had disembarked at Sigoe, there's a good chance they're among them."

"Agreed," he said, squeezing his knees against his horse. "Let's ride!"

Cybella sat on a plush velvet stool behind a dressing table and mirror, scanning an array of accessories laid out in front of her. She sighed.

A female servant stood beside her and pointed at a pair of earrings. "The Countess often wore that set with this dress, your highness."

Cybella rolled her eyes. "Yes. Thank you. I think I can manage." She inspected the pearls embedded in the blue silk dress the young woman had helped her put on moments before and grabbed a pair that matched — a different set than had been suggested.

"I'm sorry your highness," said the girl, "but the Count insisted I not leave your side until you depart for dinner."

"Fine," Cybella said, sighing again, looping the second earring through her ear. *It's bad enough Vernik makes us wait on his precious paperwork*, she thought. *Must he subject me to frivolous entertainment too? It's hardly the time for it!*

She gazed into the mirror and spotted the portrait of a young woman which hung on the wall behind her.

"She was quite beautiful, wasn't she?" asked the girl.

"Yes, indeed. The Countess, I presume?"

"Yes. Niranda, of the house of Graznov."

"It must have been painted quite some time ago, was it not?"

"Oh no, the Count commissioned it only a few months before she died."

"A few months...?" Cybella said, taking a breath. Her eyebrows furrowed. "So young... what caused her death?"

A knock came from the door.

"Excuse me," the girl said, bowing before she turned to open it.

"Good evening, your highness," said Reeve Garecht, bowing after he entered the room, "I hope I'm not too early?"

"Not at all, Reeve," said Cybella, springing from her seat. She held out her elbow and pulled him along as he took hold of it, whisking him out the door. "Let's get this over with, shall we?"

They turned down the hall and headed for a grand staircase.

"How's your family?" she asked.

"Hmm?"

"Your family. When we spoke in the Guildhall you said you had to attend to your family's safety. I didn't see you again until we departed. I assume you evacuated them along with the townsfolk? They didn't ride with us so I was wondering—"

"Oh yes, I had my men take them to my family retreat in the mountains. They'll be safe there."

"Safer than the fortress?"

Garecht took a breath. "In a way, yes."

"What does that mean?"

"It's nothing. I'm embarrassed to say... my wife and the Count have a little history between them. I'd sooner not elaborate. Suffice it to say she'd rather be where she is than here."

Cybella tightened her grip on his arm and slowed her pace.

"Something troubling you, Bella?" asked the old man.

She stopped halfway down the stairs. "Doesn't it seem a little odd to you that the Count would go to the trouble of hosting a formal dinner on such short notice, especially under the circumstances?"

"The Zuelan fleet you mean?"

"What else?"

"Well, Vernik's always been a little odd. He's been a headache to deal with for years. He holds the county seat; commands the fortress and its garrison, but I'm the Reeve of its biggest town and have the trust of the Merchant's Guild. We quite often lock horns. As for the Zuelans, Kortova was attacked at least a dozen times during the war and never fell, so I imagine talk of a menacing fleet doesn't really faze him. His troops have saved Sigoe at least as many times."

"Well, he didn't save Sigoe this time, did he? These aren't the Zuelans of yesteryear, Reeve Garecht. You were wise to evacuate the town. I'm not quite sure what they have, but their powerful new weapons allowed them to overrun Trianon in a matter of hours. Who knows what they did to Rivenrach. The country is in grave peril. All I need is safe passage to the Duchy."

Garecht's arm tensed in her grip. Cybella studied his features. He'd carried himself with such a strange, detached ease since she'd met him — and the way he seemed lost in time whenever he spoke to her, as if she was still the little girl he'd met years before — all amounted to an air of gentle senility. Why only now did talk of the Count cause him such angst?

"I wish I could do more to help, Bella, but he and I have an understanding. He handles the military decisions, I handle the civil ones, and it's a good thing too."

"Really, why is that?"

"He's got no head for finances. Never has. He's up to his ears in debt and I won't lend him any more money. So now he's beholden to the bankers in Nova Engaric. He's ever wining and dining them when they come. I think he's entertaining one of them now. I saw him greet a gentleman in fine southern attire in the Great Hall while you were dressing. I expect he'll be joining us for dinner. Vernik probably thinks he can bolster his reputation by having you by his side for a few hours."

The nerve. She released Garecht's arm as they neared the door to Kortova's opulent dining room. "Well, we'll see about that."

"Her royal highness, the Crown Princess Cybella of Cortavia," bellowed a footman as she entered the room.

Vernik stood in front of a tall window, next to another man who stood with his back to the entrance. Cybella heard the double doors swing closed behind her. The latch snapped with a heavy click. She looked back. Garecht was gone. The footmen each took a step in front of the door. She pivoted back to see Vernik hasten toward her.

Vernik took her hand and kissed it as he bowed. "Your highness, you look positively radiant! Come, there's someone I'd very much like you to meet."

He led her across the floor. Cybella gasped and yanked her hand free as Vernik's mysterious guest turned to face her.

Vernik gestured toward the rigid figure. "Princess Cybella, may I present the Liester of Luthargrad."

Gavek snatched the document and rushed for the door.

"Leaving so soon?" Pel asked, rising from his high-backed chair. He raised his bushy eyebrows and held his palms in the air. "You barely read it."

"I assure you, Mr. Pel," snapped Gavek, holding the door open for Khloe, "I read it in its entirety. Thank you."

Gavek slammed the door and the pair scurried down the hall, headed for the exit to the courtyard.

"Ugh, that was gruelling!" Khloe lamented, dropping her hips and stomping her feet. "Is it wrong that I thought about shooting him after he insisted it also be translated into Voldovian?"

"Yeah, but I might have let you anyway," he said, shaking his hand. "My hand's cramped from all that transcribing."

"Oh, my poor bookworm, what shall we do with you?" she said, taking his hand.

A gust of wind blew raindrops against their faces as they entered the courtyard. They hurried toward the keep, dodging a column of soldiers who ran past them on the way.

Gavek pulled up his hood. "I'd take a hot meal, for starters. Hope there's some left." He shook his head. "What a day."

"Ya think? Orin gave you quite a walloping. Does your face still hurt?"

"Only when I talk," he said, winking, pushing out his cheek with his tongue.

Khloe giggled and gripped his arm. She pulled up her own hood.

"You're still better off than poor Nicah."

Gavek exhaled. "Yeah, you're right."

"I hope the others are doing okay with him."

"Me too," he said, bounding up the stairs. "They should be half way to Kessa by now. They'll make it to Cairhn in time." He grabbed the handle of one keep's double doors and swung it open.

Khloe stopped a few steps inside and shivered.

"Khloe?" asked Gavek, noticing she was no longer by his side.

"Gavek, something's wrong."

"No kidding, we both haven't eaten in ten hours and we've got to deliver this, come on."

"No," she said, catching her breath. She whispered and pointed at the floor. "There's something dark here. A vile presence."

Gavek studied her eyes for a moment. He ran his fingers along his belt and touched the hilt of his dagger. "Okay... let's stick together. No more splitting up."

Khloe nodded. Gavek took her hand. The pair whisked across the polished floor and ascended the staircase to the second level to reach the dining room doors.

Gavek shook the handle. "It's locked." He pounded the door with his fist. "Hey, open up! Princess Cybella is waiting for this!" He waved the parchment in the air.

"Can I help you, sir?"

They gasped and turned to face the strange voice. A servant tightened his white gloves while he looked down on them with glassy eyes.

"Yes," said Gavek, "I'm a special adviser to the princess; she's expecting these orders delivered post haste, and... I'm hungry!"

"I'm afraid I cannot let you enter the dining room, sir. The Count allows no interruptions when he's entertaining."

"No interruptions...?" Khloe blurted, mouth gaping. "She's gonna be Queen someday, ya know."

A pair of armed guards moved down the corridor, aroused by their voices.

"You'll simply have to wait," white-gloves responded with a strained smile, "Count's orders. I'm sure the kitchen can supply you some refreshments while you bide the time. Your other companions dine there as we speak."

The guards arrived.

"Is there some kind of problem here?" asked one of them.

"Nope," answered Gavek, pulling Khloe away. "Which way is the kitchen then?"

White-gloves pointed back the way they came. "First floor. Follow the smell of food."

"Oh, that's clever," Gavek remarked, squinting. "Thanks. We'll be going now."

Gavek grabbed Khloe's hand and they took off down the stairs.

"We're not just gonna do what he says, are we?" Khloe asked.

"Not a chance."

Back on the first floor and a few turns later, they burst through the kitchen doors to find their Tzyani companions sitting around a table with the kitchen staff.

Sibia jumped from her seat and reached for her bow.

"Oh, it's you guys," she said, withdrawing her hand with a sigh of relief. "Something wrong?"

"Sure feels like it," answered Khloe.

Gavek snatching an apple from the table. "They won't let us in the dining room."

Sibia asked, "Isn't Cybella anxious to—"

"That's what I said," interrupted Gavek. He took a large bite out of the apple and motioned Sibia to his side. His voice now hushed. "There's something fishy going on here. I intend to find out what. Did they assign us quarters for the night?"

"Yes," answered Sibia, "one of the apartments on the third floor."

"Perfect. I'll need a couple of you to stand lookout and the rest to stay here to keep up appearances."

"Siobe," called Sibia to the dusky girl at the end of the table.

Siobe nodded. She grabbed her bow and quiver and rushed out the door after the others.

Wrytha yanked the reins, weaving her horse through the crowd of refugees as they trudged up the winding mountain trail to the fortress. "I don't see them yet, do you?"

"No, keep searching," Arghan replied. He drove his mount to the higher side of the trail to get a better look. It was then that he noticed the sunset and the countless number of long, blurry shadows cast across the river.

"Heaven help us — Look!" screamed a woman clutching an infant to her bosom. She pointed back down the mountain slope to the river valley. "Their ships crowd the river from one side to the other! I can see raiders coming ashore!"

"Keep going, keep—" cried a Sigoan watchman, pointing up the slope, rocking in his saddle, jostled by the multitude that flowed past him. The lead group of riders broke away from the crowd and galloped up the path.

"They're abandoning us!" shouted another civilian.

The throng erupted in shouts and screams, stumbling against each other in a mad fit to race up the path. First, an old man fell, then a cripple. The crowd stampeded, trampling those too weak to keep pace.

"This is madness, Arghan," Wrytha cried, standing in her stirrups, "they're going to kill each other trying to escape and we'll never make it."

"We'll leave the horses," he shouted back to her, positioning his mount near a boulder at the edge of the path. He held out his hand. "Jump!"

Wrytha wriggled to the top of her saddle and leaped over the crowd onto Arghan's horse. He pushed her up onto the outcropping and took her hand. She grunted, straining to pull him up.

"Where to now?"

"Up the slope," he shouted, "we'll head them off."

"Head them off?"

"Just follow my lead."

Arghan and Wrytha scrambled up the incline, grappling the branches of the rugged evergreen shrubs that dotted the slope. They reached a higher section of the road. Arghan ran into the middle of it ahead of the mob.

"Father of Lights help me," he whispered. He drew his sword and paced the width of the trail until riders at the head of the pack reached his position.

"Halt!" he beckoned, reaching with his wounded left hand while he twirled his weapon in the other.

"What's the meaning of this?" cried the lead cavalier. "Make way!"

The horseman attempted to race past him. Arghan swung his sword in a tight, steep arc, severing the man's saddle strap, sending him flailing to the ground.

"Anybody else want to try?" he barked while Wrytha stopped the runaway horse.

The others balked, yanking their reins.

"What do you want with us, stranger?" called one of the riders. "Are you mad? Can't you see the fleet down there?"

"Who's in charge here?" Arghan bellowed, ignoring the question.

"He was," said another, pointing to the man Arghan had toppled.

"Not anymore; I am now," Arghan shouted.

"To hell with this, who's he think he is?" growled another. He kicked his heels and sped forward only to be knocked from his horse by an arrow to the helmet from Wrytha's bow.

Arghan threw off his cloak, exposing his navy blue gambeson emblazoned with the crest of the sea eagle and spun his sword hilt over his knuckles.

"By my brass boots — that's Arghan of Danniker. I'd listen to him if I were you, kid," chided a grey-haired soldier among them. "What do you want us to do, Erne Warder?"

"You two over there, ride like mad up to the fortress and tell them to lower the drawbridge for us. The rest form a line across the road. Let no one pass until the crowd yields. Tell them there's no need to panic. Count off fifty able-bodied citizens to stand aside and wait by the slope to go back for the fallen. The rest who look fit enough, send straight up the mountain, off-road. Let only the mothers with children, the elderly and cripples take the path, led by one of you. I've seen all your faces. Fail to do this and I'll find you. Somewhere, someday, I'll find you. You're soldiers! Now act like it!"

The veteran who recognized him saluted then led the others back down the path while two other riders split away and sped forward.

"What about us, 'captain'?" teased Wrytha, riding down to him on the fallen leader's horse.

He leaped onto the steed and sat behind her. "To the fortress. Their textbook defence will only get everyone killed. If Kortova's to survive what they've got coming, they're going to need my help."

Gavek and Khloe slipped onto the terrace outside the keep's dining room.

"Wow," Khloe whispered, scanning the row of tall windows that lined the wing's exterior. "How'd you know we could get here this way?"

"Damient of Ravix wrote a treatise detailing his designs when the Count commissioned him to renovate the castle after the war. The keep's more of a palace now than a functional part of the fortress. An architectural triumph to be sure, but it all but drained the Count's purse. It follows the—"

Khloe rolled her eyes. "Got it, thanks. Couldn't you just say you read a book about it?" She giggled. "You're such a nerd."

"I thought that's what I—"

Khloe covered Gavek's mouth and pointed ahead. A silhouette paced along the battlements in the distance. She looked up and waved, signalling Sibia to pull up the rope that they'd used to rappel down from a small balcony two stories above. They waited until the guard walked past a corner and then scampered ahead to peer through one of the windows.

Khloe gasped. "What? Gavek, it's—"

"Empty," Gavek said, creeping toward a set of windowed doors. He opened one of them and nodded through it.

Khloe followed him inside. A slip of paper fluttered off one of the tables as Gavek breezed by it and landed at her feet. She picked it up and scanned the page.

"Oh, no — Gavek!"

"Shh. Keep your voice down," he said, gliding back, "what's the matter?"

"It's addressed to Arghan, look!"

Gavek snatched the page and read it. He crinkled it in his shaking fist. "That treacherous snake, Vernik! He's in league with Thurn!"

"Thurn?" she echoed.

Gavek handed the note back to her and spun around, surveying the room.

"I don't understand," Khloe said with a puzzled look, noticing the uneaten feast and empty chairs around the Count's table. "Where'd they all go? How'd they get out? We'd have seen them leave, wouldn't we? Unless of course they crossed one of the terraces outside? Maybe exited one of the corner towers, or the apartment doors?"

"No," said Gavek, his eyes darting in various directions as he scanned the room. "Everything leads back to the main corridor, or the vestibule, except..." He rushed to open one of the tall cabinets built into the wall on either side of the table.

"What's that?" Khloe said, looking inside it.

"A dumbwaiter," Gavek answered, testing its floor with his foot.

"A dumb what?"

"It's a lifting device used to bring food up from the kitchen."

"Oh. You think they used this to sneak out? If it goes down to the kitchen, wouldn't the others have seen them come out of it?"

"Yes, they would."

"So no, then?"

"Not necessarily..." Gavek turned his attention to the other cabinet opposite the table. He glanced through the windows and waited for the guard outside to move past them again, then scampered over to the cabinet and ran his fingers around its decorative mouldings.

"Gavek?"

"Damient insisted symmetry was the hallmark of good architecture. He designed everything in perfect balance. It may look like there's no door on this side but — ah, there it is! You were complaining about how much of a nerd I was?"

Something behind the cabinet clicked and a hidden door popped open, revealing a shaft. They peered down it to see a platform resting on the floor two flights below and a ladder recessed into the outer wall.

"I wasn't complaining. I think it's cute how oblivious you are to how silly you sound. You are a tad dramatic at times, but—"

"Ingenious," remarked Gavek, taking a few steps down the ladder, "not a cable in sight. The whole thing runs on gears built into the shaft."

"Gavek—" Khloe implored, looking over her shoulder.

The double doors behind the count's table sprung open, followed by the sound of a sword sliding out of its sheath.

"Hey, you two!" an armoured guard demanded, "what are you doing in here?"

"Schlika!" Gavek grabbed Khloe's hand and pulled her into the shaft with him. He pounded a panel on the wall and the door slammed shut.

CHAPTER TWENTY-THREE
Siege

"I can't see a thing in here!" Khloe exclaimed, hugging the rungs of the ladder.

"Follow me, just climb," Gavek's voice echoed from below.

The shaft brightened as they descended. They reached the bottom of the pit and dropped onto the lift platform. Flickering candles glowed at the end of a narrow passage.

The floor shook. Dust fell from the ceiling.

"Was that what I think it was?" Khloe asked, looking up.

"I sure hope not," Gavek replied, accelerating through the passage, "we gotta get out of here."

They charged through the tunnel until it opened into another shaft and shinnied up the ladder inside it to reach an iron hatch. Gavek pushed it open and popped his head out, only to jump back again at the sound of horse hooves thundering by.

"Ow!" Khloe groaned, "you kicked me in the face!"

"Sorry..." Gavek said, jumping out of the hatch. He spun on his knees, following the sound's origin.

A cluster of riders raced across the courtyard, headed for the rear gatehouse. Seconds before the riders disappeared through the tunnel archway, Gavek glimpsed Cybella hanging from the back of one of the horses, gagged and bound.

"Cybella!" he cried as he sprinted after them. He ran through the archway and watched the gatehouse portcullis slam shut and the riders race away.

Khloe bumped into him, panting. Kortova's defenders scurried along its battlements. A thunderous crack echoed in the distance, followed by a whizzing sound that grew louder until the roof cone of one of the forward towers exploded in a hail of flaming timbers.

"Back to the castle!" Gavek cried, pushing her.

Khloe watched the debris smash to the ground. "Back to the castle!" she echoed, recoiling. She hesitated. "No, wait, you said the keep's not a real castle anymore!"

"It's better than standing out here! We need to find the others; take refuge in the barracks."

They charged around the northeast corner of the old keep, headed for the front door.

Another projectile wailed through the air and struck a heavy tower inside the curtain wall near the keep, collapsing one of its corners, sending dislodged stones and mortar crashing to the ground beside them.

"Don't tell me—" Khloe gasped, "I'm guessing that was the barracks?"

"Keep running!"

They sprinted the rest of the way. As they neared the front steps, Sibia and Siobe came running down them with Reeve Garecht following, along with the rest of the Tzyani zealots.

"What happened?" Sibia implored, "where's Cybella?"

"You mean he doesn't know?" Gavek said, flashing his teeth at Garecht. He brushed past Sibia and grabbed Garecht's lapels. "Weren't you supposed to escort her to the dinner? How much did the Count pay you to hand her over?"

Sibia tugged Gavek's shoulder. "Gavek—"

"Calm down, son," said Garecht in a placid tone, his chin close to his chest. "It's not what you think. Immediately after Bella walked through the dining room door, Vernik's ruffians slammed it shut and bound my hands in fetters." He showed Gavek his bruised wrists.

Sibia stepped between them and said to Gavek, "After you disappeared we spotted some men pushing the Reeve across the terrace to one of the towers. It was short work to set him free."

"Do you know what became of poor Bella?" asked Garecht, his voice cracking. "What has that deviant Vernik done this time?"

"Deviant?" Gavek asked, with a look somewhere between perplexity and apprehension, his eyes darting from side to side. His eyelids narrowed and his expression morphed into a scowl. "Thurn took her;" Gavek said, "the Count's in on it."

"I knew he was up to something," said Garecht, shaking his head.

"Thurn?" Sibia asked. "How'd he get here? What's his connection to the Count?"

"Not sure, but I saw them riding out the north gate together a few minutes ago."

"Wait," interrupted Khloe, "you did?"

Gavek held up his palms. "We really gotta get inside. Come on, I'll explain lat—"

The tunnel beyond the front gatehouse echoed with shouts and clopping hooves. The group looked toward the commotion. A crowd of refugees rushed through the gate, led by figures on horseback. Gavek's jaw dropped and he staggered back when his gaze fell on one horse in particular.

"Arghan! Wrytha!" he exclaimed. "Over here!"

Clutching Rhodo's empty lead, Khloe ran beside the horse as it trotted to a stop next to the stairs. "Mother!"

Wrytha jumped down and embraced her. "Khloe! Praise the Maker, you're okay." She took the leash from Khloe's hand and looked into her daughter's eyes. "Oh, Khloe," she sighed, hugging her even tighter than before.

Gavek embraced Arghan. "You're a sight for sore eyes. I feared you might be dead."

"Not yet, son," he said, smiling, "not yet. Come, let's take shelter under the portico."

Garecht cleared his throat as the group followed them up the steps. "Excuse me Sibia, who are these people?"

"That's our Clan Mother, Wrytha Pan-Deighgren. The big guy's her new beau, Arghan of Danniker. They rescued Cybella from being executed by the Archprelate."

Garecht's eyelids widened. "Arghan of Danniker... rescued... it would seem I need to keep better abreast of what's going on in Trianon."

Arghan looked to Gavek and Khloe as they reached the landing. "Where's Cybella? Where are the others?"

"Yes, and Nicah and Orin?" Wrytha asked, leaning past him to scan the group.

Khloe and Gavek exchanged looks.

"Where's the wagon and the manuscripts?" Gavek responded.

Arghan looked to the ground for a moment, then traded glances with Wrytha.

"It would seem we all have some tales to tell," Wrytha said.

Another projectile whizzed overhead, missing the keep by an arm's length.

"But not here and now," Arghan urged, "Zuelan troops will likely reach the fortress in less than two hours. All of you need to take shelter." He waved toward the door.

"No," said Sibia, clutching her bow, "we're ready to fight!"

Arghan gave Wrytha a deferring look.

Wrytha raised her voice and pivoted toward the zealots, "I disapproved of Teighthra's teachings, but there's a difference between recklessly looking for trouble and the choices you make when trouble comes looking for you," she said. She turned back toward Arghan. "Perhaps it's time we took a stand, Arghan. There must have been at least seven thousand refugees on the road. How could we live with ourselves if we fail to help defend this place?"

"So be it, but not like this." Arghan leaned against one of the portico's columns and squinted, surveying the clusters of soldiers massed behind the battlements along the curtain wall. He grimaced and shook his head.

"They'll get slaughtered up there. Gavek, find the princess. Get her out of here while there's still time. We're going to need the Duke's help and she's the only one who can get it. Avoid the river. Take the Borga pass—"

"I can't Arghan; she's gone, look." Gavek handed him the handwritten note left by Thurn. "Count Vernik tricked us."

Arghan's fist trembled while he read the note. He gritted his teeth. "Thurn! When I get my hands on that fiend...If only we didn't have these Zuelans breathing down our necks."

"What happened?" Wrytha asked Gavek, grabbing the note.

"That creep Thurn was here waiting for us in the castle;" interrupted Khloe, "probably got here right before we did."

Arghan pounded the column next to him with his fist. "After all we went through, he's got her again! He wants me to journey to Ondar Falls. Says he's going to murder Cybella if I fail to meet him there in thirty-six hours."

"Thirty-six hours?" Wrytha exclaimed. "He must have assumed we were aboard the *Duskrider*. That's barely enough time by horse. You'd have to leave immediately and ride all night to make it. Why Ondar Falls? Why not here?"

"He wants his precious treasure, remember?"

"So give it to him, Arghan. Is any amount of riches worth your daughter's life?"

"Of course not. If it were that simple that's the first thing I would've done. But the vault at Ondar Falls is different than the rest. Von Terrack didn't even mark it on his map, and when he confided in me about its existence he issued a dire warning. He said any man who possessed the riches stored inside it would conquer the world. There must be something of incalculable value inside it. Can you imagine what a man like Thurn would do with that kind of power?"

Wrytha shook her head. "I dare not. There has to be a way to stop him."

"Duke Weorthan could," said Gavek, waving the document he drafted with Pel. "Thurn wouldn't even need to know Weorthan's men were there. He could encircle the falls. Prevent Thurn's escape. I've got orders from Cybella right here that authorize him to cross the border."

"That'll be impossible if Kortova falls," Arghan interjected, "he'll need every man he can spare to stop the Zuelans, unless... "

Arghan looked skyward. Another missile wailed through the air and struck the roof of the curtain wall's easternmost tower, destroying it instantly.

Arghan touched Wrytha's shoulder. "Get us some horses. Take the others and meet me at the north gate as soon as you can."

Arghan hastened down the stairs and headed toward the curtain wall.

Wrytha called from the portico, "Arghan, wait, where are you going?"

"To find the garrison commander. He needs to radically change his defence posture, otherwise everyone inside these walls are doomed."

Standing on the deck of the Kaighan's flagship in the middle of the Onya, Haracht-Wan stared down the sight of the dread weapon his master called the Dragon's Breath and signalled his comrades to stand aside. Stripped from the waist up and drenched in sweat, the men leaped backward, wiping their brows and sighing as they let go of the levers and handles that controlled the pitch and rotation of the massive bombard. They joined the ranks of armoured raiders who stood at attention in a circle around the rails the weapon rode on and a hush spread throughout the assembly.

"It's ready, my Kaighan," called Wan, stepping aside.

The Kaighan approached a flaming brazier and lifted a long, red-hot spike from its basin. "Warriors in the service of Zuel, lord of darkness and flame; god of all gods, this day he gives you victory!"

The men cheered, beating their shields with their swords and axes.

"The infidel called you barbarians!"

The troops called out with boos, hisses, and curses.

"They called you savages!"

The men's jeers intensified.

"But I say, when did any ignorant, superstitious fool from the great halls of learning across the obstinate, stubborn and contemptible continent of Eskareon ever dream of such magic as ours!"

"Never!" cried a voice above the others.

"Hail Haracht-Wan, master alchemist!"

"Ho! Ho! Hooo-Ohhhh!"

"Hail Zeneg-Kal, master of the Kaighan's foundry!"

A stout Zuelan who stood beside Wan bowed his bald head.

"Hooo-Ohhhh!"

"Hail Zuel!"

"Zuel, Zuel, Zuuuueeel!"

"Hail our mighty Kaighan, Zuelkar the Great, god among men," cried Haracht-Wan.

"Zuelkar! Zuelkar! Zuelkaaarrrrr!"

The men erupted with screams and whistles as Zuelkar touched the blazing spike to the fuse on top of the weapon. The fuse burned away. The Dragon's throat shot backward and its mouth spewed smoke and flames, rocking the ship with fury as it ejected a polished stone sphere the weight of three men through the air, blazing like a meteor toward the walls of Kortova.

A man in plate armour and waffenrock peered through a spyglass from one of Kortova's gatehouse towers. He pressed a voice horn to his mouth as tightly as his grizzly beard would allow. "Crossbowmen, pick your targets! Wait 'till they're in range to fire," he bellowed out a side window. "Oilers, stoke your fires! Engineers, load the catapults!"

Another soldier rushed through the door. "Sir Radu," he called, tipping the wide brim of his kettle helmet with a cautious bow, "there's an Ostergaardian knight outside who—"

"Ostergaardian?" Radu asked, still looking through his spyglass. "That's impossible, sergeant. The Count could've only just sent his courier! Did they come of their own accord?"

"No, but I did." Arghan barged past the sergeant and strode across the dusty timber floor to stand in front of the commander. "Your men need to retreat to the north wall immediately."

"The north wall? Are you mad, sir? Their entire force is coming up from the river." Radu stepped down from the step stool he used to reach the window. "Who the blazes do you think you—" His gaze fell on Arghan's gambeson.

"Arghan of Danniker," he answered, looming over Radu with his Twin Talon held upside down to reveal its distinctive crossguard and pommel.

The sergeant's eyelids widened at the sight of the polished blade.

"By the black beard of Saint Keil, you are alive," Radu exclaimed, looking him over. "Seems I owe the men a payment for a wager. I'm Sir Radu, garrison commander. Perhaps when this is over you can entertain us all with the tale of how you managed to dodge the axe. But right now we've more pressing matters to attend to, as you can see. Whatever you want to say, you'd better make it quick, Erne Warder."

Arghan sheathed his blade. "Listen to me, you must order your men to the north wall. Set up a firing line to cover the middle of the bailey. Get your engineers to turn the north mangonels southward."

"Southward? Why would I do that when I have six perfectly good ones on the south wall zeroed into the mountain slope?"

"Because they're about to get blown to splinters, that's why, and the bulk of your force along with them."

"Ha! The years have dulled your memory, Danniker. Kortova's never fallen." He slapped the wall with his gauntlet. "Her walls are as thick as they come!" Radu offered Arghan his spyglass. "Look, the foreign devils are coming straight up the mountain like last time. It'll be a turkey shoot once they're in range. Feel free to ask the stable master for a horse on my order. You can chase down the stragglers with that elegant sword of yours afterward if you like, but right now we have matters well in hand."

Arghan pressed his finger against Radu's breastplate. "You don't understand, the Zuelans—"

The telltale boom of the invaders' deadly invention echoed through the arrow slit where Radu had perched with his spyglass, this time deeper and more thunderous than the ones Arghan had heard during the siege of Trianon. A sonorous whooshing sound intensified like the climax of a dramatic symphony.

"Get down!" Arghan shoved Radu to the floor, then tackled the sergeant as he dove out the door.

The top of the gatehouse tower exploded, showering the dry moat with falling stones. The floor above the chamber where the three men had stood collapsed, bringing the conical roof above it down on top of Radu.

"Sergeant?" Arghan called, pushing himself up.

The sergeant nodded as he staggered to his feet.

A cacophony of lesser explosions erupted from the river.

The sergeant yelled to the men who now cowered behind the battlements of the curtain wall, "Off the wall, all of you!"

Radu groaned through the wreckage. "S-Sergeant H-Hanuke... D-Danniker..."

Hanuke leaped over the debris. Arghan followed. They stooped over Radu, who lay pinned, his head sticking out from below a heavy beam.

"Sir Radu!" cried Hanuke. "Hang on, we'll get you out—"

Blood oozed from Radu's mouth. He gasped. "N-never mind that, Hanuke. I c-can't move. M-my neck broke. D-Danniker... Danniker's in command. You hear me?"

Hanuke blinked, then nodded.

Arghan gripped Hanuke's shoulders. "The Zuelan gunners won't be able to sight the back of the summit from their position. They'll destroy the south wall first then send their troops in, which will force them to stop firing. Get the men to the north wall. Tell the engineers to start turning the mangonels to fire south onto the slope to thwart their approach, but don't let them fire until a significant number of Zuelans have breached the south wall. Line your crossbowmen up to fire into the bailey. Tell the mace-wielders and pikemen to hide behind the barracks until the Zuelans cross the courtyard, then encircle them as they pass. Got it?"

"Yes, sir," Hanuke replied, saluting. He bowed to Radu before he scrambled off.

"S-save my m-men... D-Danniker... a-and t-the civilians..."

"I'll do my best," said Arghan, rising to follow Hanuke.

Radu's voice diminished to a gurgling whisper, "Danniker, wait. One more thing."

Arghan stooped again and turned his ear to Radu's mouth.

"The armoury... i-inside the b-barracks to the left... a bronze chest. Key's round my neck. You'll be needing what's in it. God h-have—"

"God have mercy on your soul," Arghan said, closing Radu's eyelids. He snapped the glittering chain from Radu's neck and raced for the stairs.

Arghan raced across the courtyard and headed for the barracks, followed by a throng of Kortova's defenders. Reeve Garecht intercepted him, attended by a few of his cavalrymen.

"Danniker! A word please," he called, cupping his hands around his mouth.

"Make it quick, sir, I've no time for introductions," Arghan responded, looking back to watch the Kaighan's missiles assail the curtain wall.

"I'm Reeve Garecht of Sigoe. What's going on? Did you find Radu?"

"Radu's dead, I'm taking command. There's little time to prepare. Now if you'll excuse me—"

Garecht flung his cloak open, exposing a Talon sheathed at his hip. "You're not the only one who escaped the purge. I may be a frail, old man now, but was a commodore long before your time. A dear, old friend of mine had a pint with me recently. He said he talked to you at my docks several days ago. I thought it was the drink talking. I'm happy to see I was wrong. Tell me how I can help."

"Sir," Arghan said, gasping and shaking his head in disbelief. "I'll take that if you'll permit me," he said, pointing at Garecht's sheath.

"Oh, don't tell me you're one of those," Garecht said, drawing his blade with a smirk. He handed it to him.

"Trust me, I'm not," he answered, sheathing Garecht's weapon in his empty scabbard, "but I may need it before the day is out."

"Anything else, Warder?"

"The civilians. I have a plan that will save them and stop the Zuelans dead in their tracks, but to pull it off my friends will need to go on without me. For it to succeed, someone will need to lead the refugees into the dry moat on the north side of the fortress. It's crucial for their survival. The north gatehouse keeper will know how to reach it."

"No need. I know the way. There's a hidden ramp next to the north gatehouse. Its exit is hidden under the drawbridge. Vernik used to graze his herd of cattle out there in case of siege, at least he did before he was forced to sell them to pay off some of his debts. The Sigoans trust me. I will lead them there. "

"Good. One more thing. On the way, tell the young fellow named Gavek to come see me at the barracks armoury. I need a word with him before they depart."

"Yes, I know him." He interlocked his thumbs and made the sign of the Sea Eagle across his chest, then bowed. "Godspeed, Erne Warder."

Arghan returned the gesture. "Same to you, commodore."

Arghan stormed into the armoury. "This better be what I think it is," he muttered, blinking in the flickering lamplight, scanning the room.

Weapons of every shape and size hung from the walls inside the octagonal chamber. Suits of armour from bygone eras stood on stands in front of them along with several large, heavy chests.

"Can't see a dreaded thing in here, which one of them is bronze? Ah!" he said, spotting a reflected glimmer.

He dashed to the chest and opened it. "By the black beard of Saint Keil, that's even better! There's a whole suit in here."

He lifted out a cuirass made of pointed, shimmering scales resembling eagle's feathers in the hue of burnt umber. He grabbed a pair of vambraces made from the same material and tied them over the leather ones he already wore.

"What's going on?" Gavek huffed as he spun into the room. "The others are ready to leave, but the old man insisted you wanted to see me?" He noticed the open chest. "Holy bathwater, is that what I think it is?"

"Yes. Get over here. Help me put it on while we talk. Start with the cuirass."

"Okay." Gavek grabbed the glittering vest. "It's light as the feathers it's made to resemble. The scales can't be steel?"

Arghan threw it over his neck. "They're ceramic. Tougher than diamonds. Cast from molten lava from the dormant volcano on Erne Rock. Satisfied? Tell anybody and I'll have to kill you. Now shut up and listen. We've got precious little time."

Arghan held out his arms while Gavek tied the sides of the cuirass against his ribs. "Tell me everything you know about the Kinnessarat dam."

"The dam? What do you want—"

"Never mind, never mind. Just spill it. Pauldrons next. Quickly, quickly."

"Well, not as much as I thought. Khloe told me some fascinating new details recently though, about how they let off water from the reservoir every fall and spring—"

"Never mind that. Structurally I mean. How it's built. I remember you telling me you read a controversial treatise once—"

"Oh yes! That one! Damient of Ravix wrote it. Funny, I was just telling Khloe about him today—"

"On with it, Gavek, and hand me those greaves while you're at it!"

"Right, well, the college of architects in Lyrance threatened to revoke his license over it. In fact, they banned its publication. But I bought the plates for it from a printer in Straskost for a song that day we stayed there two years ago. He was so angry he'd spent all that time typesetting it that he refused to throw it out—"

"Who cares! The dam! What did Damien write about the dam!"

"Damient."

"Whatever! Continue. Knee-cops now."

"Well, the College reveres the Kinnessarat dam as one of the eleven wonders of the ancient world. But Damient claimed it has a fatal flaw. He said the builders used the wrong material in the foundation and it relies too heavily on the buttresses that support the downstream side. He claimed that if just one of them were to fail—"

" — The whole thing would collapse," Arghan interrupted, "bringing lake Kinnessarat down with it."

"Yes, exactly. The results would be quite devastating, and — as if the resultant deluge wouldn't be terrible enough — his drawings illustrating how portions of the scree slope on the south side have crumbled over the centuries predicted there would be a landslide of apocalyptic proportions to go with it."

Arghan's gaze grew distant. "That's what I thought I remembered. Had to be sure. What about the lock the Ostergaardians built into the north side of the gorge after the war to allow their ships to descend to the river?"

"Oh, that's not going anywhere. It's cut into the mountain. Damient designed it himself, with such a potential failure in mind. Both ends can be sealed. He wrote the treatise about the dam while supervising its construction."

"And the Zuelans have never even seen it," Arghan muttered under his breath. "They only got as far as the battle lines — the Duchy's current border... "

"I'm sorry, what?"

"Belt and helmet."

Gavek handed Arghan his arming belt, and while his mentor fastened it around his waist he paused to admire the ensemble's final piece. The helmet resembled a Gothan sallet with a long tail at the back, but it was a distinctive feature at the front that caught his eye.

"Fearsome," Gavek said, handing it to him, "the way the visor curves to a point like an eagle's beak. Nice touch."

"I always thought it looked a bit silly myself," Arghan replied, "but the Zuelans empty their bowels whenever they see one. The angel of death in their twisted religion is a great eagle that flies out from the sea."

Arghan lifted his visor to look Gavek in the eyes.

"You're not coming with us, are you?" Gavek said, looking back at him.

"No. But I hope to meet you in Straskost as soon as I can. Ride like mad to reach it. Warn the Duke. Give him those orders. Tell him your plan to encircle the falls; I couldn't have devised a more brilliant solution myself. The sooner you get there the better. If things go as planned, we may yet beat Thurn at his game. Failing that, well, if there was a man born who could figure out how to disarm Von Terrack's ingenious contraptions its you. You're the best man I've ever known, Gavek of Cairhn. But don't tell Pattron I said that."

Gavek snickered, fighting back tears. "Hey, it's 'Master Librarian' now. I'm an adviser to the future Queen don't you know."

"Well, pardon me 'Master Librarian', you still got that notebook and wadd stick of yours?"

"Yes, right here."

"No, you do it. Can't write in these," Arghan said, waving his gauntlets, "I need you to take down a letter to Wrytha."

Gavek bounded through the maelstrom, dodging running soldiers and fallen debris, and dove through the door into the fortress stables.

"Ready to go?" He implored, throwing his cloak back over his shoulders.

"Ready when you are," answered Wrytha, turning her horse. "That kind old Reeve gave us his knight's best horses, we ought to—" Her eyes turned toward the front door. "Gavek, where's Arghan?"

"He's not coming," Gavek asserted, jumping onto the one horse left with an empty saddle. "There's been a change of plans."

Khloe sighed and dropped her head only to look up again when her mother stirred.

Wrytha dismounted and headed for the door. "Oh no he doesn't, Khloe just finished telling me about what my foolish son and his friends did in Sigoe. I'm not leaving here worrying about him too."

"Wrytha, wait," called Gavek, himself dismounting. He rushed past her and grabbed her shoulders.

"There's no time. He gave me this." Gavek handed her the note Arghan dictated to him minutes before.

Wrytha opened it and read. Tears burst from her eyes and she covered her quivering lips with her free hand.

"That stubborn, selfless man," she said, weeping. "The whole country hated him for years and he's still fighting to defend it. He may wield a sword, but I've never met a man of deeper faith. How could one with a heart like that ever be thought a criminal?" She folded the letter and carefully stuffed it under the folds of her tunic. She jumped back into her saddle. "Let's go."

The riders burst out the stable and headed for the gate.

Reeve Garecht stood behind the battlements of the gatehouse and watched them gallop through the tunnel. He commanded a nearby infantryman, "Drop the portcullis the moment they're over the drawbridge."

Arghan walked into the middle of the bailey and tied his left hand around the hilt of Garecht's Talon with a leather strap. He watched the portcullis close, then turned to face the gap between the old keep and the barracks.

The last stones of a widening gap in the south wall exploded, collapsing the section between the south gatehouse and the next mural tower. A massive projectile bounded across the courtyard and crashed into the entrance of the old keep. A shriek rose up from beyond the wall, followed by the pounding rhythm of war drums and the chanting of a thousand voices.

Arghan dropped his visor and drew his second sword.

The first wave of Zuelan raiders poured through the gap, wailing like demons set free from hell. They rushed between the keep and the barracks, headed straight for Arghan's position.

Arghan threw up his left sword, signalling the men-at-arms behind the buildings. They rushed out from either side and closed the gap.

Arghan whipped his right sword into the air and crossbowmen fired from the north wall into the bailey, dropping the Zuelans' front line. A hail of flaming missiles launched from mangonels atop each of Kortova's north towers, streaking like meteors through the night sky over the south wall until they crashed and spiralled in a chaotic landslide through the ranks of Zuelans still scaling the approaching slope.

Arghan screamed a Gothan battle cry and a rushed the Zuelan horde. Swords clashed, gleaming in the moonlight. Black lacquered armour ground against polished steel. Blood and spit sprayed through the air. Soon the first wave lay dead at the surviving defenders' feet.

Arghan flicked open his visor. "Starting positions!" he bellowed to the defenders, whipping his blades clean.

Garecht paced along the north wall. "We might live through this yet, Hanuke," he said, patting Radu's sergeant on the shoulder as he passed. "Danniker's a born tactician. If only the Count had been as brave as her defenders. I know Radu would be proud of you."

Another wave breached the wall, then another; each one increasing in number. The cycle repeated through the night until the sun cast long shadows over Kortova's ragged, stumbling defenders and the silent corpses of the dead.

A horn sounded from the base of the hill. Arghan lifted his visor and staggered forward, squinting as he watched some of the other knights chase the last group of the Zuelans back through the gap in the wall. He grabbed a waterskin from the hand of a squire who stood nearby him transfixed with a vacant stare, trembling.

Arghan emptied the waterskin in one breath. "C'mon, lad," he said, tugging the boy's jerkin, "snap out of it. G-go to the stables. Fetch me a h-horse."

The boy nodded and Arghan snatched a stalk of bergaroot from his pocket before he scampered off. Arghan dropped to his knees and chewed the bitter plant, willing the fingers of his left hand into motion while he plotted his next move.

CHAPTER TWENTY-FOUR
Crucible

Arghan drove his mount down Kortova's zigzagged path, slashing the retreating raiders as he rode. Any trepidation that remained about the task ahead vanished at the sight of what lay before him. He grimaced as he passed the spot of the stampede where he and Wrytha had dismounted roughly twelve hours before. Despite his timely orders to the town guards, more Sigoans than he hoped to see lay fallen, too frail to survive the trek or trampled by the panicked townsfolk. Zuelans too littered the path, each man clutching the site of a fatal wound.

He would put an end to war in this land once and for all, or die trying.

He soon reached the shoreline and jumped his horse over a toppled supply cart the Zuelans had brought ashore and landed among a crowd of stragglers who limped across the pebbled beach toward their landing craft. Steam blew from his horse's nostrils, its moisture revealed in the cool morning air. Arghan slid from his saddle and strode toward the waterline.

"He's one of the undead," cried one of the men in his native tongue, diving into the river, "come to exact vengeance on us for invading their land!"

"Nonsense," muttered another, drawing his two-handed war cleaver, "he's mad, driven out of his wits by battle fever. Perhaps the Kaighan will pay us a better price if we bring him a trophy."

He screamed and lunged at Arghan. Arghan dodged his blade and threw him over his shoulder and onto the ground.

He kicked pebbles at the man who attacked him and shouted at the others in their own language, "Mercenaries! No wonder the Kaighan spent your lives so freely." He leaped into one of the boats. "Take me to him, if you dare! I wish to speak to him." He threw a handful of coins onto the floor of their craft, sat down at the stern and folded his arms.

The men dove into the boat, hands clawing each other until every Regalian doubloon had found a place in their pockets.

"Perhaps he is mad," said another. He bit one of the coins with rotting teeth. "Sounds like suicide to me."

"He can kill himself if he likes, as long as he pays the ferryman," said another, snickering as they picked up the oars.

Wrytha stirred from her bedroll. Rubbing her eyes, she rose and looked down over the highlands of the Borga Pass, southeast toward the Onya river. Even from there she could see the smoke billowing from the towers of Kortova. Had the defenders prevailed? Or like Trianon, Rivenrach, and Sigoe before it, had it become the Zuelans' latest prize? Or worse, would Arghan be counted among the dead? She shuddered and marked the sun's position in the sky.

She kicked dirt over the glowing coals at her feet. "Everyone, get up, get up!" she said, spinning in a circle. "Time to leave! There's a long way to go and we've only a day to do it!"

"My Kaighan, you'll want to see this spectacle!" cried Haracht-Wan, rushing into Zuelkar's cabin. "It seems you have a visitor."

Zuelkar opened one eye at first. He snuffed out the candles beside his bed and bowed to a dark idol carved from obsidian glass. He touched the tip of each of its eighteen tentacles and then kissed its dragon head before rising to face his celebrated alchemist.

"If you were any other man I would strike you down for such insolence," Zuelkar sneered. "But you and Zeneg-Kal have proven your worth this day." He cracked the joints of his neck. "Those cursed mercenaries may have failed to take the fortress, but the Dragon's Breath proved their walls are no longer a match for our might. Now it's only a matter of time. Keep it loaded and ready to fire." He looked out the aft windows. "I see the rest of the fleet has arrived, and with them my best warriors. My own guard and I will lead the final assault. Kortova will finally be mine and I shall build an idol to Zuel atop her towers. Come, let us see this so-called 'spectacle' of yours. I enjoy a good laugh before going into battle." He headed for the door, pausing to run his hand over a map of Cortavia spread out over a table. His fingers lingered at a vacant section of the page northwest of Kortova.

Zuelkar strode past Haracht-Wan and stepped out onto his flagship's deck. Arghan stood erect, defiant, a few steps in from the port side, surrounded by a crowd of jeering raiders.

Zuelkar's black-painted eyelids flashed with delight. "An Erne Warder," he said, circling him, grinning. "It would seem Zuel has answered my prayers at last." He cocked his head. "Have you got a death wish, infidel?"

The crew whooped and whistled.

"I'm here to challenge you to a duel to the death," Arghan said, removing his sallet.

The younger men erupted in laughter. The older ones hushed and murmured. Hands started passing coins.

"That is if you have any honour left."

The crew hissed.

"I assure you my honour is quite intact," said Zuelkar, smiling.

"You're sure about that? Last time I saw you, you sailed back home to the whore you call a mother with your tail between your legs."

Two warriors jumped toward Arghan, drawing their sabres. Zuelkar laughed and held out his arms. They spat at Arghan's feet and sheathed their blades.

"And the stakes?" Zuelkar asked.

"If I fail to return to the fortress within four hours, her defenders have been ordered to abandon it to you."

More murmurs ensued. The mercenary who attacked him on the beach stood nearby. He chuckled and called out to one of his fellows, "See, he is mad. He thinks there's still a chance they'll prevail."

Zuelkar heard him. He grabbed the man's cleaver. Steel flashed. The mercenary's head rolled across the deck. "Get this lice-ridden cur off my deck," he said, dropping the blade on top of the man's body.

"You were saying, infidel?"

"If I win, you quit this hopeless campaign to regain your faded glory and leave this continent forever."

Haracht-Wan tugged on Zuelkar's sleeve and spoke into his ear, "Why not simply detain him, my Kaighan? Your leadership is too important to us. The fortress will be yours and we can—"

"You think I'll lose? I don't need your magic to defeat one man."

"Plus if he refuses," Arghan interjected, "he'll prove to his men here he's nothing but a coward with big toys."

"I am no coward!" Zuelkar screamed, lunging to within inches of Arghan's face.

There's the nerve I was looking to step on, Arghan thought.

"Challenge accepted." Zuelkar threw off his silken robe, exposing his chiselled physique, naked except for the loin cloth wrapped around his pelvis. A sable-hued tattoo matching the figure that stood on his altar spread from one rippling pectoral muscle to the other. "Fetch me my Kapkul[1]!" he commanded.

The crowd backed away. A shorn-headed attendant rushed into Zuelkar's quarters and back out again carrying a long, curved sabre. Zuelkar grabbed it and rolled it around his knuckles.

"Prepare to die, Erne Warder."

Arghan put on his helmet. "Take your best shot." He drew his Talon and gripped the hilt with both hands.

---

1. Kapkul – a bladed weapon of uniquely Zuelan design, similar in some respects to a Mongolian cavalry sabre, but fatter at the end.

Zuelkar lunged at him, cursing. Arghan dodged his thrust and batted Zuelkar on the back with the flat of his blade. A mercenary laughed. Zuelkar took his head. Arghan swung. Zuelkar ducked and punched him in the front of his hip. Arghan grunted, stumbling. Zuelkar feigned an attack and sidestepped at the last moment, scoring a heavy blow on top of Arghan's wounded shoulder. Arghan wailed.

"Did you think I could forget that smug face on account of the grey beard?" Zuelkar taunted, "or the sound of that arrogant voice? Do you recall the day I myself shot you there from my horse, Danniker?"

"How could I forget," Arghan replied, recovering his stance, "it was the same day I bedded your wife."

Zuelkar lunged again. Arghan spun around him. Zuelkar's topknot fell to the deck.

The raiders gasped.

Zuelkar attacked again. They locked blades. Zuelkar glared down at him, flashing his teeth. He shifted his weight and flicked his wrist. Arghan's failed. His Talon flipped through the air and splashed into the river. He drew Garecht's Talon. Zuelkar struck with a downward thrust, shattering the blade, his own only stopped by the beak of Arghan's visor. Zuelkar grabbed the back of Arghan's head and slammed his face into the deck.

"I forgot how resilient that amazing armour of yours was," Zuelkar mocked, "too bad your steel wasn't."

Blood oozed from Arghan's bevor. He coughed and slid off his sallet. "If you think my armour's resilient, wait 'till you face the Duke's fortress. Your pathetic invasion will fall dead in its tracks. I doubt that metal monstrosity of yours can penetrate its walls. Then the Duke will crush you after your men wither from scurvy next winter." He chuckled. "Kortova's no triumph. It's as brittle as my last blade. But the Duke's fortress is as strong as my armour, perhaps more."

"Finish the insolent cur, Kaighan!" cried one of his own men.

"No, he's unworthy of our master's blade," said another, "allow me, Your Greatness." He drew his weapon and raised it over his head.

"Silence!" Zuelkar commanded, waving his hand. "Tell me of this fortress, sea-eagle and perhaps I'll wait a day or two before I boil you like a crustacean in that splendid suit of yours."

"It's built over a waterfall, between two unscalable mountains, a day's sail upriver. As high as heaven and as deep as the sea. It would take a far braver man than you to destroy it."

"We'll see about that!" Zuelkar said, flashing his eyes. "The Great Wall of the Nibu-Khan fell at my hand." He pointed at Arghan. "Lash him to the foremast; front and centre. The Erne Warder will get a front-row seat to my triumph. I'll force his God to bow to Zuel like all the rest!"

"Zuel, Zuel, Zuuuueeel!" shouted his crew.

The same pair who had wanted to finish Arghan seized his arms and dragged him across the deck.

"What about Kortova, Mighty Kaighan?" asked Haracht-Wan.

"It'll be waiting for us when we return. Weigh anchor; signal the fleet," he called, donning his robe. "Set sail upriver. We'll attack at dawn."

Wrytha and Khloe, Gavek, and the remaining zealots turned a corner where the trail to the Ondar River gorge diverged from the pass. They looked down the mountain slope and out over the rooftops of Straskost toward the shimmering waters of Lake Kinnessarat. Adorned with the golden banners of its master's house, the Duke's castle loomed over the town, perched at the edge of the Onya River gorge opposite the ship lock, near the northern side of the ancient dam.

"Straskost, at last," said Wrytha. She goaded her horse onto the descending path. The mare's knees buckled and it threw her from the saddle. Wrytha rolled out of her fall, flinging her braid back over her shoulder. "But not on these poor things," she said, watching the horse collapse by the wayside.

" 'Fraid not," said Gavek, dismounting. "Mine's done as well."

"Mine too," said Khloe, following.

The others did the same.

"We'll have to proceed on foot," said Gavek, taking off down the trail. "At least the rest of the way is downhill."

"You haven't hiked many mountains, have you?" Khloe quipped, tugging her pack down from the back of her horse.

"No," Wrytha said, waving her hand as she stood up.

Gavek pivoted back. " 'No, I haven't hiked many mountains' or 'no, we won't proceed on foot'?"

"Neither. We're splitting up. Drop your packs. You and Khloe go down the mountain. Take the orders to the Duke. Remember to tell him everything Arghan wrote in his letter to me. The rest of us are going to the falls."

"What?" Khloe said, holding her arms out by her sides. "Mother, no!"

"We're not going to debate this, Khloe. Sibia and Siobe, you're with me. Lahmech, Zorhen, Kaleth — I'm counting on you three to make sure Gavek and Khloe make it to the castle. Go."

"C'mon, Khloe," said Gavek, tugging her hand. "Your mother knows what she's doing."

Khloe embraced her mother and kissed her on the cheek before following him. "Come back to me, mother."

"I will," she said, wearing the most stoic expression she could muster. If she looked worried, Khloe would too.

She turned to the three boys. One at a time, Wrytha looked each of them in the eyes and gave them a tender hug. She could tell by their dejected expressions they hated her, thinking she had chosen the older girls because of their prowess as archers of the wood. This was a pain she could live with. Of all of Teighthra's disciples, the three brothers were the only ones directly related besides her own, and among the youngest. She knew what might face her at the falls. As Clan Mother, she couldn't bear having to return to Nova Elkahrn with the death of one woman's three sons and only children on her conscience. There were already too many sorrowful memorials to observe. She watched them run with unveiled reluctance to catch up to Gavek and Khloe before turning away.

"Let's go," she said, hurrying up the path to the falls.

"Master Librarian? Of Trianon? Right… and I'm the Marquis of Husselstein," scoffed one of Castle Straskost's gatehouse keepers, standing at his post opposite Gavek. He lowered his halberd and pointed back into town. "Do you have any idea how often visitors say they're important people on important business? No way I'm letting you in, you don't even look the part! Shove off before I arrest you."

"Listen you dim-witted oaf," replied Gavek, waving the parchment he'd drafted with Pel. "I'm telling you for the last time, I've got legal orders here saying—"

"Off!" the soldier yelled through the grizzled strands of his red beard. He thrust the spiked end of his weapon at Gavek.

"Whoa! Okay, okay," Gavek said, reeling backward. He hurried across the street to where Khloe and the others stood waiting.

"Nice going," said Khloe, folding her arms. "Once again I'm in awe of your powers of persuasion."

"Ha, ha," Gavek said, sighing.

"What are we going to do now?" she asked.

"We have to reach Weorthan somehow. We'll have to sneak in or something, but security looks pretty tight. Any ideas?"

"I've got one," piped up Zorhen, beckoning his brothers as he stepped off the curb. "It's been forever since we've had a proper game of tossball, boys, wouldn't you say?"

Lahmech jerked his head, flinging his long black bangs away from his eyes. "Oh, has it ever."

"Longest toss wins," called Kaleth, following after them.

The boys ran across the street, headed for the barbican.

"Guys, no!" Khloe said, chasing them.

Gavek followed. "What are they doing?"

Zorhen sprinted past the guard and raced over the bridge.

The guard spun toward him. "Hey! Get back here!"

Lahmech kicked off a nearby wall and flipped in mid-air over the guard's head, snatching the man's helmet before he landed.

"What? Hey! Given me that you—"

The guard lunged to grasp Lahmech's tunic but missed. Lahmech tossed the sallet to his brother Kaleth, who snatched it out of the air with a dive.

Another soldier emerged from the guardhouse on the opposite side of the entrance. "Halt! Give that—"

Zorhen grabbed the second man's headgear and tossed it to Lahmech. "We've never played with two before, I think we might be on to something!"

The boys led the guards farther into the street with each pass of the helmets.

"I see what they're up to," said Gavek, "c'mon!" He grabbed Khloe's hand and they bolted across the stone bridge and over the moat to the second, larger gatehouse which stood beyond a drawbridge on the opposite side.

They were about to rush through an open side door when the main gate creaked open and a horse galloped past them, mounted by a rider in a pointed feather cap and cloak, bearing a bow and quiver. A second rider followed soon after; this one in a suit of black velvet embroidered with gold trim, white cuffs and a collar. A hooded falcon clung to a heavy leather glove on his left hand. A pack of long-legged, steel-grey hounds kept pace with him, as did a pair of cavaliers wearing swords and brigandine jackets. A second capped archer took up the rear.

Wide-eyed, Khloe looked at Gavek. "Did you see the caparison on black velvet's horse?"

"I did," Gavek replied. "Same colours as the standards flying from the towers."

"It's the Duke!" they exclaimed in unison.

"He's gonna outrun us—" Gavek shouted, taking after the cavalcade.

Without hesitation, Khloe dropped to one knee and nocked an arrow to her bowstring. She fired a shot through the bulging waterskin hanging beside Weorthan's right leg, exploding its contents over his trousers and boots.

"What the — ? Hold up," exclaimed the rugged, golden-maned Duke, contorting his stubbled face. He yanked his reigns, turning his horse in a circle while he attempted to figure out what happened. He spoke to the archer ahead of him, "Schlika! Daft thing sprayed all over me, Reihner, look."

"Might have something to do with that, your grace," the man said, pointing at the arrow dangling from the waterskin's tattered leather. "An excellent shot. But who—"

Weorthan's eyelids widened. He spotted Khloe still kneeling.

Gavek caught up with the group who by now all had stopped. "Duke Weorthan, a word please sir."

"What's the meaning of this?" called one of the Duke's knights. "Guards!" He dismounted, drew his sword, and marched toward Gavek.

"No, wait, it's not what you think," said Gavek, holding out his hands.

"I'll bet it isn't," scoffed Weorthan, brushing off his trousers. "Can I not get one day's peace? I thought we put an end to this nonsense, Reihner. Where are the gatekeepers? If I find them asleep it'll be their—"

"Duke Weorthan, we're here on behalf of Princess Cybella of Cortavia," Gavek pleaded as the knight grabbed him by the collar and pushed him against the wall that bordered the bridge.

"Cybella?" said Weorthan, his ears perking at the sound of her name.

"Don't fall for it, your grace," said the man he called Reihner. "Probably another trickster hired by the barons of the south trying to lure across the border again. Surely your lady love would have written you if she'd been found."

"We're telling the truth, Weorthan," Khloe called, lowing her bow. "My friend's got written orders from Cybella herself. Have your man check his pockets. The country's in danger! There's a Zuelan fleet ravaging Cortavia, headed upriver."

Weorthan gave Reihner a quizzical look and replied to him in a quieter tone, "You're probably right, but… the girl wears a braid over her shoulder. Why would a Tzyani have anything to do with one of the barons of the south?" He arched his eyebrows and cocked his head as if to contemplate the scene.

The second knight dismounted, drew his sword, and headed toward Khloe. "There's one way to find out." He seized her bow and threw it to the ground. "We'll handle this, your grace. We'll send a fresh escort straight after you with a fresh supply of water. Enjoy your hunt." He grabbed Khloe's arm and shoved her toward the open gate.

"Ow, you're hurting me," she said, wincing.

The first knight sheathed his sword and seized Gavek with both hands. He pushed him toward the castle. "Get moving."

Weorthan watched for a few seconds, shook his head then remounted his horse and continued across the bridge.

Gavek twisted his torso and slipped out of his cloak. He pulled it over the knight's head and scrambled past him. "Weorthan! Wait! D-Deighn Renzek — Deighn Renzek died trying to free Cybella from the Traitor's tower."

Weorthan yanked his reigns. "Set them free!" He slipped off his horse and handed his falcon to Reihner.

"Your grace?" Asked the knight handling Khloe.

"I said unhand them," he replied, walking back across the bridge. "Give this gentleman his cloak." Weorthan strode past Gavek and stood between him and the knight who accosted him. He grabbed Gavek's cloak from the knight and handed it to him. "Apologies, friend." His countenance grew sombre. He drew closer and whispered, "I'm the only man alive this side of the border who knows about Renzek's mission. I feared the worst when his reports stopped, but not this. I beg you tell me, how did he die?"

"Perhaps there's someplace better we can talk?" Gavek responded, eyeing the guards who continued to glare at him.

"Agreed. This way," Weorthan said, beckoning Gavek to follow him into the castle.

"Oh, your grace, one more thing," Gavek said, nodding over his shoulder. "The kids playing tossball out there with your gatekeepers' helmets are with us."

Weorthan looked back and saw the early teens jostling with his men, then looked at Gavek and arched one eyebrow. Finally, he grinned. He called to one of his knights, "Sir Wagnacht, rescue those poor men, will you? Have the lads brought into the castle as my guests."

Wagnacht looked at him side-eyed and nodded. He mounted his horse and headed out. As he neared the gate on the town side of the bridge, a commotion broke out in the street caused by another rider who galloped his horse through a crowd of bustling pedestrians, headed for the gate. The frantic rider whizzed past Wagnacht and skidded his horse to a stop a few strides short of where Weorthan and Gavek stood.

"Duke Weorthan," cried the hooded rider, gasping as he sprung from his saddle, "I'm glad I caught you, sir. I've just come from the south tower. Sentries report a large fleet sailing up the river. A witness said they attacked Roe before dawn and are headed this way."

Weorthan looked at Khloe and she nodded back at him.

"Boenhoff," Weorthan called to his second knight, "tell Sir Wallitz to dispatch archers to the dam at once."

"No!" Gavek interrupted. "Forgive me, your grace. You must keep your men off the dam at all costs. I can explain."

"Tell me everything you know," he said, nudging Gavek's back. "But please talk fast, Mister... ?"

Gavek bowed sideways as they walked. "Gavek of Cairhn, special adviser to her royal highness Cybella of Cortavia, Master of the Royal Archive and Chief Librarian of Trianon, at your service. This is my lovely assistant, Khloe Pan-Wrikor."

"Enchanted," Weorthan said, nodding with a smile as he passed.

Khloe scowled at Gavek as he walked by. "'Lovely... assistant'?" She slapped him on the arm, picked up her bow and scurried to catch up. She whispered in his ear, "Got that half right, haven't you? We'd be in his dungeon right now if I hadn't made that shot and you know it."

"I was only trying to be funny. That wasn't funny?"

Khloe rolled her eyes and they disappeared behind the gatehouse doors.

Arghan awoke to the sensation of warm liquid splashing across his face. His eyes stung and the stench of ammonia filled his nostrils.

A gravelly voice grunted beyond the blur, "Rise and shine, sea-buzzard, we've arrived. The Kaighan demands you watch."

Arghan shook his head and groaned. A familiar pain oozed through his shoulders and arms. Lashed for the better part of a day and all night to the foremast of the Kaighan's flagship he had passed the time severing his fetters with the razor-sharp burrs concealed in his gauntlets. Then, with the job nearly done, he'd finally surrendered to slumber a few hours before dawn. It had been the first time he'd slept since that night with Wrytha in the vineyard barn north of Tolpa. The thought of it brought to mind the fragrant smell of her raven locks and the gentle way she snored. Though they'd both been too exhausted for any temptation to overcome them, the experience had deepened his longing to be with her, away from the madness that had stalked them both since they'd met. Would he ever get the chance? Had she made it to Straskost? Would his daring gamble pay off?

The stinging in his eyes subsided and he gazed out over the deck. The Kaighan's crew scurried from one side of it to the other, readying the ship for their attack. Beyond it churned the black waters of the Onya, shadowed by the soaring cliffs on either side of the towering, fjord-like gorge that formed the first fifty leagues of the river. Framed by mountains to the north and south of them, the arched buttresses of the ancient dam of Kinnessarat loomed high in the distance. An open gate at the base of the wall, in the same place where a waterfall had existed long before its construction, spewed a jet of frothing water, which fell in an arc over a cliff that plunged the remaining distance to the waterline.

"Faster you curs!" bellowed a Zuelan, whipping a team of half-naked slaves below him. "We've a schedule to keep!"

"It's no use, you've driven them too hard," said the Kaighan's metalsmith, Zeneg-Kal. "Fetch some of the captives to help them push the wheel."

"Yes, Master Gunsmith," said the slave driver. "Keep pulling 'till I get back," he yelled to the slaves before scurrying off.

Arghan's gaze fell on the slaves who marched in leg irons below him. The men pushed the rungs of a giant wheel that used the foremast as an axle, driving the mechanism that hauled massive stone spheres up from below deck to feed the mouth of the Kaighan's Dragon. Watching their muscles strain under their sweat-drenched ebony skin, it sickened him to see such powerful men debased as they were, and saddened him to think of the cruel fate that would end their lives if his plan succeeded. How many proud and noble nations had the Zuelan empire shackled to their ambitions of conquest? He thought of his own dear friend Pattron — one of the gallant Hospitallers of Trenegal who escaped the Zuelan conquest of their own country and later fought for Cortavia during the war — and prayed he could someday forgive him for what soon must be done.

Chains rattled up the stairs to the forecastle deck.

"Take the empty rungs," the slave driver demanded, pointing at the wheel. "Your Kaighan demands it!"

A line of prisoners hustled past him and took their places on the wheel. Arghan's eyes flashed as the whip-stricken bare back of the last man in line came into view. Leaner and paler than the rest, the raven-headed figure wore a tattered Khevet around his neck.

"Orin?" Arghan shouted.

The youth glanced up at him, squinting through bruised and swollen eyelids.

"Never mind him!" screamed the slave driver, slashing Orin's back with the whip. "Take your place!"

Orin moaned and stumbled behind one of the rungs, bleeding.

Arghan's arms trembled. His eyelids narrowed into fiery slits.

Haracht-Wan emerged from the top of the stairs and directed a team of assistants to pack the throat of the Dragon with a charge. The slave driver commanded the captives to turn the wheel. Seconds later a polished granite sphere rolled down a set of iron rails past Arghan's head and dropped into the Dragon's mouth. Wan's men finished the procedure by packing in a layer of mud and straw and stood aside. The slave driver pushed a gear. The team turned the wheel again, this time spinning the Dragon's carriage around a circular track until its muzzle pointed forward toward the dam. Wan leaped over the rails to peer down the weapon's sight then waved to his team, who turned a set of winches to adjust its pitch. He looked down the sight again and waved toward the bow before scurrying to the side.

Horns blew from behind Arghan's view, echoed by similar sounds across the fleet. The Kaighan marched up the stairs and strode to where Wan had stood.

"Today is a historic occasion," Zuelkar began. Bizarre symbols, freshly painted on his face contorting as he smiled. "Prepare to witness the might of Zuel and the fall of a civilization. Hail Zuel!"

"Zuel, Zuel, Zuuuueeel!" his men chanted in refrain.

"So it ends," Arghan whispered, staring at the dam.

An attendant handed him a glowing iron taken from a burning brazier. Zuelkar took it and waved its red-hot tip toward the cannon's dangling wick. The crowd hushed.

Then he stopped.

"Schlika," Arghan gasped, his mouth gaping.

"Did you take me for a fool, Erne Warder?" Zuelkar said, lowering the rod. "Thurn told me what lies beyond that wall. I just wanted to see the look on your face when I dashed your hopes. Thank you for not disappointing me." He grinned and nodded to the slave driver. "Turn the Dragon toward the Duke's fortress," then to Haracht-Wan he said, "adjust for maximum angle."

Arghan's pulse raced. He gritted his teeth and flexed his wrists, ripping through the remains of his restraints using the razor-sharp barbs on his vambraces to slice the cords. He dove off the platform and landed on the slave driver, tackling him to the ground. He snatched a ring of keys from the man's belt and tossed them to one of the prisoners. "Free yourselves!" he shouted, narrowly dodging Zuelkar's blade before it struck the boards of the deck.

A squad of warriors rushed the platform. The first to reach him swung his blade. Arghan blocked it with the jagged edge of one of his vambraces and ducked, vaulting another attacker over his shoulder. Two more attacked. The first of the pair thrust his sword. Arghan turned his torso at the last second, extending his left arm over his attacker's opposite shoulder and seizing the man's weapon with his right. He dropped his weight, sending the man barrelling to the floor. The next man swung low. Arghan jumped, trapping the weapon between his forearms as he landed, then finished its wielder with a strike to the chest and a kick to the ribs.

"Kill him you fools!" cried Zuelkar, taking another swing.

Arghan ducked and landed a blow in the middle of Zuelkar's bare chest, winding him. The Kaighan reeled away, gasping.

The man beside Orin tossed him the ring of keys. The youth unlocked his irons and stuck out his leg the moment Zuelkar passed, tripping the Kaighan, who stumbled onto the deck with a thud.

Another group of warriors charged up the stairs. Before they could reach him, Arghan jumped on top of the Dragon and chopped its wick short, then jumped down again and grabbed the burning poker from where Zuelkar had dropped it. He lit the wick. The Dragon roared, shooting its projectile into the base of one of the dam's buttresses. The round exploded, leaving a gaping crater where it landed. A crack sprung from the point of impact and widened as it shot upward toward the arch. The column collapsed. Stones fell from the dam's face. The south slope rumbled. More boulders fell. Others were hurled through the air, propelled by jets of water that shot out from the lake behind them.

Arghan beckoned the liberated Askhavahni, "Follow me!" He grabbed Orin by the elbow and pulled him overboard. The others followed under a hail of arrows fired by Zuelan archers who reached the guardrail seconds after they jumped over it.

Arghan burst from below the water's surface. "Swim for the platform, there, at the edge of the river," he yelled. "Go through the door when you reach it."

Aboard the *Leviathan*, Zuelkar scrambled to his feet and looked up at the crumbling dam. "Weigh anchor! Turn the fleet! Hard about!"

Crewmen and warriors alike ignored him, scrambling over each other as they too dove into the river.

"We'll never make it in time," cried Orin, glancing up at the dam as the top third above the widening fissure gave way, releasing a fall of water several times mightier than the one far below it, now a trickle by comparison.

Arghan saw it too. "Keep swimming!" he shouted, subconsciously reciting a desperate prayer.

Seconds later the scree slope on the south mountain collapsed, hurling boulders the size of houses into the water. The ships of the Zuelan fleet rocked into each other, tossed like toys in a child's bathwater by the ensuing wave which hurled the swimmers against the opposite cliff, dropping both them and a soup of debris from the Zuelan ships onto the stone platform, steps away from the man-sized iron door that led into the lock.

Arghan vomited water and shook his head. He looked skyward. "Not quite what I had in mind, but thank you." He scrambled to his feet and wobbled over to the door. He gripped its heavy iron wheel and strained to turn it. "No use," he grunted, slamming the door with his fist, "thing's rusted shut!" He dropped his head against it and took a breath, preparing for another attempt.

The platform quaked. Another column collapsed into the river.

One of the Askhavahni called to Arghan in Trenegalian, "Let us help you, oombutu[2]." He fetched a Zuelan spear that the wave had washed onto the platform and threw its shaft through the rungs of the wheel. Arghan gripped it with the others and the men strained together to open it. The wheel loosened.

Arghan spun it free and opened the door, waving inside. "Thank you friends, you first."

The Askhavahni raced through the door.

Orin followed. "Shut it!" he cried.

Arghan watched another column fall. The dam's wall exploded, showering the Zuelan fleet in a hail of massive stones. Arghan snatched the Zuelan spear, jumped inside, slammed the door, and threw the weapon through a set of rings behind it, barring it from inside. "Run to the

---

2. Oombutu - a Trenegalian word meaning "new friend".

top, run!"

The men scrambled up a stone staircase, feeling their way in the dark.

Outside, the waters of Lake Kinnessarat gushed through the breach, pummelling the entire Zuelan fleet in a sudden deluge, sinking them almost instantly. The gorge flooded to the brim. The lake swept the south mountain out with the flow, filling the river with mud, trees, rocks and all sorts of debris as it raged southward.

Outside Castle Straskost, Khloe Pan-Wrikor clenched the balcony's railing and gaped at the raging tsunami unleashed by the dam's collapse. Voices hollered from below. She leaned over the rail and spotted a group of sentries pointing through the gaps between the battlements.

She followed the tangent of their outstretched arms and noticed a door had opened from one of the pavilions on the platform surrounding the lock. From it, six dark-skinned figures emerged, followed by another of shorter build and lighter complexion, and finally by another tall figure in a bronze-coloured suit of armour. The armoured one fell forward and rolled onto his back, discarding his helmet with a toss while the others scrambled to the edge of the retaining wall next to the cliff and proceeded to leap and dance.

"Is that… could it be… ?" she whispered, zeroing in on the armoured figure. "Arghan?"

She turned and raced through the door to a suite inside Weorthan's keep. Inside, she dove over beds, slid across floors, and rode down the handrail of a grand spiral staircase to land in the vestibule, spinning. She wobbled through another doorway leading into a darkened corridor. Several twists and turns later she barged through a door at the edge of the lock and dashed across the platform toward the pavilion.

"Arghan!" she cried, dropping beside him.

"W-Wrytha… ?" he murmured, blinking.

"No, you goof, it's me, Khloe." She kissed him on the cheek and fell on his shoulders. "Oh, thank the Maker! We thought you might be, y-you might be—"

"Dead?" he said, coughing up water. He turned onto his stomach and tried to push himself up. "Nah, I'm in way too much pain to be dead..."

"Khloe?" called Orin, limping over to where they lay.

She sprung to her feet and embraced him. "Orin!"

A tear escaped his swollen eyelids. He pulled away and looked at the ground. "Khlo, I'm so sorry, It's all my fault. If Gavek hadn't fought for you—"

"What happened?" she asked, furrowing her brow as she lifted his head.

"Dannika. Zedekael. They're dead. The Zuelans — they did unspeakable things to her... tortured him... It's all my fault. I should've listened to mother. I should've... Khlo, I don't even know why they let me live. Why did they let me live?" He dropped his head on her shoulder and sobbed.

"Sorry to interrupt you both," said Arghan, lurching to his feet, "but time is short. Khloe, where are Wrytha and Gavek?" He looked up at the keep. "Did they speak to Weorthan? Is he going to help?"

"Mother went up to the falls with Sibia and Siobe—"

"What?"

"Gavek's gone there too, with Weorthan."

"To do what?"

"They're going to try Gavek's plan, you know, surround them or something."

"I'd better get up there. Who knows what other tricks Thurn might have up his sleeve." He took a few steps and collapsed again, missing the waters of the lock by a hand's breadth.

"Arghan!" Khloe cried, rushing to him.

"Dizzy... can't see very well..." he muttered, his breath deepening.

"Stay here — Orin, watch him. Pull him away from the edge. I'll get help."

CHAPTER TWENTY-FIVE
Ondar Falls

Wrytha dropped to one knee and held up her fist. She flashed two fingers and motioned to the right. Her two companions darted into the brush. She followed and kept her eyes fixed on the two men who stood in the middle of the trail until she passed out of sight.

"Sentries. Why so soon?" said Siobe. She unrolled a buckskin map onto her knee. "We've only just reached the first set of falls. The ones we're looking for are a few more leagues upriver."

"We'll hug the river the rest of the way," replied Wrytha, stuffing her cloak under a fallen pine. "Stow your outer garments here. Looks like the brush gets pretty thick on the way down."

The women descended further into the gorge, clinging to trees and digging their heels into the damp ground to control their pace. Gradually, the once gentle rustle of distant waters grew into an omnipresent roar. They stepped onto a moss-covered crag and dropped behind a ridge overlooking Sirat Falls.

"More of them," whispered Sibia, pointing at a cluster of figures standing on the rocks on either side of the drop. "They don't look anything like the two on the trail."

"Zuelan raiders — the professional kind," said Wrytha.

"Look, there's even more of them up ahead," said Siobe.

The women peeked over the ridge. In some places, the escarpment rose from the riverbed at a steep, yet traversable angle cluttered with rocks, moss, and trees; in others, sheer crags jutted into the river. As far as they could see, warriors in black armour stood at every turn.

Wrytha drew an arrow and slid it through the fingers of her bow hand. "Siobe, I want you to go back. Warn the others. Tell the Duke what we're up against."

Siobe nodded. "What about you?"

"Sibia and I will work our way up either side. Cybella's got to be here somewhere. If we can at least find her, it'll give us an advantage we didn't otherwise have. I'm still hoping Arghan will arrive in time."

"The Maker guide you, Clan Mother," Siobe said, touching Wrytha on the shoulder before scurrying off.

"You too," Wrytha whispered, still watching the warrior. She pointed at Sibia. "You stay on this side. I'll take the right."

Sibia crept away. Wrytha dropped into the shadows on the pebbled shoreline and peered past the edge of the crag. A bulging shape hanging from a branch over the falls caught her eye. She nocked her arrow and fired, striking the top of a large hornet's nest. It plummeted onto the rock and crashed open at the Zuelans' feet. The men dashed in various directions, batting the air as they fled.

Wrytha bolted, skipping over a series of stones across the river and scurried up the opposite slope. From there she scaled an incline to the upriver side of the falls and navigated her way along the jagged escarpment. Using the dense foliage for cover, she snuck past several groups of warriors, weaving in and out of the treeline until the river narrowed at a turn, where a babbling spout poured into a basin between two cliffs. She scanned the cliff sides around here. One way remained. She gripped a set of dangling roots and clawed her way up the gentler of the two slopes until she reached its narrow summit, where she stopped to peer over the other side. The base of the gorge widened ahead. To the southeast, bare cliffs rose up from the river basin to the treeline — a height of at least forty men. To the northwest, precipitous hills of dense fur trees and deep, shadowed gullies rose to the foothills of the mountains. She scanned the treeline toward the sound of the falls and flinched at the sight of a slender figure slouched inside an iron cage, suspended from a rope spanning the chasm.

"Cybella," she whispered. She gazed to the right and traced the line upward, trying to spot the origin of the cord. It passed out of sight behind a balancing rock along the cliff side. A quick glance to the left revealed a similar obscurity. "It would've taken some effort to hoist," she muttered, "it must be connected to a winch or pulley system on one, perhaps both sides." She licked her upper lip and darted her eyes toward the towering cascade. Her gaze lingered there while she surveyed the exposed volcanic rocks surrounding it and then finally focused back on the cage. She peered down to the ledge below and started to descend but halted at the sound of voices. The corner of a black pauldron appeared just past the slope. She scanned the cliffs around her. "Aha." She fired another arrow, this time aimed at a fallen branch teetering at the edge of a crag on the other side of the river. The branch fell, cracking as it spun over an outcropping.

"Nah ach ney?" said one of the voices.

"Boh-untu, shobi," replied the other.

Boots clomped across stone.

Wrytha slipped down to where the men had stood, scrambled over the rocks next to the river and disappeared around a bend. Almost an hour later, and after several similar encounters, she crept out from the treeline and stood at the top of Ondar Falls. After a quick glance over her shoulder, she peered out over the gorge and followed the line's course again to see where it was anchored on either side.

"Winches," she pondered aloud. "Just as I thought. A man on each side. Wish I had Arghan's spyglass right about now."

"Do you now?" called a voice from behind.

Wrytha spun around and gasped. Omhigaart Thurn loomed over her, clenching a sabre dripping with blood. Wide-eyed, she glanced through the gap between his legs and spotted Sibia's mangled, lifeless body floating headfirst down the river. Thurn flashed his teeth and swung his blade. She dodged and stumbled backward into the river, nearing the falls. He lunged again. Teetering, she fired an arrow that struck him in the hand, causing him to drop his sword.

He drew a dagger and bellowed, "Where is Danniker? Tell me or I'll gut you like a pickerel, you Tzyani witch!"

She nocked another arrow while she struggled to find her balance. Her back foot slipped across a rock covered in green algae the moment she released the string. The arrow whizzed past Thurn's head. He leaped into the water and clenched her neck before she could recover.

"Does he take me for a fool? You saw where she is. Does he really think this little game of yours will buy her some time?"

Wrytha kicked him in the groin. He released his grip and swung his dagger, narrowly missing her nose. She lurched backward and slipped again, this time finding nothing but air beneath her feet as she plunged over the falls.

Bobbing atop decorated warhorses, Weorthan's knights crested a stone bridge beside a lonely sawmill near Lake Sirat.

Siobe burst from the treeline and rolled across the road, blocking their path. She whipped her braid over her shoulder and held out her arms. "Stop."

Weorthan raised his gauntlet and the armoured cavalcade skidded to a halt; their horses snorting in disapproval.

"What's the meaning of this? Make way." Weorthan waved. "Reihner, see her to the wayside, would you? I'm not sure what your game is, miss, but if you'd like to rob us, It may be wise to bring some friends next time."

The knights chuckled.

"Your grace, wait," called a voice behind him.

Reihner glanced at Weorthan for confirmation. Weorthan nodded. "Siobe?"

"Gavek!" She ran past the others and met him beside his horse as he dismounted. Weorthan and his aids did the same. She exchanged glances between Gavek and Weorthan. Her rosy cheeks bulged as she exhaled.

"Where's Arghan? He isn't with you?"

"He hadn't arrived by the time we departed," Gavek replied. "We—"

"Cybella's safety is my top priority," Weorthan asserted, stepping in front of him. "Where is she? Did you find her?"

"No. We got as far as Sirat Falls. Wrytha sent me back to warn you. Thurn came with help, and lots of it."

"So did we," said Weorthan.

"You don't understand. Wrytha said they look like Zuelan regulars, and they're well positioned." She unrolled her map and showed it to him, tracing her route with her finger. "They're blocking the path. The river too. If their numbers beyond the point we reached are as dense as they were there, you're in for a terrible fight."

"We don't have to fight," said Gavek. "We need only surround them; keep Thurn from fleeing. Arghan said that was a sound plan."

"You can't surround them, not in this terrain," she retorted, circling the area on the map with her finger. "You'd have to cover a vast distance. You don't have enough men here."

"The girl's right," said Reihner, stroking his beard. "I've fished up here often, your grace, incognito of course. There's only two ways in or out: either back the way we came or further up the road to Lake Trieehd and we'd have to traverse the mountains on either side to reach it if we want to avoid the road." He shook his head. "There's no time for that."

Weorthan strode to the edge of the bridge and rested his hands on top of the retaining wall. He watched a trout snatch a fly from the surface of the river. Finally, he spun back. "We'll split the force. Sir Wagnacht will lead the bulk of the men up the road as a diversion, but don't engage. Take Mr. Gavek with you. Tell them Danniker's been delayed and sent his apprentice in his stead. This may buy Danniker some time. If it doesn't, at least we'll be in range to act."

Gavek approached him. "I'm not sure that's such a good idea, your grace. Thurn's a devious foe. May I remind you I'm here as the future Queen's representative. Arghan said—"

Weorthan's blue eyes flashed. "To hell with Danniker! I'm here, he isn't. You only serve Cybella; I love her. Discussion over." He started unbuckling his armour. "Wagnacht, I'll lead Reihner's mountaineers up the south ridge. We'll rappel the cliff and come down behind the falls. Thurn wants his treasure. Cybella's the only leverage he has to get it. He'll be close to it and have kept her even closer, I'll wager. Miss Siobe, you look at home in the woods. Will you scout for us?"

"Of c-course, sir," she answered, meeting Gavek's gaze with a fleeting, apologetic glance, "whatever I can do to help."

"Good. This way, men." Weorthan mounted his horse and offered a hand to Siobe who took it and jumped in the saddle behind him. He and the unarmoured men rode ahead while Wagnacht signalled some of the knights to join him in a huddle.

Gavek glared at Weorthan as he rode away. He jumped on his horse and looked over his shoulder, sighing. "Where are you, Arghan?"

T'kuk tightened a bandana around his head and leaned on his spear, staring at the vacant trail. "I wonder what the fleet's up to." He swatted a mosquito against his neck. "They've certainly got to be having more fun than we are."

"Never mind that," Zeng chimed from his perch on a nearby rock, whittling a stick, "if this treasure is as big as Encani says it is, we'll be having all the fun we can handle soon enough."

"Hope you're right," said another warrior, pacing across the road. He cleared his throat, closed one nostril and blew out the other. "The sooner we're out of this cursed country, the better."

Zeng's eyes flashed. He dropped his stick and stood up. "Do you hear that?"

T'kuk straightened up and nodded. "Horses... a lot of them. They're coming up the road."

Zeng held his fingers to his lips and whistled into the woods. The men were soon joined by several others who ran down from an adjacent hillside. Zeng stared up the road, his hand ready at his hilt. A golden banner emblazoned with a black eagle was the first thing to appear over the top of the hill, followed by a polished steel sallet. The trail soon flooded with mounted knights in plate armour, thundering toward them.

"Blow the horn," insisted T'kuk, pointing at a curved ivory instrument hanging from Zeng's belt.

Zeng shook his head. "Not yet. See what they want first. Danniker might be with them."

T'kuk took a breath and put on his helmet. He thrust out his spear and spoke in broken Cortavian, "Halt! Who goes there."

Wagnacht signalled his column to slow, then stop. He and three other knights dismounted and approached the Zuelans. Gavek followed close behind.

Wagnacht stopped several steps away from the raiders and answered in his own version of garbled Cortavian, "We're knights of his grace Weorthan, the Duke of Ostergaart." He nodded back at Gavek. "We escort the squire of Arghan of Danniker, who, being detained, has sent him to bargain for the princess's release in his stead."

Gavek walked up and stood beside Wagnacht. "That's not exactly accurate, you see I can—"

"Bargain?" T'kuk spat on the road and cocked his head. "You're stalling. Thurn wants Danniker or the princess dies. No bargain! You go tell him that."

Wagnacht gripped his hilt. "Listen, you dimwitted ingrate, you're not dealing with a bunch of Cortavian cowards here now. I'll go easy on you if you cooperate. At least take a message to your master for—"

T'kuk stuck out his chest. "He's not our master, beer-guzzler."

An insect bit one of Wagnacht's men in the neck. He jerked his head against his shoulder, swinging his crossbow forward suddenly. Zeng saw it. He blew his horn and a horde of Zuelans came screaming down the hill.

"It's an ambush!" cried Wagnacht, drawing his greatsword.

The knights did likewise. The Zuelan line dove onto the road, hacking at the horses as they landed. Swords flashed. Lances thrust. The roots across the trail soon oozed with blood.

Gavek bolted southward through the ferns.

Weorthan looked up the slope at Siobe. "What is it?" he called, crouching behind a pine tree.

"Best see for yourself, Duke," she answered, waving him up to the ridge.

Weorthan signalled to Reihner for him to follow and scrambled up to where she lay, slipping on some loose rocks as he went. The men dropped beside Siobe and Weorthan scanned the canyon with his spyglass. Their vantage point high above the expanse revealed the locations of both ends of the rope that suspended Thurn's devious prison, as well as the men who stood near them ready to destroy the line, either by pushing a lever that would loose the rope instantly or to light a fire to burn through it, delaying its release. Either method would plunge Cybella nearly twenty statures[1] to her doom. The cage hung directly over the place where the fall's dark, frothing plunge pool overflowed a monolith, forming a swift-flowing, shallow slide on the downstream side of the massive rock. Weorthan aimed the spyglass back up at the cage. The sight of Cybella's golden locks hanging out between its grey bars confirmed his worst fears.

"The devil," he said, gritting his teeth as he turned onto his back. "If we take out the man on this side it'll surely alert the other. How then could we hope to deal with him?"

"It's much too far for an arrow, I know that much." Siobe propped her torso up with her elbows. "I'm a good shot, but not that good."

Weorthan looked at Reihner. "I'll bargain with him; offer my life in exchange for hers." He handed him his spyglass. "Look, that must be him there, the ghoulish looking bald one in black, on top of the falls."

Reihner spotted him. "He doesn't strike me as the kind of man who likes to cut deals. What if he doesn't listen? He'll have two hostages instead of one."

Weorthan turned back on his stomach. "Do you see a better way?"

Reihner handed him back his spyglass without answering.

"Give me your rope," Weorthan said, "I'll go down alone. Tell the

---

1. Stature – a common measurement throughout Eskareon for vertical distance, one stature being the average height of an adult male.

others to follow close behind in case something goes wrong. Siobe, stay here. I assume you could hit the man guarding the line on this side?"

"Easily."

He handed her his spyglass. "Look for my signal. If I hold my arms straight out to the sides, take the shot."

Siobe nodded and watched the men scramble away.

Arghan grunted and slid forward in his saddle. "What's the matter? Why are we stopping?"

"There are bodies strewn all over the road ahead," said the young knight ahead of him. He twisted back in his saddle. "Looks like there's been a fight. The whole trail is blocked."

Arghan reached into his tunic and sighed when he realized his spyglass was long gone. "That's okay, I'll go in on foot. Thanks for your help, lads, I'll take it from here." He slid off his horse and stumbled onto the trail.

Khloe dismounted her horse and scurried over to help him up. "I'm not sure that's such a good idea." She glanced at the sweat dripping from his forehead and then down at the blood-stained, white linen straps that bound Arghan's left arm to his chest. "Weorthan's physician didn't even want you to leave the castle."

"I had places to be. Besides, he kept threatening to saw my arm off." He didn't dare tell her why.

She cocked her head. "Listen, your charming wit might work on my mother, and your bossy bravado on Gavek, but you're dealing with Khloe now. You're going to need some help. Let me at least come with you."

"Out of the question," he said, his eyelids flicking. He opened them and stared at her with bloodshot eyes. "Khloe my dear, what a bright, lovely young woman you are. You've had made a fine daughter. Gavek's got my purse. There are enough diamonds in it to feed you and your mother for the rest of your lives — your whole village for that matter. If anything happens to me, it's yours."

"Don't talk like that, Arghan. The Maker's given me no dreams that show that's gonna happen."

"If there's one thing I've learned, my dear, the Father of Lights likes to keep his end-game under lock and key, even from gifted seers like you."

"Whatever. I'm coming with you anyway."

"I said no! Your mother would kill me if I—"

She pointed at the slope below the treeline. "Arghan, mother's down there somewhere. Gavek too, perhaps. If you fail, it stands to reason neither one of them will make it out of there to hold a grudge."

Arghan smiled and limped off the trail. "You sound just like her — your mother. I love her with all my heart, you know. Have done since the moment I saw her on that dock."

"I know. Everybody knows. We all see it. Why do you think we all put up with you?"

Arghan chuckled. Khloe threw his right arm over her shoulder and led him into the woods. "Keep your purse. But if you're gonna be my dad, we'll have to negotiate an allowance. You really like to put us all to work."

Arghan laughed again and they disappeared behind the trees.

Gavek rushed through the woods, red-faced and panting, counting his steps. He checked the sun's position in the sky. Visions of every map of the Trieehd region he'd ever laid eyes on scrolled in front of his mind's eye. He slide across a granite boulder and broke through the bushes at the river's edge, just north of the falls.

"What the—" he exclaimed. He gaped up at the cage suspended over the gorge, then jerked his head toward the sound of voices beyond the rushing current.

Thurn stood on the opposite bank holding a sword to the Duke's throat, surrounded by his crew. Gavek could tell by the weapon's hilt and a nick on the blade it was the same one Arghan had lost in Trianon. Weorthan and Gavek locked gazes. Noticing Weorthan's distraction, Thurn turned to look. Then he grinned.

A sharp pain shot through Gavek's ribs. He looked down to see a rapier point pressed against his torso and traced the length of the blade to the hand of the man who held it.

"Move it, slim," Dreighton sneered. "I don't know what you're all up to, but it's not gonna work. Let's go see the captain, shall we?" He prodded Gavek with the tip of his sword.

"Ow," Gavek said, holding up his hands. "Relax, ugly, I get it. There's no need of that."

"Well, well, what do we have here?" Thurn asked, widening his grin.

"Gavek of Cairhn," he answered. "Special adviser to her royal highness Cybella of Cortavia, Master of the Royal Archive and Chief Librarian of Trianon."

Thurn stared at him for a moment then erupted in laughter. "So what?"

Gavek stuck out his chin. "Arghan's been waylaid. The Zuelan monsters you loosed on the country proved a bigger problem than he thought."

"So said the Duke here."

"Well, you might want to reconsider doing something like that next time you set a deadline. Just a suggestion. Ow!"

Dreighton withdrew his rapier. "Let me run him through." He looked at Weorthan. "I'll do 'em both."

"No!" said Gavek, waving his hands. "I'm Arghan's apprentice. He sent me here in case he didn't make it. Told me everything about the vault." He pointed toward the falls. "I can get you in and out of it. Let the Duke go."

Thurn laughed again. "Oh Mr. Gavek, you're an entertaining fellow indeed. Why on Earda would I let the Duke go? We're just getting acquainted. He just finished an eloquent speech offering his life in exchange for his lady love — truly touching. Unfortunately, he mistook me for someone with honour and morals. Dreighton—"

"Wait!" said Gavek, "the door's inlaid with a strange script you can't decipher, isn't it? It's ancient Tzyani. I'm the only man alive who can read it, you know. The whole reason Solstrus was out to murder Cybella was because she and Wardein discovered manuscripts of the forbidden scriptures under the library of Trianon and he was afraid they'd get out."

Dreighton squinted and cocked his head. "Isn't that what the old man in Metacartha said those symbols were when you showed him the rubbings you took, captain?"

Thurn narrowed his eyelids and glared back at him. "Yes. Yes it was." He lowered Arghan's sword and kicked Weorthan to the ground. "Tie him up. He can watch his beloved die if this one's lying." He turned back to Gavek and waved the Talon toward the falls. "Okay, Mr. Gavek, you've intrigued me. Dreighton, take him down. We'll keep watch for Danniker here." He looked at the sky. "Arghan's got another hour to go. We'll give him that. But God help the princess if he doesn't. It took such effort and planning to string her up like that. Part of me would like to see her fall, just for the satisfaction of it."

Thurn's words resounded in Gavek' mind. He stared at the cage high above the canyon while Dreighton prodded him down a damp, steep path to the midway point of the cataract. Not too long ago, Cybella had been nothing more to him than the object of a quest; the source of a riddle. But now, after getting to know her, the deep and near-instant trust she'd placed in him — amplified by Arghan's own confidence in his powers — awakened a sense of duty unlike anything he'd felt before, except perhaps for the high calling he sensed was his to translate the lost Scriptures. But the look in Arghan's eyes when he'd asked about the fate of the manuscripts told him that quest was over. Gone was the game of words or numbers. Now, a human life other than his own — her life — hung in the balance, and quite literally too. He'd let her down by failing to anticipate Count Vernik's duplicity. He dared not do that again.

"Some stunt Thurn pulled at Kortova," Gavek said, still eyeing the cage. "He must've promised Vernik a high percentage of the take to walk away from his castle and county like that. Probably more than you're getting."

"Ha, nice try, 'librarian'. The old 'make the henchman doubt his boss routine' won't work on me." He shook his head with certainty. "The captain and I go way back, almost as far as he and Vernik. As for the Count, well," he snickered, "he was looking for an excuse to get out of there anyway, so I heard. He'd be off whoring somewhere right now waiting for payday if he could've kept his pants on long enough."

"What do you mean? I don't understand."

"Vernik wanted more than a payoff. He wanted to have his way with the princess. It was that or the cash or nothing at all. Omhigaart didn't see the harm, as long as she was still alive afterwards. So he let him."

Gavek stopped and clenched his fists, trembling.

Dreighton poked him in the back. "Don't get your britches in a bind, now, keep going. Her virtue's intact. The romance wasn't meant to be, sadly. She fought him off, and hard too. He's at the bottom of a cliff out there somewhere."

Gavek glanced up at Cybella's cage one last time and breathed a prayer before they passed behind the raging flow.

The misty air chilled. Dreighton and Gavek stopped in front of a moss-covered stone door. As predicted, its entire surface was inlaid with carvings, each of them a glyph from the Tzyani alphabet, displayed in random order across the slab.

"So? Here we are. Can you open it or not?" said Dreighton, poking him with his rapier.

"You know, I'm really getting sick of that," Gavek said as he scanned the stone portal. "Be patient." His head stopped panning when his gaze fell on the top line.

"Vash gomen sirat gomena osh?" he read aloud.

"What the devil does that mean?"

Gavek rolled his eyes. "Somebody like you might never know. It reads, 'which name is above every other name'?" Gavek scanned the door again, speaking the letters aloud as he pushed the corresponding tiles, "Yod, Shin, Vav, Ayin."

The slab vibrated and the door popped open, releasing a gust of air from the cavern inside.

"You did it," Dreighton exclaimed, peering through the opening. "What was the name?"

"Yeshua," Gavek said, making the sign of the Three-in-One over his chest.

"Never heard of him."

"Trust me," Gavek replied, "I think you will soon enough."

Dreighton took a small lantern from his belt and lit it. The pair descended a steep staircase into a cavern. Shafts of water streamed down the jagged walls on either side of it, flooding a darkened pool at the base of the stairs where a short ramp led to another door.

Gavek paused on the ramp and looked up at the ceiling. "Do you hear that?"

"You mean the falls? Who can't? It still rattles my teeth all the way down here."

"No, not that. Wheels... cogs... " He surveyed the various holes cut into the higher sections of the walls. "There must be some kind of machinery hidden behind those walls."

"Who cares," Dreighton chided with another poke of his rapier. "The only hidden thing Omhigaart cares about is the treasure. The door — now."

Gavek stepped toward it, still looking up at the holes. It wasn't until he bumped into it that his eyes turned toward its carved face.

"Circles within circles, within circles," said Dreighton. "And a bunch more of that funny writing. Looks like a big mess to me."

"Of course it does."

Dreighton poked him again. Gavek winced.

"I thought you said Danniker told you all about these. Why then do you need to stop and think it over?"

Gavek glanced sideways and paused, then looked back at the carvings. "It has been twenty years since Arghan was told the answers to the riddles. His wits aren't what they used to be. Too much drink and bergaroot I suspect."

Dreighton chuckled. "Well, you'd better solve it, otherwise the pretty blonde out there won't be the only one taking a dive today."

Gavek stepped back and let his eyes fall out of focus. "That's it! Wheels within wheels."

"What's it?"

"A pair of circles, always together but in orbiting positions to each other, a greater and a lesser sphere, following and elliptical arc around an even greater circle at the centre of the door."

"So?"

"The Other World — where the Saviour died to save the cosmos!
"I think it's a celestial calendar. The lesser sphere is the Other World's solitary moon. Does that mean the Other World is a disc as well? If the Other World is a disc, that would have to mean Earda is a disc also, wouldn't it? No, not a disc, a —"

"Listen, you'll have plenty of time to ponder the nature of the universe once we're long gone. Can you open the door or can't you?"

"Of course, this one's easy." Gavek rearranged one of the sets of sphere's, triggering a click inside the door. It opened like the last one.

"What did you do? How—"

"The circles in question represent positions of celestial bodies over the course of a year. The set I moved was out of position in relation to the rest. When I turned it, the larger sphere's inlay shifted to solid for one-eighth of the rotation — the day the Other World turned to darkness for three hours. This represents the year in which the Saviour died and rose from the dead."

Dreighton rolled his eyes. "More spooky nonsense. Come on, you're on a roll, but time's ticking. What's next?"

Gavek shook his head and swung the door wide open, revealing another room. A shaft of light from a crack in the chamber's stone canopy cast a dim glow throughout the cavity. A course of water flowed across their path, bridged by no less than seven crossings leading to a platform on the opposite side where a simple wooden door hung open.

"Well that's just perfect," Dreighton huffed. "Looks like somebody's been here ahead of us!"

"Not necessarily," said Gavek, inspecting the bridges. All of the wooden crossings were identical in breadth, broad enough for three men to cross shoulder to shoulder. But the floorboards of the fifth one from the left was unique in one regard, containing a narrow middle row of planks, perpendicular to the others forming a straight line across the length of the span.

"There's one way to find out." Dreighton marched past Gavek and stepped onto the middle bridge.

"No, wait, you'd don't understand." Gavek swiped Dreighton's sleeve but the salty buccaneer yanked it away.

Gavek dropped to his knees and folded his fingers over his head. Dreighton's boot heel depressed the bridge's middle board, triggering a clunking sound below it. Dust fell on his head seconds before a steel blade swung down on a timber pendulum and took it off. His headless corpse dropped with a thud.

"Broad is the road that leads to destruction," Gavek whispered, peering through his fingers at the bridges. His eyes darted from side to side while he listened to the noises beyond the walls. More cogs and wheels. The last door slammed shut behind him and a portcullis dropped behind the bridges.

He was trapped.

CHAPTER TWENTY-SIX
Treasure

Arghan and Khloe slid down the last few feet of the escarpment and trudged across the wet sand toward the riverbank. They emerged from the shade of the canopy and started up the pebbled shore. Moments later, they rounded a boulder and stumbled headlong into a circle of pacing Zuelans, who drew their swords in the blink of an eye.

One of them whistled up the gorge. "It's him, the Erne Warder. Tell Encani he's arrived."

Another one of them tried to seize him and pulled Khloe away.

Arghan flashed his teeth and drew an Ostergaardian long sword from the frayed scabbard at his hip. "The girl stays with me or I'll cut all of you down right where you stand."

"Ha, with that old thing, one-handed?" scoffed a smooth faced warrior, his faint moustache curling at the edges as he grinned. "It looks like an antique, just like you."

The Zuelans chuckled.

"An old sword like this one and the eagle on my jacket was all I needed to send your fathers to the bottom of the river, son. You think you'd fair any better against me? Now give me back the girl and take me to Thurn or I'll cut the lot of you into bear bait."

The fair-skinned one started for Arghan. His grey-bearded comrade caught his sleeve. "He looks weak, but he's more trouble than he's worth, kid. Besides, if we kill him we won't get paid." He waved to the one holding Khloe and the man released her. Arghan sheathed his borrowed sword and put his arm back around her.

"That was close," she said.

"For them, yeah."

They took a few steps past the band. Khloe glanced up to the sky and froze.

"Arghan... look."

Arghan squinted against the glare of the midday sun. "Describe it to me kiddo."

"There's a cage hanging from a rope strung across the gorge. There's a girl inside it in a fine dress. It looks like—"

"Cybella," Arghan said. "When Thurn demanded I meet him here it crossed my mind he might try something like that. I hoped he'd forgotten that old trick. We used to do the same thing to the Dai-Kaighans we took prisoner in the war. There's little chance of getting her out of it now unless I do exactly what he says."

They travelled on to the place in the river where it widened into a plunge pool at the base of the falls.

Arghan held two fingers to his lips and let out a shrill whistle. "Omhigaart," he bellowed, "I'm here."

A figure ran upriver from the spout and disappeared behind the cliff. Two figures returned.

"It's him," Khloe said. "That's the man who stood staring at us when we escaped the dock at Onya Landing."

Arghan nodded.

One of the Zuelans pointed to a trail that zigzagged up the cliff. "This way."

The entourage started up the path. Khloe hesitated for a moment, then continued.

"What was that about?" Arghan muttered. "Did a cliffhawk swoop down on us or something?"

"No," she whispered. "Something better than a hawk. I just made eye contact with mother. She's scaling the cliff on the far side of the gorge."

Praise the Maker, he's alive. But what's he doing bringing Khloe here? Wrytha crawled onto a ledge beside the cliff overlooking the mechanism that anchored the rope to that side of the gorge and the sentry who protected it. She crouched behind a rock, turned her gaze toward the falls and watched Thurn's crew tie Khloe to the opposite side of a tree on which a man wearing a black and yellow waffenrock was already bound, while Thurn led Arghan down the path toward the vault door. The two men disappeared behind the cascade and the buccaneers followed shortly thereafter.

Moments after the sailors disappeared behind the mist, a line of gleaming figures broke from the treeline up and down the riverbank and clashed with the Zuelans. A black and yellow banner waved by one of them looked just like the huge ones she spotted hanging over the walls of Weorthan's distant castle. *The Duke's knights!* She breathed a sigh of relief. Siobe had made it back. Movement at the top of the falls caught her eye. A band of men in huntsmen's scarlet descended the short slope to the shoreline above the falls. No sooner had they freed Khloe and the man bound to the tree beside her than a crowd of black figures raced out from the woods and set upon them.

Now's my chance. The only ones looking at the cage are the men on either side of the rope.

But Wrytha wasn't the only one to witness the unfolding struggle on top of the falls. The rope watchman nearest her signalled his counterpart with a mirror. His partner signalled back. The watchman struck a stone and lit a pile of firewood under the rope.

Wrytha bolted from her perch and dove onto the overhang where the man and mechanism stood. She thrust her heel into the side of his knee. The joint collapsed with a crunch. He screamed and stumbled off the cliff. She kicked the firewood away, jumped on top of the rope and started to run. A quarter of the way across she saw the other sentry's mirror reflect another flash. *He didn't see it happen*, she thought. *He's waiting for a response.* Wrytha dropped onto the rope and gripped it with her legs as she spun upside down. The sentry flashed again. She nocked an arrow, drew her bowstring and aimed into the wind at a place high above the light. She loosed the string. The arrow whizzed high in the air as though it followed an invisible arc in the sky and passed through a rainbow of mist flowing off the falls. It slowed at the climax of its ascent, almost pausing in mid-flight as though nudged by the finger of God, then dropped, spiralling downward until it plunged into its target. She watched the mirror fall, twirling off the cliff as smoke started to bellow near the place the man had stood. She shimmied up the rope. Several moments later she reached the cage.

"Cybella," she called. "Can you hear me? Are you okay?"

Cybella gasped and sprung to her feet, gripping the bars of her prison, blinking. "Wrytha! How did you—"

Wrytha glanced at the growing flames near the anchor on the other side of the canyon. She slid down the outside of the cage and braced her feet on its floor. She inspected the heavy iron padlock on the door. "Never mind that. We don't have much time. You see that pouch on my hip?"

"Yes."

"There's a file inside I use to sharpen arrowheads. Take it out and stick it in the lock. Wiggle it until you hear a click."

Cybella did as she said. After a few attempts the padlock popped open and plunged into the river. Wrytha swung the door open and jumped inside the cage.

"Now comes the hard part. I hope you're not afraid of heights."

Cybella's eyes bulged. "What are you going to do?"

"Follow me to the underside of the cage. Pace yourself. Keep a tight grip at all times. It'll be just like hanging from a tree limb. You did that as a kid, didn't you?"

She swallowed, trembling. "Yes, but never over a chasm like this!"

"It's this or death, princess. Follow me." Wrytha slid out the door on her belly and gripped the bottom rungs of the cage. She swung from one to the next until she hung near the back of it, facing the falls. "Now you!"

Cybella followed, looking only upward as she gripped the rungs one to the next until she hung beside Wrytha. She closed her eyes. "Now what?"

"Swing your legs in time with mine. I'll guide you. When I tell you to let go, don't even think, just do it."

"Ah, okay, okay."

"Swing!"

The cage started to move back and forth.

"Swing!"

The cage's arc widened.

"Swing!"

The cage rocked higher and higher.

"Last one now, at the highest point toward the falls, let go."

The cage swung forward. Wrytha let go and plummeted into the plunge pool with a splash. Cybella winced and closed her eyes again, continuing to swing.

Wrytha swam to the surface and whipped the water from her face. "Jump, Cybella! The rope's going to break any second!"

Cybella kicked her feet at the high end of her swing. When she opened her eyes, her gaze fell toward a little blonde girl standing in the water near the spout of the falls. A wave of peace spread through her chest like the heat of the summer sun. She reached the apex of her forward movement.

The rope snapped and she let go.

"This isn't going to work if your rabble follows us in, you know," Arghan said, cringing at the fetters around his wrists. He took a deep breath and tried to forget they were there.

"And why is that exactly?" Thurn asked with an air of suspicion. "Trying to get me alone so you can overpower me, are you?"

"Do I really look like I could overpower anybody?" Arghan showed him his darkened eyelids and twitched his tethered limb. "I spent the last of my energies sending all of your Zuelan friends to a watery grave. I just want to get this over with, okay?"

Thurn eyed one of his men. "So do I, but I don't trust you. Besides, I'll need them to carry out the loot."

Arghan stopped. "They'll be carrying nothing if they're dead. Every trap inside this temple of doom is hair-triggered, driven by machines powered by the flow of the falls. Get too many bodies in there and who knows what might happen. The whole mountain might come down with you inside it."

Thurn cast another questioning look at his men.

"Look, do you want your treasure or don't you? Your men will be free to enter and carry out whatever you want once I've disarmed the traps, but they must be done in sequence and with minimum distraction. You've got the daughter of my flesh strung up over the gorge and the daughter of my heart lashed to a tree. What more insurance do you need? You know, I'm beginning to doubt you'll get much enjoyment out of whatever riches lay inside this trove, given your paranoid senility."

Thurn's face grew red and twisted into an expression somewhere between a grin and a sneer. He whipped off his long coat, threw it to one of his crew, and thrust the point of Arghan's lost Talon toward him. "Try anything stupid and I'll deprive you of your manhood with your own sword." He cocked his head over his shoulder. "The rest of you stay here. Guard the entrance. Nobody gets in or out." He looked back at Arghan, narrowed his eyelids and pointed down the path. "March."

Arghan made an about-face. Thurn followed, goading him down the trail with the tip of the sword until they reached the first door.

Arghan saw that it was open. "What? How—"

"Oh, I was so excited to see you it slipped my mind. Your young apprentice arrived not long ago insisting you had sent him here to act on your behalf. I was curious to see if he was lying so I let him have a go. Seems he was more successful than I gave him credit for."

Arghan called through the door, "Gavek?"

The sound of rustling water and the muffled din of the cavern's hidden machinery were the only reply.

Arghan cast Thurn a questioning look. Thurn nodded and pointed inside. They descended the steps and reached the second door. Arghan turned the circles into proper alignment the same way Gavek had done and the door opened, triggering the portcullis beyond the bridges to retract into the ceiling.

Gavek sat on the floor of the chamber with his head between his knees. He sprung toward the sound of their footsteps. "Arghan!" He smiled and threw his arms around his mentor. "Man, am I glad you're here. Did you—" Thurn's entrance answered his unfinished question. His countenance soured.

"Hmm. What happened here?" Thurn said, poking Dreighton's headless corpse with Arghan's sword.

Gavek glanced at Arghan before he answered, "Dreighton lost his head, twice. First when he ran ahead of me and second when the trap he sprung finished him off. I knew the way. He took off before I could warn him. It's his own doing, I swear it."

"Prove it," Thurn said. "Lead the way, Mr. Gavek."

Arghan nodded. "I'm certain you know what to do."

Gavek strode past them both and walked down the centre spline of the fifth bridge, placing one foot directly in front of the other as he went. He jumped onto the platform on the other side of the stream. "Enter through the narrow gate, for wide is the gate and broad is the road that leads to destruction."

Thurn looked at Arghan. "What's he going on about? A riddle from some ancient fable?"

"Ancient, yes, a riddle, no, not to those who understand it." Arghan shuffled past him and duplicated Gavek's route. "Walk only on the middle planks."

Thurn sauntered over to it and placed a toe on the first plank and ducked his head, searching the roof with his eyes. He took a step and allowed his weight to rest on the bridge. He stepped again, then again until he reached the other side.

"Continue," he said, waving the sword toward the open wooden door, "Gavek first, then you."

Arghan again nodded to Gavek. Gavek passed through the threshold and stepped onto a hard floor. The stone beneath his foot sunk under his weight and he heard a click. Twenty-four oil lamps built into alcoves around a cylindrical chamber ignited simultaneously, flooding the room with light. Intricate carvings adorned every wall, gilded in gold and encrusted with jewels.

"Now this is more like it," Thurn said, plucking out a ruby from one of the carvings.

Gavek started, dropping into a crouch with his hands over his head. "Please, be careful!" He rose again when it appeared nothing had happened.

Thurn laughed. "Jumpy one, aren't you?" He held the ruby up to one of the lights. "The only thing I don't understand is why such a fine chamber would have such a pitiful doorway, and why anyone would leave it open like that if all this was inside."

"There's nothing pitiful about it," said Arghan. "In fact, it's quite exquisite. Did you notice how there are no nails in it? Each plank is perfectly fitted into the other by notches and grooves. A master carpenter made that door and without a handle, I might add. Had he not opened it, how could anyone hope to make it inside? The bridge was the test."

"Hmm. I suppose you're right," said Thurn, plucking a diamond from another part of the wall. "But don't for a minute think I'm fooled. As impressive as this room is and though I see no other door, I can't believe this is the end of it. Other troves across Cortavia had more loot than this. I warned you not to play games. We both know what great pains Thulrek took to keep this place a secret, and why."

"There is another door here," Arghan answered. "We simply have to find it."

Wrytha and Cybella crawled onto the damp gravel shore beside the plunge pool and rolled onto their backs. A trout flipped out from under Cybella's skirt and wiggled its way back into the water.

"You okay?" Wrytha asked, springing to her feet. She held out her hand.

"I will be, I think, once the world stops spinning." She took Wrytha's hand and stood up. Seconds later she buckled over and vomited on the ground. "On second thought, maybe not."

"Hang in there, kid, you did well." Wrytha patted her on the back while she surveyed the riverbank. Wagnacht's forces continued to pour down the hillside, driving the Zuelans into the rapids. Something moved across her peripheral vision. She looked up toward the path the others had used to reach the vault door and saw members of Thurn's crew scrambling back up it to meet Weorthan's scarlet rangers, who pressed down on them from the topside of the falls, accompanied by Khloe and the blonde haired man she'd seen tied up with her. Though firing in rapidly from the advantaged perch of the high ground, few of the archers wielded anything more than a dagger besides their bows. Thurn's men rushed up the hill and began to cut a path through them with their sabres. It wasn't until the Duke drew his longsword and charged to the head of the line that the carnage abated.

Straightening up, Cybella staggered back and stared up at the trail. "Weorthan!"

Weorthan kicked one of Thurn's sailors off the path and called back to her, "Cybella!"

"Stay here, keep out of sight," Wrytha said, scrambling up the escarpment.

"Where are you going?"

"To even the odds."

Wrytha scaled a massive boulder along the hillside and knelt on top of its mossy canopy. She pulled off her quiver and dumped its contents in front of her. She grabbed a shaft and took aim. One after another, her arrows thudded into the backs of the buccaneers. Distracted by their falling comrades at the rear, their middle ranks turned back and soon they too fell by the dozens as the rangers launched another volley. The fierce Tzyani huntress continued to fire from the left; the Ostergaardian rangers from the right, until the last of them fell by Weorthan's sword. The remaining Zuelans not cut down by Wagnacht's knights or swept away in the current staggered into the woods below the south bank.

The Duke led the others back up to the top of the falls and together they raced down the same path Arghan and Khloe had used less than an hour before. Weorthan slowed when his boots touched the gravelled shore.

"Cybella, my love."

Cybella ran into his embrace. "I feared I'd never see you again," she said before she kissed him.

Khloe intercepted her mother as she jumped back onto the bank. "Mother, you were awesome! I saw the whole thing!"

Wrytha threw her arms around her daughter and held her tight. "Love can make you do some pretty crazy things, can't it?"

"Yeah it can," Khloe said, looking back at the amorous couple. "I saw Cybella lose her lunch a few minutes ago and Weorthan's still kissing her. Yuck."

Wrytha giggled, pulled her close again, and stared back up at the falls, her smile disappearing as a tear fell from her eye. At that moment a pair of figures in grey robes appeared at the top of the falls.

"Who are they?" Wrytha said to Khloe, scrunching her eyebrows. "Where'd they come from?"

"Don't know," Khloe answered. "They weren't around when I was up there."

Finding the gilded chamber's exit proved no greater challenge to Gavek's powers than the previous two riddles. Though Arghan knew the solution himself, he played along, content to let Thurn believe what Gavek had told him was true, that Arghan had confided in him all the vault's secrets. It allowed Thurn the illusion of control, keeping Arghan on a short leash while Gavek did the work.

At first glance, the cylindrical chamber's carvings were nothing more than an eloquently decorated abstract. In reality, the motifs were divided into horizontal rings that spun around the room when pushed. Gavek had stumbled upon them while looking for a clue, pretending for Thurn's sake to simply be trying to pinpoint something he already knew was there: the beginning step of the next door's unlocking mechanism. By holding Dreighton's lantern close to the wall as he went, he'd dispelled the shadows cast by the light of the chamber's own lanterns and revealed the tiny seams — each no thicker than a hair — between the rings. The rest was simple. When properly aligned the carved rings formed a scene depicting the lost story of creation, a tale passed down by the Cantorvarians since the forbidden Scriptures had been lost.

Gavek finished turning the last ring into position. As the scene aligned, so did a set of vertical seams. He pushed between them and swung open the door.

"Clearly, that was built to be a false end," Thurn said as they exited the room, "gilded to look like a treasure vault, and yet left empty enough to appear as though it had already been looted. Von Terrack was a clever man indeed."

They started down a spiral staircase hewn into the rock.

"He was," Arghan said. "But he had nothing to do with its construction. Unlike the rest of the troves throughout Cortavia, these chambers have existed for centuries. At least that's what the man in Saasbourg who sold him the map showing its location said. But he did give that up for another bottle of Lyracian wine, so take that story for what it's worth. Your guess is as good as mine as to what's inside it."

Thurn sniggered. "Nice try, Arghan. I know there's something of incalculable value hidden here. You'd not have risked your own daughter's life for a fool's errand. No use trying to convince me otherwise."

They spiralled farther and farther underground. Arghan stopped and leaned on the wall, panting with drool dripping from the corners of his mouth.

"Give me a minute, p-please," he said, blinking and clutching his chest. "Need to catch my breath."

Thurn sighed. He moved closer to Gavek to see his belt by the light of Dreighton's lantern and sheathed Arghan's sword. A trickle of water dripped down his face and he looked up at the ceiling. "We must be well below the falls by now, how much further is it?"

Arghan exhaled. "Ah, o-one more chamber and a d-door. Beyond that is the treasure vault."

"Good. Break time's over. Get moving. Danniker, you take the lead."

Arghan soldiered on. With each new step, his gait grew slower and more erratic. They exited the stairs and stepped onto a narrow shelf at the edge of a dark, cylindrical chasm. A polished granite statue of a seraph holding out its arms and six wings stood atop a sculpted column that rose up from the seemingly bottomless pit.

"I don't understand," Gavek admitted. "How do we get across and how would anyone carry any treasure back?"

"You mean you don't know?" Thurn said, arching an eyebrow.

Caught in his lie, Gavek attempted to compensate with another one, obfuscating it with the truth, "No, I don't. I-I know how to open the door, just not how to get there."

Arghan took a few steps backward. "Don't fuss, Omhigaart. The means of retrieval are triggered from inside the vault. As for how to get there, the chasm's uncrossable. You must be carried over. I'll show you. Stand aside." Arghan tore off his sling and threw it over the ledge. He inhaled sharply and gritted his teeth, mustering what remained of his strength. He sprinted toward the drop and leaped through the air, flailing his limbs. His torso bounced against the statue's cold exterior and his foot slipped, narrowly catching the edge of the sculpture's pedestal. He dropped, scraping his chest against one of the seraph's feet. He caught its toes with his right hand and dangled below it, struggling to recover.

"Arghan!" Gavek exclaimed, reaching toward him as though by gesture alone he could stop his mentor's fall.

"If he falls, it'll be down to you, you know," Thurn slithered. "Don't distract him."

Arghan screamed and grunted. He whispered, "The heartland's throat I shall ward, 'gainst all who serve the devil's horde..." He let out a bellow and pulled his body up by his right arm, steadying it with his limp and stiffened left until he rose above the statue's feet. He sprung forward and hugged the statue's legs then shimmied up until his face fell past its neck. He hung from it and shifted his weight backward. The column tilted like a level then sprung back again to the opposite side. The statue swivelled on its pedestal to face the opposing side of the shaft, turning him with it. He repeated the procedure, this time jumping off it when it lurched toward the ledge in front of the vault chamber's sealed door.

Arghan collapsed on the ledge. "See... it's a... it's a piece of... piece of Trionnian pound cake."

Thurn pushed Gavek's shoulder. "Your turn."

Gavek straightened his tunic and brushed past him. He secured the lantern to his belt, then ran and jumped onto the seraph's feet and gripped its torso. He repeated Arghan's moves and soon he too was across.

Gavek helped Arghan to his feet. "You okay?"

Thurn readied for his attempt.

Arghan fell onto his shoulder and coughed up blood. "No son, I'm not. This is the end of the road for me. Surgeon in Straskost said if he didn't take my arm I wasn't long for this world. I couldn't let any of you down. I'm so very proud of you, son. You'll become a better man than I ever was. Take care of the others when I'm gone. You know where my treasures are. There's a pool of water inside. If anything goes wrong, and you're near it, dive in. It leads to a shaft that will take you to the surface." He laid his hand on Gavek's heart and watched Thurn jump.

Thurn landed on the platform beside them. "You must've really taken a beating, Danniker. I'm twenty years your senior and yet I managed that."

"Good for you," Arghan said, turning away.

The final threshold loomed over them, its double doors sunken into the recess formed by a series of inlaid arches that decreased in size the nearer they were to the opening like the portal to a grand cathedral. The height of two men and the width of one, its amber-painted exterior shimmered in the lantern's light. Life-sized statues of men flanked on either side. The one on the left was bearded, wearing a long robe and hood; the one on the right was bare-headed and clean-shaven.

"Gavek? If you please..." Arghan said.

Gavek studied the door. He reached for the doorknob, then stopped. He glanced at the statues on either side of the door. The bearded one held a quill in one hand and a scroll in the other. The clean-shaven one also held a quill in its right hand but its left was open and cupped as if to grip something that wasn't there. A dove perched on the right man's shoulder, looking toward the door. Gavek pulled the statue's hand and it swung out on hinges, and the hand enveloped the doorknob. A click echoed through the silence. The doors swung open. Oil lamps inside it ignited, revealing the chamber within.

Thurn strutted into the room and kicked over one of several lamp stands, spilling its flaming oil across the floor. "If this is supposed to be some kind of joke, Arghan, I'm not laughing. Where in the name of all that's sacred... is... my... treasure?"

Aided by Gavek, Arghan limped into the chamber, gaping. Gavek's mouth dropped open also. He stopped and stared, eyes bulging.

The vaulted room spread long before them, bathed in amber light. A pathway of tightly fitted stones divided the room and stopped in front of an elliptical pool of calm, still water as smooth as glass which reflected a high-backed, opulent throne that stood beyond it. Twenty-four crowns stood atop short pedestals around the pool. At either side of the aisle, water trickled over the soft clay-filling grooves cut into the floor. Beyond those stood bookshelves divided into square cells. The shelf on the left had thirty-nine of these while the shelf to the right had only twenty-seven. All of them were filled to the brim with parchment scrolls secured with silken ribbons. A stone table stood halfway down the aisle between where they stood and the reflecting pool.

Thurn's face turned red. He started to vibrate. "Well? Where's my treasure, Arghan? Where's the prize so valuable Von Terrack claimed would allow me to conquer the world?"

Gavek rushed to one of the cells and grabbed a scroll. He whipped off its ribbon and unrolled it, translating the Tzyani script on the fly while he read aloud,

"...Surely he took up our... pain

And... carried our suffering,
yet we considered him... chastised by God,
stricken by him, and afflicted.
But he was... run through for our transgressions,
he was destroyed for our iniquities;
the punishment that brought peace to us was on him,
and by his wounds we are healed.
We all, like sheep, have gone astray,
each of us has turned to our own way;
and the Maker has laid on him
the iniquity... of us all."

Gavek replaced the scroll and raced to unseal another, then another, reading excerpts aloud as he went.

"Arghan... I can't... I can't believe it, it's a complete set of the Scriptures... multiple copies, five, maybe ten times more plentiful than the one we found under the Library of Trianon!"

Arghan collapsed against the stone table and broke into raucous laughter. "There's your priceless treasure, Omhigaart! One that would allow any man in true possession of it to conquer the world." He stood up and pointed. "But only by expressing things you have no desire to possess: faith, hope, and love."

Thurn's teeth cracked audibly. He grabbed another burning lamp stand and rushed toward the shelves.

"No!" Gavek cried, jumping onto his arm and kicking the lamp away as it hit the floor.

Thurn drew Arghan's sword and swung it back, readying to strike. Arghan lunged toward him and grabbed his Talon by one of its side rings, yanking it out of Thurn's grip with a twist. He threw it across the floor to Gavek's feet. "Whatever you do, stay by the shelves!"

Gavek picked up Arghan's Talon and braced himself for another attack, but it never came. The two old foes grunted and twisted in each other's grip. Thurn broke free and tackled Arghan against the table. He grabbed him by the beard and slammed his face into the stone slab, then grabbed him by the scruff of the neck and threw him into the pool. Thurn turned back to Gavek, pacing like an angry tiger behind a cage while Gavek swung the sword. Arghan scrambled out of the water and jumped into the seat of the throne. Something clicked below him. Metal doors dropped from the roof into the clay-lined grooves in the floor, sealing Gavek and the selves away from Thurn and the rest of the chamber. A large hatch high above their heads dropped open, releasing a gushing deluge of water that quickly filled the room.

Thurn screamed, sloshing through the rising tide. "You motherless cur! You know I can't swim! I can't swim, damn you!" He dove at Arghan again. At the last second, Arghan sprung from the throne. Thurn's forehead struck its stone exterior and he fell limp into the water, a cloud of red flowing from his skull.

Arghan wobbled, stumbling through the swirling current. He took a deep breath and dove below it, headed for the centre of the pool. He felt his way to the bottom, then through a narrow, horizontal tunnel leading to a vertical shaft. He struggled upward, or so he thought. Wide-eyed he saw only darkness. His lungs started to burn. His limbs ached. The burning intensified. The tunnel remained black. He screamed and inhaled, flooding his lungs with water.

His limbs fell limp and he floated upward.

Wrytha, Khloe, Cybella, and Weorthan huddled next to the edge of the plunge pool, surrounded by members of Wagnacht's knights. Some of the Duke's rangers came running down the path.

"It's no use, your grace," called the one in the lead, "we tried, but the cavern's sealed. They're trapped inside."

Weorthan turned to his trusted officer. "Wagnacht, ride like the wind back to Straskost. Summon my siege engineers. Tell them to come here post haste. Maybe they can get it open."

Wagnacht nodded and raced away. At that moment, a pile of rocks beside the falls toppled over and Gavek crawled out of the hole below it.

"Gavek!" Khloe cried, spotting him first.

The friends ran to him and pulled him out.

"Where's Arghan?" Wrytha asked him, peering down the narrow tunnel. "Isn't he with you?"

Gavek shook his head. Tears streamed down his cheeks. "I'm sorry Wrytha. There's nothing I could do, I—"

"No." Wrytha said, batting the others aside, "no, no, no, no..." She started up the trail toward the door.

Khloe screamed and pointed at the plunge pool. "Arghan!"

Arghan's lifeless body floated to the surface amid the spewing torrent.

Wrytha froze. A dull chill spread through her limbs. She snorted, raced to the water's edge, and dove in. She pulled him to the shore and cradled him in her lap, listening for his breath. "Arghan, Arghan honey, wake up. Please, please, wake up, wake—" She held her fingers to his jugular, then collapsed on his chest, sobbing, finally releasing a guttural wail that echoed across the canyon.

"I love you," she repeated over and over, rocking over him.

Gavek and Khloe shuffled through the crowd and dropped down beside her, crying.

A murmur spread through the crowd of knights. Their armoured bodies parted, allowing two figures in grey robes to pass through.

"Gavek?" asked a familiar voice, touching his shoulder with dark brown fingers.

Gavek looked up as the man pulled down his hood. "Pattron! How—"

"I saw this place in a dream two nights ago," answered a female voice. Sister Agape knelt beside him. "Prior Arthos found himself in grave distress. We left at once and came here."

"I had the same dream, on the same night," Pattron said. "Brother Gavek, have faith, it's going to be okay. His mission on Earda isn't over." He stepped past him and knelt beside Wrytha. "Excuse me, madam, you must be the one called Wrytha?"

Wrytha nodded.

"May I?" Pattron asked, taking one of Arghan's hands.

Wrytha looked at Gavek with a desperate, quizzical look. He nodded.

She did the same to Pattron.

Pattron placed his hands on Arghan's chest and projected his voice so the knights could hear him, "I command this body to life in the name of Yeshua, the Anointed One!"

Arghan's eyelids started to flutter.

Khloe gasped and covered her mouth with both hands. Wrytha moaned, her face now awash with tears.

Arghan's limbs started to tremble. His torso shook. He opened his mouth and twisted to the side, spewing water all over the shore. Eyelids fluttering, he tore off his bandages and opened his eyes, blinking in the sunlight.

The knights knelt down one by one. Awe-filled mutterings spread through their ranks.

Khloe stood up and looked at Weorthan and Cybella, pointing down at him. "I-I watched the surgeon in Straskost re-wrap his arm. He'd been shot through with an arrow, but now, now there isn't even a scratch!"

Wrytha gripped his cheeks. "Arghan, oh, Arghan! How is it possible?" She kissed him and fell on his neck.

"Wrytha, my love..." he finally said, his lips broadening into a smile. "Your son's alive, he's safe."

"It's true mother," Khloe said, kneeling down again. "Arghan rescued Orin from the Zuelans. He's waiting for us in Straskost."

Wrytha's eyes sparkled.

"No, I mean, yes, that's true," Arghan said, "but that's not who I meant. I'm talking about Nicah."

"Nicah?" Wrytha asked, looking over at Khloe.

"How do you know that, brother?" Pattron asked. "The others brought him to me several days ago. The brothers and I prayed for him fervently. I gave him my best medicines, but he was still in a deep sleep when we left the monastery. I wasn't sure he would make it."

"Yeshua told me, my dear friend. Right before he sent me back." He looked into Wrytha's eyes and caressed her hand. "Yeshua wanted me to tell you your son will live. You believe me, don't you?"

"I just watched a dead man come back to life. Of course, I do," she said, squeezing his hand. "Do you think you can stand?"

"Yes," he said as she helped him up. "But I could do with a hot meal and a nice long nap."

Weorthan called to his men, "One of you, please, get the Erne Warder a horse?"

Sixteen knights turned at once and started for their mounts.

Wrytha and Arghan both chuckled and sauntered after them, hand in hand.

Weorthan gestured to the others. "All of you, please come to Straskost as my—" he paused, looking Cybella in the eyes when she squeezed his arm, " — as our honoured guests."

Gavek, who had been staring at the falls ever since Arghan's miraculous resurrection trying to make sense of it all, stood up and looked at Pattron as he passed. "Why didn't you just... you know, do that thing you just did there with Nicah?"

"It doesn't work that way, little brother," Pattron said with a smile. "Yeshua works in mysterious ways. He heals when he wants to, not when I want Him to. I simply do as the Spirit leads and today he led me here."

"Well, I'm sure I speak for everyone when I say we're glad he did," Arghan quipped as one of the knights helped him and Wrytha into his saddle.

The friends all laughed and watched them ride away.

CHAPTER TWENTY-SEVEN
Epilogue

Leaves of fiery red and brilliant amber twirled to the ground while the limbs they fell from rustled in the afternoon breeze. Arghan and Wrytha stood bathed in sunlight on either side of the shadow of the gnomon while friends and guests looked on from the circle of the Oratory: Cortavia's newly crowned Queen Cybella and her betrothed Weorthan, the Duke of Ostergaart — attended by his knights, the monks of Cairhn, the Tzyani villagers of Nova Elkahrn, Wrytha's twins, The Reeve of Sigoe and the Queen's own Archers — the youthful band once known as the Tzyani zealots.

Pattron signalled Khloe and Gavek, who stood next to the couple and each handed them a coloured ribbon: a white one to Arghan and a violet one to Wrytha. Working together, the couple wove them into a single strand. When finished, Pattron took it and used it to tie their right hands together.

"What the Father of Lights has bound, let no one separate. What the Shepherd King has nurtured let no one stifle. What flame the Spirit has lit, let no one snuff out. The Maker-Three-in-One bless you this day and always."

Pattron took a step back and waved his hand. "You may kiss the bride."

Arghan lifted Wrytha's veil and paused.

"What's the matter?" she whispered. "Did a fly land in my teeth?"

Arghan chuckled. "No, you look radiant... I just don't want this moment to end."

"You sentimental fool," she said, cocking her head and pulling him to her. "We'll have plenty more moments. Now be a good Lord and kiss your Countess."

He smiled. "As you wish, my lady."

THE END

About the Author

Aaron Babcock has worked as a graphic designer for over 25 years, but he's always been a storyteller at heart. He has been creating characters and plotting their fantastic adventures since childhood. However, life always seemed to find a way to keep him from committing a completed work of fiction to paper (though he does have a few unfinished projects laying on the shelf). That all changed with the release of The Erne Warder, his first published novel.

He is the author of two blogs: ***Dayhiker Adventures*** (dayhikeradventures.wordpress.com, a chronicle of his hiking adventures — some of which inspired locations described in The Erne Warder), and ***Rod of Aaron*** (rodofaaron.wordpress.com), a collection of articles related to matters of faith.

He is an active member of the Christian community in Nova Scotia, especially the intercessory prayer movement, and currently serves on the board of directors of Fundy Camp, a Christian summer retreat in Kings County.

He lives in Cole Harbour, Nova Scotia with his wife Stephanie, daughter Avelyn, and their two dogs, Cagney and Billie.

There once were three swordsmen of Pereon,
Encaro, Dahn Torio and Tereon;
Sharp were thier blades,
Sharper still were their wits;
And they foiled every brigand
in Eskareon...